D1003010

PRINN&JUNZT

Tom Hillenbrand

DRONE STATE

Translated from the German
by Laura Caton

DRONE STATE

Title of the original German edition:
Drohnenland

Copyright 2014, Tom Hillenbrand.
All rights reserved.

Translated from the German by Laura Caton.

Published by Prinn & Junzt.
www.prinnjunzt.com

Design: wppt:kommunikation gmbh
Süleyman Kayaalp, Sascha Zerbe, wppt.de

ISBN 978-3-00-060513-0

"Reason is often the source of barbarism; an excess of reason always is."

– Giacomo Leopardi

CHAPTER 1

He's by far the best-dressed corpse I've ever come across: welted calfskin shoes; a bespoke Milanese suit worth more than what I take home in a month; and a Steinkirk tied with deliberate disregard—including a matching pocket square.

Everything about him is immaculate except his face.

His remains are spread in a semicircle across the sandy ground. The rain's already washed some of them away, the blend of blood, brain matter, and bits of flesh creating a pinkish halo around his shoulders.

"Something high-caliber," I say to Paul.

The forensics expert looks at me and shakes his head. His white Tyvek coveralls rustle with the movement. "Nah. There's too much skull left for that," he replies.

"Then what are you thinking?" I ask.

Paul contorts his unshaven face. My question's coming at him too soon. Like most forensics experts, he'd prefer to let the humming-drones and mollies do their work first and have the entire crime scene replicated. Then, ideally, he'd poke around in the data they extracted for a week before he'd even make a call about the victim's gender.

I take a licorice stick out of my pocket and slowly put it in my mouth. Now Paul has plenty of time to compose and then regurgitate a well-informed hypothesis. I chew and wait—all for nothing.

"I'm not going to hold you to it later, Paul. How many mugs have you seen blown to bits in your life by this point?"

"Too many."

"I bet you could tread the boards on the net with that act," I continue. "Based on 360-recordings of faces shot to pieces, Paul Leclerq can, within seconds, determine the caliber and make—"

"What did I ever do to piss you off, Westerhuizen?" he growls.

I put my hands in my coat pockets. "You woke me up at four in the morning."

It was a priority call over the sound system in my apartment, with the volume and intensity of an air-raid siren. As I staggered to the underground parking garage a few minutes later and got into my car, Terry had already sent the first pieces of information to me: corpse near the E40 at Westrem. According to the biometric scans and signature, the dead man is Vittorio Pazzi, forty-seven years old, from Northern Italy but living in Brussels's Anderlecht district.

Strictly speaking, a corpse in a Flemish marsh isn't a reason to get up this early. Usually I'd have had myself replicated into the crime scene from home to give the data hounds a few instructions, then gone back to bed afterward. But things are different with Signore Pazzi. Unfortunately, I can't leave him lying around all alone in the rain, since he's a representative in the European Parliament. Or rather, that's what he was before someone blew to pieces his political mind and his good looks.

Using a firearm whose make I still don't know.

"Well?" I look at Paul expectantly.

He decides to play ball. "I'd bet on a caseless high-velocity shot. Probably 3.7 millimeters. Not from close range, like I said, otherwise the mess would be bigger."

"Who'd use something like that?"

"The guys from Taurus. Or the military, it's standard caliber for an assault rifle. Otherwise, almost no one requires a special permit."

Paul's answer raises disagreeable questions. But for now, it'll do. I thank him and walk a few steps in the direction of the street. The adjacent terrain slopes slightly from there, enough for me to get a good overview of the crime scene. This must have been farmland or a pasture at some point, as evidenced by the hedgerows and ditches surrounding the sandy field. It's not a pretty place to die, but at least it's a peaceful one. There's absolutely nothing here, and it's probably been days since a single living soul has laid eyes on this spot. Which certainly begs the question of how Pazzi was found so quickly.

"Operation report," I mutter.

Information pops up on my rain-flecked specs. Evidently Pazzi owned an implanted vitals transmitter. It's an expensive toy, even for a representative. As soon as the pea-sized plastic projectile started to cut a swathe through his brain at fifteen hundred meters per second, the transmitter notified emergency services that its client could use medical care. Pazzi must have had pretty good health insurance, since a Helijet drone was on the scene within twenty minutes. When the local cops figured out an MEP was involved, they shat a brick and called us up.

From my vantage point I look out over the bustling activity on the field. Although I didn't give a command to this effect, evidently someone was on the same page, even though I don't have any idea who that someone could be. And so the crime scene's already swarming with humming-drones, floodlight drones, and other machinery buzzing around the dead man in concentric circles, snapping high-resolution images from every conceivable angle.

"Message to Paul Leclerq," I say. "Text: Don't we have any mollies on the scene?"

A few seconds later the answer pops up on my specs: "Molecular scanners are good for nothing in this kind of shitty weather."

A Dutch expletive slips out of my mouth. I set up a voice link. "Paul, I want the mollies anyway. Terry and Ava can try to make sense of the data later. And I don't want just the crime scene to be replicated, I also want a radius of two square kilometers, at least."

"That's way too much work. We'd have to gather almost everything from scratch. This podunk town only sees a flyover from a land-survey drone once in a blue moon."

"I couldn't care less, Paul." I pause for effect. "Or

would you like to explain to Vogel why we didn't replicate all the data we could get related to the death of an MEP?"

Our head forensics expert grunts in a way I take as a sign of agreement. I cut the connection and let my gaze run over the plain again. It's completely empty—what had Pazzi been looking for out here? He must have come from the road, unless he had a long night's walk behind him. I rewind the video recording on my specs by a few minutes, to the point where I stood directly over the corpse and studied its shoes. The still image shows the soles and sides of Pazzi's shoes covered in muck, but not as muck-covered as they should have been if he'd trekked a long way in this rain. According to my specs, it's 153.34 meters from the road to the corpse, and part of that distance is a gravel path. Pazzi likely didn't go any farther than that. Which in turn suggests he arrived by car, though there's no trace of it.

"Is there anything around here at all?" I ask my specs.

"You are located 31.37 kilometers to the west of Brussels's District Européen," I'm informed by a woman's voice that sounds much too well-rested for this time of day. "This abandoned agricultural area is in the possession of—"

"Disconnect," I snap. Why are these things always so moronic? I wish Ava were already up. But I don't want to wake her, since it's barely 5:00 a.m. and my analyst will definitely be of much more use to me later if she's well-rested. Besides, it could be a while yet before the forensics team has replicated everything anyway.

I try it another way. "Display the nearest houses and businesses. List view."

The search results scroll by in front of my eyes. There's not much. There's a distribution facility off the westbound side of the highway, with a farmstead and a truckers' bar past that, though everything's at least two kilometers away from the crime scene. In other words, there's no logical destination nearby that Pazzi could have been headed toward. I take a fresh look at the crime scene and the surrounding area. It's unlikely there happened to be any random witnesses, given the time of the crime and how far we are from civilization. Apart from the gnarled poplar trees enclosing the field on the north and west sides, looks like no one saw anything.

The rain starts falling harder and the wind picks up. I can smell the North Sea, which isn't too far from here. I pull the wide brim of my rain hat closer to my face and decide there's nothing else for me to do here. I walk back to where my Mercedes is parked in an emergency pull-off by the highway and get in.

"To Galgenberg, Gottlieb," I say. The car gets under way. I take my specs off and lay them on the passenger seat along with my rain hat. The sky is dark gray and doesn't look like it'll get lighter anytime soon. As the car accelerates with a purr, fat raindrops burst on the windshield—*Pruimenregen*, as the Flemish say, plum rain. I truly hate summer.

I send a message to Ava, telling her to come to

my office as soon as possible. According to her official schedule she has something else on the docket for this morning, but it'll just have to wait. When my boss Jerôme Vogel gets wind of this case, which should be right around 7:30, I'd like to know a bit more than the deceased's name and shoe size.

I tell the Mercedes to make the windshield opaque and set up a link to Terry. The integrated media screen turns dark blue, the Europol logo appearing in the middle. It's really an analyst's job to communicate with the police computer, but I'm in a hurry. Besides, Terry isn't quite as stupid as the software in these French smartglasses.

"Good morning, Chief Inspector Westerhuizen," comes through the car's stereo system. "How can I be of assistance to you?"

"Précis for Vittorio Pazzi."

"How extensive would you like it, Chief Inspector?"

"Enough material to keep me busy and stop me from falling asleep until we arrive."

"One moment, please. Your précis is being compiled."

An official-looking photo of Pazzi appears on the screen. He's sitting behind a massive desk, flanked by two flags: on the left, the dark-blue banner of the Union; on the right, the azure-blue flag of the Northern Italian League.

"Vittorio Pazzi, forty-seven, born in Merano. Comes from a well-to-do family of entrepreneurs. Studied applied economics in Milan and Uppsala. Unmarried, no children. Member of the Liberal party, has sat for them the past four years in the European Parliament, deputy party leader, chairman of the Committee on Foreign Trade. Named Man of the Year last year by the business journal *Il Sole 24 Ore* for his efforts at improving Europe's competitive position."

As the police computer continues its recitation, the pictures on the screen change: Pazzi on a skiing holiday in the Alps, at an awards ceremony in Berlin, at the Christmas market in Strasbourg. Terry plays a video of the MEP giving a speech at some congressional session: "And only through a subsequent tightening of trade relations with our Brazilian friends, in simultaneous compliance with existing customs regulations, can the Union's economic power be—"

Maybe I'll end up falling asleep before we get to Brussels after all. It's the usual politician's drivel: like most of his party, Pazzi talks a lot about cooperation and free trade at the same time he tries to limit imports from South America. Instead of listening to him, I consider him closely. He commands a certain charisma, definitely more than the average representative. And he's always well-dressed. Even his ski suit looks custom-tailored.

Terry's now talking about Pazzi's successes in agricultural policy reform. I interrupt him. "You said he doesn't have a family. Was this guy gay?"

The police computer stops talking and a short pause follows. If I didn't know any better, I'd think I struck a nerve.

"There are no official statements from Vittorio Pazzi concerning the matter, Chief Inspector."

"Could be. But I'm sure you can conduct a congruence analysis."

"I'm required to warn you that, in the case of MEPs, such data is protected from governmental access by the Enhanced Privacy Act."

"He's dead, Terry. And this is a murder investigation."

Another short pause. "Access to such data will be logged and noted in case records. Furthermore, it must be of direct concern to an investigation. I am obligated to warn you that, according to Article 23 of the Code of Criminal Procedure—"

"Keep your shirt on."

"Please reformulate the question."

"Answer my question about Pazzi's sexual preference and log whatever you want."

A photo appears on the screen showing Pazzi in a circle of people. What I can see of the venue in the background is incredibly ugly. That makes me think it's somewhere around the EU Parliament building. The computer flags a man in his late thirties, standing a short distance away from the deceased. He's sandy-haired and somewhat chubby. His cheeks are flushed, probably from the glass of red wine he's holding in his right hand.

"No official information about Vittorio Pazzi's sexual orientation is available. An analysis of his characteristic speaking style, word choice, taste in music, frequently visited locations, and other data sources, though, suggests a close homosexual affinity."

"How reliable is that?"

"The probability is approaching 95.1 percent. The flagged person in this photo is Peter Heuberger, parliamentary assistant for the Conservatives. Parts of Pazzi's email correspondence have been sealed due to his status as a representative and must first be approved for digital forensics analysis by magisterial order. Available patterns of private communication, as well as joint check-ins at airports in Brussels, Berlin, and Lisbon, however, indicate a close relationship."

Through the side window, I see we're passing Saint-Gilles. We'll be there in a few minutes. I'd like to poke around more in the data about Pazzi's movements over the past twenty-four hours; but, unlike his corpse, Pazzi's digital cadaver is largely inaccessible, at least until the examining magistrate unseals the damn thing, which will be in two hours or so. That's when the early shift gets into the office. I instruct Terry to submit an emergency motion to unseal all data trails concerning Pazzi. Then I turn off the display and look out at the Brussels morning commute.

CHAPTER 2

I get out at the Café Amsterdam and tell the car to park in the underground garage beneath the Europol Palais. I enter the bar and order coffee. At the counter, large and covered with media screens, tired-looking men are sitting and reading the news. I take a seat at my usual corner table, open up a window, and search for news reports related to Vittorio Pazzi. There are a few recent mentions; happily, though, the articles are all under the assumption he's still alive. That buys me some time. As soon as Pazzi's death comes over the feeds, the higher-ups will be stepping all over my toes.

I order a second cup of coffee. The news round-ups are showing pictures of emaciated Persians or Saudis in some refugee camp or other. Workers in hazmat suits screen the new arrivals with Geiger counters. Other refugees stand in line to get something to eat, guarded by soldiers with assault rifles. According to the caption, the scene is unfolding in Calabria.

The guy at the table next to me leans over and points at the table top. "Poor bastards, huh?"

I look him over. He's the type of guy who could get a close shave in the morning and still have a five o'clock shadow by noon. His greasy jacket follows suit: it's coming apart bit by bit. He smells like Wallonian beer and apple brandy.

"Sure," I answer, "but at least they're still alive."

"But is that really living," he counters, "to be so completely homeless?"

This conversation is becoming decidedly too philosophical for me, so I grumble, "Not our borders, not our problem." A heartless remark, but it has the desired effect. My neighbor turns back to his drink without another word.

A message from Ava pops up on my specs: "There in ten minutes—replication's ready."

I stand up, place a few hundred-euro coins on the counter, and nod at the bartender. Then I leave the café and head in the direction of Europol headquarters. Even after all these years, I still feel a shiver down my spine as I get closer to this enormous palace of justice. The Palais is a failed attempt to fuse together quite a number of classical styles. The result is bigger than the Basilica of St. Peter and distinctly uglier.

The building is much too big for our purposes. The entire Belgian justice machinery used to occupy the space, but now the Palais only houses the Union's criminal courts and us. Since there aren't that many of us, the majority of the rooms are slowly gathering dust. Some of our fussier contemporaries were critical of the move to bring the Union's police and prosecutors under the same roof, arguing that it isn't an appropriate separation of powers.

As a small concession to this scolding, separate

entrances were established for judges and cops: the former use the main door off the Poelaertplein, while we gain entrance to the building around back, via the Jacobsplein, which as far as I'm concerned means the powers are plenty separated. One consequence of this arrangement is the hike from here to my office, located in the front section of the building. Another is that the entrance via the Jacobsplein has lent itself to my agency's nickname: locally, we're known as Jacobins. It's meant as a compliment.

As I pass through the security perimeter, a humming-drone follows close on my heels. It whirrs around me repeatedly, matching my physical appearance and gait against the database. The results are evidently to its satisfaction, since the security checkpoint slides open without a sound. I say hello to both of the gendarmes stationed at the entrance and continue inside.

The effect of the Palais's interior is even eerier than its façade. The building is made up of staircases to nowhere, halls and archways whose logic their architect must have taken to the grave, and columns, columns everywhere, most more than twenty meters tall. There are probably more columns in the palace of justice than there are public servants.

I go up to the main hall via a winding stairwell full of dusty art-nouveau sconces. It's the length of a football field and so overstuffed with columns— some round, others square or fluted, yet others present only in outline—that even a sunny spring day wouldn't let in enough light through the tiny windows to chase away the eternal twilight. From there, I take the stairs to the first floor. When I get to my office, I see Ava's already here, leaning over the conference table. It's a sight I find by no means unwelcome.

I clear my throat, and at the noise, she turns to face me. She's wearing skintight Japanese jeans tucked into tall lace-up boots, plus one of those new tracksuit jackets with rain neutralizers built into the shoulder pads. Ava Bittman is in her early thirties and has the body of an ancient Babylonian temple dancer with the mind of a nuclear physicist. She's the best analyst I've ever worked with, not to mention the prettiest. Most of the data forensics experts are women these days. Supposedly, it has something to do with feminine intuition, the cliché suggesting women should get along better with Terry. Whereas most of the inspectors are men. Against the odds and contrary to custom, I'm not sleeping with my analyst.

"Good morning, Ava."

"Hi, Aart. You look tired."

"I'll look even more tired before this is through. Assuming we can rule out suicide?"

Ava leans against the edge of my desk and studies the framed *Casablanca* poster hanging on the wall across from her. Bogart looks back. He appears not uninterested.

"As you're about to see, the line of fire makes suicide impossible. The projectile was fired from a distance of around a hundred meters."

"Paul says Pazzi was shot with a high-velocity weapon."

Ava tucks a coffee-brown lock of hair out of her face and nods. "That's true. It was this model." She clears her throat and says, "Terry, show the Pazzi murder weapon."

The media screen in the conference table changes color and shows a short-barrel assault rifle made of black plastic. Floating beside it are a few bright yellow streaks that look like little heat-sealed packets of ibuprofen.

"It's a Jericho 42C. Israeli make."

I reach my right hand out to the gun and pull it toward me. With a flick of my left hand, the weapon rotates along its length. I have memories of this model.

"You know, I've shot one of these before," I say.

"Really? When was this?"

"You're forgetting how old I am, Ava. I was in the military police during the first Moroccan crisis."

She looks at me, her coal-black eyes showing surprise and maybe, too, a hint of disgust. "The military used caseless high-velocity ammo during the Solar War? Against civilians?"

"Against terrorists," I answer mildly. "But let's not worry about yesterday's news. Who uses the 42C these days?"

"Only the military and police are allowed to use them, since, thanks to the vibrations and the enormous kinetic energy, even a grazing shot would turn a victim's nervous system and blood vessels into a nice puree. The southern coalition forces are equipped with them, and, of course, our special forces."

"Any stolen or missing units we know about?"

"Unfortunately, quite a few. With all the attacks in North Africa, some equipment inevitably gets lost. Terry says there are about two hundred stolen Jerichos listed in the database, although none with a signature matching this weapon. But that's not saying much. Ballistics isn't an exact science when it comes to these things."

I walk around the desk and sink into my chair. I fish a licorice stick out of the tin near my filing cabinet, then offer the container to Ava.

She shakes her head. "No, thanks. That kind is way too salty."

"It's supposed to be. Why is it difficult to determine the signature on this weapon? Because of the plastic?"

"Exactly. The barrel is made of a frictionless ceramic-plastic alloy. The ammo is caseless and also made of plastic. Unlike with projectiles made of metal, it's not as simple as matching bullet to barrel. Fewer traces of abrasion. If we found the murder weapon, it might be possible. But that's unlikely."

"Says who? Terry?"

"Says me, Aart. It's a perfect shitstorm."

Instead of answering right away, I finish chewing my licorice first. Then I say quietly, "Unfortunately, I have the same feeling."

"Where do we start?" Ava asks.

"To begin with, I want to go in and check out the crime scene. The replication's ready, right?"

She nods, opens the office door, and starts walking. I follow her. We go into one of the replication rooms. Ava sits down on a rolling stool, activates two screens on the wall, and locks the doors. She looks at me with interest as I loosen my cravat and take off first my jacket, then my shirt. She hands me an escape patch, which I stick to the left side of my chest. Then I take my place on one of the upholstered chaises and pull on my replication headset.

From the comfort of this position, I watch as Ava opens her track jacket. She's wearing nothing underneath but a skimpy sports bra. She lifts it up to attach her patch. I can see the dark aureole of her nipple and notice how my penis starts to stiffen. It's no wonder so many inspectors and analysts are lovebirds.

Ava approaches me and hands me an inhaler, then lies down on the couch next to mine. I turn the dispenser so the curved opening faces toward me. Hypnoremerol, a detective's best friend. Theoretically, it's possible to go in without it, but it's not recommended. When faced with the transition to an immersive computer simulation, the human brain reacts just like an old car changing gears without prior application of a clutch—with a groan and a crunch. Doing it too often can result in dissociative fugues and amnesia, impairments that put an inspector at something of a disadvantage.

The hypnoremerol provides a smooth trip to the other side. In the presence of an activated replication headset, it triggers the transition as soon as it floods the synapses. I double check that the headset is powered on. Only then do I put my lips around the inhaler and press down on the cartridge. With a hissing sound, the aerosol shoots into the back of my throat. Like always, I consider the sort of scent filling my nose. I imagine there's a hint of raspberries, or maybe even vanilla mixed with—

Right before I figure it out, I'm gone, like always.

When I come back to consciousness, the first thing I hear is the plum rain. It's pattering against the roof of the tent Ava has kindly erected beside the freeway. I get up from the camping stool where I'm seated and walk through the drawn canvas flap out into the open air. The rain whips against my face, exactly as it did at the time of the crime. Ava's already waiting for me near the tent.

"All due respect to your realism," I mutter, "but can you please turn off the rain now and make it a bit lighter out here?"

She murmurs something incomprehensible. The sun comes up in fast forward and the rain stops abruptly. Tiny fluffy clouds cover the Flemish sky. It's the first time in three weeks I've stood outside without getting wet.

I take a few steps across the field and look around. A strange feeling comes over me. As always, something in me rebels against the replication. I feel slightly queasy and then start having difficulties focusing. It has nothing to do with the simulation itself, which is excellent. It's all in my head.

I breathe in deeply. The air has a crispness it only

gets right after the end of a rainstorm, smelling like sea salt and soil. This whole damn thing is well done. Terry gets better with every passing year.

The dead man lies across the field, a tad less wet and less pale than he was a few hours ago. That's because this Pazzi and the three-dimensional orthomosaic of the surroundings have been computed from hundreds of thousands of individual images taken at the crime scene before I ever arrived. Even the footprints left behind in the marsh by Paul and his lumbering forensics team have disappeared. My specs tell me the replication of the crime scene corresponds to 3:29 a.m. Central European Time, twenty-nine minutes before I arrived this morning. In a certain sense, then, Ava and I are time travelers. Best not to think about it too much, though, since it's enough to drive a person completely insane.

I'd really like another licorice stick, but I don't have any with me and so I'd have to ask Ava if she could generate one in the replication for me. In lieu of that, I go over to Pazzi and take another look at his gunshot wound. "Captions," I say. Glowing blue letters and numbers appear near the corpse, along with arrows pointing to various body parts. I can hear Ava approaching from behind me.

When she's standing next to me, she says, "Time of death, 2:19 a.m. According to his mediwatch, he was dead instantaneously. One bullet to the back of his head."

"Not very sportsmanlike."

"Maybe, but technically speaking it's an excellent

shot, given the distance and the lighting conditions. The high-velocity shot punctured his parietal bone. The enormous vibrations instantly destroyed his brain, with further damage to his spinal cord, a ruptured carotid artery, and burst eyeballs."

"I get the picture."

She keeps going, unperturbed. "Exit wound centered beneath the eye sockets. So although there's still something left of his skull, the path of exit means his face is mostly gone."

"Show me the path of the shot."

Ava gestures with her hand. A red line appears, leading from our position to a thicket of eight poplar trees on the west side of the field. The line ends at the third tree, just above a branch that looks stable enough that a gunman could've sat on it.

"Original weather," I say.

Ava turns the rain on and the sun off. I can now see what I was already expecting. The poplar is 104.34 meters away. Through the sheets of rain, the tree's outline is just distinguishable in the darkness. Unless Pazzi coupled his specs with a scout drone at exactly the right moment, there's no way he'd have been able to see the gunman.

"Any drone activity before the murder, Ava?"

She seems to listen to something inside her own head for a moment. Then she says, "Nothing at all. According to Terry's database, the last registered drone flew over this field two days ago, a small heli-courier from UDS."

I notice how the water running off my trench coat

is forming little puddles on the ground. I point a finger at the clouds. "That's enough, thanks."

The rain stops.

"What else do we have, Ava? Can you run through it once?"

She nods, makes the dead parliamentarian disappear, and points to the road. "The mollies found some particles from his leather soles back there. That's where the trail begins."

"So that's where he was dropped off. Do we have the car?"

"Terry says no vehicle stopped here at the time in question."

"No registered vehicle, at least."

"Correct. According to the Enhanced Privacy Act, every car with an EU license plate, as well as all transport trucks, have a geosignature whose movements are stored indefinitely. Of course, an experienced criminal could disconnect that. Our drones, though, would be on it in less than an hour. They don't care much for any car that refuses to be identified. But maybe the vehicle sent out a counterfeit signature from another registered car. It'd stay under the radar a long time that way, at least until the original car got reported as stolen."

"The good old glass-diamond trick. Like those separatists in Munich, back in the day."

"Exactly. The only sure thing is that he must have gotten here somehow." She makes a gesture in the air and Pazzi appears at the side of the road. "Here's the next part."

The MEP walks in our direction at a measured pace. He moves very smoothly.

"Nicely done," I say, impressed by my analyst.

She shrugs her shoulders. "Public figure. Terry has thousands of hours of video footage. It's child's play."

Pazzi walks down the slope. Then he stands still and lights up a cigarette, which makes me feel a twinge of envy. After he's had a drag, he keeps going. Now he's 29.34 meters away from us. Pazzi takes another pull, then tosses the butt away and stands still. He tilts his head back slightly, lets his arms hang loose, and murmurs something to himself. That can only mean one thing.

"He's looking at something on his specs."

Ava freezes the playback and says, "According to Terry, he sent a message to Peter Heuberger."

"At this time of day?"

"A message with delayed send. It was supposed to be delivered at 8:30 a.m."

"Contents?"

"It read: 'Need to talk. Dinner at 7:30 at the Hotel Lotte.' He seemed confident Heuberger would accept, since he reserved a table for three at the same time."

"Why for three? Who else was invited?"

"According to Terry, there's no data about that."

"Any predictions given earlier meetings?"

"Based on his social connections and his restaurant history, the most likely candidates are Alan Thompson, a British MEP; Heidi Garcia, lobbyist for the Association for Solar Energy; or Jong de Klerk, a jazz musician. All of them were friends of Pazzi's. But according to Terry, the likelihood of any of them joining is less than twenty-five percent, since in ninety-one percent of all recorded cases, Pazzi and Heuberger ate alone—and what's more, if I understand correctly, always in restaurants outside the European Quarter."

"Very discreet, these guys."

"Seems that way. After making the reservation, he didn't use his specs again. There's also no point-of-view recording." Ava murmurs something, and Pazzi starts moving again. He walks closer and looks through us into the rain. A meter to Ava's left, he stops and stands still. He waits, walks a few steps back and forth, looks in different directions—at least according to Terry's interpretation of his footprints. Then Pazzi's face morphs into a pinkish cloud, and he goes down. In the course of the fall he pivots, landing on his right shoulder and rolling onto his back. Just before he hits the ground, I hear the gun's supersonic report.

Pazzi has to die quite a few more times before I'm satisfied. Ava sets him marching across the field again and again. I watch from various angles as he topples in real time, in slow motion, in stop motion.

"Let's go to the poplar," I say. Ava could teleport us over there, but I'm old-fashioned. These special effects give me a headache. So I walk. When I get there, Ava's already standing on the branch in question, 5.21 meters above me. She looks down at me with an amused expression.

"But you don't want to climb up here on your own, right, Aart?"

"Actually, that's exactly what I want."

"But why? I can fly you up here. Or if that's too surreal for you, I could create a hydraulic lift that would—"

"The world is full of obvious things which nobody by any chance ever observes."

"Was that a quote?"

I nod. "Arthur Conan Doyle. One drawback to virtual forensics is that they let the obvious be overlooked."

Ava rolls her eyes like a teenager listening to an old man dust off a story from back-in-his-day. I ignore the gesture, take my trench coat off, and start to look for a good foothold.

"The obvious in this case," I wheeze as I swing myself up on one of the lower branches, "is, namely, that we can fly. The murderer, on the other hand, must have climbed the tree using a more conventional method."

It takes about two minutes before I'm up. I decide against asking Ava for another rainfall, though that certainly would've made my climbing excursion more realistic. I might have fallen from the slippery pixelated poplar into the virtual mud, and I don't want to give my analyst the satisfaction. But now I'm also reasonably certain that any man in decent shape could reach the branch without the help of climbing equipment. Once we're sitting beside each other and looking over at Pazzi as he stands motionless in the middle of the field, it becomes clear to me that this must have been a shot to rival William Tell. Not only was there the rain, the darkness, and the too-steep angle. There's also the fact that, to get a shot to the heart, the gunman must have held the weapon very steady. From a foothold on solid ground, it's doable. From a crouch on a damp branch, it's extremely difficult.

"Any leads?" I ask.

"The molly drones found traces of his clothing and equipment, but no usable DNA. Hold on, I have a projection."

A man without a face appears beside us on the branch. He looks a bit like one of those holographic display mannequins at the Galeries Lafayette. He wears black combat boots, black cargo pants, and a chameleon poncho whose colors have changed to match the bark and foliage. He's holding a Jericho 42C in his hands, pointed in the direction of a Pazzi still awaiting his inevitable fate.

Ava has the killer pull the trigger. "The plastic in the ammunition boils away and leaves almost no residue behind, but a few molecules stuck to the trunk. He only fired one shot."

I shake my head. "It doesn't make sense. That's not the way it's done."

"And here we go with another piece of military wisdom from the Solar War, am I right?"

"Right. If I want to shoot someone from behind using an assault rifle with no kickback to speak of, I'm putting it on automatic."

Ava furrows her brow. "While you're balancing on a tree branch?"

"Okay, maybe just the one shot after all. But, after the first contact was made, I'd fire a few more rounds, just to make sure."

"But he was clearly dead right after the first shot to the head. So the gunman could save himself the ammunition."

"And how could he have known that? From here, Pazzi's just a tiny little speck. In any case, professionals never skimp on ammunition. And they never aim for the head."

She murmurs something, then nods. "Terry agrees with you. Based on the cases in his database."

"What's he got?"

"Europol forensics, replications of separatist operations, attacks by North African terrorists, contract killings by the mafia, things like that. In all of these instances, Terry's analysis gives a range of fifty to three hundred meters for the lethal shots. His prediction is that a professional gunman in the given scenario would have a ninety-three percent likelihood of opting for a body shot to the upper part of the back."

It's nice to be backed up by the numbers, even when I already knew what they'd say.

Ava looks at me expectantly. "Where would you have shot, Aart?"

"I was never a sniper. But the upper back is the best target. Then you can rip up the spinal column, the lungs, arteries, and maybe even the heart. It doesn't get much deader than that."

"But he shot at the head," she objects. "What does that tell us about the gunman?"

"That he's probably pretty arrogant. Convinced of his own powers."

"Apparently not without reason."

I gesture to the surrounding area. "Do we know where he came from and where he went off to afterward?"

"According to the traces we have, he came from the road, like Pazzi, although it's impossible to say exactly how much earlier. Terry's guess is an hour. He went back the same way. There's no vehicle signature for this one either."

This whole case is one stroke of bad luck after another, as every further detail—or, rather, every further lack of detail—makes clear. With a probability approaching certainty, we're looking at a politically motivated assassination. The only usual criminals with the knowledge of how to erase their traces so professionally are the Britskis, but I'd rather not think about that.

And as if it weren't all bad enough already, Ava says suddenly, "You're getting a priority call."

I rub my eyes. "Send it through."

Polite people finesse their unannounced intrusions into a running replication by choosing the subtlest possible method of communication. One popular option is to send a butler over with an old-fashioned rotary telephone on a tray; once, a white pigeon with a note in its beak actually landed on my hand.

But such niceties are, of course, foreign to Vogel. He simply bellows into the replication, his thundering voice seeming to come from somewhere on the other side of those fluffy white clouds. This is what Moses must have felt like when his irate Old Testament God dressed him down yet again. I wonder if this is an intentional effect, or if Vogel just can't carry it off any better. I'm leaning toward door number two.

"Westerhuizen! Get out of there. I want to see you in my office right now."

"With pleasure, Commissioner." I signal to Ava and everything goes dark around me.

As always after a replication, I feel like I polished off a bottle of genever the night before. At most, it was three or four glasses. Apparently, my hangover is obvious to look at me, since when I run into Marquez and Kaczynski in front of the elevator, they both hold off on cracking one of their usual dumb jokes. Instead, Marquez looks at me almost sympathetically through his blue-tinted specs.

"The Pazzi case, Westerhuizen?"

I nod and rummage around in the pocket of my jacket for another licorice stick. Marquez and Kaczynski have been working for weeks to root out a smuggling ring that's been bringing drugs and weapons into Union territories from overseas, probably via Sicily. Looks like they haven't made any headway on the case.

"Still on the smugglers?"

Marquez grunts. He has the face of a bulldog left out in the sun for too long. Since it's been pouring in Brussels for more than three weeks, my money's on tanning drops. He rocks his big head back and forth as if he's trying to loosen up his neck muscles. "It's shitty, that case. But not as shitty as yours, yeah? Dead MEP, must be causing quite a stir."

"Is it true there's almost no trail?" Kaczynski asks.

Marquez may look like a guard dog, but his Polish friend resembles a vulture: a long neck with an Adam's apple hectically shuttling back and forth, topped by disheveled wheat-blonde hair already a few years into its retreat, allowing his pale scalp to shine through. A few of Marquez's tanning drops would do him good.

His duplicitous question makes me furious. He could get the main points of the Pazzi dossier from Terry at any time. Maybe he's even reading the damn thing on his specs right now. But he's asking me anyway out of pure malice.

"We don't know how Pazzi and his killer got to the scene of the crime, and we don't have a signature for the weapon. But it'll come along soon enough."

An idea comes to me. "Of course, you boys are experts on smuggling. How would someone get an assault weapon from a war zone into the Union undetected anyway?"

Kaczynski shrugs his shoulders. "There are a lot of ways."

"What's that? Even though the two of you have been digging for gold on this case for weeks, you still don't know how it's happening?"

Just as I expected, Marquez's bulldog jaws snap open and closed angrily in response to this suggestion. He tries to look fierce. "We know exactly how it's happening, Westerhuizen."

"And that is . . . ?"

Marquez pauses for effect. Maybe he thinks he can build suspense that way. But the only thing he builds is boredom. After an eternity he says, "Human couriers are passé. Terry's predictive software can identify smugglers before they've shoved the goods even halfway up their asses. The newest trend is hobo drones."

"What's a hobo?" I ask.

"It's an English term. That's what they used to call tramps in America, people who traveled the country as stowaways on trains."

"They hung underneath the cars," Kaczynski chimes in. "Back then, those didn't go faster than forty kilometers an hour."

"That must have been quite a long time ago," I counter.

Marquez grunts in agreement. "Around 1970. These hobo drones do the same thing. They find a train or a semi-truck and hang themselves underneath. Then they turn off all the systems so you can't detect anything using scanners. When they reach their destination, they detach themselves. These things don't have much storage space, they're only about this big." He indicates a space with his hands about the size of a mop bucket. "But that's plenty big enough for disassembled weapons, explosives, organs, you name it."

"Interesting," I reply in a monotone. "If you'll excuse me, I have to go see Vogel now."

The two look at each other and grin. "Oh, Vogel? My sympathies," Kaczynski says. "But better you than me."

"Don't worry, my friend. If you spend a few more fruitless weeks investigating this smuggling ring, I'm sure you'll have an audience yourself soon enough."

Without another word, I leave them both standing there and get into the elevator. I tell it I'd like to go to the prefecture, located on the top floor of the building. Before a visitor is permitted to enter the office of Jerôme Vogel, he has to go through no fewer than three security checkpoints. I walk down the long hallway with measured steps, giving the humming-drones and scanners ample opportunity to inspect every fold and wrinkle in my skin. At regular intervals on both sides of the wide corridor, there are neoclassical statues, more than likely reproductions stuffed full of security and defense technology. There are stucco-embellished gold picture frames hanging in between, their media screens showing major landmarks from across the Union. I pass the New Brandenburg Gate, the Eiffel Tower, the Colosseum, and the Temple Mount. Directly beside the entrance to Vogel's office are Buckingham Palace and Stonehenge, lending a kind of comic irony.

I stand in front of the entryway. Since the system has already announced my arrival, I go inside without knocking. Vogel sits at an immense desk. Behind him is a picture window reaching almost to the floor with a view of Regentschapsstraat, home to the old

Palais Royal, now the seat of the European Commission. So Vogel's masters are always breathing down his neck, but the setup doesn't seem to bother him.

In any case, it's difficult to imagine anything in existence that could bother Jerôme Vogel. Not only does he have all the subtlety of a hippopotamus, but also the thick skin of one. He's in his late sixties and has already survived a half-dozen Commission presidencies, dozens of intrigues, and at least four murder attempts. He weighs a hundred and forty kilos and leaves his desk chair only when it's absolutely necessary—so, thanks to ever-better replication technology, almost never. When he sees me, he rubs his right hand along his shaved neck and fixes his piercing steel-blue eyes on me.

"Good morning, Westerhuizen."

It's the friendliest greeting I've heard from Vogel in at least two years. That puts me on my guard right away.

"Good morning, Commissioner."

He points to the visitor's chair. "I was just on the phone with Özal. As Commission president, she's extremely concerned about Pazzi's death."

"More likely she's concerned about the constitution vote."

"It's six weeks until the vote, so yes, this case is coming at an inopportune time for her. For all of us, if you don't mind my saying so."

"You follow the political circus much closer than I do, Commissioner. Was Pazzi involved in the constitution issue?"

Vogel tries to shake his head—not so easy with no neck to speak of. "He wasn't the one calling the shots, if that's what you mean. But he was always against Britain's exit and for the cohesion of the Union."

"There's a certain irony in an Italian saying something like that."

The Commissioner makes a dismissive gesture. "We'd have liked to have kept Great Britain, unlike Southern Italy. Wasn't your wife from England?"

Vogel again displays his considerable tact by bringing up my dead wife. "She was from Wales."

"I see. Anyway, the United Kingdom is out, the exit clause will go into effect in six weeks. Pazzi was neutral on the issue."

"Is that what the political commentators are saying?"

"It's what Terry says. After all his data streams were unsealed, I had a political congruence profile drawn up." He throws an accusatory look my way. "Which you obviously neglected to do before now."

"I thought it was more important to reconstruct the crime first thing, Commissioner."

"And I'm already waiting for your report. Terry's congruence analysis showed Pazzi's public and private statements as a seventy-seven percent match with the Liberal party platform."

"Not too bad. Almost an honest politician."

Vogel, a member of the Conservatives, ignores my observation. "When it comes to constitutional reform, though, the situation is less clear. There's a fifty-seven percent probability he would have voted yes."

"That's Terry's way of saying he doesn't know how Pazzi would've voted, right? Then do you suspect a political motivation?"

Vogel spreads his meaty hands across the oak desk. "We have to assume the worst. What do you think, Westerhuizen? Separatists? Mafia?"

I shrug my shoulders. "Nothing in his précis indicates Pazzi had any contact with the Britskis or the 'Ndrangheta. The usual terror groups only come into question because he was an MEP. The only thing we know for sure is that professionals were at work here. There's almost no usable evidence at the crime scene."

"What the hell is that supposed to mean?"

So much for the friendliness from earlier.

"I ran through everything in the replication two or three times. Molecular scans, humming-drones, the whole nine yards. But we still don't know how Pazzi got to the field. However, everything points to a premeditated execution. Although if it was terrorists we'd have a claim of responsibility by now—and the web would probably be full of 360-videos of Pazzi's head exploding. You know how these guys love their execution videos."

I tell Vogel everything else that came out of the replication, that Pazzi was probably bumped off with a weapon used by coalition forces. His expression becomes even stormier, if that's possible.

"From now on, you're working only on this case, Westerhuizen!"

"Understood, boss."

"I want this matter cleared up within forty-eight hours."

I notice my throat going dry. "I can't promise you—"

"I'm not expecting you to solve the entire case in that time. I do expect the investigation to be at a point where I can feed a story that makes Pazzi's death look as boring as possible to these guys," he points his thumb over his right shoulder in the direction of the Commission Palais, "and to everyone in Parliament, on the Council, and of course all of the goddamned general public. The media will go nuts to begin with, but after that I'll have to calm things down again."

"I'll do my best."

"For your sake, I hope so. What do you need?"

"All of Ava's time. Probably a stack of replications. And I'll have to take a few trips as well—to Northern Italy, for one, where Pazzi's from."

"Bullshit! You'll do it via replication. Traveling wastes far too much time."

"But it gets more results than lying on a couch."

Vogel lets loose a noise that could almost be considered a laugh with a big enough imagination. "The cop in me agrees with you, Westerhuizen. You're old school, just like me. You go out, speak personally with witnesses, sniff around the crime scene. But the commissioner in me says those times are gone. This isn't one of your Harry Bogart films."

"Humphrey Bogart."

"Whatever. We're supposed to stop terrorism,

organized crime, and other severe offenses in thirty-seven member states and eight associated territories. For all that, I have fewer officers than the municipality of Paris has garbage collectors. The name of the game is efficiency, Westerhuizen. Having boots on the ground is just a romantic notion from 2D movies. But don't worry about it. I'll make sure you have the right tools to move your investigation forward considerably."

"And what are those, Commissioner?"

"As of now, you can operate as a ghost."

"In the mirror space? I thought that was only for the intelligence service."

"Normally, yes, since it's expensive and eats up an enormous amount of processing power. But I need fast results. And so you're getting access."

"Thank you very much, Commissioner."

Vogel waves away my thanks. "And now see to it that you get to work. I expect an interim report by this time tomorrow."

He puts his hands in his lap and concentrates on his desk, which I take as an invitation to see myself the hell out. I stand up and walk to the door.

"One more thing, Westerhuizen."

"What's that?"

"There's a new iteration of TIRESIAS. One that's a lot more . . . independent. It's still classified. I'll try to get you access to that as well. Maybe it'll help."

"Thank you. I'll speak with my analyst about it."

"It might be that in the future you won't need her anymore."

"Why not?"

"The next Terry will work with inspectors directly. That's the idea, at least. At the beginning the analyst will still act as a go-between, like before, but probably not in the later stages."

"Has he really gotten that advanced?"

"Remains to be seen. Personally, I was very impressed by the first tests. And now, out with you."

I leave the office and head in the direction of the elevators. Digital forensics without analysts—how's that supposed to work? Europol's hormonal equilibrium will go completely off the rails.

CHAPTER 3

On the way back to my office, I give my analyst a call.

"Hello, Ava."

"Hi, Aart. How were things with Vogel?"

"He was friendly, in his own way. But he's not going to stay that way for long if he thinks we're working too slowly. We're focusing on Pazzi from now on."

"And what about this creeper-feed story?" she asks. "I had new illegal recordings come across my desk. Crazy stuff."

"Vogel says we should ignore everything else, so that's what we're going to do. Perverted sex videos will have to wait."

"Damn."

In the course of our conversation, I've arrived at the elevator, heading directly to the underground garage. "I'm going to see Pazzi's apartment for myself."

"Okay. Should I prepare a replication?"

"Yes, just to be on the safe side. But I'll go to his apartment anyway and look around in the real world. Can you share the address and access codes with my car?"

"Will do."

"Thanks. And after that I need to speak with the leader of Pazzi's party. Who would that be, again? The Danish woman?"

"Exactly, Jana Svensson, Liberal party leader."

"Good. Though Pazzi's lover, Peter Heuberger, would be even more useful. He's in Brussels, right? Can you pinpoint his location for me?"

"Easy. He's only a parliamentary assistant, so he doesn't have immunity." There's silence for a moment. As I'm stepping into the parking garage and summoning my car, Ava says, "Peter Heuberger isn't in the District Européen."

"Why not? I thought he had a date with Pazzi for dinner tonight?"

"Yes. But he took the express train to Berlin at 7:30 this morning. He arrived around ten."

"And what's he doing there?"

"At the moment he's in the House of Representatives at the Bundestag, along with his MEP, Tanja Boll. Would you like Terry's predications, based on his earlier movement patterns?"

"Please."

"It's a quick trip, lasts five and a half hours. Heuberger comes back on the same day. Probability: eighty-seven percent. Or it lasts longer than planned, then he'll have dinner at the Viaggio restaurant in the Gendarmenmarkt and stay overnight at the Hotel Lotte. Probability: ten percent. Terry says that in the first case, Heuberger will probably arrive back at Bruxelles-Midi on the 6:33 express train tonight."

"Okay. Terry should let me know a half hour before

he gets there. If he stays in Berlin, I want to know right away. Assign drones to him, too, if necessary."

"We're not going to send Heuberger a summons?"

"No, I'll wait for him at the train station tonight. Does he already know Pazzi's dead?"

"Hold on. We have all of his phone and email records and Terry can't find anything about it in there."

Vogel's still keeping it under wraps. But the media will catch wind of it by early afternoon. Heuberger will find out around the same time, probably during his return trip. Not ideal, finding out about something like that in a crowded train. That means he'll be at his wit's end when I run into him. It's how I like my witnesses best.

I consider talking to Ava about the new version of Terry but decide against it. "See you later, Ava. Could we go through everything we have again tonight?"

"Of course. But we'll have to do it at my place, if that's okay?"

I've never been to Ava's house before. Our relationship is, as previously mentioned, of a strictly professional nature. But why not? "Sounds good. I'll come by as soon as I've squeezed everything I can out of Heuberger."

"Okay, that's great. See you later, Aart."

I get into my Mercedes and direct it to drive to Pazzi's apartment. As we leave the parking garage, I can hear a familiar pattering sound. It just keeps pouring rain—if anything, it's getting worse. The rain management system is a dead giveaway about that. A few years ago, the city administration installed drainage pumps throughout Brussels, since the boulevards and avenues were constantly turning into streams. Normally the pumps carry the water away with no problems, but today the water is ankle-deep. Traffic is practically at a standstill because of it, even though rush hour hasn't started yet.

"Priority access," I growl. Right away, Gottlieb commands the other cars to make way for an urgent police matter, and the traffic parts in front of us.

After about twenty minutes, I arrive at Pazzi's place of residence. It's a boxy building, a bit past its prime, probably from the late twenties if the New Art Nouveau style is anything to go by. The bottom part, comprising the first five floors, is made of once-white sandstone, with a glass cube almost a hundred meters tall stuck on top of it. In spite of, or maybe precisely because of, all the floral motifs and fairy tale designs, the building looks like Snow White's coffin. Thanks to my Europol codes, the car can drive right past the double security perimeter into the parking garage. It drops me off in front of the elevator.

As my specs have shared with me, Pazzi lived on the fifty-seventh floor, the penthouse. I make a pit-stop in the lobby. In the foyer, I'm greeted by even more Nouveau aesthetics, a group of chairs, and a reception desk with a concierge sitting behind it. I give him a friendly nod. He smiles back at me. When I hold my Europol badge under his nose, the smile goes away.

"Good afternoon. You must be here because of Mr. Pazzi, Mr. . . . " He eyes my badge. "Inspector Westerhuizen?"

The concierge is a small man with a thin mustache on his upper lip and a habit of looking around nervously. According to my specs his name is Reza Yekta, fifty-seven years old, Persian, limited residency permit, lives at 15a Lombardstraat, not married, no kids, problems with deciphering police badges.

"Chief Inspector," I respond gruffly.

The concierge turns pale.

"When was the last time *you* saw Vittorio Pazzi?"

He mumbles something, calling up some data or other on his bargain-basement North Korean specs. It takes some time. "According to the building's security system—"

"He left his apartment yesterday shortly after noon. Our forensics experts have already checked over the data, you don't have to read it to me."

I activate the slim LED bars on my specs that indicate I'm recording. In old movies, the police always directed harsh lamps at their witnesses during interrogations, but today the same devastating psychological effect can be achieved with a small red light-emitting diode. In actuality, I've been recording everything since the beginning of the conversation. But the concierge doesn't need to know that.

"So instead I'd like to know when you saw him last." I pause for effect. "Mr. Yekta? 15a Lombardstraat?"

I see fear in his eyes. "When he got home yesterday, I'd guess around seven o'clock, I saw him briefly," he stammers.

"Did you notice anything about him in particular?"

"He looked like he'd been through the wringer. And he was carrying a deck of playing cards."

"Playing cards? What kind of cards?"

"A very ordinary kind, I'd say, Inspector, I mean Chief Inspector. In a cardboard box, I saw it very clearly."

"Anything else?"

"No, Chief Inspector."

"Good." I turn the red LEDs off. He looks relieved. "Have a good day, Mr. Yekta."

I walk to the elevator and tell it to take me to the penthouse. As soon as the doors have closed, I send the recording of Yekta's statement to Ava, asking her to compare it to the video records from the building's camera system. In addition, she needs to find out if Vittorio Pazzi had a weakness for poker or bridge.

As the elevator doors glide open, I mutter, "Site map" and walk a few meters along the hallway before standing still. The inside of the building is certainly in better shape than the outside. The ceiling is stuccoed, as are sections of the walls. More of the New Nouveau style, elves riding on whales, halflings with giant manga-eyes, wizards in pointed hats hurling thunderbolts. According to the blueprints on my specs, there are a total of four apartments on this floor. I go to the door at the far right, behind which Pazzi's penthouse lies in wait, and ring the bell.

The door opens and Paul Leclerq appears in the entryway. "You again already, Westerhuizen. Can't you let us do our work in peace and quiet? Just look at the replication afterward."

"How far along is your team?"

"As good as done." He takes a step to the side and lets me through. Pazzi's penthouse is 151 square meters. The lion's share belongs to the living room, where I'm now standing. A humming-drone buzzes past me, stops short, and inspects me with its infrared camera. It takes a few fractions of a second before the little drone realizes I'm not some Nouveau-style sculpture of a troll that's part of the inventory it's meant to be scanning. The humming-drone flies away.

Pazzi's retreat looks different than I imagined. Generally speaking, bachelor pads are all the same; there are only two variations. The first is owned by the unorganized bachelor, with sauce-encrusted cartons of Brazilian takeout, old socks, and bits of weed under his coffee table. In contrast, the apartment owned by bachelor number two is unbelievably spick-and-span, as if the occupant is counting on the arrival of his dream woman at any moment, the woman who will finally put an end to his lonely existence. Whether tidy or untidy, time seems to freeze in single men's apartments. Most are full of Swedish student furniture, the sort of thing any woman would have taken to a recycling plant years ago.

Considering his bespoke Milanese threads, though, I should have known Pazzi wouldn't fall into either of these categories. In the first place, the man had money; second, he had taste; and third, he was no bachelor. I'm thinking too much in heterosexual stereotypes—maybe I'll have to go back to one of the diversity seminars held by Commission management. Pazzi's furnishings are expensive and tasteful without coming across as showy. He, or maybe an interior designer he hired, made sure the designer pieces decorating his apartment were arranged in a way that doesn't resemble a furniture warehouse. Basic everyday items are lying around everywhere, not tidy or untidy, but lived-in. I remember Pazzi's deliberately untied cravat and the open cuffs on his linen shirt. The apartment fits his style.

I wander through the penthouse. In the kitchen, a member of the forensics team is setting more drones in the fridge and on the countertops. They scrabble around the milk cartons and opened yogurts like cockroaches, sniffing for chemicals that have no business being in a normal fridge. The kitchen alone must have cost about as much as my Mercedes, though I doubt much cooking was done in here.

"Is there an interior security system?" I ask the forensics worker with the robo-cockroaches.

He shakes his head. "No, nothing at all."

That means Pazzi valued his privacy. I peek briefly into the bathroom, then enter the bedroom. It's dominated by a king-sized bed. There's a tray on the floor nearby with tumblers and a bottle of whiskey. I reach for it and check the label: Shimizu Gold, eighty-three years old. I put the whiskey back and go to the closet, sunk into the wall. I don't see a door handle. After the closet and I have stared at each other for a few seconds, I say, "Open closet."

A portion of the closet glides to one side, revealing

suits behind it—there must be dozens. I've heard of closets like this, but never thought I'd actually see one myself. I say, "What should I wear today?"

One of the closet walls—obviously completely covered with media screens—changes its color. A strange-looking man appears out of a white background, some kind of virtual construct only a stoned programmer could have come up with. The man is in his mid-fifties, strangely gaunt, with a white ponytail that looks as if he's powdered it.

"Good morning," the man says in French. "The outside temperature has reached twenty-one degrees Celsius. I recommend a linen two-ply. What color would you like today?"

"Something muted, in blue," I answer.

The man on the screen nods, and the suits in the closet set themselves in motion. They clatter by me like shirts on a dry cleaner's rack. After about thirty seconds, three different suits push toward me and come to a stop, though they keep swaying. I pick up one of them. The virtual fashion designer nods appreciatively. An array of miniature shirts and cravats appears next to him.

"A recommendation, please," I say.

"For you, I recommend a light blue cotton shirt by Pietro Wong and this cravat by Iguaçu."

"Okay."

There's more rattling in Pazzi's wardrobe. Then a drawer to my left opens with a whir. Inside are a neatly folded shirt and a bright red scarf with a South American Indian motif.

I leave the room. Apart from the bathroom, kitchen, and bedroom, there's just the living area. The panoramic window on one side looks out in the direction of the city center. The other side looks over the surrounding countryside, though more will be visible whenever it finally stops raining in such torrents, maybe in September. The space is dominated by a walnut dining table and a sofa set with coffee table. In between are several statues by Giacometti. Since I was able to marvel at Pazzi's wardrobe in the course of my work, I know for a fact the man must have been outrageously rich—as I approach the statues, I pull up his bank account balance on my specs—but real Giacomettis are a bit unlikely even given his wealth. Not that there's a substantial difference between these copies and the real sculptures in a museum. A 3D printer must have utilized the same metal alloy to fabricate them, with the help of replicated measurements precise down to a thousandth of a millimeter.

"Are they real?" I ask my specs.

"My scanner is not able to determine this."

Good copies, then. And a stupid answer. I consider a statue, this one depicting a bulimic woman. "Précis for the sculpture."

"Alberto Giacometti's *Woman of Venice*, from 1956. Housed in a private collection in São Paulo. Art critics consider this sculpture—"

So it is a copy. Against one wall is a small Biedermeier secretary desk, with its slatted cover rolled down. I push it up. On the work surface is a Montblanc fountain pen and a stack of handmade paper printed with Pazzi's home address. Next to those is a small metal box. Its surface is made of hammered silver, etched with tiny cherubs and grapevines.

"Has this already been replicated?" I ask no one in particular.

"No, still need to get the inside," one of the forensics team calls.

I open the little box. It's lined with red velvet. I'm mostly expecting to find drugs. Instead I find playing cards—a poker deck, then a Rider-Waite tarot pack, both somewhat worn. The box also contains assorted dice in different colors. Most of them have six sides, though some have eight, twelve, or twenty.

Further down I find what appears to be a homemade spinner. It's made out of a round, gray cardboard disk with a small hole through the middle. A red arrow has been fastened inside so it can be spun around. The disk is divided into a total of ten sections. In them is written "go for a walk," "library," "museum," "opera," and so on. A useful toy for someone unsure of the best way to kill time. I pick up the disk and spin the arrow. It recommends that I take another trip to the zoo.

Under all this game paraphernalia are brass coins with a square stamped out of the middle. They're Chinese I Ching coins. Their surfaces are black with oxidation and somewhat hollowed out. I remove a few of them, lay them on the tabletop, and run my finger over the raised, glittering gold symbols. Then I turn around. No one's looking at me. With my gaze averted, I lay my palm flat on the table so one of the coins sticks to it, releasing it only after my hand has slipped into my jacket pocket. Then I set the rest of the I Ching coins back in the little chest and close the lid.

On the way back to the elevator, my stomach begins to growl. Unfortunately, I can't do much for it. It's already 3:12 p.m., I have a lot of things left to do, and taking a break isn't one of them. On the ride down, I eat my last two pieces of licorice, a few glucose tablets, and whatever else I can find in the pocket of my trench coat. Then I take a seat in my Mercedes and call up Jana Svensson's office.

A Southern European woman with black corkscrew curls appears on my specs—she's very pretty, but with a face that's been perhaps a bit too obviously optimized.

"Office of Jana Svensson, a very good afternoon to you," she chirps.

"Good afternoon. Chief Inspector Westerhuizen. I need to speak with the representative on urgent business."

I transmit my Jacobin ID card to her. As always, that puts a damper on the mood. Still, the curly-haired woman tries to keep on smiling.

"About which matter would you like to speak with Ms. Svensson?"

"An investigation into a homicide."

"I'm terribly sorry, Inspector, but she's currently in a very important meeting that could last a few more hours."

I nod my head sympathetically. "Understood. But I'm afraid the case can't wait that long."

She grins in amusement, with the air of someone who's managed to brush off many appellants in the past. "And what do you think I should do?"

"Simple. Get the representative out of her meeting. Is she in Brussels?"

"No, Copenhagen. And I can't—"

"And then," I cut her off, "set up a holo-conference for us immediately."

"Inspector, it is highly unusual to summon a representative on such short notice like this. At the end of the day," she straightens up a little, "she has diplomatic immunity." She tries to give me an accusatory look.

I consider simply telling her the truth. But if I did, in fifteen minutes the entire EU Parliament would get word of Pazzi's death, and another fifteen minutes after that, the entire District Européen would know. Worst of all, Svensson wouldn't hear it from me, but from her curly-haired Cerberus.

So instead I say, "It's also highly unusual to impede an investigator from the European public prosecution office in his work like this, Ms. . . . Petrarca. We're investigating a murder case, and it's of the utmost necessity that I speak with Ms. Svensson right away." In a more conciliatory tone, I add, "This isn't a formal summons, and the representative isn't a suspect, but the case could become very delicate politically. The dead man was a well-known figure."

The look in her eyes takes on a certain nosiness.

"And who is it?"

"That's confidential. Now, send my request to Ms. Svensson right away, or—"

"Or what?"

"Or maybe I'll have to send one of my Danish colleagues to this meeting in person? Of course, I wanted to steer clear of that. But if you're sure you'd like there to be a scene . . . "

She capitulates much faster than expected. I'd really like to know why.

"Okay, Inspector. I'll try to get her out of the meeting as fast as possible."

"Thank you."

Then I hang up. During the drive back to my office, I read through a précis on Svensson. She's fifty-six years old, studied history in Rio and Lisbon, and has been a member of the Liberals for over four years. Before that, she was the Danish minister of defense, and before that an army officer. In one of the photos attached to the report, Svensson is jumping out of a military helicopter, dressed in desert camo and a Kevlar vest. She really looks the part of a lieutenant colonel in the Union coalition, one who sniffs out rebel nests before breakfast—she has the right merciless look. According to the précis, though, Svensson has never breathed the sands of the Sahara; instead she kept comfortable in an outpost for recon aircraft. I'm jealous. Sitting beside a pool in Malta with specs and an ice-cold Heineken, using the nearby satellite dishes to hack a few Tuareg guerillas, sounds a lot nicer than the things I had to do back then.

If the commentators are to be believed, Svensson is the type of politician who routinely goes after anyone and everyone: real and imagined enemies, underachievers, people who have the misfortune to be nearby at the wrong time. Many believe that, because of this tendency, she'll make it all the way to the top. If Pazzi might have held Svensson back in her career, that would be the first inkling of a motive in this case. Clearly, I do need to eat something before my conversation with Svensson after all. She doesn't look like someone whose path I want to cross with low blood sugar.

I close out of the précis and set up a link to Terry. The windshield turns opaque and the Europol logo appears. Underneath it reads "TIRESIAS."

"Good evening, Chief Inspector Westerhuizen."

Terry is the perfect Union citizen. He speaks a total of forty-one official languages fluently and accent-free. To me, he speaks in wonderful Dutch, light as a flower petal. It's almost enough to break my heart.

I have plenty of questions for our police computer and consider which I should pose first. Terry waits faithfully, with more patience than any Montessori kindergartener.

"Was Pazzi a rival of Svensson's, Terry?"

"In his function as deputy party leader, Vittorio Pazzi was theoretically in competition with Svensson. An analysis of his communications, however, reveals that he was quite loyal."

"What do you mean by 'quite loyal?'"

"Audio and text records from the past four years document only small differences of opinion, largely in trade policy. There are no indications, though, that Pazzi was involved in any intrigue against his party leader. All signs point to harmonious cooperation between these two party members."

"How bizarre."

"I don't understand the question, Chief Inspector."

Instead of explaining the concept of sarcasm to Terry, I ask, "Are you by any chance the . . . the new Terry?"

"Yes, Chief Inspector. You are speaking with TIRE-SIAS, Version IV, beta."

"You're a test version?"

"That is correct. This iteration of my software is still in the development stages and is therefore in use by only a select number of people."

"Who in particular?"

"That is confidential information, accessible only by clearance from the Commissioner. Should I request it?"

"No. In what ways are you better than the last Terry?"

"New semantic algorithms allow me to communicate data forensics directly to those without special training. Furthermore, my predictive capacities were improved considerably."

"That means you could use the data history to help an idiot like me, for example by generating a list of delivery services in the area that'll deliver something to eat to the Palais and arrive at the same time we do, despite the lousy weather and rush-hour traffic?"

"I have access to all traffic patterns and payment transactions associated with delivery services in Brussels and could provide a very accurate prognosis. Though I am obligated to inform you that it is a violation of service regulations to use my resources for an overtly private matter."

"I'm not saying you should order me a pizza. I just want to test your predictive algorithms and I happen to be doing it by asking you for the name of a delivery service that fulfills all of those conditions."

That gives him something to chew on, but naturally, it doesn't take long. "What sort of cuisine would you prefer, Chief Inspector?"

"Traditional Dutch food."

"There are no delivery services that meet your criteria."

I sigh. "Korean food?" There's always a Korean restaurant.

"There's a branch of Pyongyang Five nearby. It offers delivery via courier drone and is extremely punctual."

To avoid giving Internal Affairs anything to complain about, I complete the order via my specs. While I'm at it, I give my inbox a look and see Svensson has already agreed to speak with me and will call me as soon as she's available for the holo-conference.

I look out the window. We're already in the city center, traveling east along Antwerpselaan. Brussels's inhabitants manage to stay halfway dry by going about their business on the covered sidewalks, while Brussels's cars get thoroughly soaked in pushing their way through rush-hour traffic. About a hundred meters in front of us I notice a road block, with floodlight drones hovering above the cars. Police officers are there, too, in the process of lugging several people out of a car and bundling them into a police van.

"Terry, I need a complete précis about my current resources. Vogel said he added to them."

"As of 2:21 p.m., you have been authorized to order and carry out live replications in the EU mirror space."

Vogel was as good as his word. That makes things a bit easier.

"On what scale?"

"There are no stipulations about the computing power, bandwidth, and budget of your unrestricted pass to the mirror space."

I whistle through my teeth. Unlimited access, not bad. "Anything else?"

"As previously discussed, you have full access to my newest iteration, TIRESIAS IV. That's also the case for Chief Analyst Bittman."

I disconnect from Terry. The Mercedes is now passing the Parc de Bruxelles. I look out at the Commission Palais, visible despite the overcast skies. Unrestricted access to the mirror space doesn't come along every day. We usually only get something like that to solve terrorist attacks or especially high-profile cases. I'm thinking of my colleague Wesslinger, who went after the so-called Mirror Killer a few years ago—a serial killer who expertly dismembered his victims, filming himself with drones the whole time, and uploaded the result onto the net as a high-definition 360-orthomosaic. Wesslinger also got unrestricted access to the mirror space.

But why am I getting it? Vogel's gone to the trouble of getting me resources that would make every one of my coworkers green with envy, and all for an overdressed second-string parliamentarian. Forcing something like that through the system requires powerful friends. I turn around and look in the direction of the Commission Palais until it disappears behind the streaming rain.

Before I go upstairs, I pick up my food in the mailroom. "When was it delivered?" I ask the mail worker on duty as he hands me the box.

"The delivery drone just left, Inspector. Your food's been here for one, maybe two minutes."

Impressively precise—if Terry IV doesn't live up to expectations as a police computer, we could still use him for procuring junk food. I wedge the red paper box under my arm and head to the exit.

As I walk past the mail worker, he sniffs with interest. "Bulgogi?" he asks.

"No, kimchi pizza."

When I'm back in the office, I settle in with the paper box. As I wolf down the pizza, I call up the Europol ticker on my specs.

In Duisburg, militant Christians have attempted to blow an abortion clinic sky-high. Probably Templar Knights, a splinter group that's already made itself famous with similar attacks in Lille and Turin.

Another tunnel was uncovered in South Andalusia, its construction indicating that it belongs to smuggling operations inside the Italian mafia. Its exit on the Union side is over three kilometers behind the fence. It's still completely unknown how something like that was built without drawing anyone's attention. Even our mole drones couldn't detect the construction work.

The Europol prefecture has raised the overall security alert level from two to three. The reasoning is that, in the coming week, six new solar arrays will be activated in the Western Sahara. Our intelligence service thinks it's possible someone may try to blow up their panel towers.

I shake my head. They always keep trying. Before I've even polished off half the pizza, I get an incoming priority message. Svensson is ready for the conference and is already waiting for me online. I look regretfully at my food. But really, the only thing that tastes worse than cold kimchi pizza is reheated kimchi pizza. I toss the carton in the trash on my way out.

On the way to the conference room, I lick my lips a few times and wipe my mouth with a less-than-fresh paper napkin from the pocket of my trench coat to get any possible sauce remnants off my face. The required etiquette dictates that each party in a holo-conference appears to their counterpart in a way as true to life as possible. It's considered poor etiquette to use digital makeup or projections based on historic data that can make someone look ten years younger. I open the door to the conference room and go inside. I can't smile too widely or show any teeth. There might still be some kimchi scraps between them.

The room looks exactly like every other conference room in the world, the same chairs, the same lighting, the same oval table made of cherry veneer.

"Refresh projection data and connect to conference with Jana Svensson," I command.

A small drone whirrs into the room through an opening between two boards in the wall. It begins to circle me frantically, refreshing my avatar in a database somewhere and adding a few new gray hairs and a couple of sauce stains. I wait until my specs signal that I've been replicated, then sit down on one of the chairs.

The air in front of me starts to flicker and the wall behind it seems to disappear. After a second or two, a holographic projection of a wiry woman in a black pantsuit appears on the other side of the table. Svensson has short blond hair. Her eyes are green, as green as emeralds, and they exude just about as much warmth. This woman is not here of her own accord, and she can't be bothered to hide it. If anything, her facial expression says she'd rather be taking a stroll through a Moroccan minefield than speaking with me. Since nothing better occurs to me, I decide to try and kill with kindness.

"Good afternoon, Madame Representative. Aart

von der Westerhuizen from Europol. I thank you for taking the time out of your very busy schedule and apologize in advance for the inconvenience."

Then I bow in the Japanese style. That's become the vernacular, since it's difficult to shake hands with a conversation partner in a holo-conference. In response, Svensson gives a barely noticeable nod of her head.

"Good afternoon. Would you like to go ahead and tell me who's died, Chief Inspector?"

"Vittorio Pazzi. We found him this morning in the vicinity of Westrem."

Her reaction isn't easy to pin down. She looks taken aback, but not at all upset or shocked. It could be she's not the emotional type. Or it could be she's using software to modify the hologram projected on my specs. Those kinds of programs could give a poker face to a manic-depressive junkie. When Ava examines the raw data from the video later, she'll be able to determine if Svensson is using something like that.

"How did he die?"

"High-velocity projectile," I answer. "Shot in the head."

She nods casually, as if that were to be expected. "Who knows about it?"

In one of my old black-and-white films, this would be the moment when the police detective would yell, "I'll ask the questions here, sweetheart!" But that's not my style.

"Up till now, not many people. But it'll be coming over the feeds soon, maybe even today."

I stand up and walk a few steps along the wall, my hands in my coat pockets. "Ms. Svensson, when was the last time you saw Pazzi?"

"If you've unsealed the data, you must already know the answer."

"But I'd prefer to hear it from you, if you don't mind. TIRESIAS can check it against the records later."

She pushes back one of the chairs and sits down. "Last Tuesday we had lunch together, in the historic district. On Friday we had another short holo-conference with our party's executive committee about the upcoming vote on the new constitution."

"How are the Liberals going to vote?"

Svensson sets her hands in her lap. "I've never made a secret of the fact that I'll vote in favor. As soon as the Brits are gone, we can finally restructure things. It's long overdue. The only way to protect the Union against challenges and threats from the outside is stronger cohesion.— Why are are you grinning, Inspector?"

"Pardon me. But you sounded exactly like a politician."

If she finds it funny, she does a great job of hiding it.

"In any case, on the record, we've stated that the vote is to be kept secret. But of course, the leadership's recommendation is to adopt the new Union constitution."

"Was Pazzi of the same opinion?"

"Officially, yes. But I think he was still undecided."

"As deputy party leader?"

"It was difficult for many members of Parliament to come to a decision. Nation states are still a beloved fetish. Not everyone has the far-reaching perspective that we have here in the District Européen."

"Do you think he had enemies?"

She considers for a moment. "None in particular. Just the usual suspects."

"Like who, for example?"

"He was vehemently against the British leaving. So maybe English separatists. North African guerrillas, due to his stance on solar politics. Or Christian zealots."

"Because of his homosexuality?"

"These people don't need a reason, Chief Inspector."

A short pause follows. Svensson grins. Little by little, I'm surmising that she is using software. It seems increasingly unlikely that this woman is capable of smiling without the assistance of a computer.

"Have you already checked my alibi, Inspector?"

"Why should I? After all, you're not one of the usual suspects."

"You'd be doing me a favor."

"You'll have to explain that one to me, Ms. Svensson."

"This case will make waves. When the press asks me about it, I'd like to be able to tell them Europol has already looked into my alibi."

"To do so, you'd have to agree to a complete unsealing of your movement and communication data."

"You'll get it from my attorney in no more than an hour. And I'll look into getting you similar approvals from all members of the executive committee."

I smile indulgently. "Thanks very much. If only everyone would put so much energy into helping the police—"

"—the world would be a better place, I know."

"And what do I get in return for doing this?" I ask.

She glares at me. "What do you mean by that? I'm meeting you more than halfway with this unsealing."

"From where I'm sitting, there's no reason to vet the data profiles of half the Liberal party. But if I do it anyway, it's like a get-out-of-jail-free card for you, isn't it? No one could possibly suspect you of having anything to do with Pazzi's death, even though you'll probably exploit it thoroughly over the next few weeks. The great bearer of hope, a martyr for the liberal cause, the Kennedy of Merano."

"Where are you going with this?"

"Where I have to in order to solve the case. Don't misunderstand me; if you approve the unsealing, you'll be absolved of all sins, no problem. But in return, I'd like to know who exactly has an interest in this case."

"And how am I supposed to help you with that?"

"There are indications that people in the highest ranks of the Union are intervening in the investigation, even though Pazzi was only a representative of middling importance. It's said you have good contacts in the security apparatus due to your membership on the Defense Committee, not to mention direct connections to the very top of the Commission."

"Go on."

"If you hear something, Ms. Svensson, call me. This is a political case, and I'd prefer not to step on a landmine."

"Understood, Chief Inspector. Is that all?"

"Yes, many thanks for your time. Although there is one more thing: Do you know Peter Heuberger?"

She shakes her head. "No, the name doesn't ring a bell."

"Good. Have a nice evening, Madame Representative." I walk around the conference table in the direction of the door and turn back to give Svensson another nod from that position. But she's already dissolved into thin air.

CHAPTER 4

It's just before six when I leave the Palais de Justice. The rain has let up and only a few drops dampen my face as I walk through the checkpoints. In front of the building, I'm greeted by a large crowd standing behind a wire fence. At first, I assume the press has gotten wind of the Pazzi case by now and are laying siege to the police entrance. But on second glance, these aren't journalists, they're Christians. Religious groups aren't my area of expertise, but I'd bet on Lanze Christi or Sturm Jesuits. The demonstration produces an impressive amount of noise and smoke, the acrid smell of incense wafting toward me.

The special forces unit on my side of the barricade looks incredibly bored. Small wonder, since in the end this is all just for show. At least half a dozen humming-drones are swarming above the zealots. If any of them does something rash, like smacking a censer against a policeman's skull or drawing a weapon, they'd be registered and identified by Terry within fractions of a second. Not to mention a police drone would powder their noses, as we like to put it—thousands of tracking devices no bigger than dust particles raining down on the troublemaker and sticking like burrs. After being tagged like that, they'd have to flee as far as the Arabian nuclear desert to avoid getting caught. And even that might not be far enough.

So the Christians have to content themselves with brandishing their wooden crucifixes threateningly in the air. "Sanguis martyrum, semen christianorum!" they scream over and over again. As they do, they look directly into the lenses of the aerial drones, fully aware that not only cops but also some of the media and droggers are behind them.

I give a friendly nod to the officer-in-charge. He lets me out through one side of the barricade. The Bruxelles-Midi station is barely a kilometer away from here, and so I walk to the Poelaertplein, where an elevator leads from the city on the surface to the city underground. Then I make my unhurried way through the Marollen quarter in the direction of the train station. According to my specs, Heuberger's Euroexpress will arrive right on time. I have a short précis on the parliamentary assistant read to me on the way, but I'm only half listening. It's hardly worth it. Peter Heuberger is one of these Eurocrats who graduate from management academies in Paris or Lisbon by the dozen. Party membership at fifteen, first EU internship at eighteen, by twenty-five more foreign visits than pairs of underwear. Wealthier than normal for someone his age, especially an assistant to a representative. Someday he'll be a candidate himself—Terry gives a likelihood of eighty-nine percent. Either his current MEP will make sure he gets a place on the party list, or he'll inherit the mandate from his daddy.

"Are Heuberger's parents involved in politics?"

"His father was governor of the province of Carinthia and is now in Parliament as a Conservative representative from Austria."

So it's the latter. Like Pazzi, Heuberger wasn't born with just a silver spoon, but with the whole place setting. I'm eagerly awaiting the chance to meet such a likable young man. He's apparently never so much as considered committing a crime; his criminal record is comparable to that of a Wallonian saint. The probability that Heuberger has ever committed an undiscovered offense is, according to Terry, under one percent. This stick-in-the-mud hasn't even done drugs, not once. His future prospects are equally good, at least they were before Pazzi's death.

There's not much to arouse my curiosity in the lighter parts of his personality either. Heuberger has terrible taste in music, all top-of-the-pops. He used to have an affinity for popular German literature from the previous century, Suter, Simmel, that sort of thing. Later he switched over to impenetrable Frenchmen, Houellebecq, Djaout, Sartre. I can't find any proof that all these books made him a more interesting person.

Heuberger is a creature of habit: he always eats in the same brasseries and goes to his local bar near the Rouppeplein once a week. Tuesdays and Fridays, he takes a yoga class, electro-stim Bikram. According to his active search routines, he's scouring the net to find a bigger apartment: prewar, around a hundred square meters, not too far from Parliament, ideally with a balcony. In addition, Heuberger wants to buy a new car and has been shopping around for over a year. He can't seem to decide between the Peugeot Envoyé and the VW Cygnus. I wouldn't be able to either. They're both awful.

At Grondwetplein I take the escalator down into the underground labyrinth of the south train station, sprawling out in all directions. My specs guide me to the Euroexpress platform and mark the place where, according to his seat number, Heuberger will exit the train. I consider double checking if his representative is also on the train but toss the thought aside. Instead I buy some black licorice from a kiosk. I chew on a piece and wait for the express train, considering the graffiti some vandal has used to adorn the partition of the waiting area next to me. It's not a slogan or symbols but crooked white rectangles and triangles, around two dozen of them in various sizes. I think I've seen these things in my neighborhood as well— must be modern art.

A few minutes later, Euroexpress 231 from Berlin glides noiselessly into the station and comes to a stop. I can only catch the passengers' outlines through the reflective windowpanes. With an audible hiss, the doors open. Tired-looking people pour out of the doorways and hurry along the platform in the direction of the exits, followed by dozens of rolling suitcases that have a hell of a time keeping up with their owners in the crush of people.

Heuberger's not among them. I call Ava.

"Hi, Aart, are you with Heuberger?"

"I'm not seeing him. Where is he?"

"Hold on, I'll find him for you."

A bright blue overlay appears on my specs. Contrary to what we expected, Heuberger must have been in one of the cars further up and exited through one of the other doors. In the meantime, he's already gone through the train station, up the escalators, and is now heading for the taxi stand.

Ava's disbelieving laugh comes through her mike into my ear. "I think he's trying to make a run for it."

With a curse on my lips, I run along the platform. In the process I almost collide with a suitcase coming at me from the right. After a few more evasive maneuvers and some pushing and shoving, I reach the aboveground plaza where taxis are waiting for customers.

Heuberger has already driven away. On my specs, I see a small red dot traveling north along the Slachthuislaan.

"Should I stop him?" Ava asks. "I can tell the taxi computer to pull over and lock the doors."

"No. Let him be." I climb into a taxi and give the GPS an address north of the city center, since I know the car's computer will refuse to follow another taxi.

"Ava?"

"Yeah?"

"A surveillance drone would be nice. Not a humming, a jet drone."

"I already requested one. It's estimated to reach Heuberger's taxi in two and a half minutes and not let it out of its sight after that."

My taxi, a tiny Peugeot, turns onto the ring road with a hum. "Can you couple my taxi with Heuberger's so it'll follow him?"

"The taxi dispatch center is kind of touchy when it comes to things like that. But if there's a reason for it, no problem. You just have to tell me that there's imminent danger."

"There's imminent danger."

In actuality, nothing is imminent. Heuberger isn't the kind of guy with the know-how to make himself invisible. If we conducted a Union-wide manhunt for him, ten thousand cameras and drones would be on the lookout for his face twenty-four hours a day. Fleeing is futile. That's the reason Ava laughed with disbelief when it dawned on her Heuberger might be running away.

Although he's not running away. At least not from us.

"Where's he headed, Ava?"

"According to his taxi, he wants to go to the seaside."

"What's his exact destination?"

"The beach on the other side of Bruges."

Heuberger doesn't seem to notice he's being followed by a jet drone and a taxi. Given the present circumstances, he's probably not noticing much of anything. During the drive, I do a little more digging into his data corona, as well as Pazzi's—two lives archived digitally. It's easy to see the relationship between the two was very genuine. I find reservations for vacations together, visits to restaurants, hundreds of hours of video chats. Somewhere in the midst of all this an invoice comes up, paid by Pazzi eight weeks ago. He ordered a ring from a goldsmith in Munich. It's simple, made of platinum, with a narrow gold stripe running around the middle.

Ava pulls me out of my thoughts. "Are you still coming by when you're done?"

"Of course. As soon as I've spoken with Heuberger."

"I don't understand why he's running away from you. And why you didn't take him into custody in the city to begin with."

"He's not running away from the police."

"What, then?"

"He's just running away."

"But why?"

"If your fiancé had been shot dead this morning, wouldn't you also think that was a reason to run?"

"He's in a state of shock, clearly. But I'd probably react differently."

Could be. No one knows beforehand how they'll react in any given situation. Some people go catatonic, others pass out. Still others cry like professional mourners after the bombing of Tehran. And some run away, just like Heuberger. It could be because he spent hours locked away in a train with his grief and the body odors of hundreds of strangers. Maybe that's the reason. Then again, maybe not. It's irrelevant.

Once we're past Bruges, the Nieuw Dijk appears in front of us. Heuberger's car stops at the bottom of the dike. He gets out and walks up the concrete staircase to reach the seaside. He moves as if he has a thirty-kilo field kit on his back. I wait a minute, then get out of my taxi as well and follow after him. The seaside consists of a cobblestone path gradually leading into a mudflat and ending in a pile of granite boulders covered in tar. Approximately two hundred and fifty meters to the left of the stairs is a wooden pier jutting out into the gray North Sea. It's still comfortably warm, and since the rain's let up, people are setting up camping chairs and picnic blankets on the dike's lawn.

I follow Heuberger as he heads for the pier. His green cravat has come loose, the wind threatening to rip it off. It doesn't seem to concern him. After he's walked halfway out on the pier, he stands still and looks out at the sea. I stop ten meters behind him and wait until his sobbing fades away.

"Mr. Heuberger?"

He turns around slowly and looks at me with disinterest. His wrinkle-resistant bespoke suit hangs sadly off him, his slicked-back brown hair is disheveled, and his reddened eyes are vacant.

"You're from the police."

I hold my identification out to him. "My sympathies, Mr. Heuberger. I'm leading the investigation into this case."

"I only heard about it just now," he murmurs. It doesn't sound like he's saying it to me. "Who could have done it?"

"That's what we're trying to find out," I answer patiently.

He looks in my direction but seems to have problems maintaining his focus on me. "What am I supposed to . . . Do I need to identify Vito?"

I shake my head. "Things like that are only done in the movies anymore. We know without a doubt that we're looking at the death of Vittorio Pazzi. And that it was murder. Come with me."

Without resisting, he lets me lead him to the dike steps. On the other side, there's a thatched house with a restaurant inside. We go in. I lead Heuberger to one of the low plastic tables and order two genevers. He knocks back the schnapps wordlessly. I recognize Pazzi's engagement ring on his right hand.

"Mr. Heuberger, when was the last time you saw your partner?"

"I spent the night at his place the day before yesterday."

"You don't live with him full-time?"

"No, no."

"And tonight, you had plans to meet him at the Lotte for dinner."

"What? No, I didn't know if I'd have to stay overnight in Berlin."

"But he did book a table for the two of you. That's straight from his data history."

"Maybe I missed one of his messages, my day was very hectic. But actually, tomorrow we wanted to . . . we wanted to fly to Salzburg for the weekend." Tears run down his cheeks. I don't need to ask Heuberger about an alibi. His overpriced apartment sits right on the Kanaal Charleroi, in a luxury apartment complex riddled with cameras and drones. If his movements had taken him anywhere else, for example to the branch of a poplar tree in a thicket near Westrem, Terry would have found out about it a long time ago.

"In your opinion, who could have done it?"

"He didn't have any enemies. He had such a good heart!" Heuberger weeps. He's taken off his cravat and is using it as a handkerchief.

"Influential politicians like Pazzi always have enemies," I argue.

He sits up slightly and looks at me properly for the first time. "He might have been the target of a terrorist plot, you mean? For the separatists?"

"Theoretically, that's a possibility."

"But he was only the deputy leader of the fourth-largest party in Parliament."

I nod. If someone wanted to bump off a high-standing EU functionary, there would definitely be fifty or a hundred targets worthier of their time than Pazzi.

"Can I escort you back to the city, Mr. Heuberger?"

"My taxi is waiting," he answers. "If you'll allow it, I'd rather travel alone. Or do I need to come into the station with you?"

I shake my head. "Go home. If something occurs to you, please give me a call."

He nods weakly. Then he notices that I haven't touched my genever, reaches for it, and knocks it back. I stand up and head in the direction of the door. Then I turn back for a moment.

"Mr. Heuberger?"

"Yes?"

"Did Vittorio Pazzi like to play card games?"

He looks at me in confusion. "No, not that I know of. Why do you ask?"

"We found a number of card games in his apartment, dice, not to mention I Ching coins."

"He wasn't a gambler." Heuberger looks into the empty genever glass. "But he was superstitious."

"How so?"

"Before making any important decisions recently, Vito was in the habit of consulting an oracle. The Rider-Waite tarot or the I Ching. Sometimes he rolled dice or tossed coins."

"You said 'recently.' So he wasn't always so superstitious?"

His lips quiver. "He always liked star signs and horoscopes, but he never really took them seriously. The stuff with the oracles began a few months ago. He used them often. For all important decisions. Before he proposed to me, he asked the I Ching for . . . for the ideal moment." Then his head sinks down, and he begins to sob again, uncontrollably. I say my goodbyes quietly and go to my taxi.

CHAPTER 5

There's nothing else for me to do today except drive to Ava's house and go through Terry's research one more time. Somehow I already have an idea what the outcome will be. I sink back into the taxi seat, exhausted, and listen to the hectic hum of the servomotors trying to accommodate my orthopedically unsound posture.

I close my eyes for a moment and drift off. I dream of a gray sea beating relentlessly against a dike. The water is at most a foot or two below the ledge and I can tell that the inside of the dam has the consistency of custard. It won't hold for much longer.

The taxi rattles over a speedbump and I wake up. My specs let me know I've only been out for two or three minutes. Two or three hours would be more to my liking. I watch the outskirts of the city going by outside. They're like the Parisian suburbs, their own microcosm with no bearing on life in historic Brussels. On the left we pass a cluster of nested apartment buildings painted a dusty pink; the locals, inspired by its concentric layout and predominantly Persian tenants, have dubbed it the "Rose of Tehran." The Arabian and North African quarters sit adjacent to the Rose, and somewhere past those is Little Amsterdam.

I ask the taxi how much longer we'll be to Ava's. It gives a remaining travel time of nineteen minutes. I use the time to catch up on the news via a media screen I find in the front seat pocket. Not a lot going on. The French authorities were able to foil an attack near Bordeaux at the last minute; the Japanese have easily conquered new territory and advanced almost as far as the Amur River; off the coast of Brazil, there's been a seaquake probably caused by a methane explosion. None of the headlines interests me, so I decide to find myself a movie instead. By the time I get home it'll be past midnight. After a day like mine, some people would just pass out cold. But I already know I'll never be able to fall asleep without a movie.

I open my video library and swipe through the old titles on the touchscreen. I just watched *The Big Sleep* for the first time last week, ditto *The Maltese Falcon*. I can't choose between *Key Largo* and *We're No Angels*, which I've seen twice; it's one of his few comedies. The movie poster shows him with Aldo Ray and Peter Ustinov. All three men wear prison jumpsuits. The jailbirds hold their Panama hats against their chests and gaze out innocently with the sort of look I get all too often in my line of work.

Wait a minute.

The three gangsters give me an idea. A group of three men—Pazzi had planned on meeting with two others tonight.

"Thanks, Bogey," I mutter. Then I call Ava.

She picks up right away. "You'll be here soon, right, Aart? You want something to eat?"

She sounds kind of eager. She tries to hide it, which just makes her come across as overeager.

"Absolutely."

"In the mood for something in particular?"

"Anything but Korean, if that's okay."

"No problem."

"Ava, Pazzi had plans to meet Heuberger and a third person at the Hotel Lotte tonight. Do we have any leads yet on who that could be?"

"Nope. According to Terry, Pazzi let his fiancé know about the meeting via email, but it looks like he invited the third member of their group some other way. Nothing we can trace."

"Nothing at all? Maybe he sent him a carrier pigeon?"

"Even a carrier pigeon would probably have shown up on a feed somewhere. All we know is that a reservation was made for three people at the Schönbrunn."

"The restaurant at the Hotel Lotte is called the Schönbrunn?"

"Yeah. And it looks like it, too." She laughs. "Koreans for you!"

"I'd like to have a look around there in person. Maybe the third guy doesn't know Pazzi's dead and he'll still show for their meeting."

She shakes her head. "The Lotte's all the way over in Woluwe-Saint-Pierre. You'll never make it in time. The meeting's in fifteen minutes."

"But I'm only five minutes from your place."

"You mean we could piggyback on the hotel security cameras?"

"Too low-tech. I want a real-time replication."

"You want to go in the mirror space? And how's that going to work? Only the intelligence service has access."

"I've heard rumors I was recently granted clearance, thanks to Vogel. Is that true?"

Ava mutters something. Then she says, "There is actually an authorization in your dossier. An unrestricted pass for the mirror space, valid until revoked. Although there is a note stating you should contact the RR before you use it."

"Those bastards would want to keep tabs on whoever's snooping around using their toys."

"You shouldn't say things like that, Aart."

She has a point. You can never be sure exactly who's listening in. The only sure thing is that someone is listening in. And it's safe to assume that someone is with the Récupération des Renseignements, the RR, the Union's intelligence service.

I think of who I know at the RR. Then I tell Ava she should prep the replication. After I hang up with her, I call Piet Ververke. He's the highest-ranking RR officer I can think of. We served together in Ain Salah, Sixth Division, through three years of sand dunes and attempts on our lives. Aside from that, Ververke's also from Amsterdam, which means we're connected by a pair of unfortunate experiences.

As expected, he picks up right away. There's no image and no signature, just a somewhat hoarse voice.

"Yes?"

"This is Aart van der Westerhuizen. Hello, Piet."

"I had a feeling you'd call sooner or later. Hmm, hold on a minute, this connection's not secure."

I anticipate hearing a click or a beep, but there's nothing like that. After a few seconds of silence, Ververke says, "That's better. So, you're a chief inspector now, hmm?"

"I'm just as surprised as you are."

"And now you want to waste agency resources on some minor-league Italian."

"Why should you get to have all the fun all by yourselves, Piet?"

"Hmm, yes, why should we? Because we need every available teraflop of processing power to keep the lunatics at bay. It's not the sort of stuff you'll hear about on the news, but we lost four big solar arrays this week alone. They have bionic drones armed with C24 explosives now. Desert salamanders, bury themselves in the sand."

"Really."

"Hmm, ingenious construction, really. We can barely take out a nest before another one pops up in its place."

"Where are they getting all this cutting-edge equipment?"

"Our best guess is from the Brits. Via Crete."

"I'm not going to use much of your precious processing power. I just have to load a couple replications."

"Have you been in touch with Yvonne Müller about it?"

"I wanted to, but it looks like I must have misplaced the direct number for the head of the EU intelligence service."

"Very funny. I can forward your request to her, Aart. But I don't know what her decision will be."

"Piet, there's been a misunderstanding."

"Hmm, and what's that?"

"I'm not asking you for permission to use the mirror space. I already have passcodes."

"What? How?"

"Beats me, ask Vogel or TIRESIAS if you want to try and make sense of the exact administrative protocol. But according to my brand-new unrestricted pass, I can go in whenever I want."

"I don't believe it."

"Then look it up. The mirror space doesn't belong to the agency, it belongs to the Union. It just so happens that you use it the most. I'm a public servant from an allied agency, and I have authorization. And because friends keep each other in the loop, I'm paying you the courtesy of letting you know before I go in."

For a moment Ververke stays silent. Then, deliberately, slowly, he says, "Do whatever you think is right, Aart. Do whatever you think you're allowed to do. But be careful."

"Is that a threat?"

"No, it's a well-intended piece of advice between former war buddies. I'm going to report this to the RR brass. And then I'm going to go hide under a rock somewhere. Maybe you should do the same."

"Point taken, Piet."

"You can still change your mind. Steer clear of the mirror space. Use Terry's creeper-feeds instead."

"They're not creeper-feeds, they're unsealed, and therefore legal, video recordings."

"Hmm. Do what you want, Aart. Over and out."

Then he hangs up.

The taxi idles in front of Ava's house, waiting patiently for me to get out. I let the interior camera scan my retina to authorize payment. With a concerted effort, I clamber out of the back seat; something in my back got bent out of shape during the trip. I have to pause for a minute on the sidewalk until I can stand up straight again.

My analyst lives in the sort of neighborhood I'd like to call home. Her street is lined by two rows of narrow three-story houses with lopsided, pointed gables; the houses' open curtains offer a peek into their living rooms, just as it was in Flanders. Ava's building is painted forest green and must be at least three hundred years old. It has a small garden in front, where sunflowers and chrysanthemums struggle to bloom without being drowned by the rain. I ring the doorbell and wait. After a few seconds I can hear the rumble of footsteps down a flight of wooden stairs; the door—also wood, painted over countless times with coats of white paint—opens, and Ava smiles at me. She's put in an effort to make herself look pretty—very pretty. It's the first time I've seen my analyst wear lipstick. She's also wearing a short summer skirt in Prussian blue, a white knit top with a deep neckline, and a black souvenir hoodie from

Marajó. She's pulled her hair back in a ponytail with a ribbon the same color as her skirt.

"Come on in, Aart."

The entryway is a real mess. Bicycles and a pile of mismatched shoes cover the knotted Inca rug; age-yellowed cross-stiches of canals and windmills hang on the walls.

"Let me take your coat. And then we'll just go straight upstairs to my office. When we're ready to eat we can sit under the awning in the garden, it's much more comfortable outside. You want to go in the mirror space first, right?"

"Right."

She goes up the steep stairs in front of me, and I follow after her tanned legs.

"Does anyone else live here?"

"Yeah, another Israeli, he works for Daimler Military. And a Brazilian guy, but he's hardly ever around. The house belongs to him." She looks over her shoulder and smiles. "Word on the street is that something like a third of these houses belong to guys like him. Pretty soon they'll have bought up all of Brussels, not to mention Lisbon, Paris . . . "

She leads me into an office that looks as if she's just moved in and is still waiting on the moving company to bring the rest of the boxes. I guess when half the day is spent behind a pair of specs or under a headset, it's hard to care about interior decoration. The room is mostly taken up by two sofas. They're cheap, made in North Korea, upholstered in Alcantara fabric, but despite that they look surprisingly comfortable. For a single person there's really only one reason to push two sofas together. I tell myself to focus on getting my mind out of the gutter and onto the matter at hand.

I loosen my collar and take off my shirt. Ava points at the circular scar on my right shoulder. "I've always wanted to ask where you got such an awful scar."

"Laser carbine. Tuareg guerillas."

"And the one on your arm?"

"Compound fracture."

"Also in the Solar War?"

"Sport injury. Rugby."

She looks interested. "You still play?"

"No. If you ask me, anyone over the age of thirty who still plays rugby has a death wish."

I pick up my jacket from where I've placed it across the back of a chair and take my headset out of the inside pocket. "Let's get this over with."

"You don't seem very enthusiastic. I'd give my right hand to go into the mirror space. I went in once during training, but never since."

"As far as I'm concerned you're welcome to come along."

"I already checked into it. The pass states expressly that it's only valid for you." She makes a face. "No analysts allowed."

"In the past few years I've only been in static replicas, Ava. My last live run was an eternity ago. Anything I should know about ghosting in the modern age?"

She puts her left hand on my bare shoulder and sticks an escape patch on my chest with her right.

I can smell her perfume. "It's more sophisticated, not like a forensic replication, but also not exactly a concert at the Sydney Opera House or a tour through Amsterdam."

"How so?" I ask.

"The mirror space is a continuous real-time replication. All of the data we can compile—from security videos, humming-drone pictures, recordings from survey drones, signatures from all cars and people—is used by TIRESIAS to generate a high-definition, three-dimensional orthomosaic."

"And what if there's no data? If there's no camera somewhere?"

"That almost never happens. But if it does, there's always the mobile network to pick up the slack."

"The net generates data?"

"How do you think the motion controls on your dishwasher and your air conditioner work, Aart? Your body produces an electromagnetic field. It collides with the radio waves in the cell network. The controls in your apartment use the resulting interference to determine your exact location and body position at all times, and of course Terry can do the same. Think of the replication as a digital map, and you can zoom in wherever you want. The mirror space overall is broadly pixelated. But Terry focuses in on the areas that a ghost is moving through. He can even order drones in the real world to go to the actual places you're visiting in the mirror space."

"Hordes of humming-drones? Isn't that conspicuous?"

"Who even notices drones anymore, Aart? Anyway, most of the time he uses mites. Tiny little bionic flies the naked eye can't distinguish from real house flies. Terry can order up swarms of them by the thousands. They come from all over the place. And if it still looks like there's going to be a hole in the map, he fills in the missing pieces. He creates a projected image with the help of the data history."

"Is there the possibility of interacting with the images?"

"With the people in the mirror space? No, they're just constructs created by Terry. Although they behave in exactly the same way as whatever they're doing in the real world. But you'll be invisible to them, like a ghost. That's why operatives refer to the whole process as ghosting. You can even walk right through people."

"So I can't hurt myself either."

"At least not badly. Obviously, it's possible to configure a simulation in such a way that a collision would hurt—think sports feeds of rugby or boxing. But that's not the case here. In the default setting another ghost can't even grab hold of you to my knowledge, much less take a swing at you."

"And what happens with objects?"

"Terry will try to make all sense interactions possible for you. You can pick up a rock and turn it between your fingers or snag some fries from the food cart behind the Palais and have yourself a snack."

"Sure, but how will they taste?"

Ava only now removes her hand from my bare

shoulder. She goes over to her desk and takes an inhaler out of a drawer.

"Terry has stored all common sensory impressions in his optic databases. The scent of a rose, the taste of freshly made fries, the touch of a kiss. Although admittedly the impressions can be somewhat generic."

I pull my headset into position. "So in Terryland all the fries taste the same?"

"No, he's too clever for that."

"You mean Terry can outsmart me?"

"Exactly. If you were to put him to the test and eat three different orders of fries in a row, or sniff three different roses, he would build in subtle variations to make the illusion even more exact."

I nod. For a moment I consider whether I should follow Piet Ververke's well-intentioned advice after all and mind my own business. But instead I heave myself onto the sofa in one sudden movement and activate the headset. There's a hissing sound as the hypnoremerol escapes from the dispenser and enters my lungs.

The Hotel Lotte Saint Pierre is part of a Seoul-based hotel chain that has spread throughout Europe in the past few years, like all things Korean. From the outside, the building looks like a huge black stone slab, towering above the surrounding office buildings by at least a hundred meters. I've apparently just exited the nearest metro station and am riding the escalator up to the surface. The nearby glass palaces are already casting long shadows; the street lies in a twilight glow.

I pause at the top of the escalator to look up and down the Avenue Helmut Kohl. All the details extracted from the real world by Terry's thousands of eyes and reassembled for the replication match almost exactly with my recollection of Woluwe-Saint-Pierre: the four-lane roads, the storefronts, even the smell in the air is correct. But then, if all the details are right, why do I feel so out of place here? I try to ignore the pounding in my temples and start walking.

There's a little kiosk near the escalator, the sort of place that sells candy, bottled drinks, and single-use media screens. I stand in front of the display and stare at the vendor. He looks right through me and focuses on his specs instead, gesticulating as he argues loudly with someone in Farsi. I pick up a package of licorice whirls and put it slowly into my jacket pocket with as obvious a noise as possible. He doesn't react. I take the package back out of my pocket, rip it open, and eat a piece of candy. It's too sweet for my taste, but I guess beggars can't be choosers. Still chewing, I walk to the end of the kiosk, open the door on the right-hand side, and go through. The space inside the kiosk is miniscule and I have to be very careful not to bump into the still-gesticulating vendor. I can see the dandruff on the back of his head, his drooping shoulders, the dark hair spilling out of his shirt collar like soot. He smells like cheap cologne that clearly lost the battle against his considerable body odor hours ago.

I wonder how Terry captured that detail. Are there mites with scent sensors buzzing around the kiosk owner? Maybe Terry's databases have stored the olfactory profiles of ten different kiosk vendors, and those were used to generate a representative odor on this guy for me. As the vendor talks on the phone, he sticks his right hand down the back of his pants. He lets it slip deep down and scratches thoroughly between his cheeks. I take a step back and leave the kiosk. As I walk past outside, I can see he's removed his hand from the depths of his pants. He holds his thumb and pointer finger under his nose and takes a scrutinizing sniff.

I check my specs. It's 7:20; I need to hurry if I don't want to be late. I walk up the street, dodging the people coming toward me, which is more difficult than I'd have thought. Evasive maneuvers like this usually involve the attention of both parties, but these passersby don't deviate even a millimeter from their set paths.

At this hour, things are still relatively busy, as the second rush hour is in full swing. Overtime workers have finally left their offices by now, and they're in a particular rush. They have to hurry if, after their commutes and family dinners, they still want to spend at least an hour vegetating in front of their media walls before they pass out from exhaustion.

The commuters bear down on me. They can't see me, and anyway they're much more interested in finding a gap in the end-of-day melee and trying to push through. I only manage to avoid a series of near-misses by dodging in every direction.

When I'm almost at the hotel, I pause for a moment and consider how I should cross the street. As I stand on the edge of the sidewalk, a taxi stops in front of me. The sliding door opens with a swish and reveals the unoccupied passenger seat inside.

Why can the taxi see me?

Suddenly, something pushes out of my chest, something round and purple-colored, followed by something green. I stagger back a step and clutch at my upper body. It's a man. He looks Brazilian and has a surgically modified forehead with bulging eyebrows. His hair is dyed purple and he wears a green designer suit. With a purposeful stride, he walks to the waiting taxi, gets inside, and drives away.

I feel sick as a dog. I lean against a nearby wall. Beads of sweat roll down my neck and my knees are shaking. I try to do meditative breathing the way we were taught in training for the replications: "Breathe in, recognizing white light and positive energy. Breathe out, releasing gray light and negative energy."

After a while the nausea vanishes. I notice the texture of the concrete against my palms and the back of my head. Does actual concrete really feel so rough? I shouldn't think about it too much. Even with the help of hypnoremerol and conditioning practice, the human mind can only handle so much, and it's only natural for such blatant deviations from deep-rooted laws of physics to trigger stress responses. I could probably ask Terry to render the passersby so they'd sidestep me at the last second. But then I'd be in just another run-of-the-mill feed and not in a perfect depiction of reality. No, I'd better learn to be a good ghost and dodge them instead.

And that brings me back to the problem of how I should cross the street. Cutting across the lanes of traffic like I normally do isn't a good idea. Just like the pedestrians, the drivers can't see me. Although none of the vehicles Terry is sending down the avenue can run me over, I still walk to the next intersection and wait until traffic stops there at the next red light. Then I cross the street and enter the hotel through a revolving door.

In the lobby I'm greeted by a statue of the eponymous Lotte. A lovesick Werther kneels at her feet with a bouquet of roses. I ignore the lovebirds and head for the bank of elevators. To emphasize that its guests are treated in the tradition of the old grand hotels, the Hotel Lotte has assigned a boy in a gold-trimmed uniform to stand in front of the elevators and relieve its guests from the effort of having to input the floor selection themselves.

I have a soft spot for such old-fashioned things, but this old-fashioned thing poses a problem for me. For a moment I stare helplessly at the elevator boy as he waits for customers behind his podium. Then something flashes on my specs.

"Elevator 2, please."

Terry and Ava are apparently on my wavelength. As the elevator boy continues to stare through me, I head for Number 2. The doors glide open. I step on and the elevator sets itself in motion. The walls of the car are covered with 3D media screens set to appear like windows looking out on a view of an idyllic landscape in springtime. Ladies in Biedermeier dresses stroll with their parasols through fields saturated with flowers and flooded with sunlight. In the background, a cute little German city is just visible.

As the elevator stops, a sonorous voice informs me the Schönbrunn restaurant is located on this floor. I step off and find myself in another room dominated by huge oil paintings. Waiters hustle past me, dressed in uniforms meant to look like the livery of the Austrian imperial family. I pass by the bar and enter the main dining room. On my left, I walk past the maître d', who stares right through me, and with the help of my specs I look for the place reserved for Pazzi. It's a beautiful table, located in an alcove behind two rose-colored marble columns and set for a multi-course meal.

I wend my way over and sit down on one of the Louis-XIV chairs, fitted with servomotors. Since it's clear no one is going to offer me an aperitif or hand me a menu, I snack on some of the licorice whirls I swiped earlier. I let fifteen minutes pass. No one comes by except the head waiter. He checks the position of the knives and forks and looks at his watch with a frown. I nod at him sympathetically. "No sense of punctuality, young people these days," I say. He ignores me.

I go to the next alcove over, about five meters away. There's a man and a woman sitting inside, both in their early thirties, attractive and rich. They slurp oysters. My specs inform me he works at Itaú as an investment banker. She's never worked a day in her life and will never need to. The two of them exchange dirty talk in pleasant tones. She describes to him in picture-perfect detail the plans she has for him later today, after this mating ritual. She does it in a hushed tone so no one outside the alcove can hear it. But since my face is no more than thirty centimeters away from hers, I can hear her better than anyone.

This dirty talk is entertaining, but it distracts me too much from my actual task. I go back to my table. Five pieces of licorice later, I come to the conclusion no one else is going to show up. The third man apparently found out about Pazzi's death far enough in advance. As I stand up from the gilded chair and start to push it under the table, my specs show an incoming priority call. I let myself sink back in the seat and answer. Vogel's stout face appears, filling almost the entire screen.

"Commissioner, good evening."

"Westerhuizen! I couldn't find you anywhere! Where are you?"

"In the mirror space, conducting an observation." I briefly consider telling him about the situation with the RR. But then I decide it's better to say nothing.

"Our meeting tomorrow's been moved. Two p.m."

"And that's why this is a priority call?" I ask skeptically.

"No, no. There's been a new development. The press has got wind of the situation. The news is full of it."

That was to be expected. "And that's why this is a priority call?"

"Don't be a smartass, Westerhuizen. I wanted to tell you Johnny Random called me."

Johnny Random is, despite what his name might indicate, not a lobotomized K-Pop DJ, but one of the most disagreeable investigative journalists in the Union. Random runs his own 360-show, and he's already ruined the careers of dozens of politicians and businessmen. It's rumored no one knows his real identity. I wonder why the Pazzi story interests him. Maybe there's still a police commissioner missing from the trophies on his mantel.

"And what did he say?"

"The usual. He wants privileged access to the results of the investigation. Otherwise he'll turn over 'every digital stone,' those were his exact words."

"And?"

Vogel snorts. "He's getting nothing from us. Got it, Westerhuizen? Nothing at all!"

"Understood, Commissioner."

I actually want to add something to that, but Vogel has already hung up. I heave myself out of the much-too-comfortable chair and walk through the dining room in the direction of the exit. Then suddenly I hear a voice. At first, I think it's Vogel still on the line. But this voice is clearer, more deep-throated. And it's not coming from my earpiece, but from the space around me.

"Keep walking," it says calmly, but firmly. "Don't let on that anything's happening."

The voice belongs to a man, probably middle aged. I walk with a measured pace through the dining hall, which by now has filled up almost entirely. I stop walking in front of the bar.

"I had a feeling you'd come here," says the voice.

"I wanted to know who the third man is," I reply. "It looks as though I've found him."

"Interesting theory."

That's enough of an answer for me. "Let Piet Ververke know it's not polite to send someone to chaperone a colleague in the mirror space," I say. "And also, as a tail, you shouldn't accost the object of observation. I'd have thought the RR would be more professional than that."

"I'm not a member of that club."

I set a hand on the counter. The bar is massive and made of the same dark wood as the shelf behind it, reaching all the way up to the ceiling. It's fully stocked with Japanese whiskeys and other liquor. In the middle is a giant, half-blinding crystal mirror, where the bartender's reflection is visible. I look directly at the mirror. I don't show up myself. No one is standing behind me.

I lean my arm against the counter and, in the process, turn my upper body inconspicuously sideways so I can look behind me. There's still no sign of the man. I turn myself back to the bar.

"Is it really necessary for me not to see you? You are actually in the mirror space?" I ask.

"Partially."

"What's that supposed to mean?"

"It's useless to ask me any questions. You should be looking for answers instead."

"And how am I supposed to do that?"

"Golden trail. Look for the golden trail."

"I think I've heard that phrase before."

"You have indeed. And something else, Inspector."

"Yes?"

"Don't tell anyone about this."

For a fraction of second, I think I see a person in the blinding mirror. They're standing a few steps behind me among the tables, almost entirely hidden by a marble column, looking in my direction. It seems to be a Korean man in his mid-thirties, with a ridiculous, towering, bottle-blonde hairdo. I turn around with a jerk, reaching instinctively for the Heckler & Koch I keep in my shoulder holster. I run toward the man and take the safety off the pistol. Crosshairs and munitions gauges appear on my specs. "No targets located" blinks in red font underneath.

I walk closer to the man. He doesn't react. When I get right up to him, I notice he's looking through me. I reach my left hand out toward him but grab at only empty air. The man walks in the direction of the restrooms, unperturbed.

From a distance I think I hear a deep-throated laugh. With legs planted and weapon drawn, I stand in the midst of a dining room full of Brussels citizens who are, so it seems, politely ignoring me.

CHAPTER 6

After my journey back from the Lotte, we sit on the patio. The rain drums on the roof above us. Ava serves homemade hummus and olives. Then she tries to pick my brain about the mirror space. But I can barely speak a word, much less get down any of the food. It's probably thanks to the replication, which was more detailed and more disorienting than anything I've experienced before. After a few glasses of red wine, I'm in better shape.

"Did you notice anything in there that might help us, Aart?"

"I don't know. The third man wasn't there. I'd like to take a look at a recording of the replication later. What did you and Terry find out in the meantime?"

If she's angry about my evasive answer, she keeps it to herself. "Just a sec, I'll show you."

Ava gets a flip chart from the living room and sets it up in front of us on the flagstones. She mutters something into her larynx mike, and the media screen fills itself with a collage of graphics, photos, and video clips.

"The autopsy found Pazzi was in great shape. He wasn't a health nut, but he could afford any treatment you can think of—cellular regeneration, nano-cures, muscle-tone treatments. Despite the stress of his lifestyle, he was in peak form. Biological age: twenty-nine. Life expectancy, according to Terry's prediction: a hundred and nineteen years."

I sip my wine. "Well. Retrospectively, maybe a bad bet."

"Here," she zooms in on a 2D map, to a red dot slowly moving around, "Terry's marked where Pazzi was in the past few weeks. We compared it with the recordings from your discussions with Svensson and Heuberger. There aren't any discrepancies."

"Damn. Did Svensson maybe use masking software in our holo-conference?"

"No. That's really what she's like."

"And did she get us the data from the Liberal party's executives?"

"Yes, she did. Terry analyzed it already. Everyone has good alibis. And they're not just substantiated by spec signature—these people can be seen on dozens of video feeds. Which also proves none of them were near the crime scene."

I wrinkle my forehead. "That only rules out the possibility they killed their colleague with their own hands."

"You're right, in theory. But Terry also didn't find anything in their phone calls, emails, or patterns of movement from the past couple weeks."

"What exactly was he looking for?"

"For example, Terry looks to see if the suspect's communication with the victim changed recently. Either in quantity—were there more meetings or phone calls, were there fewer, or was there a complete stop in communication? Or in quality—were there noticeable variations in the semantics in the emails or conversations, something that would indicate animosity or at least tension? Anything like that."

"Were the members of the executive committee in close contact with our fiddle-fit corpse?"

"All of them had their final contact with Pazzi during the executive conference last Friday."

"Do we have the recording?"

"Yes, but it strikes me as irrelevant. The content lines up with the information from Svensson."

I sigh. "Any other meetings that could be of interest?"

"In the last seven days, other than the previously mentioned meetings, just one with his father in Merano, via hologram. Seems like it had to do with family matters, about Pazzi's mother's birthday. Other than that, appointments with journalists from *Il Messagero*, *The Voice*, and *VNN*. According to Terry these were off-the-record conversations, like Pazzi gave every few weeks. And then another meeting with someone from the Conservatives, his name is Alan Thompson. Also an MEP, he and Pazzi played squash together every Tuesday evening."

I shake my head. "So that's a dead end. Let's do another round of research, maybe we'll be able to shed light on something."

"Okay. Should I link to Terry now?"

"Yes, please. But wait just a minute." I sip my wine

and consider Ava. "Before you do, I have a confession to make."

I stand up. Her brown doe eyes look at me in anticipation. Those brown doe eyes are about to be disappointed.

"It's about Terry."

"Oh. What about him?"

I explain to her what Vogel told me about the newest iteration. How the new Terry works much more independently and that I've already spoken with him directly. And I repeat Vogel's assessment that there will be lots of analysts out of work and out of love in the not-so-distant future.

"He said that?"

"In that peerlessly sympathetic way of his."

With her thumb and pointer finger, she flicks an olive pit into the shadows. "It won't work. I mean, when are they finally going to get it?"

"What do you mean by that?"

"Terry is a computer. A very smart computer, but that's all. At the turn of the century, programmers and system designers were confident computers would be smarter than us someday. In particular they were counting on the emergence of AI, artificial intelligence. They called it the singularity, since afterward everything would change."

I smile grimly. "But they're still waiting, right? For the breakthrough, I mean. Although I have heard the Cantonese developers are supposed to be getting close."

She wrinkles her nose. "The singularity is only

ten years away, and I'll be damned if it hasn't been that way for a few decades. Look, I could ask Terry to compile us a list of all the mistaken predictions on the subject of AI. In a few milliseconds he'd have it drawn up and would start rattling them off."

"But?"

"But could he also tell us why the attempts at AI didn't work? No, that he couldn't do. He's like the golem in Jewish mythology."

"The golem? Isn't that some kind of Frankenstein's monster made out of clay?"

"*Golem* is Hebrew, it means 'unformed.' In the Sefer Yetzirah, the Book of Creation, there's a Kabbalistic ritual where certain combinations of letters and numbers can be used to awaken inanimate material to life."

"I take it you mean that metaphorically."

"Of course. But it's a good metaphor. Bringing letters and numbers, bits and bytes, to life is exactly what the programmers of highly developed computers like TIRESIAS, Xianhe, or Pensador 5 are looking to do. It's exactly like the saga of the Golem of Prague. The Rabbi Löw brought a clay figure to life. The golem was very useful to him. It never got tired, it never grumbled. It could sweep the synagogue on Shabbat and schlep hundreds of buckets of water through the shtetl."

"What point are you trying to make with this, Ava?"

"Just that Terry is like the golem and always will be. He's untiring, he always does everything correctly. He's obedient and never asks questions. He just carries out orders. And when he doesn't have any on the docket, then he does—nothing! Like the golem. Most of the time it sat on a footstool in the kitchen, dumb and deaf. Terry has no ideas of his own, no creativity, no soul. And that's also why he's not intelligent."

"Maybe you're right."

"I'm definitely right." Ava has stood up and looks very agitated. She points to the media screen. "Terry packaged this whole thing up for us very nicely. But is it getting us anywhere? No, we still have to come up with the ideas that'll actually find the murderer ourselves. And that's why the only thing they'll achieve by eliminating analysts is a decline in the number of solved cases."

"Then let's show our electronic golem how clever we are. You ask the first question."

Ava sits back down, looking somewhat embarrassed by her little outburst. After she's sipped a bit of her wine and murmured something in her larynx mike, the collage disappears and the Europol logo appears.

"Did Pazzi have any ties to Christian groups?" she asks. "In particular, any groups in Southern Italy?"

Not a bad question. If any of the usual suspects have our Tirolean fashion plate's blood on their hands, the militant arm of these fanatics is definitely a possibility. Pazzi's family is apparently filthy rich, which could indicate connections to the mafia. And after all, there's a lot of overlap in the workforce for the 'Ndrangheta, the Catholic Christians, and the

Southern Italian government.

"Based on his data, there are no indications of a relationship, Chief Inspector. I've also checked if other members of the Pazzi clan are rumored to have links to the Calabrian-Sicilian mafia—"

An anticipatory answer. The new Terry is quite good. I'm not so sure if Ava's golem theory will end up holding water. After another couple of updates, this computer will upstage at least the bottom third of our department, all the Marquezes and Kaczynskis.

"—connections between Pazzi and the Christian groups can accordingly be ruled out with eighty-eight percent probability."

"Britskis?" I ask. "The short answer, please."

"Connections between Pazzi and British-Russian syndicates can be ruled out with ninety-one percent probability."

"Were there any death threats against Pazzi? Or anything at all that would indicate he was in danger?

"Negative in both cases, Chief Inspector."

And so it goes for an entire disheartening hour. We find out the only notable similarity between Pazzi and Svensson is a fondness for Tuscan cuisine. Terry calculates a thirty-seven percent probability that the murder weapon came from the coalition troops and predicts who will get Pazzi's job as deputy of the Liberals. Ava fires questions at him about the North African guerilla groups and English separatists, two more of the common suspects.

I drink even more wine. As a former soldier, I'm fairly resistant to alcohol. But then again, I'll be falling off my chair drunk before the police computer gives us a piece of useful information in this case. I rub my eyes and stare at the screen, where the star-encircled Europol logo can still be seen. Behind it is TIRESIAS. It's a typical EU abbreviation. Someone or other thought it was a good idea to name our police computer after Homer's all-seeing prophet. And then later some PR employee had to pull a response out of thin air about what the abbreviation is supposedly short for.

"What does the acronym TIRESIAS mean, Terry?"

"It stands for 'Telemetric Immersive REenactments and SImulations of ActualitieS.'"

No wonder I forgot it.

I suddenly feel hungry, so I polish off the rest of the hummus and flatbread. While I chew I say, "Can you think of any more questions, Ava?"

"Maybe," she stretches like a tired cat, "if I drank some coffee."

She makes us two espressos. I'd really like to get into bed with Bogart and Ustinov as quickly as possible, but before I stand in front of Vogel empty-handed tomorrow morning, I'll torture myself with Terry a little longer. Not that our super computer is to blame. He has an answer for literally everything. We're just too stupid to ask the right questions. Or maybe too cowardly.

Ava comes back with two small dark cups, filled with even darker contents, and sits across from me. I sink four cubes of sugar in my coffee. It's time to ask the long-shot questions.

"Terry?"

"Chief Inspector?"

"This vote on the new EU constitution—why is it even happening and how do the odds currently stand?"

Ava looks at me, bewildered, while Terry's sonorous voice provides the answer. "Since the exit of member states was not foreseen in the EU agreement, according to prevailing interpretations of the law a new constitution must be put in place so that the United Kingdom can leave the Union."

"I'd be curious to hear the minority opinion," I interrupt him.

"Critics argue the exit of Great Britain serves merely as an excuse for pushing through a new constitution that will further weaken the member states of the Union and strengthen centralized power."

"And what are the chances of ratification?"

"A two-thirds majority is necessary for ratification of the constitution. According to current polls, sixty-seven percent of MEPs are for the new constitution, thirty percent against, three percent still undecided."

"Undecided, just like Pazzi?"

"That is correct."

Ava sits up. The espresso appears to have had the desired effect. "Show the polls about the constitution on a timeline," she says.

A diagram with a blue and a red line appears on the screen. The latter shows the portion of Union parliamentarians planning to vote no. It moves in a downward direction, while the number of supporters has gone up sharply within a year, from forty-eight to sixty-seven percent.

"Why did the pro-constitution camp make such headway?" I want to know.

"The most likely factors are: changes in public opinion, pressure from party leaders, corruption."

"Come again? Someone's bribing the representatives? Can you prove that, Terry?"

"Pardon me, Chief Inspector. But that's not what I said."

"That is what you said, but apparently not what you meant."

That gives him a few milliseconds' food for thought. I use them to take a licorice whirl out of my pocket, only to find there aren't any. Mnemonic echo from the replication—I need to get to bed soon.

"My observation was meant in a general sense, Chief Inspector. What I wanted to express was the idea that rapid changes in voting behavior among politicians can typically be traced back to one of the three previously mentioned factors. That holds up based on historic analysis of voting behavior in a total of one hundred ninety-seven available states."

"I'm shocked by your low opinion of politicians, Terry."

"Could you rephrase the question, Chief Inspector?"

"Forget it, Terry. So, to recap: it's not implausible to assume someone bought this increasing number of yes votes, but there's no supporting evidence."

"That is correct."

"Maybe," Ava speaks up, "Pazzi hadn't locked himself in yet because he wanted to drive the price of his vote even higher."

"Maybe. Or maybe he just found the decision difficult to make. Or he had to toss a coin first."

"Are you talking about the I Ching coins and tarot cards, Aart?"

"Exactly."

She shakes her head. "Important decisions like that can't just be left to chance."

Stranger things often happen, but I don't say so. For a moment no further questions occur to either of us, but then Ava says, "Terry, were there any other murdered MEPs in the recent past?"

"The last murder of an EU parliamentarian was over eighteen months ago. Status: solved."

"Guy Rodange," I mutter.

"That is correct. Representative from Luxembourg. Domestic violence, stabbed to death by his girlfriend."

"And how many parliamentarians have died in the past three months?" I ask. "Doesn't matter how."

"Nine people have died."

"Seems to be something of a dangerous profession."

"According to the classification of the Commission's General Directorate VII, there are a total of a hundred and thirty-four other professions in the Union with a demonstrably higher mortality rate."

"Sarcasm, Terry. Tell me more about the dead MEPs."

"In particular, I'm referring to the following people and causes of death: Otto von Beurenthal, heart attack. Gideon Abramov, hunting accident. Joanne Schultz, complications from cancer. Anna Plekszy-Gladz, stroke. Irene Gruber, sporting accident. Valérie Dupond, car accident. Jorge Perez Milar, traffic accident. Beat Füßli, sporting accident. Tryphon Gryzbowski, complications from cancer."

"Any suspicions of foul play?"

"No, Chief Inspector. All of the deaths in question were extensively investigated by Europol and by the authorities in each member state. There were no irregularities and no indications of criminal offenses."

"Shit."

"Agreed," Ava says. "Nothing else is occurring to me right now either, Aart. I can look over the circumstances of these deaths tomorrow, but I don't have much hope."

"I wouldn't mind seeing the live recording of the hotel now."

She nods. "Terry, Aart's ghosting in the Lotte, isometric axonometry."

A video appears on the screen, showing the Schönbrunn restaurant in an aerial view tilted forty-five degrees up. The perspective reminds me of the first-person computer games I played as a kid over thirty years ago. The isometric view is centered on a figure. It walks through the dining room and sits down at a table.

"This part's not interesting. You can skip forward to when the bar shows up."

The video moves forward. I see an athletic man in his mid-forties, at least six feet tall, standing at the bar with his hand on the counter. He wears a khaki-colored trench coat and comes across as decently attractive. Although he could do with a shave. There are dark circles under his eyes and his white over-shirt is wrinkled. The man talks to himself and he looks around, harried, as if he thinks some gangster's going to spring from behind the bar at any moment and open fire on him.

"Who are you talking to there, Aart?"

"Vogel," I lie.

And here comes the moment when the play-back-Westerhuizen draws his service weapon and storms back into the dining room.

"Terry," I ask. "Was I alone in the Lotte?"

"Yes, Chief Inspector. There were no other ghosts in the vicinity."

"No RR agents?"

"Negative."

"Is it possible someone could have hacked in?"

"Theoretically that's possible, Chief Inspector. In this case, though, I see no indications of it. Furthermore, in the entire history of the mirror space, there are no hacks known to me that were carried out successfully."

"Look at it again. Data transfers, all deployed drones, my specs. Everything."

This time Terry needs much longer than a few milliseconds. Ava looks at me quizzically, as if she wants to say something, but I put my finger against my lips to indicate she should stay silent.

"My analysis has concluded that, at the time in question, there was no illegitimate access to the mirror space."

Ava can't conceal her anger any longer. "Aart, could you please tell me what you're doing, damn it?"

"I'll explain everything to you, I promise. But not now. Tomorrow, at breakfast."

"Just tell me now, I'm your analyst!"

"Ava, I know it seems completely crazy. But give me time until tomorrow. Café Amsterdam, around nine?"

Before she can renew her protests, I've taken a few steps toward her and kissed her softly on the cheek. "Thank you for dinner." Then I leave her behind, alone on the patio.

CHAPTER 7

When I tell my coworkers my apartment is located in the super-fashionable Châtelain neighborhood, they're invariably impressed. I've yet to invite a single one of them over to my place. If I did, they wouldn't be so impressed. And they wouldn't have to waste any time gossiping about how a low-paid inspector can afford an apartment only a short walk away from the Europol Palais.

After I've pressed my thumb against the keypad, the front door opens and I enter the hallway moving in a sideways scuttle. It's the only option, since otherwise I'd run into the armoire that takes up half the entryway. One long stride and I'm standing in the living room, one more and I'm in the kitchen, office, and bedroom. If the bathroom space is included in the total, I have 8.43 square meters. It's enough for me. Back in the military barracks in Aoulef I had even less space.

I hang my jacket and my shoes on their designated hooks and pull them up on a drawstring until they dangle just below the ceiling. I grab the metal ladder on my loft bed, climb up, and activate the media screen hung on the wall at the foot of the mattress. I stretch out, fold my arms behind my head, and start

We're No Angels. Bogey, Ustinov, and Ray break out of prison. Every few minutes they toss pearls of jailbird wisdom at each other: "A man sentenced to life can always spare a few minutes." Or, "If crime showed on a man's face, there wouldn't be any mirrors."

I make it through half an hour and then can't take it anymore. I climb quickly down the ladder and put all nearby electronic devices, including my specs and service badge, into my little safe. Then I close it and leave the apartment.

It's relatively quiet outside. Only a few stray night owls are still walking through the neighborhood in the spitting rain, on the hunt for a bar still open this time of night.

There's only one. It's called Globoskop and is on a side street near the Church of the Holy Trinity. The club isn't the sort of place anyone over thirty would normally stumble into, not even when plastered. I'm too old and too sober, but I go inside anyway. The decorations in the place look like they were shaped out of a single block of milk-white polyethylene by a 3D printer. I'm hit by a mix of teenaged sweat and booming baile funk. But the worst part is the colors and lights. The owner has attached media screens to every single surface in the establishment. He might also have used those newfangled spray screens, since it's not just the walls, ceiling, and tables pulsating in every hue across the Pantone spectrum. The door handles, the barstools, and the waitresses' trays are all projection surfaces the guests can fill with images or videos as they see fit.

I try not to look too closely, shoving my way through the throng to an empty corner table whose surface shows Tom and Jerry on a wild chase. As I go to sit down on the chair, I notice some prankster has drawn a dozen neon-colored penises on the seat, ejaculating continuously in time with the music. I wipe them away before I have a seat.

After a few seconds, a waitress appears. Not only is her tray pulsing, but her bustier and miniskirt are also surfaces for playing back whatever comes along. I order a negroni. She's never heard of it but promises to ask the bartender. While I wait for my drink, I look up at the ceiling, where video material from North Africa is playing. A solar tower explodes in an endless loop; its warming storage tank bursts open and hot liquid sulfur salts rain down from the sky at more than 2000 degrees Celsius. The enormous tower falls in on itself and leaves behind a smoking swathe in the array of solar panels clustered around it, over and over again.

The waitress comes back. I exchange a two-thousand euro bill for a brown-colored cocktail I only wish were a negroni. I take a sip. It's nice and cold, in any case. And now I get to work. I wipe the table clean, pull up a search window, and enter "golden trail."

"*Golden trail* is a phrase appearing in the Union's anthem," comes up on the table. I call up the text from Beethoven's Ninth. And, in fact, there is another verse after "Joy, radiant beauty of the gods" and "All the world shall be encircled":

At the breast of Nature joyful
All creation drinks its fill;
All of goodness, all of evil
Follow down its golden trail.

I wipe the table clean and call up another search window.

"Alternate meanings for 'golden trail'?"

I get two results—a florist in the Brussels-Louiza metro station, and an encyclopedia entry.

"Project Golden Trail: name of an alleged financial scandal in which members of the Union Parliament supposedly received kickbacks for giving preferential treatment in weapons contracts to the company Tallan Consolidated, abbreviated TalCon. In return for being approved by defense and trade committees, the multinational corporation invested large amounts of capital in the electoral districts of the representatives involved. However, this was never conclusively proven. A newsmagazine that published the accusations was required to pay a large amount in damages to TalCon. Arne Jürgensen, the editor-in-chief at fault, was fired, and the publishing house slipped into insolvency soon after."

According to the entry, this happened barely ten years ago. Tallan Consolidated—I know the name, like everyone who was in the war. Our recon drones were made by Tallan. They were about as reliable as seventy-year-old Russian Ilyushins, but at least they looked better. Our specs also came from TalCon. Supposedly, everything the business produced was only the finest European craftsmanship. But of course, we knew there were cheap North Korean electronics buried inside the products, guaranteeing us a lower life expectancy and Tallan a higher profit margin.

I search for Tallan, an arduous task since the search engine isn't very clever and offers me an archaic list of results rather than collating the information into a précis. But it's clear to see Tallan Consolidated earned a lot of money in the Solar War with its tumbling drones and kimchi guns. The corporation has grown enormously in the meantime and now belongs to the mega-conglomerate known as Jébol.

In times of peace, if they can be called that, the corporation utilized its profits to diversify: house-hold drones instead of flying assassins, mass-market electronics instead of targeting systems. I look at the sales figures for the company, charting its as-tronomical growth. In no time flat, Jébol succeeded in besting the established competition in every new arena Tallan ventured into, or, to put it more accu-rately, it blew them out of the water. It's rumored the corporation doesn't shy away from sabotaging or intimidating its rivals. That doesn't surprise me. It's like the old joke: What's the difference between Jébol and an international crime syndicate? Answer: Jébol is listed on the stock exchange.

When everything went to hell in the United States, Tallan bought up an array of companies in Silicon Valley. Today, the corporation is the Union market leader for specs and all kinds of other technology. Profits last fiscal year totaled almost a billion, company headquarters in Frankfurt. The really astonishing thing about Tallan Consolidated, though, is that the corporation is apparently still lead by a member of the founding family. The last head of the company, George Tallan, has been dead for over twenty years. Since then, his son John has been the CEO.

John Tallan—the name rings a bell. I enter it in the search engine and find out his full name is John Tallan-Furlough, and he's the Earl of Mertonshire. Now it's becoming clear to me why I've heard of him before. Tallan is the owner of a spectacular estate a hundred and fifty kilometers northeast of Brussels, referred to by the media as the Water Palace, even though it definitely doesn't look like one. It rests on gigantic pontoons and was of interest to me at the time because it's located in what was once Dutch territory.

I clear the display and lean back. The table unfortunately doesn't stay blank, starting to play baile funk videos—that is, pornos—after a few minutes. I take one more drink of the poorly made negroni and leave the club. I need Ava for the rest. My analyst is very smart and very pretty. It remains to be seen whether she's also discreet.

CHAPTER 8

It's ten past nine when I arrive at the Café Amsterdam the following morning. The regular crew is hunched over the bar watching the news. Ava is already there, settled at a small table in the corner. She makes a face as if she's already had to turn down a dozen invitations for coffee. I'd guess it was three at the most.

I greet her and get us something to drink at the counter. Ava watches me expectantly, arms crossed across her chest. After I've hung up my dripping-wet trench coat and sat down across from her, I say, "I'm sorry."

"Good. You owed me an apology. And if you follow it up right now with an explanation for why you behaved so strangely, we might be able to be friends again."

"An informant made themselves known to me."

"When?"

"Yesterday, after I spoke with Heuberger." That's not technically a lie.

"And who is it?"

"Don't know. An anonymous call."

She laughs derisively. "There's no such thing anymore, at least not since the amendment to the Enhanced Privacy Act. I could definitely have traced the call for you. Or Terry could have identified whoever it was based on their tone of voice or word choice."

"Maybe. But I was afraid the source would run dry the minute we tried to follow. So for now I just want to analyze the information they gave me."

"That's a strange approach."

"It gets a lot stranger," I reply. "I want to leave behind as few traces as possible while doing it."

Ava bites her lower lip and looks at me. "Because it's a politically sensitive case?"

"To tell the truth, I still don't know what kind of case it is. All I know is that Vogel or someone else is taking the whole thing very seriously, otherwise I wouldn't have been granted blanket access to the mirror space. A little discretion certainly can't hurt."

I tell her my RR contact gave me a warning, and so did my anonymous source.

"And what tip were you given by this strange informant of yours?"

"Not much. They suggested I look into a possible connection between Pazzi and Tallan Consolidated."

"The conglomerate? I can do it."

"Can you do it without attracting attention?"

"You mean without using a Europol database and without alerting Terry to the fact that it's happening?"

"Exactly."

"That sort of thing wasn't on the curriculum at the Leuven Academy of Digital Forensics. But it was still one of the first things everyone learned there."

"Thanks, Ava."

"No problem."

I pay for our drinks at the counter. We leave the café and head over to the Palais. As we do, I can admire not only Ava's graceful way of walking, but also her track jacket. Although the lotus coating on my trench coat has allowed the Brussels plum rain to roll off it in a very conventional way, the field generator in Ava's shoulder pads stops the rain from coming into contact with the fabric at all. I have no idea how it works, though I do wonder if the technology would also help against the ubiquitous seagull shit.

Inside the Palais, I say goodbye to Ava and go to my office. I open a browser and reluctantly attend to my correspondence. Four journalists have asked if they could interview me about the Pazzi case. Johnny Random isn't one of them. I decide to follow Vogel's orders for the time being and close all the requests without answering them. The chief is right, after all: there's no sense in going to the trouble of making up lies when there's a press office to handle that.

After half an hour, there's a knock at my door. I activate the media screen embedded in it. A three-dimensional image of the person on the other side appears. It's Ava. I open up for her.

She comes in and sits on the edge of my desk. "Bingo, Aart."

"So there is a connection between Pazzi and Tallan?"

"Yes. Apparently TalCon invested large amounts of capital in Pazzi's district. Six years ago, the corporation built a manufacturing center for courier drones near Merano, with a total investment of a hundred and thirty billion euros. But that's not all."

"What else is there?"

"A few years ago, there was a corruption scandal Tallan was allegedly involved in."

"Is that so?"

"The press called it the Golden Trail scandal, since that was supposedly the internal codeword. But it was never proven."

She's telling me the part I already know.

"Good work, Ava. If Pazzi was also involved in this scandal, we need to check into the company. Vogel will be overjoyed."

"Are you being sarcastic, Aart?"

I shrug my shoulders. "Maybe he'll be happy with an initial suspect. Maybe Tallan's CEO is also a buddy of his. Doesn't matter either way. In any case, I'll have to tell him once we have something more concrete."

I take a piece of black licorice out of my tin. "But first things first. A scandal from ten years ago, especially one that was never proven, isn't exactly a hot tip."

She crosses her arms in front of her chest. As a rule, that doesn't bode well.

"What's wrong?"

"Do you think I'd be standing here if that was all I had?"

"Sorry, no, of course not."

"There were supposedly even more representatives

dragged into the whole thing. A court in Frankfurt forbid the magazine that broke the story at the time from circulating the names of the guilty MEPs. The editor-in-chief, Arne Jürgensen, was fired."

"And then what?"

"The magazine article in question doesn't exist anymore, it was expunged from the net. I researched Jürgensen's biography and tried to track him down. Proved to be quite difficult, it was like pulling teeth from my search routines. Like this guy disappeared off the face of the earth. I also checked into all MEP districts where Tallan invested large amounts of capital in the past few years."

"And how many did you come up with?"

"Eight in total. And all the MEPs in question were or still are members of the Economic or Defense Committees. And you already know two of them."

"Svensson and Heuberger?"

"Wrong guess." She smiles triumphantly. It suits her quite nicely. "Milar and Füßli."

I stop chewing. "Both of them are on Terry's list of representatives who died in the past three months."

"Exactly. Jorge Perez Milar, delegate from Lisbon-South. Tallan opened a regional headquarters in his electoral district four years ago, creating thirteen hundred jobs."

"Remind me how he died?"

"Traffic accident. He was run over by a train belonging to the historic Lisbon tram line 28."

"How quaint. And the second?"

"Beat Füßli, electoral district Aargau. Tallan has

sponsored a jazz festival for years and also con-structed small manufacturing plants there."

"Was that the sporting accident? Something Al-pine?"

"No, Aart. MEP Füßli was struck dead by a golf ball."

"Come again?"

"At a driving range near Zurich. He was hit by a very unlucky shot and died shortly after from a cerebral hemorrhage."

"No one on earth would fall for that. This is a damn killing spree."

"Possibly. But it's just as likely it's a coincidence. If you want to know the probabilities, I have to run the information through Terry."

"Later, Ava, later. Right now, I want to take a look for myself from up close. What's the situation with the data?"

"The crime scene for Füßli's accident was uploaded by the local canton police. They did a thorough job, but unfortunately it's just a static 360-video. Milar, on the other hand, was run over near the Praça Luís de Camões, right in the middle of the city center. The place is full of drones and cameras. Which means we can view his accident as an immersive replication."

How wonderful. What better way to start the day than with a fatal traffic accident? Without exchang-ing another word, we stand up and head to the rep-lication room.

We enter the Praça Camões from the eastern side, via an elevator that's apparently brought us up from the parking garage below. I've been here once before, but it was at least five years ago. All signs point to the fact that the richest country in the Union has only gotten richer since then. Buildings, stores, cars—everything smacks of too much money. Then again, even though the Portuguese did make a mint with their wave energy plants, most of the things here don't actually belong to them anymore, but to the even-richer Brazilians. I look around at the plaza, paved with marble and alabaster. I'm managing to keep my sympathy under control.

"Where's it going to happen?" I ask.

The tracks run all the way around the plaza and then disappear down various streets that lead away from the Camões.

Ava points to a junction on the other side. "Over there."

We stroll across the plaza. There's a drizzle, making me feel right at home. According to my specs, we're looking at the third of June, 6:04 p.m. A few people are heading out early for the evening, but the majority are evidently still in their offices, which means it's comparatively quiet. Brand-new Toyotas and Hyundais buzz past us. A white-and-yellow tram turns the corner, rattling and shooing away a few pedestrians and pigeons.

The tram is rendered well. It looks like the old Lisbon eléctricos, including a false patina, peeling paint, and a mechanical sound when it drives. The historic husk is hiding modern power and computer technology. The man behind the wheel is also a decoration—the tram naturally runs all on its own.

Which will make it all the more interesting to see how this guy manages to get himself run over by a streetcar outfitted with the most modern vehicle technology available. We situate ourselves on a corner that provides a good view of everything. Ava marks Milar for me as he comes straight toward us from the other side of the plaza. He seems to be in a hurry. The Portuguese representative is short, I'd say 1.6 meters tall at most. My specs say 1.63 meters. He wears a dark-blue suit as immaculate as it is boring, with an open white shirt and no cravat. Milar is coming closer.

"Where's he going, anyway?" I ask.

"Milar has an appointment with his mistress, he promised her new earrings. They're supposed to meet at Cartier, right around the corner from here, and he's running a bit late."

Milar reaches the east side, where the Praça opens up in the direction of the Rua Misericordia. He starts to cross the street as a vehicle from line 28 approaches from the left. If I had to place a bet, I'd say he'll make it. He seems to be light on his feet. And anyway, he's a local and knows how fast the eléctricos go.

The odds are a thousand to one against the tram. But that's not going to do Milar any good.

The eléctrico is still about three meters away from him as his right foot crosses the first rail. I hear the jingling sound of the bell. It looks like the train's sensors have registered Milar and are braking the tram. He just has to keep putting one foot in front of the other. Then the vehicle will, at most, graze him. The only injury he'd sustain would be a few streaks of oil on the tails of his hundred-thousand-euro jacket.

Instead, he makes an evasive maneuver to the left. I can't tell exactly what or whom he's evading, but he stumbles in the process and falls right in the path of the tram. No pedestrian sensor in the world can help him now. First, his head bangs against the metal on the exterior. Maybe he'll be knocked unconscious by it. At least, hopefully he was, for his sake, since the eléctrico proceeds to mow him down his entire length. Horrible sounds come from Milar as his spine, skull, and other large bones break like balsa wood. He's dragged along for a few meters until the bloody formless thing that was a distinguished statesman only a minute ago bursts like an overripe fruit and spreads his innards across the tracks and the street.

The tram comes to a stop. Chaos ensues. The women nearby are shrieking; the men are retching. A few people stand frozen still from shock, while others run away. I decide to look at things a little more closely.

"Rewind and pause."

The tram drives backwards and moves away, Milar comes back to life and freezes with his left leg firmly on the ground. I go over to him and study his face. It doesn't show any indications of fear or terror; all I see is the faint concern of a man who's keeping an impatient woman waiting.

"Play in slow motion."

Milar takes a step, the tram bell rattles, and the disaster runs its course all over again. Just before he takes the sidestep that will cost him his life, I have Ava pause the replication again. I kneel down.

"It's not real," I say.

On the rail, exactly where Milar planned to put his foot, there's something perching that might once have been a pigeon. Now it looks like a failed Brazilian genetic experiment. I have no idea what environmental poisons or pesticides came into contact with this animal, but it's ridden with festering sores and boils and most of its feathers have fallen out. Presumably, it can't fly anymore. It's a miracle the pigeon managed to get this far into the intersection without being run over.

"Extremely slow motion."

The animal hops toward our man from the right. Milar sees the mutant pigeon and, understandably, he doesn't want this cooing boil to ruin his expensive suede ankle boots. He therefore steps around it, to the left. In the process, he steps in something that looks like fresh dog shit. He slides a few centimeters. I stare at his face. He looks a bit surprised, his eyes staring at the tram and taking on a quizzical expression. Maybe it's dawning on him that a pair of ruined ankle boots would've been the better option.

"Normal speed," I mutter. Then I take a little jump back to keep the rails clear for the line 28 tram.

I have Ava fast forward a bit, to the point where the forensic recording reset the tram. I walk along the five or so meters of track where Milar's remains are scattered, searching for the pigeon. I'd like to know if it survived. But the animal has disappeared. Hard to say if it hopped away or if, in death, it became one with the MEP.

"Did the forensics team find any traces of the pigeon in his remains, Ava?"

"They did. Bits of feathers and blood. Otherwise the autopsy didn't reveal anything of note. No drugs in his system other than a bit of nicotine. Death occurred at the site of the accident."

"Yeah, I thought as much."

I glance at the red puddle at my feet. Even though I've seen similar things hundreds of times before, it's always astonishing to me how much blood can come out of a human body. I feel slightly queasy. It's not due to the mess in front of me—my aversion to replications is making itself known again.

"Everything okay, Aart?"

"Yes and no. It's like somehow everything here is coming across as too real to me, the tram, the corpse, the bystanders."

"Too real? But staying faithful to reality is the point of a simulation."

"Maybe it's also too artificial, hard to say."

Ava looks at me uncomprehendingly.

"Forget it. I think we're done here, Ava. Let's check out this guy Füßli."

She nods. We go to the elevator leading to the underground garage. Ava picks the lowest parking level. When we get there, the steel doors open onto a view of a lush green meadow where multiple caddies are standing. I step out and feel how the hairs on the back of my neck stand up. The canton police constructed the crime scene as a static replication using a handful of simple infrared cameras, and the data quality is correspondingly poor. Terry probably inserted a few additional details to make the whole thing seem more realistic. But I still feel like I'm walking through the backlot of an old B-movie. The turf looks like it's made out of plastic, no breeze blows through the trees, no birds are twittering.

"This isn't much to look at," I say. "Maybe we'd be better off watching it as a desk hologram."

"But it won't be any better that way, Aart."

I shrug my shoulders and take a look at the driving range. There's a small clubhouse with all the amenities, though it's still trying to pass itself off as a spartan ski chalet. In front there's a terrace with a total of ten driving stalls. Behind that, there's a sprawling, gently sloping lawn. A point is marked in red at a distance of 57.3 meters from the driving line. That's where Füßli came into contact with the golf ball.

"Am I right in saying we have too little data to run it?"

"Unfortunately, yes, Aart. There aren't any camera recordings of the accident."

"What about panopto photos?"

"No such luck. Panopto drones only surveil cities, and sometimes not even those. But we do have the golf data from the players."

"What kind of data is that?"

"This is a very exclusive golf club. Did you notice

144

this driving range doesn't have any of the usual distance markers?"

"No, but whatever you say."

"That's due to the fact that the members all have golf software on their specs. It not only leads players to the next hole, it also saves the ballistic data of all the balls they hit. On the driving range, it shows the player how far his ball went, what the wind conditions are like, that sort of thing."

"And what results came up from analyzing the data? Do we know which ball hit our man?"

"Yes, Terry can reenact it. Should I display the trajectory?"

"By all means."

A blue line appears in front of us. It begins on the far right of the driving range and traces a high arc. Instead of remaining parallel to the long edge of the range, though, the line goes across it and disappears in the woods to our left.

"Completely whiffed it."

Ava nods. "Totally. But the ball did have a lot of momentum. After fifty-five meters, when it hit the back of Füßli's head, it was still at a height of 1.81 meters and, according to the GPS chip integrated into the ball, a speed of 127.4 kilometers per hour."

"And why was Füßli walking around here?"

"He was hiking. According to the camera footage from the wellness hotel behind this hill," she points with her thumb over her shoulder, "he set out at 7:31 a.m. He was headed to a scenic overlook nearby. According to his specs signature, he arrived at

11:13 a.m. After a snack break, he started back down, but using a different path."

"And then he came right by here?"

"Yes, he took a seldom-used shortcut that brought him in the vicinity of the range. After the golf ball hit him, he collapsed on the spot."

We go to the place where it happened. On the edge of the golf course, there's a chain link fence with a gate. On the other side we have to tramp through about ten meters of undergrowth covered in burning nettles before we reach the clearing where Füßli and the golf ball had their little introduction. The representative lies in the middle of the narrow trail. He's in his mid-fifties, slightly overweight, with the skin tone of a man who's already spent a few days in the sunny Alps. But that's not to say he has a healthy glow. A few coils of hair adorn Füßli's balding skull, where a bruise is spreading. Surprisingly, it's golf-ball-sized.

I kneel next to him and point to the bruise. "How exactly did this kill him? Skull fracture?"

"No, cerebral hemorrhage. The medical forensics said Füßli would have survived easily if he'd been operated on within an hour, maybe two. But it took a while before they found him."

"Why was that?"

"It was Sunday, which meant he had no appointments. And anyway, it's not unheard of for hikers to come back only when it starts getting dark. Since he was here alone, no one missed him during dinner at the hotel."

"And who found him?"

"The ball boy, at around seven o'clock on Monday morning. But by that point, he'd been dead for hours."

I stand up again and walk a few steps to a point marked in red behind a birch sapling. A golf ball lies next to a stump.

"Did the ball boy often check the woods for balls? Seems strange to me. There can't be that many here."

"The balls all have chips. The ball boy could see their locations on his specs."

"Do we know anything about the guy who managed this kind of involuntary kill shot?"

"Name's Peter Bruckner. German, lawyer, works for a bank in Frankfurt."

"Good golfer?"

"Passable. His handicap is -25. Means tee-offs are his biggest weakness."

We turn back to the clubhouse. I take one more look at the empty space, with no one else in sight. "Ava?"

"Yes?"

"How many fatal accidents have occurred during golfing in the past few years?"

She makes a hand motion and reads something on her glasses. "More than you might think. Around ten to fifteen annually, according to Eurostat."

"And they were all killed by low-flying golf balls?"

"Not all of them. Lightning strikes are one cause of death, not to mention accidents with golf carts. But head injuries aren't a rarity. The first golfer to succumb to one was in the year 1632, according to the database."

More information than I wanted, but I just nod. Then I indicate Ava should end the simulation. Before I open the door to the clubhouse, I say, "I need a real-time search routine, Ava."

"What for?"

"As soon as Terry registers the death of an EU representative, I want to be informed, immediately, by priority message."

"All of them? Or just the ones that might be foul play? Do you want to rule out any deaths by natural causes?"

"No, I want all of them, and also all former MEPs. It's doesn't matter if they're hit by meteorites or if they pass peacefully in their sleep at a private clinic in Geneva at the age of a hundred and fifty."

Ava's brow furrows. "Understood. Do you not believe Füßli and Milar were accidents? The circumstances look totally plausible to me. Unpleasant, no question about that, but well-documented."

"Plausibility doesn't count for anything in this case," I respond. "Please take another look at the data. I'd like it even more if we could close the files on both of them. Our focus is Pazzi, and it'll stay that way. His death definitely wasn't an accident, and Vogel won't be happy about the fact that we still don't have any suspects."

CHAPTER 9

I spend the rest of the morning taking another look at Pazzi's and Heuberger's précis. I also speak with Pazzi's father. There's almost nothing more uncomfortable than speaking with parents whose children have died. Even when the child in question was a grown man, it doesn't make things fundamentally better.

Even worse, though, is that Pazzi Senior doesn't have the faintest idea who could have shot his son. After the conversation, I contact the CEO's office at Tallan Consolidated and request an appointment. I'm told it will be enormously difficult at this time. I reply that my concern is enormously urgent. The secretary assures me John Tallan's assistant will contact me as soon as possible.

Afterward, I walk back and forth in my office. Instead of taking a lunch break, I look at evidence more or less at random on my media table. I eat licorice, draw lines connecting Pazzi, Svensson, Heuberger, and the two unfortunate representatives, then wipe them all away. On a map, I call up all the restaurants and shops in Brussels Pazzi frequented in the past year. I double check if Tallan is a good golf player and read the text of "Ode to Joy" another time through, including the passages taken out by Beethoven. I eat even more licorice. It all goes nowhere. Eventually I sit down at my desk and look at Bogey, who considers me disapprovingly. I close my eyes and wait, like a condemned prisoner resignedly awaiting his executioner. The only difference between the two of us is that Vogel won't separate my head from my shoulders with an axe. If anything, he'll bite it off.

Half an hour before I have to go see Vogel, there's a knock at my door. It's Ava. Her expression tells me something important has happened.

"We have a claim of responsibility, Aart," she says breathlessly.

"What? From who?"

"Can't say yet. It'd be best if you take a look yourself."

She murmurs something and the evidence disappears from my media table, leaving a blank white surface.

"Came in a few minutes ago. Anonymous delivery to the Europol press office, who forwarded it to me immediately. The data was password-protected, the entry code came at the same time on a piece of paper delivered via courier drone. Maybe the sender wanted to make sure no one on the net intercepted or traced it."

"Is it a text?"

"It's a video."

She types on the table. At first nothing happens. But then I notice the film is already playing. What looked to be a white surface is in actuality a room without walls or ceiling, a room seeming to stretch out infinitely. In the distance I can make out a dark point; as it draws nearer, it becomes recognizable as a human figure. Two other people appear behind it. All three are coming right at us, wearing suits of armor straight out of the Middle Ages. Their faces are covered by helmets with closed visors. In the distance I think I can hear drumbeats. They seem to provide a marching rhythm for the three knights.

"What the hell is this?"

"An elaborate computer animation, high resolution, extremely well done."

"What are they wearing?"

"Suits of armor. From paintings."

"From paintings?"

"I'll explain it to you later. Keep watching, it's about to get interesting."

By now the three knights have gotten so big they fill almost the entire surface of the table. The middle one, marching slightly in front of the others, wears a magnificent suit of armor made of Damascus steel inlaid with gold and carries a substantial broad sword in his right hand. I can see a coat of arms on his chest showing three golden lions.

The camera performs a kind of daredevil pan only possible in completely digital animation. Suddenly the three knights are standing with their backs to us. They seem to be waiting for something. Something approaching from the distance at high speed.

It's a bull.

With head lowered, the animal runs at the three

knights, who fan out and await their opponent, blades drawn. When the bull is still a few meters away, they scatter away from each other. As the frenzied bull races past him at only a few centimeters' distance, the golden knight in the middle turns a pirouette and sinks his sword with all his might. A fountain of dark blood spurts in all directions. The bull wheels around and I can see now that this isn't a true-to-life digital depiction of a bull, but a horrific caricature. It looks like it sprang to life from a Cantonese horror film. The animal's horns are much too large and its mouth opens onto rows of razor-sharp teeth. Black smoke billows from its nostrils. The head reminds me of some mythical creature, but I can't say which one.

The fight lasts a solid three minutes, by which time the knights have given the bull enough blows that it starts to stagger. The golden knight runs up to it with a leap that makes a mockery of all laws of physics. With sword raised high, he flies on top of the monster and swipes the blade across its neck. One more gush of blood, one last gasp, then it's over.

"Is there anything else? If so, we should see about getting ourselves some popcorn."

"Still about two minutes."

The knights are now shown in a medium shot. They stand with their legs straddling the empty space, stained with blood and manifestly in the full bloom of their manhood. They take off their helmets.

The golden knight is a woman. She's in her mid-forties and has a red-blonde mane of hair framing her stern face. Steel-blue eyes stare us down. In English she says, "The first blow is complete! The beast of Europe will fall! Awake, citizens of the continent! Albion will make clear the way!"

Then she places her armored foot on the giant shoulder of the lifeless bull and hefts her bloody sword in the air. The two other knights follow her lead. If the woman is supposed to be a kind of English Joan of Arc, then the knight to her left is a perfect Lancelot. He's tanned a golden brown and has brazen good looks: brown locks play around his perfectly sculpted face. A double eagle is embroidered on the surcoat draped over his suit of armor. The third knight is less imposing, a younger guy with a receding chin. A little mustache sits majestically over his pursed mouth, making his big nose look even bigger.

"Awake, citizens of the continent! Death to the beast! Death to the beast!" the three cry at full volume. Then the screen turns black.

I have to sit down.

"Everything okay, Aart?"

"I'm not entirely sure. That is some shit. Did Terry already watch the video?"

"Yes, but he can only offer a preliminary analysis."

"And what does it suggest?"

"At the present, that the sender of this message must be an excellent video designer. It was created completely on a computer, with no sets or actors."

"It looks very realistic for something like that."

Ava smiles grimly. "The programmer availed himself of various historical models and then pasted it all together."

"What kind of models?"

"Everything imaginable, apparently. Old Hollywood films, oil paintings from the Louvre, newsreels from last century—"

"Slow down, Ava. Give me some examples."

She murmurs something and the video starts at the point where the victorious knights are venerated in a medium shot. Ava taps on the armor of the middle knight and says, "Terry, show the original."

An oil painting comes into view in one corner. "This is Henry the Fifth, king of England, painted by Benjamin Burnell circa 1820. See how closely it resembles the golden armor in the video?"

"Yes. But that's a man," I reply. "Was the head of the lady knight also sourced from a painting? She looks familiar to me."

Ava exhales audibly. "That's Margaret Thatcher. She was the British prime minister. The animation is based on a recording of a speech she gave in the House of Commons, videotaped by the BBC."

"Thatcher? *The* Thatcher? The English separatist from the twentieth century?"

"The very same, Aart. The other two are politicians as well, and they're considered heroes in anti-Union circles."

I consider the knight with the receding chin and the giant nose. If he'd been wearing his general's uniform instead of this absurd cuirassier armor, I would have recognized him earlier.

"That's Charles de Gaulle."

"In a decorative suit of armor worn by the Sun

King, Louis XIV, from a painting by Rigaud."

"And who's the pretty boy? Judging from the crest, he's Austrian."

"Terry says it's a politician named Haider."

"Never heard of him. When did he live?"

"From 1950 to 2008, leader of the Austrian nationalists and opponent of the Union."

"I have to go see Vogel soon, Ava. Do you have any idea which separatist group created this claim of responsibility, if that's what this is? Normally they'd spend half the video bragging about themselves, and show their logo."

"True, the lack of a signature is strange. We don't know who it is yet. But I'm confident we'll find out soon."

"How and how fast?"

"There aren't many people who could create something like this. It's studio quality. The video designer must be a real art connoisseur and a cinephile, too. The bull's head, for example, comes from an old American fantasy movie. It'll have left traces behind on the net. It could take a little while, but give it two or three hours and Terry can compile enough data for a prognosis."

"Thanks. Let me know as soon as you have something."

And now to climb the scaffold.

Police Commissioner Jerôme Vogel sits enthroned behind his desk. It'd be easy to believe he hasn't moved from that position since our last meeting. His shirt looks crumpled and there are sweat stains visible on his cravat. As always, he's happy to see me.

"You're late, Westerhuizen. I hate it when people are late."

"I beg your pardon, sir. We've just received a claim of responsibility."

Vogel nods, but the expression on his face is inscrutable. He invites me to take a seat with a motion of his hand. The gesture seems to cost him some effort, probably because it's the most complicated movement he's asked of his muscles in the past few hours.

"To avoid wasting any more time, I had Terry go over some of the results of your investigation for me already," he says. He pulls down the corners of his mouth and looks at me through his service specs. "Did TIRESIAS not understand something? Or do you, in fact, have nothing, Westerhuizen?"

"As it happens, we don't have a suspect just yet."

Vogel's lips narrow. "Terry?" he says quietly.

From a speaker in the ceiling comes a voice in the finest upper-crust French, "How can I help you, Commissioner Vogel?"

"Tell me the rate of murder cases solved, Union-wide, since we put you into service."

"The rate of such crimes solved since the implementation of TIRESIAS I is 99.47 percent, sir."

"And how long does it take to solve a crime, on average?"

"The average time to solve a murder case since my implementation is sixteen hours and nine minutes."

I lean forward. "Commissioner, I'm aware that—"

Vogel keeps speaking as if he didn't hear me. "How long has Chief Inspector Westerhuizen already involved himself in this investigation, and how often does it happen that a murder investigation takes so long?"

"Chief Inspector Arthur Westerhuizen took responsibility for case 798/32936/BRU thirty-four hours and eleven minutes ago," says the pitiless voice from the speaker. "Which means that his performance is in the lowest quartile of the group in question."

The hippopotamus presses his paws against the desk and rises up out of his chair with a speed I'd hardly have thought him capable of. Then he bellows, "Not. Good. Enough!" and lets himself fall back in his chair, whose servos start buzzing and whining right away. Vogel wipes sweat from his brow with a disposable tissue ripped from a dispenser on his right.

"You're testing my patience, Westerhuizen. Do you have anything at all? Terry says you looked at two old crime scenes. What's that about? You have nothing better to do?"

Since Vogel caught wind of the whole thing, there's nothing I can do except tell him the truth. Otherwise I'll probably be off the case by tomorrow and can look forward to an interesting new assignment at some rank-and-file force in the suburbs.

"I suspected the deaths of two other EU representatives were related to the Pazzi case. Beat Füßli and Jorge Perez Milar had a connection with the victim."

He looks at me, halfway interested. "And that was?"

"They've all probably had their palms greased by Tallan Consolidated."

"How'd you come to that conclusion?"

"A combination of gut instinct and coincidence, sir."

If I'm reading the hippo's facial expressions correctly, he's disgusted by the very thought that I'd rather follow my intuition than Terry's prognoses.

"You said 'probably.' So you don't have any evidence for it?"

"Unfortunately not. There were reports in the press, but the public prosecutor never opened a case."

"And these two MEPs? In looking over their cases, did you find any hints that the causes of death determined at the time were falsified?"

"Both died in very strange ways." I tell him about the golf ball and the pigeon.

"Yeah, so?" Vogel snaps. "Stranger things happen every day. Last week in Namur a man was beaten to death by his wife with a baby bottle. I'll ask you again, Westerhuizen: Is there probable doubt about these accidents? Probable, meaning I could call the public prosecutor up and ask him to reopen the investigations without being laughed off the phone?"

"No, Commissioner."

"Then stop wandering around in ancient crime scene replications! Don't bother yourself with who might have been murdered. Stick to the faceless corpse, since that makes a murder seem like a pretty likely explanation."

Vogel wipes his forehead again and growls, "Reduce room temperature by two degrees."

Then he turns back to me. "I like you, Westerhuizen. You're a good cop. But you got completely carried away in this case. The claim of responsibility proves it."

"The video makes no direct reference to Pazzi."

"Could be. But as far as I know, he's the only EU representative who took a bullet to the head this week. Or did I miss something?"

"No, Commissioner."

"Then bring me the guys who made this moronic video. God only knows when this thing will show up on the net. Do you have any idea what would happen here if it did, Westerhuizen?"

"My analyst is confident we'll have him soon. The video is so unusual it must have a data trail."

"Figure out who it is and put them through the wringer right away. No kid gloves, got it? Maybe we'll find Pazzi's killer in the process. The man had no personal enemies, no underworld contacts, no other skeletons in his closet." He gives me a questioning look. "That, at least, was in your investigation report."

I nod.

"It follows," Vogel goes on, "that we're probably dealing with the usual suspects, which is what I've said from the start. I'm having dinner with Tansu Özal at 7:30 tonight. She wants updates on the case from me personally. You have until then to come up with something. Otherwise the case goes to Marquez. And you go off into an uncertain future. Have I made myself clear?"

"Completely clear, sir."

"Good. Then out you go."

CHAPTER 10

As soon as I enter Ava's office, I'm surrounded by darkness. Like most digital forensics officers, she works with special specs whose displays can show more information. She's dimmed the overhead light to prevent reflections on her output device, which looks like a multi-dimensional pair of sunglasses.

"Hello, Aart. How was everything with Vogel?"

"Fantastic. Looks like I might even be getting the opportunity to hand out traffic tickets in Little Tehran soon. What's Terry saying?"

She takes her glasses off and points to a chair that looks ergonomic and uncomfortable in equal measure.

"I think he'll have something soon."

She says something subvocally into her larynx mike. One of the walls lights up. My eyes protest for a moment, since they'd just started to get used to the twilight in Ava's vampire grotto. I can make out the faces of dozens of men and women on the media screen. There must be well over a hundred of them, stacked in a grid. About two-thirds of the pictures are already blacked out. As we watch, picture after picture extinguishes.

"It always takes some time at the start, but once

Terry has six, maybe seven, data points, he really gets cooking. All of the EU citizens you see here have sufficient software skills to make a video like that. We were also able to follow traces of the video's data back to a network node in Cologne, so we can rule out a few EU states right from the start: Northern Italy, Spain, Portugal, the Balkans, not to mention Israel and the Maghreb protectorate."

"And what now?"

"Now Terry's checking which of the suspects might have had a working knowledge of the details used in the video. For example, who would have heard of Haider and Thatcher. Do you see the pictures that are glowing particularly bright, with a kind of green shimmer, like the man in the upper right?"

"Our top suspects?"

"Yes. For example, that's Tasso Dupuy. Video designer, lives in Paris, calls up feeds critical of the Union on a regular basis. And on top of that, he read a book about Charles de Gaulle last year."

"Lots of Frenchmen read books about de Gaulle."

"It's all about probabilities. Furthermore, Dupuy once watched a film about Thatcher, as well as *Lord of the Rings*. That's where the bull in our video came from. There are more and more incriminating factors, and therefore Terry thinks it's likely it could've been him."

As soon as Ava's finished her sentence, the green shimmer on Dupuy's picture disappears. It's not alone: in one fell swoop, almost all the pictures on the wall turn black. Only a half-dozen remain.

"What happened?"

Ava murmurs something and seems to be listening to herself. "Terry found a well-hidden REM statement in the code of the video, a footnote by the programmer."

"And?"

"It's in German. Terry's analysis suggests a good knowledge of the language. So in one go, he can remove everyone who doesn't speak any German or whose semantic profiles make it unlikely they could've written the statement."

The police computer blots out three more pictures.

"How much longer, Terry?" I ask the room in general.

"Prognosticated time for process of elimination: three minutes and twelve seconds, Chief Inspector."

"Where are our remaining suspects located?"

"Aarhus, Hamburg, and Lyon."

While Terry continues running his search, I call up the headquarters of Europol's Taurus special operations unit to arrange possible strikes in each of the three cities. I'll have to cancel two of the missions almost immediately. Accordingly, dozens of drones will lift off for no reason, Taurus apes will get suited up in their tactical gear in vain, several skyships will warm up without an emergency in sight. My false alarm will squander taxpayer money to a tune I can't predict. But I'm more than ready for that kind of sacrifice.

Just as I'm about to shove a licorice stick in my mouth, Ava cries, "We got him!"

A large picture of the man appears on the media screen. His name is Thomas Winterfuhr, he's twenty-nine years old and looks conspicuously inconspicuous. No piercings, no notable tattoos or cosmetic modifications. Not even colored hair, which is unusual in light of his précis, which Terry projects up on the wall. Winterfuhr belongs to the Hamburg anarchist scene and plays bass in a horrorcore band. And yet he doesn't have filed teeth or pointed ears, which tells me he's paranoid. Every anti-surveillance forum tells its readers that distinctive piercings or an unusual hairstyle makes people more easily identifiable to TIRESIAS and other surveillance systems. That's correct. On the other hand, it's incorrect to think people without hoop earrings or goatees are more difficult to identify, as Thomas Winterfuhr will shortly find out.

Our man hasn't been accused of any major criminal activity, just a couple of petty offenses and one charge of insulting an officer. Based on the suspect's data corona, though, Terry has calculated a likelihood of over seventy-five percent that he's committed further unnoticed offenses. Winterfuhr's predictive criminal record is even more inauspicious. There's a ninety-one percent likelihood he'll commit a major crime in the coming decade or be an accessory in planning one. There's an eighty-five percent likelihood it'll involve a politically motivated crime, not a surprise given the circles he moves in. Winterfuhr is one of those enemies of the state who doesn't have even the faintest idea how good he has it in the Union. In totalitarian states like Canton or Russia, he'd already be in permanent preventative custody given such an unpromising prognosis. In the Union, on the other hand, we just keep a slightly closer watch on him.

Terry brings in aerial shots of the building where our man lives, or rather squats. It's a thirteen-story office building that looks as if it could collapse at any moment. Ava shows us a map. A red dot lights up near the Elbe River, southeast of the city center.

"Shit, why does the asshole have to live there of all places?"

"What's wrong, Ava?"

"The house is in the HafenCity."

"The way it looks in the picture, it's definitely in the old one, not the new one."

"Exactly right," she answers.

I slowly slip the licorice from my hand into my mouth. After I've finished chewing, I call up headquarters again. For Hamburg, I'd ordered two teams of ten men each. But for this little number, we're going to need at least twice as many.

The first difference between Brussels and Hamburg is clear before I'm even entirely through the door. It doesn't rain cats and dogs here, it rains tigers and wolves. If I found myself here in reality, I'd be drenched to the bone in a few minutes despite the nano-coating on my trench coat. But I can direct Terry to make the rain bounce off my avatar as if I had one of those newfangled jackets like Ava wears.

I walk a few steps to orient myself. According to my specs, I'm at the western end of the old Hafencity, near a place called Deichtor. The gray Elbe River stretches out into the horizon, with tall clouds towering up beyond it. It makes me think this downpour is just a prelude to a severe summer thunderstorm. In front of me, half-collapsed houses on stilts stand knee-deep in the water. A few of the bridges spanning the old waterlogged dikes look like they might be useable. At least, they would be for someone with angler's pants.

I check the position of our troops using a survey map. Two skyships, each with about twenty men on board, are circling at a few kilometers' distance. They're waiting on ground troops, which in this case means the marines—this part of Hamburg is only accessible via inflatable boats or small hovercraft. On the map, three boats draw closer from the west. They'll be here in five minutes. I take a pair of field binoculars out of my jacket pocket, where Ava or Terry must have thought ahead to stash them, and take a look at the building where our man lives. It's an enormous cube made of glass. The most conspicuous thing about it is that a part of the façade is set back from the rest, so the whole building gives the sense of a gigantic window. Many of the enormous panes shattered years ago, so I can make out the vast atrium inside, crisscrossed by floating staircases.

I pull up the plan of action. Since the majority of the building is empty for one thing and damp and draughty for another, the tactician of my Taurus unit is moving forward under the assumption that the occupants could only be located in the upper levels. Those appear to be halfway intact, while the rest are presumably occupied by river rats and other fauna. But in order to go forward with absolute certainty, I'll have to check out the lay of the land from a closer vantage point.

"Terry?"

"Yes, Chief Inspector?"

I point to the gray-green surface of the water between me and the building. It's broken only by metal bars and lampposts. "How the hell am I supposed to get over there?"

"You could walk over the water."

"Like the Messiah? Are you serious?"

"Are you referring to the biblical figure of Jesus Christ, Chief Inspector?"

"Yes. I don't want to walk over the Elbe."

"If it's a matter of your being afraid you'll become nauseated due to your spectrophobia, as in the case of your ghosting in Woluwe-Saint-Pierre, I'm happy to transmit you to the other side. Or insert a water taxi into the replication, Chief Inspector."

"The last one, please."

A few seconds later, one of the white-and-blue water taxis Hamburg is so famous for comes shooting out from the direction of the Speicherstadt warehouse district. It stops close to the quay wall where I'm standing, maybe one and a half meters under me. I jump. Without asking my destination, the taxi shoots away and stops at the occupied building. On the other side, I have to walk over a waiting pontoon leading to a metal ladder built into the wall of the quay. The squatters have planted a bunch of flagpoles on the pontoon, their black skull-and-crossbones flags fluttering in the wind.

I climb up the ladder and find myself in front of the building, which seems immense from this close up. The cobblestoned courtyard is strewn with Elbe mud, algae slime, and all kinds of flotsam. The waterline is visible a few meters up on the side of the building.

"Scouting mode," I say.

As I walk toward the main entrance, my specs point out a small object lying a few meters away on the pavement. I walk over and bend down to look at it. It's a humming-drone. One of the wings is shredded and the head looks like someone worked it over with a blowtorch.

"Determine signature," I murmur.

It's one of ours—more precisely, one of the German state police's. It discontinued its transmission three hours ago.

I look around me. "Tag all CCTV cameras."

Something like thirty dots illuminate around me. There are cameras on the front of the building, on the lampposts, on the bridges. They're all alike, though, in that they were destroyed a long time ago. Their lenses are smashed and a few are blackened with soot. That's to be expected. These anarchists are well-known opponents of the "surveillance state." They're likely to have their own drones, armed to the teeth, ready to take down anything that looks like it belongs to the police.

"Terry? Have we powdered the area well enough?"

"An hour ago, mite drones were spread throughout the entire HafenCity area, with a focus on the target in question. The verisimilitude is in a confidence interval of ninety-nine percent."

"Same goes for the areas inside?"

"The building's structure has been compromised in many places, allowing sufficient points of entry. Additionally, we were able to smuggle in a Trojan."

"What kind?"

"One of the occupants placed a large order from Pyongyang Five by courier drone forty-five minutes ago. A friendly agency was able to hide another swarm of our mite drones inside, which has since infiltrated the entire top floor of the building and replicated it."

The old delivery service trick always works. It unsettles me somewhat, though, that it was carried out by a "friendly agency." That expression is the common euphemism for our mysterious brothers in the "agency that doesn't exist," the shadow police: Récupération des Renseignements, the Union's intelligence service.

I walk through the main entrance. The inside of the building is in a much worse state than was discernible from the outside. It's not just that water has invaded the lobby every six hours for years, turning the space into a rotting mud pit. The moisture seems to have turned the entire atrium into a sort of greenhouse from hell. Immense mold colonies adorn the walls all the way to the upper floors, and stalactites formed from calcium and salt deposits hang from the ceiling. One of the catwalks stretching across the hall above me is broken in the middle. The few mold-free places are smeared with separatist propaganda—on one wall I can see a cluster of the same white squares I saw around the capital. A man with blue hair looks out from one of the balustrades surrounding the atrium. He wears a rain jacket and has shouldered a weapon that looks like a shotgun. My specs tell me he's twenty-three years old and didn't have the greatest childhood. If he wants to try and defend this ruin against dozens of heavily armed Taurus bulls with a hunting rifle, the rest of his life won't be much better.

But I have to admit these anarchists have really thought through the security in this building. The mud and high water would scare off most tenants, but they're ideal for squatters, since they act as a natural line of defense and make the building as difficult to access as a medieval fortress.

Due to the invasion of the water—or, possibly, due to sabotage—the elevators are out of service. The stairwell is still there, but the anarchists have filled the lower section with a large heap of rubble and junk. I walk closer and peer through the broken glass door. They've poured several cubic meters of epoxy resin over the rubble for good measure. There's no getting through it without a few liters of explosive gel. The only way to get upstairs is via a rope ladder, attached to the balustrade on the first floor about four meters up. The blue-haired man is standing at the other end, presumably always at the ready with a round of shot to hinder a cop climbing up.

"I'm coming up," I call to him, knowing full well he can't hear me, much less see me.

Wheezing, I climb the rope ladder and swing myself over the balustrade. Behind it, someone has stacked bricks that can be thrown onto the heads of uninvited visitors as a gesture of welcome. Several motionless spider drones, each as big as a human hand, sit on an old filing cabinet against one wall. Attached to their backs are small tubes identified by my specs as compressed-air pistols. They probably shoot poisoned arrows. These things are almost as fast as their natural prototypes. On the black market, they cost less than a palm book. I'd bet the entire building is full of these biomimetic crawlers. No wonder the Hamburg city police had no interest in coming in here.

I walk along the balustrade, past private offices full of ancient, silicone-based computers and rotting stacks of papers covered in green mold. Then I enter the stairwell and climb up the steps. It's eleven floors to the top level where Winterfuhr and most of the other squatters are staying. Every few floors, someone has constructed barriers out of tables and bookshelves, though they've been pushed just slightly to the side. If they were expecting us, they'd have barricaded the landings better, and there'd be more of those spiders on the move.

Clearly, they haven't caught wind of the forth-coming raid. That'll change soon enough. Shortly before I reach floor number 12, I contact the officer-in-charge.

"Chief Inspector Westerhuizen?"

"Yes. I'm in," I say. "Give me three more minutes, then you can get started."

"Understood. Over and out."

I take the last flight of stairs at a run. Behind a still-intact glass door, I can see a giant room of more than 1,245 square meters. The office furnishings that were likely here back in the day have largely been removed and replaced by living room furniture. In several places, the anarchists have set up makeshift partitions and a few tents to go along with them. I'd guess there are somewhere between twenty and thirty people living here. The view is breathtaking: the entire city center, from St. Michael's Church to the flooded harbor, is visible through the entirely glass walls, even if they are somewhat smudgy. At a certain spot on the horizon, anyone clued in would also notice three inflatable boats getting closer at high speed.

I cross through the room. "Where is he?" I ask Terry.

"Thomas Winterfuhr is located in a private office at the other end of the floor, Chief Inspector."

I follow the arrows my specs use to mark the way. My hand drifts to my Heckler & Koch to take off the safety, a force of habit. I enter a room that was once probably a conference room. A venetian blind has been pulled down to cover the window, and large parts of the walls are covered in media screens displaying all kinds of images: sketches of manga figures, computer animations, snippets of action movies. Thomas Winterfuhr stands in front of one wall, pushing sections of pictures here and there, apparently completely engrossed in his work. He wears a faded field jacket from the Chinese People's Army along with matching pants and combat boots. I can't make out what he's trying to cobble together. It might be because there aren't enough mites in the room. Or maybe because I lack the right sense of art appreciation.

I take a few steps back and turn around. With a finger, I push down one of the blinds slats and peer through the gap. The inflatable boats are almost here, and over the southern bank of the Elbe, I can see something hovering that looks like a cross between a fighter jet and a helicopter. Agitated yells come through from the main room, though they're drowned out only a few seconds later by a booming voice. It comes from the megaphone on the skyship, so terrifyingly loud even the heavy windowpanes in front of me start to vibrate.

"Attention, attention! This is the police! In the name of the European Office of Public Prosecution, you are commanded to clear the building immediately. Make your way to the exit. Resistance is futile. Your faces have been logged."

Winterfuhr runs to the window. "Fuck, fuck, fuck!" bursts out of him. He reaches for a backpack in the corner and leaves the room. I follow him. In the main room, people with patched-up clothes and multicolored hair run back and forth agitatedly. A woman points through the glass to a second skyship that has taken up a position against the side of the building opposite, Gatling cannons extended. I can make out the bull cockade with its border of stars on the stubby wings of the flying ship.

"We have to do something!" she screams. "Where are the snipers?"

"Are you crazy?" a boy with dreadlocks yells at her. He's maybe seventeen years old. "Those aren't normal cops! Didn't you see the steer symbol? Those are Jacobins!"

Then he grabs the woman by the arm and pulls her in the direction of the stairwell. Most of the other squatters follow his lead. It's gradually becoming clear even to the particularly clueless or stupid that something is brewing outside. A group of police drones, each the size of a calf, have swarmed the building by now, an indication that my colleagues have neutralized the drone defenses. I can see more Taurus troops taking up their positions in the courtyard. From somewhere down below comes the sound of fully-automatic weapons.

"The guy with the blue hair, Terry?"

"Correct, Chief Inspector. He was hit by several bullets. No police were injured."

Winterfuhr also runs toward the stairwell. Unlike the other anarcho-communists, though, he doesn't head down, but instead goes up. I follow him. After a few meters, the steps end in front of a heavy steel door without a touchpad. Winterfuhr takes off his specs and deactivates them, then slips them into the pocket in one leg of his fatigues. He opens his backpack. Inside is a white outfit, not unlike the Tyvek overalls we have to make sure and wear at crime scenes. Winterfuhr slips inside. Unlike our overalls, these not only have a hood but also a mask, which fits snug against his haggard face. He murmurs something. The color of the overalls changes immediately, taking on the yellow-brown tone of the walls and the slate-gray of the door. I can still see him in spite of that, and even if he were to move a few meters away, Terry would mark him for me. To anyone else, though, he'd be as good as invisible on the poorly lit roof.

Winterfuhr pulls something out of his right pants pocket. It's a key. He sticks it into the old-fashioned lock and turns it to the left. With a snapping sound, the door springs open. Warm rain whips against us. In a stooping stance, Winterfuhr goes through the door and crouches down near the wall of the building. The sounds of yells and police sirens drift up from below. We're on the short side of the building, and I can make out the two skyships to the left and right. The wind has gotten so strong by now that the jet engines have to work continuously to keep the airships in their positions. The roof lies in half-darkness, the tarpapered flooring only sporadically illuminated by a shaft of light from one of the search drones.

I ask myself how Winterfuhr thinks he's getting down from this roof—and what he plans to do once he does. The suit and the face mask are certainly helpful. But even if he can pull a fast one on the drones and cops, there are still the panoptos swarming around us, high-up and invisible. Thousands of cameras are watching the HafenCity and everything else in a thirty-kilometer radius from above; their gazes cut through every cloud and see every blade of grass. In spite of the chameleon suit, Terry will be able to identify him from the images the panoptos are taking every hundredth of a second. The camouflage isn't flawless enough to fool a computer, and anyway Winterfuhr is still casting a shadow.

But that doesn't mean the situation doesn't call for caution. "Commander?"

"Velazquez here, Chief Inspector."

"Report, please."

"All means of exit are secured. All vehicles within a two-kilometer radius have been stopped by the central transportation computer. Seventeen taken into custody. One dead terrorist. Teams I and II are inside now working their way up floor by floor. Team III will repel from Skyship Alpha shortly."

"The target is on the roof, Velazquez. He's wearing a chameleon suit."

"Oh, just give me a minute."

I hear a short snigger. "I have him. His suit doesn't have a cooling system, cheap North Korean crap. It's lighting up on my infrared like a dumpster fire. Should I send my guys down?"

"Permission to strike issued, Lieutenant."

"Copy that."

I see the nose of one skyship tipping forward as the pilot powers up the propulsion. Winterfuhr sees it, too. He takes off running straight across the roof to another bit of cover at the other end. I follow him. I'm not the only one. By now, the drones also know where they need to search. Dozens of spotlights lock on to Winterfuhr and follow his outline, barely discernible to the naked eye, as he makes his way across the roof.

He's running toward something that looks like a three-dimensional gel pill. It's mounted on a kind of ramp constructed against the edge of the roof.

"Terry, identify that object."

"It's a submersible open-water rescue capsule. Passenger capacity: one. Manufacturer: Dassault-SsangYong. Model year—"

"Velazquez!" I bellow.

"Chief Inspector?"

"He's running toward a launch ramp! That's a lifeboat!"

"Copy that."

Winterfuhr is still 10.54 meters away from the capsule. As soon as he's climbed inside, a mechanism in the ramp will catapult him high in the air. Soon after that, an engine in the stern will ignite. These things are designed to send a person as far as possible away from a flooded boat. Then they clear the area and steer for the nearest coast. In Winterfuhr's case, it's likely he hacked into the capsule's navigation system and programmed another destination. It's not a bad plan.

But it's also not good enough.

The roof in front of Winterfuhr begins to disintegrate, showering tarpaper, granite, and plastic in all directions. There's a spray of sparks as the skyship fires on the building. The whole thing only lasts a few fractions of a second, until there's not much left of the edge of the building where the rescue pod once stood, much less anything of Winterfuhr's escape plan.

Winterfuhr goes a few more steps toward the edge, as though he has to see with his own eyes that the capsule didn't survive the barrage from the Gatling cannons. Then he slowly raises his hands.

I take up a position near him, waiting for the team to repel down and take Winterfuhr into custody. Toward the northwest I can see the first strikes of lightning, enormous, jagged, and terrible. For a brief moment, they illuminate the entire sky, a mindboggling sight. Either it's the worst storm in years, or Terry has an overactive imagination.

For those physically present, it's about time to clear the roof. Two Taurus members come running toward us. They're dressed all in black, their faces hidden behind masks. The men don't wear any name badges or rank markings. Only the patches with the steer cockade on their right arms give away who they work for.

"On the ground!" yells one. "Hands behind your head!"

Winterfuhr wants to be a good separatist and disobey, but he doesn't get a chance to do it. Because at that same moment, a loud buzzing pierces my ear, drowning out even the howling of the storm. It sounds like a furious swarm of hornets. The noise is coming from the rotors of a huge police drone moving toward Winterfuhr at high speed. It makes an ugly, dull noise as its wedge-shaped ceramic body makes contact with his solar plexus. The force of the impact lifts him off his feet, he's flying backwards, he's already over the edge.

I can still see his overalls taking on the color of the gray-black cloud front behind him. Then he's gone.

CHAPTER 11

Ava lifts her olive-colored arms to her waspy waist and stares at me. "Sometimes I don't understand you. The case can be closed ahead of the deadline Vogel set for you. But despite that, you don't look happy, Aart. All things considered, the whole thing was actually an open-and-shut case."

"If a bolt out of the blue can be called an open-and-shut case."

"You know what I meant."

Of course I do. According to Terry's analysis, the drone that sent Winterfuhr flying was hit by a lightning strike and knocked off course. A malfunction with tragic consequences. Using Winterfuhr's computer, we were able to follow his trail back to a data haven in the Caymans, where there was the master copy of the video he made. The film was indisputably created on his Samsung. Amazing, how such a hopeless case can be cleared up in a matter of hours. Ava's right. It doesn't get any cleaner than this. At least if certain details are edited out.

"I got a call from Ververke earlier, my acquaintance at the intelligence service. They had a lead on someone, and now they're certain it must have been Winterfuhr."

"Go on."

Instead of answering her, I say, "Terry, the RR dossier from Ververke, the Kirchberg incident."

The wall in Ava's office begins to light up, showing the Juncker tower in Luxembourg. The plaza in front is paved in marble, with the inevitable fountains and a piece of modern art that utilizes rusty steel beams to depict the process of European unionization. In front of the plaza, there are thirty-seven masts with flags from the member states, set in rows like an honor guard.

"And that's what it looked like after Winterfuhr was done with it."

With a hand gesture I advance to the next picture.

"Looks the same as before," Ava says. "Wait a minute, the flags! The flags are all black!"

"That happened two years ago. The RR believes it was Winterfuhr's doing."

"How'd he do it?"

"Apparently he reprogrammed a couple of cleaning drones and filled their tanks with black paint. There are only a few compilers working in the Juncker, and the security precautions aren't as strong as they are here in the European Quarter. By the time they noticed, it was too late—the pictures were already being broadcast over all sorts of feeds."

"Subversive and original at the same time."

"Correct, it seems like he was some kind of performance artist. This is also allegedly one of his." I call up another picture on the screen. It shows a brass statue of a very fat man. It reminds me of Vogel. On its shoulders sits a pig's head instead of a human one.

"Where is that? And who . . . ?"

"That's the statue of Kohl at the Neumarkt in Dresden."

"And he hacked off the head and put a new one up?"

"No, the real Helmut is still there. Winterfuhr used a drone this time as well, one that could spray epoxy resin and create three-dimensional structures. They're available at any home-improvement store for a few thousand euros."

"When was this?"

"Three years ago. But it wasn't widely reported, the Germans were somehow able to sweep it under the rug."

Ava pushes off with her legs, causing her rolling chair to catapult backwards across the office. For a moment it looks like she's going to collide with the edge of the table, but at the last second, she brakes with one foot and turns 180 degrees. As she pulls up a few windows on the media table in front of her, she asks, "How come this didn't occur to the RR earlier?"

"Maybe it slipped their minds because of everything with the video and our strike on the Hafen City?"

Ava laughs.

"Most likely they held back the information on purpose. A quid pro quo, since we defiled their precious mirror-space."

"And why are they being so cooperative now?"

"Because it's become clear to them that we're solving the case. Of course they want to be a part of it now. It means they can report that this incredibly dangerous master criminal, this threat to Union cohesion, was only captured thanks to a cooperative effort between the RR and Europol."

"Is that sarcasm aimed at the shadow police or at the idea of calling Winterfuhr incredibly dangerous, Aart?"

"Both. I mean, take a look at this guy. The blacked-out flags, the pig's head, this video cobbled together out of plagiarized bits and pieces, probably a few other spontaneous operations."

"And?"

"All of his previous actions were nonviolent. Then, a murder. Why the change of heart? What was his motive?"

"Hatred for the Union? Progressive radicalization? Aart, we found the camouflage suit that matched the scraps on the branches where the shooter fired at Pazzi. And Winterfuhr was in the military. He knew his way around weapons."

"Sounds conclusive," I say quietly.

"But?"

"But nothing. Vogel already gave a press conference. The presumed murderer is dead. The case is closed."

She turns around in her chair and gives me a wary look. "Good. So we can get back to working on the creeper-feeds, right?"

"We have to. After that lecture from Vogel, we should do something about our performance statistics."

"Okay. I'll catch you up on what I've found out so far. Do you by chance still have access to Terry IV?"

"Yes, why?"

"You can put him through all his paces this week. I'm going to Tel Aviv for a few days, for the Jewish New Year." She blows me a kiss. "I'll miss the rain in Brussels, and of course you too."

I refrain from telling her I'd like to have known about this a few days earlier. It wouldn't do any good because technically speaking I'm not Ava's boss. Instead, I grab the workout ball, sit down next to her, and listen to another explanation of the creeper-feed case.

"For months now, there have been more and more videos like this one appearing on the black market," Ava says, pulling up a window. A woman's backside appears in front of us. She's quite full-figured and barely fits into the leather corset she's buckled around herself. Bulges of fat well up under her shoulders and the area around her waist. She's being fucked from behind; the video was taken from the guy's perspective. The only things visible of him are a hairy beer belly and a cock ring.

"Looks like any old amateur porn video," Ava says needlessly. "Taken with a pair of specs."

"And?" I reply. "The net is full of stuff like this."

"Yes, but one of the participants reported this one. Happened to come across it himself on the net and was furious the material was circulated without his permission."

"That also happens all the time."

"But it was the man who filed the complaint. He says he never filmed intercourse with his wife at all. We checked into it. He's telling the truth. Evidently, we're dealing with a creeper-feed."

"Does that mean someone hacked his specs and made a secret recording illegally?"

"Exactly. Someone hijacked the integrated camera and made off with the images. There are often creeper-feed crimes like this, though in this case there were no data traces pointing to it. There are no indications someone hacked the specs."

I lean back, only to recall that I'm not sitting in my desk chair, but on Ava's stupid exercise ball. As a result, I almost fall all the way over.

My analyst considers me and shakes her head. "Everything okay, Aart?"

"This ball is going to kill me. There are two things about this case I don't understand."

"And what would those be?"

"Why would anyone wear specs during sex? I mean, if he wasn't planning to direct his own private porno."

"Um, erotic software, Aart?"

"Since when is software necessary for that?"

"For tantric exercises, Kama Sutra positions. That kind of thing. The specs show what movements the participants should make or indicate erogenous zones."

"And what kind of software was being used by our leather prince here?"

"'SM for Beginners.' And your second question?"

"Why are these sex videos our problem? That's definitely something for the vice squad. And why is it even of interest to the Union? Shouldn't the local police mess around with that?"

"Why? Because the case is enormous. Buckle up, Aart. This isn't pretty."

Ava murmurs something and the wall fills with dozens, then hundreds of tiny videos. There's fucking in many of them. In others, people are beating each other to a pulp. But in their midst are other videos depicting acts of unimaginable violence. Someone uses an iron bar to beat a person tied to a chair until their head is nothing but a bloody mass. In another, someone with a riding crop is whipping a girl, maybe twelve years old, her skin hanging off her back in shreds. Based on the perspective, all of these recordings were clearly taken with specs. I see a hairy hand close around a .65-caliber Desert Djinn and shoot someone in the neck. As the man fires, his victim's head lifts clean off. I'm feeling a bit sick to my stomach.

"Turn it off, Ava. What is all that?"

"A terrier found it in a data graveyard somewhere on the net."

Terriers are small autonomous programs TIRESIAS uses to keep the Union net clean and routinely comb through it for lawbreakers.

"And then?"

"Then Terry set more trackers on the case. They found more material, thousands of snippets. All of it dates from the past three or four years. And we have no idea where it's coming from."

"Could it be someone is selling this smut? A network for snuff videos? Powered by pedophiles or other perverts?"

"Theoretically possible. But the material is very heterogeneous."

"What do you mean by that?"

"There are execution videos, gang rapes, torture scenes. But there's also totally sedate lovemaking by candlelight. We even have a ten-minute video of someone painting his garage door."

"How perverse. I suggest Terry and I take another look tomorrow and the day after, while you're on vacation. Was he able to identify any of the people already?"

"Quite a few. At the time, the cases were automatically turned over to the authorities in each member state. There have already been a dozen arrests. But the Union public prosecutor took on the larger case and assigned it to Europol due to its massive scale. Only a professional hacking ring could be behind something like this, Triades or Britskis."

"Do you have a list?"

"Already in your inbox."

I thank Ava and wish her a pleasant trip. Then I leave. On the way to my office, I call up the list of videos on my specs. There are many, too many.

Yet another shitstorm, and so soon. I'm in desperate need of some licorice.

CHAPTER 12

Back in my office, I find the licorice tin empty. This fact strikes me as so devastating that I decide to call it a day. I go down to the parking garage, get in my Mercedes, and have it drive me to the city center. Behind the La Monnaie opera house, I get out and instruct the car to find itself a parking space. Then I wander along the Schildknaapstraat up to the St-Hubertus-Galerij, where I know of a great local pub. Inside, there's a stained-glass ceiling and copper fixtures decorated with art-nouveau tendrils. The wobbly tables look as though they were arranged this way by chance, their splotched wooden tops signaling to guests that they're good only for ordering beer and not for using as monitors. The place is still fairly empty, since it's too early for dinner. I decide to set myself up at the bar and drink Hoegaarden with genever until it's late enough to eat.

As I rise from my barstool two hours later and head for one of the tables, I'm already two sheets to the wind. Maybe I should have cut the schnapps with more beer. I order a steak with a double portion of fries. They don't serve any of those in-vitro steaks here, just good old beef. After I've finished eating, I pull up the schedules of all movie theaters in the area on my specs. The text swims in front of my eyes. Basically, the only things showing are Korean blockbusters and a French comedy that's supposed to be quite good. Most of them are filmed in 360, which is too demanding for my current state. I just want to watch, lazily and passively, as the actors converse and walk back and forth for a little bit. I can do without perspective changes and panoramic views for today. I ask if there are any old 2D or 3D films showing somewhere. And, as it happens, the computer finds a small arthouse cinema somewhere north of the European Quarter that's showing a gangster flick from last century.

I buy a ticket, call my car, and head to the theater. It's called Cinematique, and it even looks like one. There's a stylized film reel on the old lighted sign above the entrance, a piece of equipment that assumedly no one other than enthusiasts like me can even identify anymore. The Cinematique unironically announces its current films in glass cases. There are no media screens hanging inside, but actual posters made out of paper. I enter an outer lobby outfitted with puffy red plush armchairs. Even more posters hang on the walls. One shows Humphrey Bogart and Peter Lorre in *The Maltese Falcon*. This place is a real gem, no doubt about it. I wonder why I've never come across it before.

At the bar, I buy licorice and a beer, and an additional mini bottle of genever, although I've really had enough already. Then I enter the screening room. The illusion crumbles a bit here, because even though it's surrounded by old theater seats and curtains decorated with gold braid, the image doesn't come from a film projector. Instead, the projection surface is made up of media screens.

On the way to the theater, I read through the database entry on the film. It's called *Reservoir Dogs* and is about an unsuccessful robbery. It starts. The film doesn't have much of a plot, but there's plenty of shooting, cursing, and stabbing. Most conspicuously, all of the protagonists are wearing the same black suits. An early American mafia signifier, maybe? Along with the suits, they all wear black ties, early variations of a cravat, and black sunglasses that make them look like bloodthirsty Blues Brothers.

The film is full of obscure references to a lost pop culture I don't understand. At the end, I leave the theater unsatisfied. I wait in the drizzling rain outside and look at my reflection in the glass panels of the poster showcases. I see a drunk, tired man. The poster behind the glass appears through him, showing four of the film gangsters. Seen through the pane, it looks as if they're running at me, ties fluttering and eyes hidden behind their sunglasses.

The car arrives. I have to use the door for support as I get inside. I direct the Mercedes to drive to my apartment. When I get there, the first thing I do is look for something else to drink. I hit paydirt under the kitchen sink, where there's a half-full bottle of Japanese whiskey. I stick it in my pocket and clamber up into my loft bed, where I can think a little more about the strange American film.

When I wake up again, I feel a sawing pain behind my forehead. Groaning, I climb down the ladder and peel myself out of my crumpled suit. After a hot shower and two cups of instant coffee, I'm awake enough that I manage to kneel down on all fours and look for my headache spray in a box under the bed. As I bend over, my brain feels like it sloshes forward and smacks against my forehead, which elicits another fit of genever migraines.

I find the inhaler in the midst of empty hypnoremerol dispensers and long-dry tubes of self-tanner. Still sitting on the cold parquet floor, I allow myself one puff, then another. The pain in my head recedes abruptly. I scramble to my feet and sit on my only chair with a third cup of coffee. I notice now that there's a media board on the small desk under the loft bed, and I clearly did some work on it last night—not that I can remember. It shows a still from yesterday's film: five of the gangsters, all in Blues Brother outfits. Someone has circled their sunglasses in red and written the model type beside them: "Ray Ban 3016 Clubmaster," "Ray Ban Wayfarer," and so on. Underneath, it says: "Ray Ban! They're all wearing the same brand!"

I massage my temples and ask myself what I should do with this shockingly straightforward discovery. Besides that, it's unclear how I was able to find out the exact names of ancient glasses frames made by a long-extinct company, and in the middle of the night to boot.

There's only one possible answer. I link to Terry.

"Good morning, Chief Inspector."

"When was the last time we spoke, Terry?"

"Wednesday, 2:37 a.m."

Meaning last night. "And what did we talk about?"

"You asked me to research details about costumes and accessories in an old Hollywood film from the year 1992, *Reservoir Dogs*."

"I was interested in the sunglasses."

"That is correct, Chief Inspector."

"Do you have an audio recording?"

"Of course. Should I play it back?"

"Yes, please."

A strange-sounding voice comes through my earbuds.

"Whakinda glasshes are those, Terry?"

"Chief Inspector, I must inform you that you may only utilize a Europol police computer for matters entirely related to official purposes."

"'S offishal! Offishal porpoises."

"Voice modulation analyses and purchase history from the past few hours indicate that you are under the influence of alcohol, Chief Inspector. Additionally, you have a weakness for North American films, according to your free-time data history. Both of these facts lead me to assume that this research is related to a private usage."

"You stupid golem, you're just an enforcement officer made out of shound, you don't even have a soul! You're an electronic Eichmann! Tell me the sunglasses mod—mottles!"

"I must warn you that I am required to inform Internal Affairs of any violations of Paragraph 13 of the official service regulations."

"Interminal Affairs can go fuck themshelves. Do

what I'm telling you, you useless piece of junk!"

"They are exclusively glasses from the United States, in a 1960s vintage style popular at the time. A list of the models will be sent to your inbox, Chief Inspector."

There's a small pause. I can hear grunting and puffing noises, then the gurgle of the whiskey bottle.

"'S all the shame! They all have the shame kinda glasses?"

"Could you reformulate the question, Inspector?"

"No, kiss my ash."

"That was the entire recording," Terry says. "I must inform you that I have advised Internal Affairs about the incident."

"You could have skipped ratting me out, my friend."

"Is there a sarcastic tone to your observation, Chief Inspector?"

"No, there isn't, Terry. The question was actually for an official purpose. And now you'll have some real work to do. I want you to analyze all of the creeper-feeds your bots fished from the data wastelands on the net."

"According to what criteria, Chief Inspector?"

"I want to know what kind of specs were used for the recordings. I'll take a look at the results in my office later."

After I disconnect from Terry, I go in search of something edible. I only find expired yogurt and black licorice. In my condition, neither of them seems like a good idea. If I don't have a solid post-bender breakfast soon, even the headache spray won't help anymore.

I get dressed and make myself look halfway present-able. Then I order the Mercedes to pick me up and drive to Café Amsterdam. It has everything a Dutchman needs for breakfast, above all what a hungover Dutch-man needs. I order herring fillets and a pot of tea. I hole up in my corner with my order, chewing intently on my food and watching TV. The news is playing on one of the video screens. There aren't any attacks, at least not on us. For that, they show scenes of war from China. Some disloyal People's Army general or other is leaving a city of fifteen million inhabitants—I've never heard the name before—in ash and rubble. The Emperor of the Greater Congo has announced he has "dozens of nuclear warheads" at his disposal. Union analysts believe it's a bluff—in actuality, it's more like four or five at most. And the weatherman is promising the downpour will let up in the coming week, but the rainy season is still not quite over.

A report about the German vice-chancellor, who apparently resigned yesterday, comes next. His name is Schneider. I've never heard of him either. The first image that appears on the screen is a politician—ro-tund, in his late-forties, with an expression like gran-ite—walking in front of the Reichstag past a row of GSG-10 tactical soldiers in heavy body armor and climbing into a fortified Porsche. Pixelated pictures follow, showing Schneider, in distinctly casual cloth-ing, with three half-naked girls. The oldest is maybe fourteen.

"So he got rid of another one of the pigs, huh?"

I turn around. The voice is coming from the stubble-bearded guy from the other day. He looks as if he hasn't stirred from this position since then. I imagine his corduroy jacket has gotten even greasier.

I still find him off-putting. But this time I'm friendly to his face.

"Who got rid of Schneider?"

"Well, Johnny Random. The journalist."

I nod and devote my attention back to the video screen, hoping Greasy Jacket will leave it at that. He does me that courtesy. I open a window and search for Random's latest broadcast. In the past, I've watched his show here and there, along with half the Union, but at some point, I lost interest. But the guy is still a phenomenon, as he's always been. Every week when a new episode airs, the feeds are full of discussions about it.

After the intro, Johnny Random enters the picture. As always, he's wearing an unnaturally white suit, lit from the inside out, and a brightly colored t-shirt. The shirt will change color at least ten times during the broadcast, just like Random's face and the color of his hair. The avatar's inconsistency is his trademark: apart from the suit, everything else about him also changes, even his gender every once in a while. Since he conducts his interviews exclusively with the help of replication technology, no one knows what the guy looks like in real life.

There are three things that make Random wildly successful. First, he's not on the payroll of any big company, so he doesn't have to take any media mogul's political opinions into account. Second, he was the first member of the media to use this new translation technology, which more and more channels have since started using. Johnny Random is clarifying the misdeeds of Vice-Chancellor Robert Schneider to me not in English or French, but in flawless Dutch. Viewers in other regions will hear his voice in their respective national language, with the translation and synchronization taken care of by a high-performance computer. The third thing is the stories. They're incredibly sordid, and Random drags them up from God knows where. Corruption, weapons sales, child prostitution—he always has excellent sources. And no one can say where he gets his incredibly volatile information from.

Seven or eight years ago, when his first broadcast was aired, Johnny Random's stories were admittedly exclusive, but not earthshaking. As time has gone on, though, he's gotten more sophisticated, built up his information network or hired talented researchers, probably hackers. Now the Union's elite quakes in their boots every week in fear of the newest edition of Random Discoveries. And not only have the stories gotten better, so has Johnny Random himself. At first, it was easy to tell he was a computer animation; now, his avatar is indistinguishable from a real person.

On the video screen, the portly vice-chancellor is about to climb into a hot tub. A girl is already sitting inside. Johnny Random has inserted himself into the video, wearing bright-white shorts with his jacket and a Hawaiian shirt underneath. The entire thing is perfectly done, outstanding video design. I regret that I can't watch it as a 360-video. Random kneels down next to the pool and pats the vice-chancellor on his hairy back. "Well, Schneider," he says, and looks at the girl. "Now I understand what you meant the other day."

Cut to Schneider sitting at the conference table of a Bavarian business, surrounded by a large group of men in traditional dress. Johnny Random is among them, wearing a bright blue felted hat. He looks right in the direction of the viewer and says, "And now, yet again, Robby Schneider will make sure we understand the thing that lies closest to his heart."

"Family," says the ex-vice-chancellor, "is, to me, the most important thing. Our children are the future. That means they stand at the center of everything we do politically, and they occupy all of my attention."

Random stands up and says, "I don't know about you, but I need to step out of the frame for a minute and puke in my pint glass."

After that, the clip comes to an end. I stab my last herring filet with my fork, then set it back on the plate and leave the café.

A little while later, I'm sitting at my media table in the Europol Palais, taking a look at what Terry's found. It isn't much.

"All of the confirmed video recordings we have were taken with newer models, Chief Inspector."

"What makes you think so?"

"The resolution of the images. It follows that none of the utilized specs are older than five years."

"And what about the makes, anything that's abnormal, any patterns . . . ?"

"I don't know the exact makes, Chief Inspector."

"Don't the videos have to carry an originating signature? Identifiers for the specs, a model type, a serial number?"

"That is correct. But someone has apparently removed such information from the video data in question."

"From all of them? Is it really that easy?"

"The signature is missing from all of the recordings, Chief Inspector. Their removal makes it entirely impossible to know the software utilized or gain advanced knowledge of the programmer."

"It's also illegal, isn't it?"

"That is correct. According to Paragraph 117a of the Enhanced Privacy Act, all data files must have a signature stating their provenance. Removal of the signature is a Union offense punishable by up to three years in prison."

So someone is looking at being behind bars from now until the next ice age. Assuming we find them. Given what we have, that's going to be difficult.

"Can't you use the resolution or the structure of the data to draw conclusions about what kind of specs were used for the recordings?"

"No, Chief Inspector. The camera modules of almost all spec models are built in the exact same way and are sourced entirely from three suppliers in North Korea and Japan."

"Let me see if I've got this right: It doesn't matter if the glasses were manufactured by Tallan or Hyundai, they have the exact same camera module from Chŏngjin inside?"

"A simplified, but generally accurate, statement, Chief Inspector."

"And you have no other ideas of how you could find out the make?"

"None, Chief Inspector."

No ideas, this new Terry. Just like the old one. "I'm starting to understand what Ava meant."

"Could you restate the question?"

"Forget it. Give me a list of all the people who have been identified in the creeper videos already. Limit results to people who are still alive."

"The list has been sent to your inbox."

I open a window where I can download the list. It contains a large number of names, must be in the thousands, from all across the Union.

"Do you have all of the local files, Terry? I mean the ones of any people who were already arrested by local police because of their hacked specs?"

"Of course, Chief Inspector. Europol has unlimited access to data of this type."

"Then search through the files and find the makes of the hacked specs, which I'm hoping the local cops collected. If they're not there, then send an inquiry, in my name."

"The information you're searching for is available in 73.4 percent of the cases, Chief Inspector."

"Put it on the table. You can deliver the rest to me later."

The list of spec models appears in front of me.

There are about twenty different varieties, including popular ones like Cougar and Horus, as well as a few exotic designer pieces. The various models come from three manufacturers: the market leader, Felton, as well as Siya and Earl.

"What a load of shit," I murmur. It would've been just too perfect if an overdose of gin and an obscure Hollywood film had contributed something to solving this case. Sighing, I pull a bag of black licorice from my jacket pocket and shove the contents in my desk drawer, apart from one piece that makes its way directly into my mouth.

"Terry?"

"Yes, Chief Inspector?"

"By chance is this company Rayman still around?"

"The name is Ray Ban, Chief Inspector. And it's not a company, merely a make. The glasses were produced up until 1999 by an American conglomerate by the name of Bausch & Lomb. The last majority owner of the make was Chungwa Industries in Tianjin, and production has since been discontinued."

"A simple no would also have done the trick."

"I am programmed to provide no misleading or imprecise answers, Chief Inspector."

"Yeah, yeah, all right. But wait a minute—if that wasn't the manufacturer, what about the others?"

"Could you restate the question, Chief Inspector?"

"Who owns the spec make Felton?"

"It belongs to the eponymous business venture Felton Ltd. in London."

"And that business belongs to itself?"

"No, Chief Inspector. Felton is one-hundred per-cent under the umbrella of Tallan Consolidated."

"And who has ultimate control over Siya?"

"Also Tallan Consolidated, though through a somewhat more complicated business structure. Would you like the details?"

"Spare me."

The only one left is Earl. The name likely gives it away already, but I ask the question just to be sure.

"Eighty-nine percent of the stock of Earl Eyewear," Terry answers, "is owned by Tallan Consolidated."

I take off my specs and look them over. They're a special model, faster, sturdier, and above all more secure than the crap most citizens of the Union care to walk around in. I run a finger over the black E etched with a laser into the ceramic side piece.

John Roberto Tallan, Earl of Mertonshire and CEO of Tallan Consolidated, is a man I urgently need to speak with.

But the real question is whether Tallan would also like to speak with me. Contrary to what most people believe, no one has to speak with the police when it comes down to it. Tallan likely has more lawyers than Europol has inspectors, and therefore he'll understand his rights perfectly. Aside from that, he'll employ an entire host of cleaners whose job is to make sure his data corona is always free from anything that might lead to awkward questions.

Furthermore, he's almost certainly in a position to put roadblocks in the path of any unwanted investigators—roadblocks as big as the Palais de Justice. Before I give the Earl of Mertonshire a call, I poke around in his précis first.

John Tallan inherited the entire company from his father, George. As it often goes, the history of the business follows the history of the family, and in this case the two seem almost to be identical. First comes the founding father, and then his somewhat spoiled but not entirely untalented offspring takes over, followed in the third act by a complete idiot.

And so it goes in this case: shortly after the hyper crash on Wall Street, a woman named Catherine Tallan (née Wieczorek) bought herself a small technological empire. When she died, her daughter Mary took up leadership of the enterprise. After her, her son George became the third CEO by the name of Tallan, and drove the group of corporations, at that time still called Tallan Networks, nearly to bankruptcy. Luckily, the fourth liver transplant for the heavily alcoholic Earl George went spectacularly to pieces, which meant his only son and heir, John, was catapulted to the head of the ailing company at the age of twenty-nine.

I take a look at several pictures of John Tallan. There are amazingly few. The 37th Earl of Mertonshire doesn't look like the usual stereotype of an incestuous English landed noble. His skin is too dark, and his full, swept-back hair is almost black. It must have something to do with the infusion of South American blood the family has used to refresh their DNA more than once in the past few decades. Like all very rich men, he looks unbelievably young for his fifty years. I look like a wrinkly old fart next to him. In most of the pictures, John Tallan wears a custom-tailored Savile Row suit and a white shirt. His only notable sartorial eccentricity is that he doesn't have a Steinkirk wrapped around his neck, but instead wears one of these old English regimental cravats. Interestingly, he's never photographed wearing his specs.

I swipe over the table and skim his dossier rather than read it. Eaton. Sandhurst. University of British Columbia. Likes dogs. Allergic to cats. Sailor. Rugby fan, owner of the Birmingham Vulcans. Unmarried. Never seen with supermodels in any of the tabloids. Spectacular estates across the whole world, include the Water Palace. Even an orbital condo that circles the earth at an altitude of thirty-five thousand kilometers—practical, if the goal is to avoid seeing anyone. No prior criminal record. Never been on trial. British citizen. Also has a Union passport, a Canadian passport, and Cantonese documents. Although those can be picked up just about anywhere.

The day before yesterday, I called up Tallan's executive office because of the Pazzi case, though the old corruption story didn't come up directly. I didn't want to scare the man away right off the bat. No one called me back.

I order Terry to find me the name and number of John Tallan's personal assistant. The contact data appears on my specs. I'm in luck, since the assistant is a person named Ivana Paul and not a computer. People will sometimes give you the time of day. I call her up.

"Good morning, Chief Inspector."

"Good morning, Ms. Paul."

"I must apologize, Mr. Westerhuizen. I still owe you a return call. But there was a lot going on here in the past few days." She laughs. I'd love to do the same again one day.

"Is this still about the death of Vittorio Pazzi, Inspector? I'm afraid Sir John didn't know him well. As far as I know, they only ran into each other at official receptions, once or twice a year at the most."

"No, the situation with Pazzi has been cleared up."

"Wonderful!"

"I'm calling about something else. It's about your specs."

"You mean the business of our specs?"

"Correct. Earl, Felton, and the other makes."

"What about it?"

"I'm investigating a creeper-feed case. Someone is hacking specs and more to the point, they were all manufactured by Tallan."

"That's hardly surprising, is it?"

"Is that so?"

"Well, it's just that we're the market leader. We produce over seventy million pairs every year. So it's only to be expected that some of the hacked glasses would be ours."

"There aren't any others, Ms. Paul. The hacked glasses were all manufactured entirely by you."

"How many cases are we talking about, Inspector?"

"That's a classified part of the investigation. But it's a considerable number."

"Listen, if you could tell me which specific models were affected, and how many, it would be easier for me to—"

"Make an appointment for me with your boss, and then we can talk about it directly. I suggest a holo-conference, very informal."

"Chief Inspector, you must understand Sir John is a very busy man. Besides that, he's not directly involved in business operations. The better person to speak to in this case would be the division manager for our specs department, Danielle Bolème. I could—"

"Do you understand the level of outrage this could lead to, Ms. Paul? All the evidence points to Tallan specs demonstrating a serious security breach that anyone could take advantage of."

A short pause. "What kind of creeper-feeds are these?"

"Felonies," I answer. "So many that the case has already been withdrawn from the jurisdictions of the member states."

I can sense my adversary floundering, how a hole is opening between her still doggedly raised fists. Time for the uppercut.

"If you organize a meeting, I promise to stick to the agreed topic and I guarantee I won't say anything to Sir John about the Golden Trail scandal he and Pazzi were implicated in."

"What? What did you say?"

"You know perfectly well what I said. Goodbye,

Ms. Paul, and my best to Sir John."

Then I hang up. I glance at the wall and can see Humphrey looking over at me approvingly.

After the phone call with Tallan's assistant, I skirt around doing any work until the afternoon. I push a few files back and forth across my media table and direct the computer to sort the 347 unread messages in my inbox by various criteria. One message contains the final report on the Pazzi case, which I'm supposed to countersign. According to the signature already on it, Ava finished up last night around 11:00 p.m. Apparently, it's easier to be bored on the beach in Haifa than I thought. I start to read it. The document's style closely resembles the user manual for a North Korean lawn-mowing drone.

"Terry?"

"Yes, Chief Inspector?"

"This report here, EPL 86786/96, you wrote it, right?"

"I completed the document according to the guidance of Analyst Bittman."

"How long is it?"

"File EPL 86786/96 contains forty-nine thousand seven hundred and sixty-eight characters, including spaces. Additionally, there are audio-visual materials totaling—"

"Okay, got it. How much of the text came from Ava?"

"Three thousand three hundred and forty-six characters, of which a total of one thousand two hundred and fifty-seven were taken from my database."

"Then you have the best knowledge of what's in it, right, Terry?"

"That is correct. I know the contents of all investigative files completed at Europol since July 1, 1999."

"Sarcasm, Terry. Go ahead and give me a short summary of the file."

"Vittorio Pazzi, MEP, was shot in an ambush by a terrorist sniper in the vicinity of Westrem. Responsibility for this deed was claimed by a separatist cell whose ringleader was the German anarchist and performance artist Thomas Winterfuhr. His patterns of movement before and after the time of the crime allow for the conclusion that he was at the crime scene. Winterfuhr sent a video claiming responsibility thirty-three hours and twenty-seven minutes after Pazzi's assassination, in which he calls on the Union citizenry to call European integration into question and return to nationalism. Shortly thereafter, Europol attempted to enforce a European arrest warrant issued for Winterfuhr via a direct strike in the territory of the member state of Germany, according to Paragraph 34a of the EuSiG. Winterfuhr attempted to flee, though he was tracked by members of the Europol special forces unit Taurus and Chief Inspector Arthur van der Westerhuizen, who was at the scene as a ghost. Due to particularly tempestuous bad weather in Hamburg at the time, Winterfuhr came into contact with a misdirected police drone and fell from the roof of the building. Later, an analysis of his data trail provided clear confirmation that

Winterfuhr created and uploaded the video claiming responsibility. Additionally, a Europol dolphin drone searched the surrounding dike and located a chameleon suit weighed down by rocks. The forensics team identified this article of clothing as the one worn by the assassin in Westrem."

"It's a top-notch piece of evidence," I say. "Are there any unanswered questions? From the examining magistrate, the prefecture, or anywhere else?"

"No, Chief Inspector. The only thing still missing is your signature, and then the case will be closed. Should I state your agreement for the record?"

"Later. First I'm going to get a bite to eat."

I stand up and walk through the bowels of the enormous Palais de Justice. Sometimes I ask myself how people found their way through this behemoth without specs. Maybe they didn't, and maybe the labyrinthine quality of the building wasn't an accident at all, but some kind of allegorical commentary from the architect. Stranger, if you've come here in search of justice, make sure to take some sandwiches and a ball of string with you.

In front of the Jacobsplein, multigender activists are demonstrating in protest of the specification of gender in their passports. A few of them wear elaborate makeup. Or rather, they wore elaborate makeup before they assembled with their media banners and whistles in the Brussels plum rain. Now they look like adults who were made up at a six-year-old's party. I give a friendly nod to the officer-in-charge, pull on my sou'wester and trudge past the demonstrators in the direction of the Louiza metro station.

I don't intend to take the train. But the rain is already particularly heavy, and it's nice and dry in the underground passages and hallways. Since it's common now to have rain for weeks on end without a break, Brussels, like many other European metropolises, undertook a massive expansion of its network of underground passageways, following the example set by the Koreans. Just like in Seoul or Incheon, the shopping areas stretch for kilometers under the city and can be used to travel long distances without getting wet. Brussels's underground city was a pet project for the Commission, and the entire area is carbon dioxide and energy neutral. The lighting, for example, comes from algae lamps, huge, green, illuminated Plexiglas holders built into the ceiling and walls. The advantage of this light source is that it doesn't require electricity. The downside is that it casts a green shimmer on everything. The shopper coming toward me as I head in the direction of the city center reminds me of a troglodyte in a network of caves.

After a few hundred meters, I arrive in the main hall under the Albertinaplein. A skylight has been installed according to the new Nouveau style, though it barely contributes to the lighting of the food court, thanks to the lousy weather. Hordes of people sit at plastic tables and eat their green food. At Pyongyang Five, I get myself an extra-large mug of kopi mocha and ride the escalator to the upper level. From the balustrade, I can look down at the troglodytes eating their lunches. Most are displaying the characteristic head position of people who aren't concentrating on their food, but instead watching something on their specs.

I connect to Terry. "Data overlay on my specs," I say. "Display all people who are wearing specs from Earl, Felton, or another Tallan make in yellow."

The food court beneath me changes into a sea of neon yellow. "Display all people with other specs in blue, and people without specs in red."

Terry does as I tell him. About two-thirds of the people are in yellow, the other third blue. If I look more closely, I can make out two or three red figures in the mix. I take a big drink of Korean coffee and continue on my way through the underground city. At Spanjeplein I head aboveground again, since from here it's possible for the street-savvy to cut through most of the historic district and stay dry, thanks to the many old and some new galleries. As I walk in the direction of the Grote Markt, brightly colored pedestrians come toward me, most lit in yellow.

At a stoplight, my gaze falls on a businessman. The dark-blue of his suit is layered over by the yellow haze Terry's using to mark wearers of Tallan specs for me. But the man isn't wearing glasses. I take a half-step forward so I can see the inside pocket of his jacket better. It's empty, not even a ballpoint pen in sight.

"Terry?" I say subvocally into my larynx mike. "The man to my right, Guy Velstraat, address 79 Rue des Echevins. Is it possible that he was indicated with the wrong color?"

"Subject Velstraat was correctly indicated, Chief Inspector."

"But he's not wearing specs."

"The subject is wearing specs of the make Felton, model Aquila One. The specs are integrated into contact lenses."

"I didn't know those things were already on the market."

"This is a prototype, Chief Inspector. The subject is taking part in a test program. The lenses will officially be on the market in three months."

"What are they going to cost?"

"Felton's MSRP is two hundred thousand euros."

So, not too expensive. It'll probably take years before they start giving us these things as service specs. I want to get another look at this technological pioneer, maybe even look him in the eyes. But the man is already halfway across the crosswalk. I decide not to follow him, since he's heading west instead of north, where I want to go. Instead, I head my own way. There are no awnings in the tiny alleyways near the opera house, so they aren't as full with Asian tourists. People from Canton and Korea aren't accustomed to the relentless rain and prefer to stay where they won't get wet. I avoid puddles and fast-flowing streams like an old pro until I reach the brasserie on Zandstraat where I like to eat lunch. I'm about to go through the revolving door when I see a small courier drone floating smoothly downwards directly next to me. Large, illuminated red letters on its body read: "Urgent Delivery for Monsieur Westerhuizen."

I wait until the drone is at the level of my face. As it hovers in place using its humming rotor blades, a woman's voice says, "United Drone Service has a personal delivery for you. Please identify yourself."

I take my specs off so the drone's laser can scan my retina. A few seconds later, a tiny flap on the front opens with a mechanical click.

"Please remove your package. Be sure that your hands remain under the red line. UDS cannot be held responsible for injuries sustained from contact with the rotor blades on this courier drone."

An envelope made of brown plastic is in the compartment. I take it out. "Thank you for choosing UDS. Goodbye." The drone disappears into the Brussels rain.

I tear the envelope open. Inside is another envelope, this one made out of cream-colored handmade paper. Someone's written my name in a jaunty script on the front. The envelope has been ceremoniously sealed with a stamp in the form of a coat of arms. It shows a yellow lion on a red background.

"Identify the heraldry."

According to my specs, it's the coat of arms of the Earl of Mertonshire. I tear open the envelope and take out a card printed on another piece of handmade paper.

John Tallan, Earl of Mertonshire,
invites you to a garden party with music.
This evening, 8:00 p.m.
Location: The Floating Castle
Dress: Black tie
Please R.S.V.P. here

I swipe a finger over the R.S.V.P. The writing on the card disappears and new text appears:

Would you like a shuttle service? Yes/No.

I press "yes." The card informs me I'll be picked up from the VIP parking lot of the Gare du Midi at 6:00 p.m. I stick the now-damp card in my coat pocket and go back in the direction of the city center. Lunch is canceled—I have to find myself a tux.

The shuttle is a metallic-blue Toyota Kimura whose doors glide open soundlessly as I approach. The interior of the vehicle looks like a miniature five-star suite: rich tropical wood, seats that can convert into a bed, camouflaged media screens. There are also heavy crystal tumblers intended to hold the forty-year-old Scotch nestled into a recess in the door panel. I take the bottle out. It's a Laphroaig, my favorite brand. I pour myself two fingers' worth and look out the window.

The Kimura has since left the ring around the city center and is approaching the entrance to the highway. It drives very fast, whisking past the other vehicles. Apparently it's been equipped with a priority code. After a good hour, we reach Tilburg. The autopilot steers onto another expressway and heads on in the direction of 's-Hertogenbosch. It can't be much farther now.

As it turns out, we drive to an industrial region somewhere north of the city and stop in front of a fenced-in complex of buildings with an entrance labeled "Maarten Hoverboats." The Kimura drives into a small hangar. As I climb out of the climatized car, the moist, muggy air slaps me across the face like a wet handkerchief.

A pretty young woman greets me. She wears something that looks like a designer's interpretation of a captain's uniform.

"We're happy to welcome you to the Dutch Everglades, Mr. Westerhuizen! If you'd like to follow me, I'll bring you on board, where the other guests have already arrived."

She leads me to the other end of the hangar, where the largest hoverboat I've ever seen is parked. I'm familiar with the small, propeller-driven metal tubs driven around the swamplands by the locals. But this boat has to be at least thirty meters long. Men in tuxedos and women in summer-weight evening gowns look out through the fully glass-fronted structure. I climb up the gangway and enter the spacious cabin. The other passengers nod at me amiably, and a steward offers me a glass of Champagne.

After everyone has taken a seat and buckled up, the captain starts the motor and opens the hangar's rolling door. Behind it stretches the endless landscape of marshes and wetlands that used to be the Netherlands. We glide out. Silently, I look out the window and observe how the swamps gradually give way to a delta landscape. There are fewer and fewer trees and houses to be seen jutting out of the water until finally there's just the open surface of the water before us. As always, the weather is awful. Bursts of rain pelt against the Zuiderzee like grapeshot.

"Ever been here before?" the man next to me asks. He looks like he's in his early thirties but is probably in his late forties, with the skin tone of an aquatic athlete and an optimized figure, achieved through muscle stimulation and surgical procedures, that identifies him as a member of Europe's upper crust.

"To Tallan's residence, you mean?"

He shakes his head. "No, I mean anywhere in New-Zeeland generally. Fantastic area for catamaran sailing."

"Actually, we're in the province of South Holland," I reply. "The province of Zeeland is further west, and this part of the Netherlands never belonged to it."

"But I thought—"

"Someone thought up that term after the dike broke and the Zuiderzee annexed Flevoland, Friesland, and all the other provinces." I look out the window and add quietly, "The new Zeeland. New-Zeeland. Funny bit of wordplay."

"My God, you're Dutch. I'm sorry, I didn't mean to offend you."

"Ex-Dutch," I respond. "Don't trouble yourself, I'm not offended."

"Did you come from this region? What kind of city was here?"

"We're somewhere around Gouda. I'm from Amsterdam."

"It must be terrible to see your homeland wash away," he says pointlessly. "Amsterdam was supposed to be a great city. I visited the replication last year."

"I'm familiar with it. Only a feeble imitation," I

reply. My neighbor doesn't have an answer to that, turning back to his Champagne glass.

Just outside Hilversum, the blanket of clouds parts slightly and the rays of the already-sinking sun touch the sea. We pass an astonishingly well-preserved windmill, its wheel jutting out of the water, shining golden in the evening light.

Over the loudspeaker, the captain informs us we'll arrive in ten minutes. Tallan's Water Palace appears on the horizon. It doesn't have anything in common with a palace except for a lookout tower, though that resembles a crow's nest more than a castle keep anyway. It looks more like a houseboat colony from Southern China. The Earl's residence is comprised of thirty or forty stone buildings of various sizes, resting on floating pontoons and connected together by narrow jetties. The outer walls of the buildings are made from white and red lacquered wood, which looks more Scandinavian than Dutch. The flat roofs are planted with shrubs and grasses.

As we get even closer, it occurs to me that Tallan's residence looks different than it did in the TV documentary I saw a few years ago. I call up a précis of the construction on my specs. Evidently, all of the elements of the Water Palace are both floatable and maneuverable. In the case of a storm, they loose themselves from their jetties and move away from each other to avoid any collisions. Afterward, they swim back toward each other, reattach together, and take up their old positions again. From the central helm, the man of the house or his steward can choose a new arrangement for the pontoons each time or pick from a list of pre-configured shapes, causing the swarm of pontoons to move immediately into position like a group of synchronized swimmers.

Today, it looks like someone has picked the "summer party for billionaires" arrangement. On the south side facing us, there's a jetty extending a long way out and ending on a helicopter landing pad. It leads to a plaza lit by torches and surrounded by a square of small pontoons. More jetties lead north, east, and west to large buildings, where various special entertainments are presumably on offer. It's shortly before nine, and I can already see plenty of guests on the pontoons, easily over a hundred.

Along with the others, I leave the hoverboat via a gangway. I move along the jetty in the direction of the plaza, where jazz music is wafting toward me. Along with the sound of saxophones, the wind carries the smell of seafood in my direction. It's coming from a large grill station, where a long line of party guests waits with plates in hand.

The plaza is about as big as four tennis courts. The biggest section is taken up by a dance floor in the middle, though it's still empty given the early hour. The prevailing category of guest resembles my neighbor on the boat: people between thirty and fifty whose families or businesses were able to emerge unscathed even after three major economic and financial crises; people who travel to Rio for Carnival every year; people who always have an insider tip at the ready for the best Hanok restaurant in the Seoul historic district; people who only start to get old at age sixty-five; people for whom Britain's exit from the Union is first and foremost a taxation problem.

I remain standing at the edge of the plaza and consider the general splendor, the trophy wives dripping with jewelry and their husbands discussing sailing regattas and offshore investments. All of them seem to be drinking Champagne, and little service drones land continually on the edge of the plaza with refills, which are then brought to the partygoers by waiters. As I step from the canopied walkway onto the open plaza, I notice that it's completely dry, although I can see drops falling on the surface of the water. I look up at the sky and see a few craft hovering over us in formation, their construction unfamiliar to me. I wonder if they're holding back the rain and if they're using the same technology found inside Ava's track jacket.

I wave off the Champagne offered by one of the waiters and walk along a jetty leading to another pontoon island upstream. There, I take a seat on a sofa.

A waiter moves discreetly from table to table and asks the people sitting at them to move to another pontoon. He indicates that I, on the other hand, should stay.

"May I bring you anything, sir? Champagne?"

"I'd prefer a cold Pils, if you have it."

"Of course, right away."

As I wait, I notice a small silver box on the little side table near my sofa. I open it and find inside a variety of cigarettes from different brands, as well as matches. I lift a Karelia out with my fingertips, place it between my lips and hold a match against it. As soon as it lights, I take a deep pull.

"Isn't it forbidden for a Union civil servant to smoke?" says a voice from behind me.

I stand and turn around. John Tallan smiles at me. The 37th Earl of Mertonshire doesn't adhere to his own policies, having decided on an old-fashioned blue-and-white-striped summer-weight seersucker suit instead of a tuxedo. Along with it, he wears a linen shirt and skinny tie that looks even more antiquated than the regimental neckcloth I saw him wearing in the pictures. Tallan looks like someone who came across this place entirely by coincidence and is observing the colorful goings-on with amused remove. He holds his hand out to me. I take it—it's warm and dry, the grip firm. I'd already decided I wouldn't like this man. But that might prove difficult.

"Good evening, Sir John. It's not forbidden, just impractical, since the Commission banned smoking in the entire District Européen. This is my first cigarette in at least two years."

"And what's your vice in the meantime?"

"Black licorice."

Tallan indicates I should take my seat again and sits down in a chair across from me. The waiter appears with a bottle of Heineken Supercrisp on a tray. Tallan is given something that looks like iced tea garnished with mint. Then the waiter steps back.

He's barely out of sight when I feel the pontoon beginning to move underneath us. In complete silence, the red-canopied raft pushes off into the Zuiderzee, away from the smell of barbecue, the small talk, and the jazz music. My specs disapprove, since out here there's not even a whiff of a network connection. I think that's unlikely. The pontoon probably has a signal jammer, or an even more complex piece of anti-surveillance technology.

"A little sphere of privacy," Tallan observes. "What do you think of my mobile island?"

"The technology is impressive. If a bit frivolous."

If Tallan feels attacked by this observation, he hides it deftly. He even smiles and nods in agreement.

"I know what you mean. People with too much money dancing on the remains of an extinct civilization, rather frivolous indeed. But just because it starts out as frivolous, doesn't mean it has to stay that way."

"What are you planning?"

"On the surface, all this exists just for my, for our, amusement. But in truth, it's a long-term test of a new way of living, of existing. My houseboat drones, as we might end up calling them, maneuver with total autonomy. They move through the Zuiderzee and the Dutch Everglades, avoiding obstructions like buildings lurking under the surface of the water, and produce their own electricity besides."

"How's that? I don't see any solar panels."

"Those would produce far too small a yield given the weather patterns around here." Tallan lets the ice cubes in his long drink glass clack together. "Too many clouds. My boat drones are facing the same problems plaguing the entire Union. As they move, they use energy from waves and the tide. There's a small power generator below the waterline, the newest Portuguese technology."

He sips his iced tea and continues. "I want to populate the entire Zuiderzee with these boats. I'm about to enter into negotiations with the wider Flemish government over the conditions."

"What kind of conditions?"

"I want extraterritoriality."

"You'll never get that. This is Union territory, and to my knowledge we haven't given up so much as a centimeter in the past fifty years. Quite the opposite."

He shrugs his shoulders. "Could be that it's some nation's territory, but de facto, we're dealing with an uninhabitable no-man's-land. I want a degree of freedom for my project, and in return I'll finance the recolonization. We'll take Holland back. One thing has been lost forever, but we'll create something new—a plan that must appeal to you, as a Dutchman."

I nod weakly and take a drag on my cigarette.

"Is that profitable?" I ask. "Since you are a businessman first and foremost."

"Everything I do must yield a return at some point, yes. But I think in the longer term. If I'm able to bring a colony of people back to this area, then I can sell the technology in another ten years."

"To the governments of every coastal state that's

been flooded in the meantime."

"I would have phrased it differently, but in principal that sums it up. Holland was the first victim of climate change, but it certainly won't be the last. I want to make money, but I also want my technology to benefit all of society."

"That's quite a statement from someone who manufactures military technology on a large scale."

For a moment, Tallan narrows his lips, but then he smiles again. "It's just as remarkable to be confronted with an accusation like that by a decorated veteran of the Solar Wars. Our military technology saved the lives of countless soldiers."

"At least when they functioned properly. They were somewhat prone to error."

"It's a fact that all new technologies are error-prone, Chief Inspector. But then it's also true that the Union could have lost the war and its place in the sun at the same time. If it weren't for all the aerial drones and panopto cameras, the coalition troops wouldn't have been able to identify and neutralize the rebellious elements in those places, and so quickly."

"Pardon me, Sir John, I didn't mean to hit a sore spot."

"That's alright. I'm often on the receiving end of hostility because of this topic—unjustly, as I see it. But those are old stories, and you wanted to talk to me about specs. Ivana said there's an investigation concerning them. And that you were trying to insist on a personal appointment with me. Why is that?"

"Amateurs may be content to talk with subordinates. But I aim higher," I counter, and fix my gaze on him.

My eyes meet his. They're icy blue and reveal as much as a glance into the Zuiderzee. Besides that, there's something about them that irritates me. Tallan doesn't blink even once as he answers, "I understand. Then please go ahead and tell me how this hacker story affects me."

"The bots in TIRESIAS have found an enormous amount of creeper-feed material on the net, including all sorts of horrible things: rape, torture, murder. Someone removed all the signatures so the sources can't be determined. But by using the identifiable people in the videos, I was able to determine that all of the specs used in the recordings came from Tallan, at least that's what the sample suggests. All affected parties reported they didn't activate the recording function on their specs."

"Is there any indication of who uploaded it to the net?"

"No. My guess is we're looking at an organized crime ring that can sell these things to perverts."

Tallan turns down the corners of his mouth in disgust. "Snuff dealers."

"Quite possibly. The videos suggest that. But it's possible even harmless creeper-feeds from your specs are being sold."

"What sorts of things?"

"We found material showing people in completely normal everyday situations, folding their laundry or cooking."

"But what would someone do with videos like that?"

I shrug my shoulders. "We live in a world where even second-tier 360-computer animations can no longer be differentiated from a real recording. These people, I mean the people who would buy creeper-feeds, want something genuine. They want to look at things that are actually happening, or already did happen. That's part of the nature of voyeurism."

I stamp out the Karelia in a crystal ashtray sitting near me on the side table and take a swig of my beer.

"The French police," I continue, "arrested a guy in Paris last year who had his entire suburban block under observation, every single apartment, for months. But most of the time there was nothing to see, not even conjugal sex."

"You mean surveillance brings certain feelings to the surface, superiority, omnipotence, that's the kick?"

"Yes, the feeling of power. In the end, that's always what it's about."

Lost in thought, Tallan looks out across the sea, then studies his glass, which has only ice and mint leaves left in it. "I'm going to order myself another. You?"

"Thank you very much. Another beer, please."

Tallan places his order into a microphone I can't see. Then he says, "And, in your opinion, why are only our specs affected?"

"I don't know. I thought you might be able to tell me."

"Maybe there's a weak spot in our software, although that's not easy for me to imagine. As I'm sure you've already realized, the differences between our various spec models are only superficial, all down to marketing. Technically speaking, they're almost identical. So if someone were able to find a back door into our operating system, it would work just as well with a Felton as with an Earl. As soon as we're finished here, I'll ask our technical director to carry out an analysis. Would you be able to give us some of the creeper-feeds in their original format?"

"Those are evidence in an ongoing investigation."

"Give us one of the cleaning videos for all I care. My boys might be able to find something TIRESIAS missed, fragments of the separated signature or other traces of data. There's always something left behind."

"That would be fine, Sir John. Many thanks for your support. Though in my opinion, there's a second possible explanation for your data leak."

"And that would be?"

"A mole inside your company. Someone with access to the servers who can siphon off the data."

"I don't believe it."

"You don't want to believe it, since it raises awkward questions."

He shakes his head. "No. You misunderstand me. I'll get my security team and technicians working on the problem immediately. But your hypothesis is based on a lack of knowledge about our technology, if I may put it that way."

A buzzing sound becomes audible, gradually growing louder. It's the drone bringing our drinks from the Water Palace, now a few hundred meters away. It sets down gently on the pontoon. I stand up, take our drinks off the tray, and hand the iced tea to Tallan.

"Where's the error in my logic?" I ask.

"When specs record videos, they send them to the user's personal server."

"But before that, the video presumably has to go through one of your data centers."

"That's exactly correct. But first the data are encrypted, and then expunged a fraction of a second later. It follows that the mole, as you call it, would have to sift through our central computers and the incoming video feeds of all 754 million active Tallan glasses out in the world in real time, with the help of a very high-performance computer. That would be the only way to grab the recordings of interest before they're expunged."

I nod. "Sounds reasonable so far. Please go on."

"The mole would also have to set up permanent search routines on our central computer to identify marketable sex and crime videos. That would attract our attention sooner or later. And he'd also have to turn on the camera functions of the glasses in question. Because you did say that the people affected didn't turn them on themselves. The mole would also have to use our central computer to hack into hundreds or thousands of specs."

"Would he not also be able to do that from your servers?"

"Hardly. If it was professionals, they went directly

to the glasses, believe me. The more localized the hack, the less likely it is to attract attention. Since we're bedfellows of a sort, I can tell you that the security of specs in the consumer realm is laughable. The security of my company's data centers, on the other hand, is extremely high."

"How long will it take for you to give me an answer about your glasses software and server security, Sir John?"

"Two to three days."

"Good. I take it you already have my priority contact information."

"Of course. And I'll give you mine as well—call me directly if there are any problems. I take this matter very seriously, Chief Inspector, and would like to clear it up as quickly as possible."

I nod and take another Karelia. The pontoon apparently got the memo that the official portion of the evening is over, since it's moving back toward Tallan's artificial island. Near-total silence dominates for a minute. Then I point to Tallan's head with my beer bottle. "Tell me, your eyes, Sir John? What's different about them? Are you wearing one of these new prototypes?"

He smiles. "You're well-informed. Yes, I am indeed wearing contact lenses with integrated specs. We're putting them on the market in a few months and believe they will be an enormous money-maker."

"Many people find contact lenses uncomfortable," I interject.

"That's true, but the resolution of the data on them

is much sharper, much less mediated. I assure you, if you wore the lenses even once, you'd never want to go back to wearing such clunky frames. May I send you a pair to try out?"

"That's very kind of you. But as a civil servant, I'm not able to accept any gifts, particularly such an expensive one."

"As a loan, of course, Chief Inspector. I'd never go so far as to bribe you."

The Water Palace is still something like three hundred meters away.

"There is one more thing," Tallan says quietly. "My assistant tells me the Jacobins are looking into the old Golden Trail story again?"

"That's not entirely true," I reply. "The matter came up in connection with our investigation into the Pazzi case."

"How so, Chief Inspector?"

"As I'm certain you remember very well, at the time, you were accused of investing capital in the electoral districts of certain representatives in order to influence their voting behavior."

"Yes, I remember. I also remember that the journalist who brought the matter to public notice lost his job because none of what he reported could be substantiated."

I shrug my shoulders. "I'm not interested in whether something illegal or inappropriate happened, Sir John. We just came across it in the process of looking into the deaths of other MEPs."

For the first time, Tallan looks somewhat unsettled. "More deaths? I'd only heard about Pazzi."

"Sir John, do you know Beat Füßli?"

"No, the name means nothing to me."

"Your company sponsors a jazz festival in his Swiss electoral district."

"Could be, I can't know every detail of our operations. We probably sponsor a dozen festivals like that throughout Europe, not to mention sports events and other functions."

"And Jorge Perez Milar?"

"Him I know. We have large amounts of real estate in Lisbon, where he's the local Union representative. My God, was he also murdered?"

"He was run over by a tram eight weeks ago. Füßli had a fatal sports accident."

Tallan looks surprised, if not exactly shocked or upset.

"That's horrible. And you see a connection between these deaths?"

"Not necessarily. But Tallan Consolidated had invested in the electoral districts of all three of the deceased."

"But Pazzi's murderer was caught. That is to say, he was killed in an accident."

I decide against explaining to Tallan that Europol was, in a sense, responsible for the suspect's death. After all, it was our drone that gave Winterfuhr an inadvertent nudge.

"That's true. In that sense, the connection could also be completely coincidental."

"That seems to be the most reasonable explanation

to me. I'd bet if you had TIRESIAS conduct a search, you'd find about half of all electoral districts receive funding from TalCon. Did you ask him how high the probability is that this pattern occurred coincidentally, Chief Inspector?"

"No. But I will do that."

A jolt goes through the pontoon as it docks on one of the jetties. Tallan stands up. "I share your concerns about these creeper-feeds. A serious matter, and I'll help you to get to the bottom of it as soon as possible. As far as this Golden Trail specter is concerned, I don't follow. We never bribed anyone. And Arne Jürgensen, this journalist, and his tabloid rag had to eat their words. And if there was no corruption scandal, then there also can't be a link between Pazzi, Milar, and this other delegate—"

"Füßli."

"Right, and Füßli."

Tallan shakes my hand. "If you'll excuse me now, I have to see to my other guests. Enjoy yourself a little while longer, Chief Inspector. Goodbye."

"Goodbye, Sir John."

As he walks up the jetty, I call after him. "Whatever happened to this Jürgensen guy?"

He turns around and tosses a cool glance at me. "The whole affair ruined him. Even years later he couldn't get work at a reputable publication."

He turns back and disappears between the pontoons.

CHAPTER 13

Ava's back the next day. Two days in her homeland were enough to change her skin tone from olive to latte-brown. If I were interested in Ava, I'd be of the opinion that the darker complexion makes her look even more enchanting. She even brought something back for me—a little basket full of candied fruit.

"A Rosh Hashanah basket." She smiles at me. "So the new year will be sweet."

We sit down at my desk and eat some of the sugared pieces. They're so sweet my fillings start to twinge.

"And what was your impression of our English billionaire, Aart?"

"He's the most pleasant manufacturer of rocket launchers and surveillance electronics I've ever met."

I point to a small package on my desk. "And he sent me these contact lenses right away, by courier drone. The newest of the new."

"Were you able to find out anything?"

I tell Ava everything Tallan said about the specs, how he ruled out the possibility of a mole in his own ranks.

She nods as she pushes various objects back and forth on the media screen. "If I were in his shoes, I'd also say it wasn't one of my people right off the bat. Tallan probably knows that if we had reasonable doubt at any time, we could unseal his corporation's network and send in a few terriers to double check what he's claiming. On the other hand, it is very difficult to crack the central computer of a corporation that size. And what he said about the possible weaknesses in his specs software also sounds reasonable. It doesn't clarify one thing, though."

"And what's that?" I ask.

"Let's say you're the star hacker of a British-Russian syndicate and are planning to skim feeds from glasses on a grand scale. Of course you'd want sex and snuff above all, since they're easiest to sell on the black market. Ideally, you'd want to scan all of the streams running through Tallan's servers, filter out the juicy stuff, and grab it."

"But that attracts attention. At least according to Tallan."

"Sure, vacuuming so much data from a company server, probably over weeks and months—that would have to attract attention. Just like TIRESIAS, Tallan's central computers also have small autonomous programs constantly on the search for intruders. They're like little white blood cells, no foreign body or virus can escape them, at least not in the long-term."

"Okay, so that plan isn't going to work. It follows that I analyze the source code for the glasses' operating system. I find a weak point and after that I can hack into any individual glasses I want to, offline."

"Exactly, Aart." Ava sizes me up. "But which ones do you hack into?"

I need the time it takes to remove a piece of black licorice from the package and chew it before I understand what she's getting at.

"That's an unsolvable problem. How could anyone know which specs wearers would—it'd be—damn it. Oh no. No."

"Tell me how you'd do it, Mr. Britski-hacker."

I lean back in my chair. Ava and Humphrey look at me expectantly.

"The videos taken from the glasses are authentic," I say, "not artificially created like most sex or snuff clips. That's what makes them appealing. The problem is that, as a data thief, I can't have advance knowledge when or if someone is whipping his girlfriend, shooting his dealer, or putting out cigarettes on the back of his six-year-old daughter's hand."

The expression on Ava's face lets me know she came to the same conclusion, though at least a full minute before me.

"That means I'd have to tap into lots of glasses and record lots of creeper-feeds," I continue. "I could use a computer to run a search on the compiled material and find usable excerpts. But that's an impractical way to go about it."

"Because there's too little blood and guts," Ava agrees.

"Right. Annually it's one murder per hundred thousand Union citizens, maybe ten rapes and two hundred cases of serious bodily injury. Is that about right?"

"More or less."

"So, as a hacker, I can't rely on good luck and tapping into any glasses at random. The probability of something usable coming through the lenses would be too low, plain and simple. I'd have to somehow know beforehand which people had a higher likelihood of committing one of these crimes or engaging in one of these interesting sexual practices."

"And how would you get that information, Mr. Britski?"

"To come up with exact prognoses of human behavior like that, you'd need enormously accurate data. And only one source of that kind comes to mind: Terry. It would require an analysis of Terry's archive of predictive criminal records, or as an alternative, the data coronas of as many citizens as possible."

"Good thinking, with one error: I don't believe someone can hack into Terry and steal that kind of information."

I cross my arms across my chest with feigned indignation. "I knew you'd defend him."

She shakes her head. "Our hacker wouldn't have to get into the Europol database just one time. He'd need a continuous link to Terry. Predictive criminal records are updating constantly since the data coronas are also changing. It's not an exact science. Maybe someone with a shitty life and an accordingly shitty prognosis meets a new woman or has some other kind of positive experience that makes a mark."

"That kind of thing only happens in Korean romance films."

"It happens more often than people think. So then the probability of this person committing further robberies or something like that goes down by twenty or thirty percent in one stroke. That's why in the Union we don't lock anyone away just on the basis of these prognoses."

"Where are the creeper-feed prognoses coming from, then?"

"Don't know. Theoretically, of course, they could be coming from Terry, and I'll ask him to run an extensive self-analysis. But obviously there are other semi-intelligent computers with the required processing power."

"You mean over in our intelligence service? They do have some kind of Terry of their own for surveillance in the sun states."

"True, he's called Georgy, well, actually, GORGON. But there are a few other A-level countries that have their own computers with the right power. Definitely the Cantonese, the Brazilians, and the Koreans. Maybe even some cartels have it by now, the Britskis or Gangpae, or a transnational company like TalCon. The things aren't as unaffordable as they were ten years ago, and the functionality is well-known."

"That means Tallan could have a little Terry of his own at his headquarters."

"Highly possible," she answers. "After all, they were involved in the development of the technology once upon a time."

"But an optic computer capable of carrying out prognoses is only half the story, as we already found out. The second necessary thing is data that can be used to predict the actions of specs wearers. Where would the hackers get the data coronas for all these people?"

Ava shrugs her shoulders. "That's the hundred-thousand-won question."

My analyst goes back to her office to occupy herself with Terry's self-check-up and to let our security team know about the possibility, however unlikely, that someone could have hacked into our police computer.

After she's gone, I remain sitting at my desk and try to think about nothing. I close my eyes and do the Zen breathing exercises they taught us in stress training, trying to project emptiness. But faces keep pushing themselves forward out of the vacuum: Tallan with a friendly smile on his face; Svensson with her icy stare; Pazzi with his stylish hairdo. They all assail me, telling me to do something. But they don't say what.

After a few minutes, I stand up and run my hands over my face. I start to pace back and forth across my office. I'd really like another Karelia or some other kind of cigarette right about now. I sink my hands into my jacket pockets and circle around my desk for what must be the sixth or seventh time. In the process, my finger brushes up against something. It's the I Ching coin I brought with me from Pazzi's apartment.

"Terry?" I call.

"Yes, Chief Inspector?"

"How high is the probability of a coincidental connection between Füßli, Milar, and Pazzi?"

"Which connection do you mean? Please reformulate the question."

I sigh. Working with the new Terry without Ava apparently means thinking less like a cop and more like a statistician. I'm not convinced my brain can handle that. I think it over for a moment, then say, "All three were MEPS, and Tallan Consolidated invested in all of their electoral districts. All three are dead. Is there a correlation?"

"I can set the demises of all three men as stochastic, dichotomous variables in integration with other MEPs in whose electoral districts Tallan invested, as well as other existing data, to conduct a regression analysis. Is that what you would like, Chief Inspector?"

"I think I'm also about to start regressing."

"Was that sarcasm, Chief Inspector?"

"Looks like it, Terry. What I wanted to say is—please conduct the regression for me."

"Yes sir, Chief Inspector. According to my calculations, there is no significant correlation between the investment relationships of the three representatives to Tallan and their demises."

"Another question: Has Pazzi already been buried?"

"The burial of Vittorio Pazzi will take place today at the Maria Trost Cemetery in Merano at 4:30 p.m."

"Will the service be replicated?"

"No, Chief Inspector. According to the obituaries,

it will take place with only the closest circle of family members present."

"That sounds a lot nicer. Record everything for me and replicate it. But discreetly, please. I don't want any humming-drones swarming around the coffin while the body's being lowered into an open grave."

"Vittorio Pazzi was cremated, Chief Inspector."

"As far as I'm concerned they can sail him up and down Lago Lungo on a Viking barge. What I mean is you should replicate the service inconspicuously. Observation mode, got it? Use mites, bionic insects, mole drones, a panopto array—all technology that can't be seen, understand?"

"Yes sir, Chief Inspector."

Not only does Terry lack a sense of humor, he also has no concept of discretion or reverence. I take my headset and hypno inhaler out of a desk drawer, put them in my coat pocket, and walk to the door. This way I can watch the funeral service at home after dinner.

CHAPTER 14

Someone once said the truth never comes to light between nine and five. I'm of the opinion that it also rarely makes a wrong turn into office buildings, and definitely never into the Palais de Justice. Finding the truth, or at least a semblance of it, is only possible away from staff meetings, official witness cross-examinations, and holo-conferences. Why else do we inspectors sit motionless at bars all night long? Why else do we drive on patrol aimlessly through Little Tehran, even though our drones could do a much better job? Because we're professional hunters, seekers of the truth. Better than anyone else, we understand the absurdity of the phrase "He who seeks shall find." He who wants to find something should under no circumstances conduct an exhaustive search for it.

So at 5:00 p.m. on the dot, I call up my car and order it to take me to the northern edge of the Zoniën-woud, a large forested area between Brussels and Waterloo. The Mercedes drops me off in a parking lot close to my favorite trail. After I've asked it to save my coordinates and pick me up later, further south near the old racetrack, I walk away. It's still cloudy, but the rain has let up, and it's almost dry under the thick canopy of leaves provided by the beech trees.

Unlike in the city, which transforms into a pea soup after every rainfall, it's a comfortable 24.3 degrees Celsius here.

I roll up my jacket and stick it into the backpack I brought with me. At first, a few joggers and dog-walking pedestrians go past me. From experience, though, I know which of the narrow side paths I need to take to get away from them. After two kilometers there's a place where a narrow path keeps going steeply downhill after a brief drop—no problem for a hiker wearing shoes with good traction, but a potentially deadly trap for blundering dachshunds, breathless joggers, and the like.

At the bottom, a gravel trail continues onward. Around the next bend, in a clearing overgrown with woodruff and flowers, there's an official building belonging to the forestry service disguised as a log cabin, with a few picnic tables nearby. I sit down for a moment, taking a drink of water from a plastic bottle in my backpack. I'm overheated. Maybe I should have left my jacket and cravat in the car. The rain has now stopped entirely, and it even looks like it's starting to clear up. Little spots of sunlight dart across the clearing and fall on my face.

Because of the backlight, I only notice them for the first time when they've already broken out of the underbrush and are coming at me. There are four of them, three men and a woman, all with ski masks pulled over their heads. All of them have pistols except the woman, who holds a short-range Daewoo Defender.

I subvocalize "enemy engagement" into my larynx mike. Right away, small crosshairs light up on my specs, as well as further information about weapon type and munition capacity. At this moment, somewhere back at headquarters, a siren is starting to howl. Taurus brigades are grabbing at assault rifles and running to their skyship, and drones are racing in the direction of the Zoniënwoud. But none of that's important. Minutes will pass before they get here. I have seconds at best.

I can gather a lot of information from the way they're moving toward me. First, they want to kill me. Second, I'm dealing with amateurs. The woman with the Korean automatic weapon is behind the men with the pistols. If she were to fire, she'd turn her murderous cronies into mincemeat.

Third, the three guys in front of her aren't running in formation—they're just running. With a probability approaching certainty, these are minor-league criminals hired by someone who doesn't want to leave any traces behind. The fourth thing I can tell is that this fantastic four aren't in agreement. One holds his pistol—a neon-colored Sig 900—pointed downward in front of him. Another one is pointing his high-caliber Desert Djinn at me one-handed, rarely a good idea. And according to my specs, the third man hasn't even taken the safety off his weapon yet. He's tall and gangly and moves as if the whole forest belongs to him. Evidently he considers himself the ringleader—or a senior forest ranger.

By now, all four have stopped still at a distance

of twenty meters away from me. The forest ranger licks his lips; apparently he wants to toss out a cool catchphrase before he shoots me down. As he opens his mouth, he takes a step forward, blocking Mr. Neon-Sig's line of fire in the process.

"Say—" he begins. The full phrase is probably, "Say your prayers!" Maybe he stole it from an old Hollywood Western, which almost makes me like him a little bit. Doesn't matter, though, since the world will never hear it.

It's been ten seconds since the amateur assassins appeared on the edge of the clearing. During this small eternity, Terry analyzed the four people with the help of my specs. Probably within the first second, he checked through his database for video material of the jailbirds. People who are willing to accept money and play murderer-for-hire don't just fall out of the clear blue sky. Setting aside a handful of invisible professionals from a syndicate or the intelligence service, murderers invariably have a criminal record. They've been in jail before, or have been under observation or interrogated. Accordingly, Terry's optic memory has hundreds if not thousands of hours of video on each of these idiots, which the police computer probably found in second number two. After another second, he analyzed the material and used it to create a predictive movement profile. He now knows the guy with the Sig has had a bum right knee since an encounter with an iron crowbar and therefore always favors his left leg. He computes a high probability that the woman would, in the case of a collision scenario, maneuver to the right.

At some point in second four, Terry completed his prognoses and shared them with the tactics software in my specs, which shows me the order in which I should handle the targets. In second five, I used my larynx mike to activate the Heckler & Koch in my shoulder holster. It asks me if I'd like to shoot it myself.

I'd like to. After all, I have all the time in the world.

If I followed my instincts, I'd definitely have shot the forest ranger first. Instead, at the behest of the H&K, I shoot the guy with the neon-colored pistol. My tactics software hedges its bets; it's decided on an explosive shot, which means that the man literally goes to pieces as soon as the projectile meets his solar plexus and detonates.

Then I move to the right. Just as the software predicted, the woman lets loose with a shower of buckshot, although buckshot is maybe a misleading term. Every cartridge shell from her Daewoo Defender is filled with thousands of ultra-hard ceramic discs with razor-sharp edges, barely a micrometer in diameter.

The place where the man with the Desert Djinn was standing turns into a red streak about two meters wide. The woman curses and swings her weapon around. I shoot her in the chest. Then I turn my attention to the forest ranger. He's gotten his weapon into position and me in the crosshairs. If he fires right now, I'm dead.

In order to do that, though, he'd first have to take the safety off his pistol.

As I fire, I can tell from the kickback that the tactics computer chose armor-piercing munitions instead of explosive shot this time. Apparently, the forest ranger is wearing one of these new sheer Kevlar undershirts. They're pretty expensive. Too bad about that.

From somewhere, I can hear the sound of jet nozzles, probably the first drone. I give a short situation update into my mike and take a few steps in the direction of the bodies, whose remains are spread over an area of several meters. The unmitigated advantage provided by Terry's smartgun software makes the deaths of these four people seem particularly senseless. It's very obvious no one told them what they were getting themselves into. I take the mask off the forest ranger, the only one who still has an intact head on his shoulders. Reza Moradi, twenty-seven years old, undocumented, Persian. He has a "26" and a "27" tattooed on his wrists, which tells me he was a member of the jail gang Les Numéros. The numbers symbolize what assignments he had there. According to my specs, he spent six years in Diyarbakir, maybe the worst lockup in the Union. The little I can glean from a quick scan of his précis tells me that he was knee-deep in shit, maybe even waist-deep: addicted to heroin, in debt, he never stood a chance.

"I'm sorry. Someone used you as cannon fodder, Reza," I mumble.

Wait a minute.

Unfortunately, tactical software doesn't just give its user the upper hand. It encourages carelessness and stupidity and discourages thinking things through. If I'd done that, something would have been clearer to me a lot sooner: no one even halfway in their right mind would have set four complete amateurs loose on a Jacobin armed with smart technology. That's a plan almost certainly doomed to end in bloody failure. It would be a much better plan to use the amateurs as a diversionary tactic so a professional stationed elsewhere would have a clear shot.

As I drop to the ground, it's already too late. The high-velocity shot doesn't hit me, just whizzes past my arm at close distance. But it's close enough that I get my share of the vibrations caused by the path of the projectile. My left arm starts to hurt like hell; I can only pray an artery hasn't been torn. Crouched over, I run in the direction of the little forestry hut and head for cover around its side.

"Analysis," I gasp.

There are two of them. They're sitting on either side of the clearing, likely in elevated positions. They're obviously using sniper weapons, most likely with smartgun software. Now that they've located me once, they could probably dispose of me even at a distance of hundreds of meters in a pitch-black forest. There's no way to escape. My only option is to stay hunkered down back here and hope the cavalry arrives soon.

"How long, Terry?"

"A Taurus skyship will be within striking distance in two minutes and thirty-four seconds, Chief Inspector."

On my specs, I see the two shooters have moved from their standby positions and are heading in the direction of the log cabin in a pincer movement.

"When will those two be here?"

"Two minutes and four seconds, Chief Inspector."

"Probability of stopping them with curtain fire without them shooting me down?"

"Four percent, Chief Inspector."

"Not a very inspiring answer, is it?"

"Please reformulate the question."

I ignore Terry and focus instead on programming my Heckler. Then I transform it. By pressing a button under the firing pin, I loosen the locking mechanism of the handle so it folds up. When it's in line with the barrel, it snaps into place. Then I flip out the stubby wings on the sides. The weapon which a moment ago looked like a completely normal semiautomatic now bears a closer resemblance to a jet plane constructed somewhat awkwardly from a model kit.

This little trick has already saved plenty of us from an ambush. In this case, though, a flight-capable high-tech pistol alone won't be enough. I need a distraction on top of it. But who's supposed to make that happen?

A shot hits a beech tree behind me, sending wood shards flying through the surrounding area. I stand up with my back against the cabin and throw the Heckler into the shrubbery in a high arch. A further shot whistles through the air, followed by a cloud of leaves and branches. I take a step toward the door on the far side of the cabin. While at first glance it looked like an abandoned log cabin, on closer inspection it's a modern building, probably storage for the forestry service's drones, sacks of wild animal feed, or other gear. I push on the doorknob. Nothing happens.

"Open the door, Terry."

"You do not have a search warrant for this cabin, Chief Inspector."

"Imminent danger, you idiot!" I roar.

The door opens. I walk inside and bolt it behind me. It doesn't look very sturdy, but it'll buy me a few more seconds. The floor of the shed is made out of bare concrete, and hay is stacked up against the walls. I sit down and use my right hand to pull my headset down over my head. Unfortunately, I don't have any escape patches with me, but I can think about that later. My left arm has gone almost completely numb and feels swollen. Dark spots dance in front of my eyes. It's looking like it did nick an artery after all.

"Terry?"

"Yes, Chief Inspector?"

"Generate a live replication of the vicinity, immediately."

"Yes sir, Chief Inspector."

As I let myself sink back onto the ground, my specs report the two men will be within striking distance in the next forty-five seconds. I bring the inhaler to my lips and wait.

"Your live replication is ready, Chief Inspector."

There's a hissing sound as my lungs fill with the aerosol. The last thing I hear is the sharp report of a weapon that seems to come from a long way away.

When I regain consciousness, I'm standing in front of the door to the windowless shed. I look back and see myself lying on the concrete floor, pale and passed out. Blood is running out of my nose. My first impulse is to run to my injured self, but of course that's not what I need to do. Instead, I pull my Heckler out of its holster and turn the doorknob.

I step outside and see the first sniper has already taken up a position in front of the cabin, in a bush to my left. A yellow crosshair comes to rest on top of him, but I resist the temptation to shoot. Instead I move a few steps away from the entrance until number two shows up.

A few seconds later, he's there. Normally, the pair of them in their chameleon suits would be difficult to discern against the bushes. But thanks to my tactical software, they light up like Christmas trees amongst the other foliage. The newcomer sneaks up to the building while his crony provides covering fire. He keeps away from the door, since as far as he knows, I could shoot at him from inside. He crouches near the wall, takes a small spray bottle from his side pocket, and begins to spray the door with a blue substance, probably octanitro. Then he gets away in a hurry.

I turn to the door. The garish blue of the explosive material turns a poisonous yellow through some kind of reaction with the air. There's no bang, but a hissing sound, coupled with a noticeable heat wave and a flash of light. Instinctively, I throw my arms in front of my face. Nausea rises in me. It's probably due to the fact that my brain can't reconcile being so close to this detonation with my continuing bodily integrity—if I really were to find myself here, I'd have gone the same way as the door, which has dissolved into ashes. Acrid yellow smoke blows toward me. Through the billows, a person is visible, lying on the floor of the cabin.

"He's inside," yells one of the pair.

I look back again and watch how the two assassins run to me, or rather the unconscious form in the cabin. I pull the Heckler up and begin to fire. Over in the real world, my smartgun drone, coupled to my virtual pistol, mirrors its shots. This time, the software opted for rapid fire, an excellent choice. As if electrocuted, the two attackers jerk back and forth before they fall to the ground.

I kneel down and look over the two dead guys. Their gear confirms what I already suspected: these two were the exact opposite of the four village idiots. Chameleon suits, tactical specs, military-grade explosives, even anonymizing generators—the best professional killers money can buy. I look at the high-velocity weapon lying beside one of the men on the forest floor. It's a Jericho 42C, the same model used to shoot Pazzi. If it's even possible, my mood gets a little bit worse.

"Terry?"

"Yes, Chief Inspector?"

"Where's Ava?"

"Analyst Bittman is on the way here. She will arrive with the Taurus unit."

"The shoes on these guys. Same type as the ones Pazzi's murderer wore, right?"

"Yes, Chief Inspector. In both cases, a jump boot used by the armed forces, model type Milway 345, production batch—"

"That'll do."

I walk through the door into the cabin. My body is in a pitiful state. The grazing shot and nosebleed have been joined by a few unpleasant burns. My left pants leg has dozens of small holes; the rubber soles on my shoes, angled in the direction of the door, have started to melt in patches.

The nausea increases; the last time I felt like this was when I ate mussels that'd gone bad. My knees shake, my temples pound, it's all worse than ever before. Maybe it has something to do with my injuries. As long as I'm in the mirror space, though, Terry will feed sensory sensations stemming from the virtual surroundings into my cortex. But he can't stop my wounded body on the other side from being thrown into turmoil, and possibly some of that is sloshing over into my brain. In any case, it's about time for me to go back to my body. But without an escape patch to free up the chemicals on my command and bring me back, I'm stuck sitting here.

"Seeing yourself so helpless. A strange experience, isn't it?"

I look around and see a man standing near me. He has a face perfect for radio: wide eyes set far too apart from each other, a slight squint. They're joined by a hawk's nose and a wide frog mouth whose hanging corners try to produce a grin. The ugly man isn't very tall, only 1.67 meters. I'm certain I've seen him somewhere before, though I have no idea where. Even more noticeable than his visage, though, and his dark hair slicked back with pomade in an old-fashioned style, is his suit. It's bright white and appears to be lit from within. There's only one man who would wear a suit like that.

"Johnny Random. What the hell are you doing here?"

"Research, Chief Inspector Westerhuizen. This is a crime scene, after all, and a somewhat spectacular one at that. Six people dead, five of them shot by a single Jacobin! And all that in the middle of the District Européen. A big story, don't you think?"

"No. This crime scene is off-limits. No press, no news coverage." I put away my H&K, which I've still been holding in my right hand.

Random's frog face squints up at me. Peter Lorre, that's it. He looks like Peter Lorre in *Casablanca*.

"Strictly speaking, I'm not here at all, Inspector."

"How did you get into the Europol mirror space anyway, Random? It's news to me if we're allowing press access. You must have hacked your way in here somehow—is this how you come by such exclusive stories? That'd make for quite a bit of jailtime."

The star journalist makes an appeasing hand gesture. "I'm not really here, not in your replication. Check your log files later—you won't find anything. I'm just a ghost."

"I thought I was the ghost here," I answer. Then

I have a moment of clarity. "It was you in the bar at the Lotte."

He nods. "I can't deny it."

"Your strange Golden Trail tip was complete crap, Random. I went after it. The connection between Pazzi and Tallan was entirely coincidental."

"Of course it was," he answers. He looks at me in the manner of an adult looking at a very slow-witted child. Random lifts his left eyebrow higher than is anatomically possible, a clear indication that this appearance is entirely the product of a computer and has nothing in common with the person behind it, whoever that might be.

I grab him by the lapels of his light-up jacket and pull him toward me. "Enough with these little games. I want answers," I hiss.

Little flashes of light flicker along Random's lapels and begin to leap over my fingers, creeping up the backs of my hands. It hurts like hell. Cursing, I let him go.

"Terry!"

"Yes, Chief Inspector?" comes from somewhere offstage.

"I need a few terriers here. We have an intruder who's—"

"Hold on, Westerhuizen," Random shouts. "I'll explain everything to you. But we don't have much time. I'm not afraid of your pathetic anti-virus software, but I have to leave soon."

"Terry, hold off on the terriers for now. Wait for my command."

"Understood, Chief Inspector."

"Well, Random?"

"Golden Trail was somewhat misguided as a lead, but there was no other way to do it. I had to give you something that would lead you to Tallan. It had to be something, though, that you could have come across on your own. Certain . . . difficulties prevented me from intervening directly."

"What exactly does that mean?"

"Lots of people are keeping you under observation, and me too. If I'd given you something that was obviously an insider tip, it would have set off alarm bells for some of them."

"Aha. Well, then I have to thank you for proceeding with such discretion, Random. I'm in awe of your finesse. I can't begin to imagine what would've happened if any alarm bells had gone off. Someone might even have set some kind of killer on my trail."

"I understand your anger, Chief Inspector. But you have to believe me when I say I'd like to help you."

"With what, exactly?"

"Helping to find Pazzi's murderer."

"We already got him."

"We both know that's not true. And that Tallan bribed Pazzi and the other MEPs."

"He denies it. Can you prove otherwise, Random?"

"No. It would've been possible years ago, but since then Tallan's data cleaners have made all traces disappear."

"And disposed of all the politicians who might have been able to remember the story?"

"An interesting theory. But it raises the question of why Tallan waited ten years to do it, doesn't it?"

I nod. "If Tallan didn't murder the three MEPs, then who did?"

"That's the hundred-thousand-won question, isn't it?" Random sticks his hands into his jacket pockets. "Though I regret it exceedingly, I have to go now. It's about to become far too uncomfortable here for my tastes."

"Random, you low-down little—"

"A good day to you too, Inspector." He glances at the unconscious form lying between us on the floor with a concerned expression on his face. "Both of you aren't looking so great. I wish you a speedy recovery. When your scorched feet are back in working order, I recommend a little leg work, old-school exercises. You spend too much time in replications, Mijnheer Westerhuizen."

And then Johnny Random gradually fades away. His body and limbs disappear first. After a few seconds, only his glowing suit remains. From a distance, I hear his high-pitched voice. "Oh, yes, right jacket pocket."

Then there's no one else in the room but me, my-self, and I.

I dig around in my jacket pocket. Pazzi's I Ching coin has disappeared. Instead I grab hold of a small piece of paper, folded over many times. I unfold it. Written on it in scrawling print is: "Tares, Malta."

The cavalry arrives a short time later, too late as always. The Taurus skyship lands in the clearing, sending leaves and dirt whirling in all directions. Men in black hoods jump out of a hatch on the side. The Union cockade is embroidered on their arms, the black bull encircled by stars. The paramilitary team crouches down and points their assault weapons in all possible directions, securing the area. Not that there's much left to secure. There are so many drones whirring through the air the sky looks like it's being eclipsed. One thing has to be handed to Europol: when it comes to their own people, they don't spare any expense.

From my position near the cabin, I can see a few other people getting out of the skyship. One of them is Ava. She wears her massive analyst specs and has evidently linked to the mirror space without entering it herself. I don't know exactly how it works, but it looks like she's able to see my ghost. Ava walks toward me. In her wake is a broad-shouldered, corpse-pale man around age fifty, whose long body is covered in a black coat reaching to his ankles. It's my colleague Cesar Crolo, known as "Count Krolock" internally. I should have known a scavenger like him would show up here. Using weapons for official police business, especially with fatal consequences, is about as tempting to the head of Internal Affairs as a rotting deer to a vulture.

Ava comes up to me, gasping. "Aart! Are you okay? Why are you still in the mirror space?"

"I got hit by a grazing shot."

"If you're injured, you shouldn't go into a replication! The transition can have very traumatic—"

"I know. But I had to take the risk, or I'd be dead by now. And now I'm waiting until the medics get here. Where are they, anyway?"

Ava looks behind her. There are indeed two men in orange-colored rain jackets coming closer from that direction, as well as a medi-drone. I'd hoped they'd get to me before Crolo arrived. But no dice.

"We'll talk later, Ava. In the office."

"Probably in the hospital, Aart."

"Take a look at the data for yourself. These guys had the same gear as Pazzi's killer."

"Terry already told me. Unbelievable."

"I have two other things."

"Which are?"

"Watch my live replication from earlier, especially the part after I shot these two guys. Look for inconsistencies or hacks."

"Why? What happened?"

"I don't know," I lie. "Just an unsettling feeling someone was watching me."

"An RR agent?"

"No, more like someone who didn't belong there."

"No one can get into the mirror space without a pass, Aart. And no one hacked into Terry. In the case of the creeper-feeds, I mean. And it's just as improbable in this situation."

"Check it anyway, okay? And then please look up a place called Tares on Malta."

"What's there?"

"No idea. Do some exploratory research."

Her lips narrow. "I have the same impression I've

been getting a lot lately, Aart, that you're not telling me everything."

"I'll explain the riddle. Promise, my hand to God. But later. For now, I have to have a chat with the rats in Internal Affairs first."

She nods, stepping to the side to allow space for Crolo, who's catching up with us at this very moment.

"Where is he, Bittman?"

"A meter away from you."

"Make a projection for me."

It takes a few seconds before Crolo can see my outline as a semitransparent hologram on his specs. Then he looks at me with knitted eyebrows.

"Westerhuizen! Get out of there! We need to talk."

"Won't work right now, Crolo. Unfortunately, you'll have to wait until the medics have gotten me out of here."

"Why's that? Don't you have an escape patch?"

"No. Besides, I'm injured. Take a walk around the cabin, you'll see."

Crolo does as he's told. He steps carelessly over one of the dead contract killers, as if he's dealing with a fallen branch. Then he peers through the door.

"Understood. Well, then I'll have my analyst build a crime scene replication first. We'll meet there after that, got it?"

"My official calendar is already quite full, Crolo."

"Internal Affairs doesn't give a shit about your official calendar. Six people! And not a single one of them injured? If I'm seeing this right, they're all dead as doornails."

"Just for the record: one was hit by his friend. But apart from that—with so many armed people coming at me with murder in their eyes, I can't exactly shoot them in the leg, can I?"

"It's my job to get some clarity around that. And so on Monday morning, when you're back in shape, we'll do a few run-throughs together and let Terry create some scenarios in which you could have avoided this bloodbath. We've been keeping tabs on you for a while, Westerhuizen."

"Why's that?"

"The murder suspect in Pazzi's case is also dead thanks to you. It seems you're not squeamish."

"Bullshit, Crolo. I never even touched Winterfuhr. I was only in Hamburg as a ghost."

He looks unimpressed. "Monday at ten. That's an official order. I wish you a speedy recovery." Crolo points to the charred soles on my shoes. "Get back on your feet."

He walks away laughing at his own joke.

Two hours later, I'm lying in a bed in the Clinique Sans Souci eating lukewarm cafeteria fries. Contrary to what I'd feared, the glancing shot didn't shred any of my arteries, just caused a few small blood vessels to burst. The result is a bruise covering almost my entire upper arm. It'll go through the entire color spectrum and hurt like hell in the next few days, but otherwise it's harmless. My feet were lightly scorched by the door's explosion. But the condition of my shoes made it look a lot worse than it actually is. The entire left sole is somewhat red, and the right is displaying some second-degree burns. A nurse has already treated both of them with a stem-cell spray, and the attending physician says I'll be able to walk again by tomorrow.

As I fish the last fries out of the plastic container with a disposable fork, I look at the recordings of Pazzi's funeral. It's fairly uninteresting: other than his family and Peter Heuberger, there's no one at the grave or at the cemetery, at least no one who doesn't belong there—no contrite murderer standing behind a bush to steal a glance at the service. Not that I was expecting anything like that, since we're not living in an episode of a crime drama, after all. But better to be sure.

There's a knock at the door.

"Yes, who is it?"

The door opens and Ava comes inside. She leans over my bed and gives me a kiss on the cheek. In her left hand she's holding a package covered in red media paper with golden stars raining down nonstop.

"For you, Aart."

"Oh, how nice. Thank you very much. Godiva pralines?"

"No, licorice."

I take the present from her gratefully. I tear the paper apart, open the package, and eat one of the black strips.

"How are you, Aart?"

"Not terrible. I can get out of here tomorrow. Theoretically I could even drag myself home now. But then the Spanish Inquisition would probably be on my case with some kind of unexplained-kill forms I have to fill out."

"You mean Crolo?"

"Yes, he already threatened me with an interrogation on Monday. But maybe I'll get lucky and some crazy Taurus cop will unleash a bloodbath on a Christian demonstration by then."

"You're horrible, as always. I'll take that as a sign of recovery."

She sits down on the edge of my bed. Her warm thigh touches my hip.

"Did you find out anything, Ava?"

"We have very good movement profiles on the assassins. The panoptos filmed them."

"They were there? I thought Brussels was only surveilled under a heightened terror threat level."

"That was also my understanding, yes. But it seems the Committee on Domestic Affairs must have issued a special ordinance a few weeks ago. It states that panopto systems can record inside Union territories on an ongoing basis. To get out ahead of definitively suspicious occurrences."

"Probably because of the vote on the constitution."

"Probably. From an analyst's point of view, in any case, it's fantastic, since the panoptos are a great data source. The resolution on these things is amazing—every person's movements are traceable. According to Terry, the amateur assassins came from the western suburbs. Reza Moradi, Firouzeh Morbier, François Nothum, and Arsham Ghasemi. All unemployed small-time criminals with no allegiance to any syndicates and a taste for robberies. Around 3:30 p.m. they all received priority calls with GPS coordinates and a recent picture of you—we're not sure who from. Then they traveled to a meeting point in the vicinity of Gare du Midi, and to the Zoniënwoud from there."

"Where was I at this point?"

Ava murmurs something. Then she crosses her arms and glares at me. "While they were on their way, you'd already had Terry conduct a regression analysis about Tallan and Pazzi behind my back."

"Nonsense. I didn't want to bother you with it, especially since the case is officially closed. I just wanted to give the new Terry a go."

"And?"

"He's horribly dense. And his eyes aren't anywhere near as beautiful as yours."

"Under other circumstances, I might be thrilled by a compliment like that. But right now, it's coming across like the tackiest kind of sexism."

"I'm sorry, Ava. It wasn't meant that way. I'd hate to imagine working without you and only with such a thick-skulled golem."

She tries to maintain her pout. But my words seem to placate her, at least a little bit.

"How could these guys know then that I'd take a spontaneous walk through the woods an hour and a half later?" I ask.

"Maybe you'd already ordered your car? Or called up directions on your specs? They could have culled that information."

I shake my head. "No, nothing like that. At 3:30, I didn't even know yet myself that I'd end up leaving my office so early. It was a spontaneous idea."

After a few seconds I continue: "Predictions. They could have used predictive algorithms to figure out my most likely destination. Is that in the realm of possibility? Are they that accurate?"

"If there's enough data, then maybe, Aart. Your preferences, your idiosyncrasies, your habits—they all create a digital pattern that can be analyzed. And we don't know if these guys were lying in wait for you in other places over the past few days."

"What do you mean by that?"

"If I wanted to kill someone with the help of predictive software, I'd find the most remote places he frequented and wait for him there. Maybe they've been watching you for a long time already. Maybe there were other, earlier predictions for the assassins along with this one, and this was the first time it worked. Terry can try to check into that. But it'll probably take some time. And, Aart?"

"Yes?"

"If these guys used predictive software, then . . . "

"Then this attack goes hand in hand with the creeper-feeds, you mean?"

"It isn't much of a leap to say so. After all, we had just come to the conclusion that the creepers also used an efficient prognostic computer."

"Hmm. What do we know about the other two assassins, the professionals?"

"Not much. Obviously Russians, probably Orelovs,

members of an assassins' guild. They have practically no data corona, must have traveled here recently. In addition, they have false identities and cleaner software to sweep away their digital traces. Terry's trying to get info from his counterpart at the FSB in Moscow, but it's difficult. Ever since all this diplomatic trouble about supplying weapons to Japan, the Russian agencies have been really uncooperative. The men's equipment, by the way, actually matches Thomas Winterfuhr's."

"How so?"

"The same boots, same guns. Different chameleon suits, though. And it wasn't the Pazzi murder weapon or the pair of boots whose prints we found on the poplar, if that's what you're getting at."

"Still a strange coincidence. How likely is it that two professional killers employed on two different murders would wear the same boots and use the same guns?"

Ava subvocalizes something. "Terry says the likelihood of a coincidental match is 19.4 percent."

I sit up and push the blankets back.

"Shouldn't you stay lying down?"

"No, Nurse Ava," I answer. "I'm not supposed to walk or play with any of my bandages. But the doctor approved sitting."

I perch cross-legged on the bed. Ava takes her shoes off and sits across from me. Then she takes a papyrus tablet from the inner pocket of her track jacket. It's made out of two long, thin tubes about thirty centimeters in length whose long sides appear to be sticking to each other. Ava grabs the papyrus with both hands and pulls it apart so a thin media screen appears in between. She lays the device on the mattress between us and the papyrus spreads until it's almost as wide as the bed.

"What next?" I ask.

"Your question about that city."

"Tares."

"Right. There's no city by that name on Malta."

"Are you sure?"

This admittedly stupid question earns me a sour look.

"Okay, okay. So there's no city."

"No, Aart, it's something much more interesting." She looks at me questioningly. "But first I want you to tell me where you got this Tares tip from."

"From my anonymous informant."

"Ah. Did he call you again?"

"No. He was in the mirror space."

"What? When?"

"He showed up suddenly during the live replication in the forest. This time I could see him clearly in front of me. It was Johnny Random, the investigative journalist."

Ava rocks back on the bed and gesticulates with her hands. "Impossible! How did he get in? Now I see why I was supposed to search the replication for hackers breaking in."

I nod. "And it wouldn't be a bad idea for you to take another look at the Lotte replication too."

It takes a moment before she catches on. "You lied

to me! This guy didn't call you at all. He hacked into a live replication twice."

I nod faintly.

"Aart, you should have told me that."

"I'm telling you now. I didn't know his identity then, what exactly was I supposed to tell you? I'll have to tell Vogel about it now, too. Random apparently threatened him a few days ago, he'll start digging around if the Commissioner doesn't give him any information."

"Shit. Now what?"

"I don't know, that's Vogel's call. I'll make an appointment with him first thing tomorrow. It'd be nice if we could find evidence of Random's hacks before then. If I know Vogel, he'll have this guy arrested."

"If he can catch him."

"What do you mean? Random has a weekly 360-show, he's a well-known journalist. Maybe he was trying to remain anonymous up until now, but he must be somewhere in Union territory. If all of Europol is after him, we'll unmask him in no time. In any case, we could get him for espionage and a half dozen data offenses."

Ava murmurs something and listens inwardly. Then she shakes her head. "According to Terry's analysis, Random broadcasts his show from a data haven in Manila. Presumably he's there physically as well."

"Any chance of getting in there?"

"Practically, none, Aart. The Philippines has the most rigid data privacy regulations in the world, and they give access to absolutely no one. The servers for their customers are coupled with completely anonymous account numbers. And there's no extradition agreement with the Union, since the entire country is a damned pirate hideout. If he's there, we won't get him. And if it's true," she adds at a lower volume, "that he can really hack into a Europol computer, I'm afraid he won't have left any traces in the course of his other activities either."

I can feel my temples start to throb. "Vogel should make the decision. Now tell me what you found out about Tares."

"Like I said, it's not a place on Malta. It's not a place at all, it's the name of a Bible story: the Parable of the Tares."

"That was a person?"

"No, tares is another word for chaff. As in, 'separate the wheat from the chaff.' Hold on, I'll get it on the screen."

A short text appears on the papyrus: "The Parable of the Tares, Matthew 13: 24–30":

"Another parable put he forth unto them, saying, The kingdom of heaven is likened unto a man which sowed good seed in his field: But while men slept, his enemy came and sowed tares among the wheat, and went his way. But when the blade was sprung up, and brought forth fruit, then appeared the tares also. So the servants of the householder came and said unto him, Sir, didst not thou sow good seed in thy field? From whence then hath it tares? He said unto them, An enemy hath done this. The servants said unto him, Wilt thou then that we go and gather them up? But he said, Nay; lest while ye gather up the tares, ye root up also the wheat with them. Let both grow together until the harvest: and in the time of harvest I will say to the reapers, Gather ye together first the tares, and bind them in bundles to burn them: but gather the wheat into my barn."

"Theologically," Ava says, "it means the following: the man who sows the good seed is Jesus, and the good seeds are the sons of righteousness; the weeds are the sons of evil; the enemy who sowed them is the devil. God will send out his angels and they will bring together everyone who transgressed His commands, meaning the bad seeds, the tares, and they'll throw the transgressors into the oven in which the fires are burning, meaning hell, and so on."

"Crazy Christian stuff," I respond. "What's that supposed to mean?"

"No idea, Aart. Goyish religion has been incomprehensible to me for as long as I can remember. But there is, there was, a Union project by the name of Tares."

"What kind of project was that?"

"It's hard to say. I tried to squeeze it out of Terry."

"But?"

"But he's not saying much. Do you want to try talking with him yourself?"

"Yeah, put him on the papyrus."

The Europol eye appears on the media screen.

"Terry?"

"Yes, Chief Inspector?"

"Précis on Union project Tares."

"Union project 183728/49236/MIL, nicknamed Tares, is classified material."

"Then unseal it."

"Tares is classified material labeled Code Q, Chief Inspector."

"Which means?"

"It's the highest level of security classification, intended for military or intelligence documents relevant to the innermost security of the Union. Access can only be ordered by the Parliamentary Committee on Domestic Affairs."

"And then I'd be able to see the file?"

"Yes, but not through me, Chief Inspector."

"Run that by me one more time?"

"Highly sensitive classified information is kept on a server managed by my counterpart at army command. In the case that access is granted, you'll have to set up a link with GORGON."

"Is there even a miniscule part of the project with a lower security classification?"

"No, Chief Inspector."

"Press reports about Tares? Parliamentary notes?"

"No, Chief Inspector."

Ava smiles smugly. It's becoming clear to me that my clever analyst beat me to the punch. I just worked on Terry in vain, since of course she already went through the same exchange hours ago. And afterward, Ava got the information she was looking for some other way—I can see it in her eyes. Some other way a clever analyst can find, but an uncreative golem or a senile inspector can't.

To signal my capitulation, I lower my head. "Okay, Ava. You win. Tell me the answer."

"Before Tares was a top-secret project, it was first a line item in the budget. Based on that, we can assume it was a billion-euro project. It follows that there must have been a call for bids."

"Even for a secret project like that?"

"The Cameralists in financial management don't differentiate. Doesn't matter if it's erasers or space stations—at the start, there are always bids. And since we know the project number, the rest was child's play. The bid's over twelve years old, but the database doesn't forget anything."

"And this old bid lays out everything to do with Tares? That's a botched job."

She shakes her head. "GORGON isn't that stupid, of course. He censored and sealed the description of the contract. But not the main points. I think you'll recognize a few of the names."

Ava makes a hand gesture somewhat too dramatic for my tastes. A data record appears on the papyrus:

Unionwide call for bids no. 183728/49236/

MIL – Construction of a system for ********

Acceptance of offer from: Tallan Consolidated SE

Contract total: ********.00 Euro

Site: Valletta, Malta

Parliamentary rapporteur: Jana Svensson

I look at the date on the bid and feel my stomach turning. The Tares contract must have been awarded around the time I started working for the military police. Maybe I've already heard the name Tares in connection with the police? Our remote recon was on Malta at that time. I think back as hard as I can. It's not easy, though, since I've spent the last eight years doing my best not to think about that time. I've tried to forget everything, to bury it deep inside me—the bombs, the sweltering heat, the death of my wife, the desert, everything.

"What's wrong, Aart? You look so pale all of a sudden."

"It's nothing. I had to think about the war for a minute."

"Because of the bid?"

I nod. "It was the exact same time I was there."

"You don't like talking about it, right?"

"Not if there's any way I can avoid it."

Without another word, she leans forward and puts her arms around me. We stay sitting that way until the nurse comes in with my afternoon snack.

CHAPTER 15

The next morning, I can once again walk without pain, thanks to the miracle of modern medicine. I use this newfound freedom to urinate extensively first thing. When I come out of the bathroom, the nurse is standing in my room with breakfast, making a big fuss because I toddled the five meters to the toilet by myself. She sets the tray down and specifically warns me to stay in bed after breakfast until the attending doctor comes to look at my feet again. That won't be for another two hours.

Five minutes later I'm standing in front of the main entrance of the Sans Souci, looking out at the rain and waiting for Gottlieb, already coming up the driveway. I use priority access to make my way to the Palais. I informed Jerôme Vogel about everything yesterday, and he scheduled an appointment for me early this morning. For once, I'm eager to talk to him.

During the drive, I pull up a browsing window and look at the news feeds. They're full of the Zoniënwoud story. I'd still held on to the hope that the whole thing would be kept under wraps since it happened in an abandoned part of the forest. But I should have known what a naïve thought that was. There are just too many droggers out there, nosy parkers with a compulsion for oversharing, people who make use of a few cheap North Korean drones to keep a constant eye out for anything that could be interesting. As soon as the first police drones jetted in the direction of the crime scene, a half-dozen drogger drones followed, nipping at their heels. It makes sense, then, that there are pictures from the Zoniënwoud by the score, of the professionally attired bodies of the assassins and, last but not least, of me. "Jacobin Serves Up Bloodbath" is just one of the more harmless headlines.

When we're close to the botanical gardens, the obsequious voice of my car says, "Query from Jerôme Vogel: 'Could we change our meeting location? Will wait for you at Club Dupont.'"

"Change destination. Club Dupont on Diesdelle-laan. Shit and goddamn it!" The Mercedes changes the route, taking the rest without comment.

The club is near the park belonging to the old Cistercian La Cambre Abbey, a green oasis in south-eastern Brussels. It's a very exclusive meeting place for lobbyists, MEPs, Commission functionaries, and other Union bigwigs. It doesn't surprise me that Vogel is also a member there, well-connected as he is. The amazing thing is that the hippo is leaving his office chair at this early an hour. I'm betting he wouldn't do so if the situation weren't urgent. Something's not right.

My car stops in front of the club, housed in a spotlessly renovated sandstone building with a view of the lake in the park, including the island with the Chalet Robinson restaurant. There's neither a sign on the door nor a bell to ring. It's meant to signal understatement but comes across as pretentious. I position myself in front of the door and wait.

It opens after about twenty seconds. Behind it stands a faithful reproduction of a British butler from the nineteenth century, including the bowtie and stiff upper lip.

"Mr. Westerhuizen, sir," he says. "Welcome. If you'd be so kind as to follow me. Your breakfast companions are already waiting for you."

I follow him through a foyer that must have cleared out a small rainforest. All of the walls and the whole ceiling are covered in dark wood. To avoid things becoming too one-note, oil paintings have been hung on the walls, depicting men on a foxhunt—presumably real foxes, mind you, not bionic ones. Two suits of armor stand by the doorway into the dining room, where we're clearly headed.

The dining room echoes the entryway—lots of wood, not much glass. The butler leads me past a reading nook where two men of advanced age sit and complete their first post-meal catnaps of the day. In the back there's a huge table made of the inescapable dark wood. Three people wait for me. Vogel sits on one side of the table and takes up practically the whole space, which is why the two women have taken their places across from him. One of them is Jana Svensson. The other is possibly the most powerful person in the entire Union: Tansu Özal, the President of the European Commission. Vogel looks blanched. I don't blame him.

The waiter bows stiffly and leaves me to my fate.

Vogel points to the only empty chair, prompting me to sit. "Westerhuizen, good morning! Have a seat. You know Ms. Svensson, and I hardly have to introduce Ms. Özal."

I greet the two women. Svensson looks back with her customary hostility. Özal, however, stands up and shakes my hand enthusiastically with such an affable smile it looks like she's about to name me Inspector of the Year. She's a small woman, a hundred and sixty-five centimeters of Anatolian cheerfulness with short hair and sky-blue eyes. Her body looks like it's made out of two pieces that don't fit together but were still mounted one on top of the other. Her torso and arms look slim, even delicate. Her immense posterior and chubby legs, though, appear to belong to another person, one weighing sixty kilos more.

As I sit down, she pours me a steaming cup of tea from a floral pot, still smiling as she does so. The only thing she hasn't done is put sugar in it for me. But she doesn't go quite that far, not yet.

"Westerhuizen, as I can see you're back on your feet," Vogel says. "I asked you here because we have concerns after yesterday's events that the whole thing is going to get out of hand, politically speaking."

"Who do you mean by 'we,' Chief?"

Vogel's fat forehead folds into wrinkles, making him look like a cured ham. "Everyone present, Westerhuizen! The Union, all of us!"

"It doesn't happen very often," Svensson seconds, "that a Europol inspector is attacked in this way."

"I'll have to disagree with you there, Madame Representative. In the past five years over a dozen of my colleagues were killed by separatists, Britskis, and other criminals."

Vogel and Svensson both want to reply, but as soon as they hear Özal's sonorous voice ringing out, they fall silent immediately.

"But not a single one of the cases involving your coworkers also involved one of the most powerful economic leaders of the Union as one of the murder suspects."

"You think Tallan hired these killers, Madame President?" I ask. "Our suspicion up to this point was actually that a huge criminal syndicate stole data on a large scale from Tallan specs using a method we've yet to prove. I suspect the same people are behind yesterday's attack."

"I read the précis, Chief Inspector. But if more about this case leaks to the media, which is the assumption we have to operate under, then the suspicions about Tallan will come to light. Simply because he's a well-known and controversial person and has a connection to your creeper-feeds."

"And that would be a bad thing?" I ask. "To me, Tallan seemed like someone who's more than capable of taking care of himself."

Özal smiles, although now it seems somewhat strained. "As you can probably imagine, at this time there are certain leanings in Parliament and government that are not friendly to Britain. Many people are of the opinion that the English are leaving us in the lurch, particularly now, of all times, when the defense situation is politically tense and we could really use the help of the British army. There are people who say we shouldn't conduct any more business with Britain at all. There's a danger that the United Kingdom will become a kind of persona non grata in the process of leaving the Union."

"It could be argued that they only have themselves to blame," I retort.

"Westerhuizen!" Vogel snarls at me. Beads of sweat run down his forehead. I've never seen him this nervous before.

Özal makes a placating hand gesture. "He's right, in a manner of speaking. But it shouldn't be approached so emotionally. This is about diplomacy and foreign policy. If we leave the British in complete isolation, who will they turn to then? The Americans are out of the game, there's not even a question of whether they'd be a strong ally. All that's left are the Russians or the Arabs. There are already signs that the British arms industry is making contacts there."

She looks at me with a piercing expression; her smile has disappeared. "Imagine what would happen if the British outfitted our many enemies in Africa and the Middle East with the most cutting-edge arms technology. Or even counseled them about military matters. Firms like Northrop Aegis, who outfitted the coalition troops for decades, know all of our secrets. I don't even want to talk about Tallan Consolidated—they not only helped in the development of TIRESIAS and GORGON, but almost all of the mirror space protocols used by our officers. There's a lot at stake, and therefore we'd like to ask you to proceed as cautiously as possible."

I don't particularly like Vogel, but I'd still gladly have spared him what's next. But since he convened this meeting, or at least condoned it, I'm left with no other choice.

"That could be difficult, Madame President," I say. "Johnny Random is already on the case."

Jana Svensson makes a noise somewhere between a groan and a sigh.

"I—I thought he was only interested in the Pazzi story," Vogel stammers.

"Unfortunately, it seems Random is also interested in the creeper-feeds. He contacted me and tried to clue me in that there was an uncovered scandal by the name of Golden Trail, in which not only Tallan played a role, but Pazzi too."

Jana Svensson snorts angrily. "Don't come to us again with that old corruption story. There's simply nothing to it."

"Tallan said the exact same thing," I answer.

Vogel displays an expression that's difficult to interpret. Either he'd like to sink into the ground from shame right now, or he'd like to strangle me on the spot. Possibly both. Özal, on the other hand, looks amused. Her eyes betray that she doesn't believe a word Svensson says. Which makes two of us.

"And why," Svensson says venomously, "do you think Pazzi's death had something to do with these creeper-feeds in the first place? Because Tallan played a role in both cases?"

"I don't believe that at all, Ms. Svensson. But this crazy journalist seems to believe it."

"We'll proceed under the assumption that it's two separate stories," Vogel growls. "The Pazzi case is closed, do you agree with me, Chief Inspector?"

Careful now.

"At the present time, I see no indications that would lead any prosecutor in the world to open the file again."

Vogel nods, satisfied. "Would you be so kind as to tell us how you intend to move forward, Chief Inspector?"

"Currently, we're waiting for a return call from Tallan, since until then we won't know how exactly this data theft could've been carried out so extensively. Additionally, we'll try to trace the paths of these contract killers. We should be able to figure something out based on one of the two data trails."

"Could we support you in any way, Chief Inspector?" the Commission president asks.

"Yes. Get this Random guy off my back. We suspect he hacked into the Europol computer."

Özal looks at Vogel. It seems she's not talking with the Commissioner about the journalist for the first time. Then she says quietly, "This time he's really gone too far."

I look at Özal quizzically. After a short pause, she says, "You know how many scandals Random has uncovered in the past few years. His methods are unconventional, not to mention illegal. He steals data, hacks feeds, spies on politicians. Until now, the police haven't taken action against him. First, because it seemed hopeless, because we never knew where he was keeping himself. And second, because the general public considers this man a hero for some strange reason. It seemed it would do us more harm than good."

"You and the Commissioner will have to handle the political trade-off," I say. "As a police officer I think he belongs in the clink, not on television."

"If he was really in our computer, we'll make sure he's finished," Vogel growls.

It comes across like he's trying to threaten a sparrow sitting on a tree thirty meters above him, but I don't say anything.

"Thank you, Chief Inspector," Vogel says. "You may go back to work now."

"Thanks very much."

As I start to stand up, my gaze falls on Jana Svensson one more time. The opportunity to interrogate her in front of witnesses of this caliber will never come again. I just have to go for it. "I do have one more question, Madame Representative."

"Hmm?"

"Random referenced a project by the name of Tares, some kind of extremely classified military project Tallan was said to be a part of. Do you by chance know what it was about?"

"Not in any detail, no. As far as I can remember, it was some sort of analysis software we wanted to utilize for identifying rebel nests. But there were programs like that by the score, and it was a long time ago. I can't tell you exactly what became of it."

It's suddenly so silent that the quiet snoring of the old men in the reading nook becomes audible. I take my leave and go to the exit. The butler holds the door open for me right away.

Amnesia is a sickness that afflicts politicians with some regularity. But it's particularly worrisome that Svensson can no longer remember a project she was responsible for as the rapporteur. When it comes to the Golden Trail scandal, on the other hand, her brain seems to function flawlessly. She can remember that even though I never told her about it.

CHAPTER 16

The morning rush hour is in full swing, so my car wasn't able to find a parking place anywhere near the club. Instead, it's going around in endless circles, running the gauntlet of the city's clogged arteries. So, despite the rain, I decide to walk in the direction of the Europol Palais until it can pick me up. I put on my sou'wester and set off on my way.

So many mistakes, so early in the day. I rebuffed my supervisor, not to mention the chairs of the Defense Committee. On top of that, I put an informant on the chopping block. Though it's not totally clear to me how I could've avoided stepping in it like this. Ava and Terry already know about Random, after all; and, as always, when three people know a secret, it's not a secret anymore. My analyst would probably keep it under her hat if I were to ask her. But everything Terry logs is accessible to the Commissioner, not to mention the examining magistrate and the public prosecutor.

Besides that, the spies at the RR must have search routines running continuously in all Union databases to sound the alarm if the name of a secret classified document comes up—a classified document so compromising not even the Parliamentary rapporteur responsible for it at the time wants to remember it.

Maybe I should call up my RR pal Ververke as a preventative measure. As of now, I have absolutely no idea if and how the intelligence service is involved. Since the Commission president is interested in the case, though, it's likely the RR is mixed up in it somehow. I think back on my time as an officer in Morocco and Algeria, on the rumors circulating then among Union soldiers. The RR, so the rumors went, was working on the development of a new technology that could be used to thwart attacks. Could that have been the Tares project? It seems possible, but on the other hand there could have been many such projects at the beginning of the last decade, all promising potential miracle weapons that manufacturers pawned off on a desperate Union.

After the nuclear attacks on Tehran and Riyadh, there was almost no more oil. We became more reliant on solar energy than ever, on our "place in the sun." But the North African countries had little interest in becoming associated Union territories, which at the end of the day was just a euphemism for occupied territory. And so they resisted, with great success. They simply had the edge on us in the desert. While the locals knew how to handle heat waves and sandstorms, our drones couldn't handle it and neither could our soldiers.

As I turn onto Louizalaan, the rain whips my face. For a long time, it seemed like North Africa was going to be a nut we couldn't crack. But at some point, the assassinations and bomb attacks began to taper off. All the rebels who had hidden away with the locals in medinas and desert villages, all the guerillas we were never able to track down, seemed to be swallowed up by the desert sand one day, though no one could say why. There were rumors the RR had taken drastic measures. But we knew nothing about what that meant or how the intelligence service had gotten their hands on so many rebels. And we really didn't want to know.

I'm so deep in thought I only notice the drones for the first time when they're hovering right in front of me. There are three, two humming-drones and a hexa-heli. Based on their colorful paint jobs, I can tell they belong to droggers.

It's already the fourth mistake I've made this morning. Since my face could be found in every newsfeed yesterday, the droggers, and likely a few professional journalists as well, have set up search routines in an attempt to get me in front of the lens. The editorial offices have to use legal, openly accessible databases to support their efforts and follow my trail—photos uploaded onto the public net by private citizens or the panoramic cameras installed every few meters by the Brussels tourism bureau. The droggers are less demure. Maybe they're illegally snatching up videos from public transportation or taxis, so as I walked away from Club Dupont, I showed up on these creeper-feeds right away, setting off all kinds of alarms.

The heli-drone is holding steady at the height of my face and has aimed a glaring spotlight at me. On its underside there's a small display where I can make out a man about twenty-five years old with colorful, flashing LED dreadlocks. He looks at me triumphantly.

"Inspector Westerhausen, good morning—Paul Poulain, 'Drogging Brussels!' Tell our viewers something about yesterday's events. Who tried to kill you? Britskis? Militant Christians?"

I pull my sou'wester further over my face and growl, "No comment."

"Is that all you have to say? You're live on the air. The Europol press office reports you acted in self-defense. But isn't this really another unbelievable act based on a Jacobin's whims?"

In the meantime, one of the humming-drones has started to jabber away at me. It's not the first time something like this has happened to me, and so I do the only thing that can be done in such a situation. Silently, and with a blank expression on my face, I keep trudging through the rain, hoping my Mercedes will show up soon. According to my specs, it's only three hundred meters away. As I keep walking, I use my larynx mike to inform headquarters about the three cases of drone stalking.

Then I catch sight of my car. It's coming toward me. I cross the street and hurry to climb inside. As we start driving, I can see a flash of light through the tinted windows. The first drogger humming-drone falls, smoking, to the ground. And then the newly arrived police drone takes care of the other two pains-in-the-ass as well.

Instead of heading straight to the office, I go home first. When the Mercedes reaches the Kasteleinsplein, I have Terry analyze the area and confirm if any more paparazzi drones are lurking outside my front door. After all, it's a cinch to find out my private address.

"A total of nine drones have taken up a position in front of your apartment building, Chief Inspector."

"Is that all?"

"Please reformulate the question, Chief Inspector."

"Forget it. Ask headquarters to get them off my back."

"Understood, Chief Inspector."

Fortunately, the building has a parking garage, so I'm spared from having to run another gauntlet. When I'm back in my apartment, I take a long hot shower right away to wash the smell of the hospital off me. Then I put on a clean suit. They gave the old one a much-needed wash at the hospital, but it still smells like I wore it at bonfire. And anyway, one of the pants legs is singed.

As I wait for headquarters to give the all-clear about the droggers, I read my messages. Internal Affairs is still of the opinion that I should've first tried talking with the six killers about their difficult childhoods. That means Count Krolock wants to go through the threatened crime-scene replication with me as soon as possible, to find out how the whole thing could have been solved "in a more conflict-free way." I'd prefer a prolonged root canal.

After I archive almost eighty messages, I check the assorted emails from Ava and our computer security department. The fact that Johnny Random appears to have successfully infiltrated the Europol system has caused a real commotion, not to mention point-blank panic. As of now, no one knows how the guy managed to do it. I call Ava and transfer her face from my specs to one of my walls. It's as if the sun has risen.

"Good morning, Aart. How are you today, better?"

"Wonderful, with a few reservations." I tell her about the droggers.

She shrugs her shoulders, displaying the same uncomprehending facial expression all young people get when old people get worked up about invasions of their privacy.

"That's to be expected, right? The price of fame."

"Very funny. And other than that, Vogel ordered me to breakfast."

"You mean asked?"

"No, ordered. Svensson and Özal were also there."

"You had breakfast with the Commission president, with Mother Europe? Wow." After a short pause she says, "And what do they want from us? Is it about Pazzi or about the creeper-feeds or about Tallan?"

"Above all, it seems they want Tallan out of the line of fire. For political reasons."

I tell her how Özal described the British exit to me, and the diplomatic and other dangers tied up in it.

She shakes her head. "Do you think that's the whole truth?"

"Since when does the truth come out over breakfast?" I reply. "Of course there's more to it, but I don't know what. In any case, we're under closer observation now. What have we gotten about the creeper-feeds and Random's hack in the meantime?"

"If you would read your messages," says the enormous face on my wall with an accusatory look, "you'd have seen Tallan's chief of security wrote to us, a woman named Stähler."

"Would I have been able to understand her message in even the most rudimentary way, Ava?"

"Fair point. Stähler says no one compromised the specs server at Tallan Consolidated, either from the inside or from the outside. She's moving forward under the assumption that the gateway for the hackers must be through some kind of hole in the glasses software."

"Just as you and Tallan guessed. Did they already find the hole?"

"No, not yet. Stähler says—and it doesn't sound implausible to me—that it may not be due to any programming error."

"So then what is it?"

"TalCon has more than twenty years of experience in spec design. Their software has been checked over and improved thousands and thousands of times, so they don't have security holes anymore. But it's possible some corrupt programmer intentionally built a back door into it and then sold the knowledge about that weak spot to the Britskis or someone else."

"And how's it going now?"

"Tallan seems to be certain this is the explanation for the thousands of hacks. So certain they've already filed criminal complaints against unknown offenders. At the moment, TalCon's semi-intelligent central computer—he's called Pythia, by the way—is openly looking into every single worker and every single line of code. That'll take some time."

"It would definitely go faster if they'd let Terry and his terriers into their network instead of using their little pocket calculator."

"We'd need a search warrant for that, Aart."

"I know. But we won't get one of those right now. Even if we could convince the examining magistrate, Özal would probably block it. But we should at least ask TalCon if they'll open their treasure trove voluntarily. Just to keep some of the pressure on. Anyway, us Union folk and Tallan are great buddies, apparently, or at least that's what Vogel and Özal tried to convince me of."

I sigh. My head feels fuzzy and it's abundantly clear I haven't eaten anything today other than a half-cup of tea. And it's hard even for a master of repression like me not to be preoccupied with having five people on my conscience. Not that they'd be the only ones. I try to shoo away those thoughts and focus on Ava's brown eyes instead.

"So any way you look at it," I continue, "we don't have any more traces on Tallan we could keep following at the moment."

"Unfortunately not. Oh, and by the way, Terry found more creeper videos."

"How many this time?"

"Five hundred clips total, for a total of eight thousand minutes. We'll analyze them right away. And as far as the Random case goes—"

"—everyone is clearly very worked up."

She looks concerned and jerks back on her rolling chair.

"What is it, Ava?"

"We don't know how he did it. Which is mostly because no one saw him other than you."

"He programmed himself into a high-definition immersive simulation, twice. How much data is that?"

She considers for a moment. "He was only in for a moment. I'd guess five or six petabytes."

"And there's not even a tiny piece of that to be found anywhere?"

"No, Aart, nothing. Some of the guys in security are saying it'd be easier to have a cortex scan done on you. Because the most likely explanation is you imagined everything. Due to the trauma you suffered and so on." When she sees my expression, she quickly adds, "Of course, I believe you."

"Thanks. Do you have a hypothesis about how he could have gotten in?"

"Yes." Ava looks at me with her huge eyes. She doesn't say anything else, but I understand her right away. I have a theory, her eyes say. But there's no way I'm telling it to you over the net.

"Oh, well," I answer, "then there's really nothing else we can do except let the local offices process the criminals from these creeper-feeds and wait until Tallan's security comes to us with more findings."

"Looks like it, Aart."

"Then I'd like to recommend a little break. Sometimes that's what it takes to get new ideas. When was the last time you went to the North Sea, Ava?"

"Before it started to rain without stopping."

"That must have been months ago."

"Yes. But to be honest, that kind of gray, beachless soup isn't especially inviting for an Israeli."

"Let me convince you otherwise. I know a fantastic restaurant there, near Zeebrugge."

"Isn't everything there under water?"

"The restaurant is on stilts. They have great seafood. We could leave right away."

Her look tells me she isn't entirely sure about the point of this conspiratorial little tour. We could also have a confidential conversation in an iso-room somewhere in the city. But she doesn't ask. I wouldn't have a convincing answer ready anyway.

"Good. You'll pick me up, Aart?"

"In fifteen minutes."

When I stop on Wolstraat near the Palais de Justice and get out of the car, I notice it's almost stopped raining. Only a few scattered drops dampen my face. A thunderstorm is supposed to roll in from the north this afternoon, but until then it seems like we'll have clear skies.

Ava comes walking toward me. Unlike me, she looks like someone who's planned ahead for spending the day at the seaside—blue chinos, sneakers, rain jacket.

"Do you really want to go to the beach in a suit, Aart?"

"Why not? I took off my cravat."

Shaking her head, she climbs into the passenger seat. After the Mercedes has gotten underway, I tell it to regroup the interior. The backseat disappears into the floor. Our chairs turn themselves until they're sitting angled toward each other. A small side table slides out of the front dash. I take two cans of Antárctica out of the cooler. We drink our sodas silently as the Flemish landscape rolls by outside, visible as barely more than streaks, since I set us on priority speed. The Mercedes drives at least two hundred and fifty kilometers per hour and uses a radio siren to force all other vehicles out of the fast lane.

It won't take us more than forty minutes to get to Bruges. Instead of talking about Ava's theory—not exactly a good idea in an official vehicle stuffed to the gills with sensors—we dig through Gottlieb's music library. Ava likes old American jazz, just like me. That's a shared interest I didn't know a thing about until now. We listen to Gerry Mulligan and John Coltrane. Ava wants to put on *Bitches Brew* by Miles Davis next, but we've already reached Moerkerke.

Moerkerke is a small village a few kilometers west of the former Belgian-Dutch border. There was just a church here before, with a few houses and many cows surrounding it. The rising sea tide, though, has since made Moerkerke into a minor tourist destination. There's a harbor, nothing in the same league as the sunken area around Zeebrugge, just a collection of jetties and breakwalls where excursion ships for tourists can dock. A sandy beach has also been piled up nearby. That's the real attraction, since most naturally occurring beaches have gotten significantly narrower in the past few years or have disappeared entirely.

We park behind Saint Dionysus and wander to the pier. The abrupt end to the rain clearly took most people by surprise, and it's less crowded than expected. I lead Ava to a small stand where I've rented boats in the past and get a small motorboat. We climb into the rocking sloop and let the lines loose. I tell our destination to the onboard computer. With a quiet hum, the electric motor switches on. We start to glide over the unbelievably calm sea. It's almost windless, cloudy, and somewhat muggy. There'll be a storm later, at 3:53 p.m. according to my specs. Beads of sweat form on my forehead. I take my jacket off and lay it on the forward seat.

"Where's the restaurant, anyway?" Ava asks.

"Further north."

"Where the beach used to be?"

"Not quite so far north as that."

The restaurant is called De lol Schol, the Droll Sole, and is just coming into view on the horizon. It towers above the sea on concrete posts; the building, made mostly of steel and glass, stays more than twenty meters above the surface of the water even at high tide.

"How did it get like that?" Ava asks.

"The owner—he's a friend of mine—he had a seafood place in Zeebrugge originally, like his father and grandfather before him. When the water came, he built a new restaurant farther inland."

"Not far enough inland?"

"Exactly. So he built another new restaurant, another one-and-a-half kilometers farther back. When the water level rose again, he decided he had to figure out something else. He wasn't thrilled with the idea of moving every five or ten years, and at the time, no one knew where the water would level off in the end. So he built it on stilts. There are pictures hanging in the restaurant. At first the building was standing in the marsh all by itself on its long legs, like Baba Yaga's hut, no sea in sight as far as the eye could see."

I tell the boat to pilot around De lol Schol in a big sweep, farther out into the sea. Then I take off my specs and my larynx mike and deactivate them both. I reach for my jacket and take my privatizer out of the inner pocket so I can check what kind of sensors are on board.

"Is that seriously a privatizer, Aart? Where did you get it?"

"It's from my time in the military. We used them so we could make ourselves invisible to the rebels' eavesdropping attempts."

"I thought it was illegal to own those things."

"Just selling is illegal, not owning."

"And using them?"

I shrug my shoulders. "An administrative offense,

maybe. But we're not disturbing any sensors or cameras used for official purposes. And anyway, way out here there are holes in the network, the connection tends to break up here and there."

The small display on the privatizer shows me a list of the various sensors integrated into the boat and makes suggestions about how to knock them out with jammers. I order the privatizer to block everything and tell Ava to put her arsenal of electronic gadgets to sleep as well. Shortly afterward, the onboard computer warns us it's lost the GPS signal, verifying that the privatizer has done its work.

Now we're halfway secure. Theoretically, there could be ghosts in our vicinity, intelligence service members who've followed us out here using the mirror space. But to get a good live replication in the middle of the sea, Terry or GORGON would have to powder the surroundings with mite drones, and those would have shown up on the privatizer. At least I hope so.

"So," I say. "What's your theory, Ava?"

"Okay, it goes like this: Based on everything we know, Johnny Random is an army of one. Maybe he has a team of a few data analysts and researchers. Maybe there's a talented hacker in there, too. But hacking his way into the EU mirror space without leaving a trace is way out of his league."

"So someone's helping him?"

"Not just anyone. These computers are among the most well-protected on the planet, even more secure than any satellite bank. There are only a handful of organizations that would have even a hint of a chance to get inside."

"And those are?"

She shrugs her shoulders. "Countries about as technologically advanced as we are, who use comparable systems—Brazil, South Korea, maybe the Cantonese. But it would be difficult even for them. I think the hacker must be part of an organization that already has access to the mirror space, and therefore has the opportunity to smuggle Random in unnoticed."

"That means there are only two possibilities," I say.

"Exactly. The first is Europol. But since I can't see why we'd let Random into the mirror space and then cover for him, it can only have been the RR. The intelligence service has full access, and many people there have administrative permissions. What's more, with Georgy at their service, they have their own analytical computer on par with Terry that could help wipe away any traces."

"But to just make a replicated person disappear without a trace—is that even possible in the first place?"

"I'm not sure. But don't forget the RR knows the mirror space much better than we do."

She's right. Although cops usually prowl around in crime scene replications in the aftermath of a crime, the mirror space works best for the very essence of what the RR does, spying on people proactively and sniffing them out.

"I don't like your theory, Ava."

"Because you don't find it compelling?"

"No, because it's playing with fire. If it's true, then there's some kind of power struggle between the Union intelligence service and Europol."

"Or between the intelligence service and the Commission. That's what Özal's sudden appearance points to, don't you think, Aart?"

I nod silently. "We have to be very careful from here on out. Lots of people are trying to take advantage of us, and we can't trust anyone anymore. Do you also have a theory of why Johnny Random is working for our friends at the shadow police?"

"No. But then again, maybe it wasn't really Random you saw. Who knows what's real in a manipulated replication?"

No clever response occurs to me, and so I switch off the privatizer. Soon after, the boat knows where it is again and corrects its course. A few minutes later, we dock on one of the restaurant's pontoons. As we enter the dining room, the owner, Pit de Graaf, greets me like a long-lost brother and leads us to an especially nice table on the glassed-in porch. I order the sole and Ava gets a medley of seafood kebabs. When the waiter brings over the enormous metal stakes, studded with crab and king scallops, I ask Ava if shrimps are kosher.

"No, they're not," she answers as she frees a shrimp from its shell. "Not for Christians, either, incidentally."

"Christians aren't allowed to eat shrimp? Pray tell where that's written."

"In the Bible. In the part you pirated from us."

Ava makes a very unladylike slurping sound as she sucks out the head of the shrimp.

"But unlike you, we have a relaxed view on seafood, at least we worldly Jews do. Don't you remember that series of attacks on the Lucky Lobster franchises, Aart?"

"Truth be told, no. Though arsons at fast-food chains aren't exactly an issue for Europol."

"They, of course, sell lobster burgers galore, popcorn shrimp, things like that. A Christian terror group torched a bunch of them at the time. In their claim of responsibility, they referenced the Old Testament, Leviticus 11:10: 'And all that have not fins and scales in the seas, and in the rivers, of all that move in the waters, and of any living thing which is in the waters, they shall be an abomination unto you.'"

Terrorists who believe the world would be a better place without deep-fried shrimp croquettes. Best not to think too much about it—it's enough to drive a person crazy.

"Speaking of your Old Testament zealots, Ava, if your theory from earlier is true, then is there a connection between them and the biblical parable we talked about recently? Tares?"

"Good question. Don't you know someone who could tell us more about it, Aart? I've already completely exhausted Terry's resources and I'm at the end of my Latin."

"I could talk to Tallan about it—he gave me his direct line. As a former contractor, he has to know what the military project was about."

"But he might still be bound by an NDA."

"Maybe. But it's worth a try."

After our meal, we sit down on deck chairs on the veranda with oversized thermoses full of coffee. On the horizon, a few billowing clouds are just visible, but there's still no clear dividing line announcing the imminent arrival of a severe weather front. I ask my specs to alert us an hour before it arrives.

I look at Ava, who's closed her eyes and is working on her tan. After an hour out here, she'll be even more coffee-colored, in contrast to me, red as a fire alarm. I lie back as well. Just as I'm starting to drift off, the alarm goes off. I look out over the sea. The horizon is already dark black.

I tap Ava gingerly on the shoulder. When she opens her eyes, I say, "We should go. Otherwise we'll have to stay here until the thunderstorm's gone by, and that could take hours."

She nods, in a daze. I offer her my hand. She pulls herself up by it and encircles my arm with her other hand. We stay standing like this for a moment, contemplating the storm front in front of us.

Ava breaks away from me and we take the elevator down to the level of the pontoons. The wind blows in our faces and our little boat dances alone on the waves. Most of the other guests have already taken their leave. Once we've climbed aboard, I direct the boat to make for the port of Moerkerke, full speed ahead.

Ava looks at the weather front behind us. "Shit,

we're too late, aren't we?"

"No, we still have enough time."

People from the Mediterranean—not used to waves and wind. The boat reaches the port at least half an hour before the storm. We only get hit by a few drops of it, arriving back at the car before the pelting rain starts.

"That was our entire summer, then," Ava says, and smiles at me. "Way too short."

I smile back and direct the car to take us to the Palais. During the drive we don't speak much, focusing on getting caught up on the work left waiting over the past few hours. I dictate a short memo to Tallan, asking to speak with him. I don't mention a reason.

When I'm done with my correspondence, I notice Ava has disappeared behind her analyst's glasses. She's probably watching a 360-video of some kind. The massive frames make her look like Housefly Puck. I look out the window. We're just passing the outskirts of Ghent.

But on the wrong side.

I call up an overlay of the surroundings to make sure I'm not wrong. Coming from Bruges, we should have taken the new E34 and then the E17, just like on the way out. The route should have taken us by Ghent on the north side. But suddenly we're on the E40, south of the city.

"Gottlieb," I say. "Why are we driving on the E40?"

"The E40 is the fastest route to the desired destination," the car computer answers.

"Since when is that the case? Is there an accident

on the E34? Or a traffic jam?"

"There are no traffic advisories for the E34."

"So then why are we on the E40?"

"The E40 is the fastest route to the desired destination."

Ava's picked up on my conversation with the navi-computer. She takes off her glasses and looks at me quizzically.

"Display route to destination," I say.

A map of East Flanders appears on the windshield, with our route marked in red. It leads from Moerkerke to Westrem. More precisely, to a nameless field directly next to the freeway near Westrem.

"Oh, fuck," Ava murmurs.

"Who changed the destination?" I demand of the Mercedes.

"The destination was not changed," it answers placidly.

"I entered the destination as—" I don't complete the sentence. It's pointless to discuss such things with a computer as simpleminded as Gottlieb. Instead I call up a display of when Westrem was entered as the destination and compare the time stamp with my own movement history.

"Westrem had already been entered as the destination when we got in. Someone must have hacked the car," I growl.

"What are we going to do now?" Ava asks. "Alert headquarters? Call in some drones as backup?"

"Tell them they should send an armed jet drone, something with guns. Terry should start preparing to take over driving, on my command."

Even if the drones set out right away, they'll probably arrive too late, but better safe than sorry. I open the glove compartment and take out my service pistol and holster.

"Do you have a weapon, Ava?"

"Sure, but not with me."

I open the hatch to the trunk and take a smart Uzi 500 out of a strongbox I have stashed there, offering it to Ava.

"For the worst-case scenario. Practically shoots on its own."

She takes the machine gun silently and couples it with her specs. Barely three minutes later, we're there. Autobahn E40, kilometer marker 537.4—the exact same place where Pazzi breathed his last. We park on the shoulder. I pull on my rain jacket and take the safety off my H&K. Then I venture out into the torrential downpour. It beats down on my shoulders and my shoes are instantly filled with water. In front of me is the familiar field, now a mud pit, though just as abandoned as ever. I activate all the sensors on my specs, but I can't make out a single soul. Lightning flickers across the skies. I regret not having any scout drones at hand.

With weapon drawn, I walk along the narrow gravel pathway and mark the spot where Pazzi lay. Ava follows me. By the time I get there, my pants legs are covered in sandy sludge, not to mention my shoes. Rain-swollen squalls sweep over the field. Whoever directed my Mercedes here wanted to make sure I noticed something. But what? I turn in all directions and squint through the rain. As I turn back to Ava, I see she has her right arm raised. She stands there as if frozen and points a finger in the direction of the thicket on the west side of the field.

A row of poplars stands there, seven in total. It's the exact same thicket from which a shot sent Vittorio Pazzi into the great beyond. The thicket looks the exact same as it did last time, only much wetter.

And then I get it.

I've watched the replication of this crime scene and the path of the shot often enough, from every possible angle, to know exactly where the shot came from without a marking overlay. There's supposed to be a poplar there, a poplar with a sturdy branch sticking out to the right from where we're standing. That's where the shooter crouched when he fired.

But there's no poplar at the spot in question. Instead, there's only a gap in the line of trees. We walk to the edge of the field as fast as the marshy ground allows. As we come closer, I see there must have been a tree in that spot at some point, since there's a stump there.

I run my hand over it. Without a doubt, we're looking at the stump of a big poplar. The traces of moss on the upper side indicate, though, that the tree it belonged to was cut down quite a long time ago.

"Can you find out when this tree was cut down?" I ask Ava.

"Maybe. Gi—give me a second, I'll look." After a pause of maybe a minute, Ava says, "There are no recordings from the forestry service, and also no removal permission from the European Agency for Sustainable Forestry Management. But a full four years ago, there's a traffic accident in the database. A semi-truck swerved, slid across this field, and crashed into a tree. I'm still waiting on pictures from the local police. But I'd bet the damaged tree was cut down around that time."

I nod. Then I put my arm around Ava. She's in shock. I can understand why: her all-digital world is dissolving around her. We walk slowly back toward the car.

"We sat on it. We sat on the tree the gun was fired from," she says.

"I know, Ava. I know."

"The mollies scanned the tree," she continues, undeterred, "and they found traces of the murderer on it."

But there is no tree. And if there's no tree, then no assassin could sit on its branch and shoot Pazzi from it. Once Ava has climbed inside the car, I close the door and stand for a moment with my head uncovered. I close my eyes and feel the lukewarm raindrops splash across my face. Water runs down my cheeks, collects beneath my ears, and runs from there into my collar. But I don't mind at all. The rain, at least, is real.

CHAPTER 17

It's still early and Lisbon's city center is deserted. As I cross the Praça Camões, I see more pigeons than people in the plaza. On the other side, I take a seat on a park bench that someone has decorated with dozens of small white rectangles. I wait, looking down the Rua Misericordia as an eléctrico from line 28 draws closer.

When it stops at the station, I climb on, go to the tinted-glass conductor's compartment, and knock.

"What do you want?" asks a voice through a loudspeaker.

"Europol. Please open the window."

A small hatch flips open. Behind it sits a man in his late forties, heavyset and somewhat pasty. Nothing in his précis indicates he has daydreams of breaking out of his daily routine, or daydreams of any kind for that matter. His name is Pedro Filucci, an eccentric bachelor with no friends who's been doing this boring job for seventeen years and four months. He'll probably be sitting in a tram until the day he starts collecting his pension. I hold my identification out to him. He studies it at length.

"What do you want?" he asks again.

"Information about the operation of the eléctricos."

"Then you'd be better off talking to somebody at the central office," he grumbles. "I have to work."

"As I understand it, these things practically drive themselves," I reply. "We could go right along to the next stop while I ask you my questions."

"Like I said, señor, the central office could tell you—"

"But I'm asking you. Informally, of course. Or would you prefer to be an official Union witness?"

His pasty complexion goes from paper to ghost. If I name him as a Union witness, he's required to be on call for us as long as we need him. Every citizen knows that being a Union witness means kissing everyday life goodbye for a long while. This case will last a few weeks. He'll have to take a leave of absence from his employer. And no one will pay him so much as a single euro in compensation for it.

"No, no, that won't be necessary, Inspector. What would you like to know?"

"How are the eléctricos steered?"

"These things drive autonomously, with a navigation computer made by Siemens-Peugeot. I really just make the announcements, it sounds more authentic. The eléctricos are also coupled with the Lisbon traffic guidance system."

"And where are the black boxes archived?"

"The live stream runs through the traffic system. That's where Carris grabs a copy and stores it."

"Who's Carris?"

"The Companhia de Carris de Ferro de Lisboa. The company that runs the trams and subways."

I thank him. At the next stop, I get off and call my rental car, still parked in the garage under the Praça Camões. If data from the trams' sensors are first routed through the traffic system for the entire metropolitan region before being archived by the management office, it would've been easy enough to manipulate it. The traffic management data is probably not secured any better than that of an average citizen.

I write a message to Ava and ask her where the tram data in Terry's Lisbon replication came from. A few seconds later the answer comes back: "Carris."

Five minutes later, my SsangYong arrives. Once I've taken a seat, I direct it to drive to the central office. Then I call the Carris office. The telephone receptionist on the other end tells me to please call back on Monday. I make it perfectly clear to him that hindering a Europol investigation could cost him his job. And so he puts me through to command central, where the trams and trains are watched over twenty-four-seven. I'm given the recommendation to call back on Monday. I also clarify the precariousness of his employment to this conversation partner.

The company's building is near the mouth of the Tagus River, not far from the bridge to Almada. As I drive up, a nervous man in his mid-forties is already waiting for me at the entrance, his mouth snapping open and closed as I go to meet him. He looks like someone who talks too much. When I reach him and shake his hand, he's off to the races.

"Chief Inspector, sir, I hope you had a pleasant

trip. We rarely get such a distinguished visitor here, ha ha, normally the local police at most, if a train or a bus is damaged by vandalism. But please, come inside, can I offer you something to drink?"

"No, thank you very much. I don't want to take up too much of your time, Mr. Arocha. Perhaps I could look over the data right away."

"But of course. If you'd please follow me, our data center is located in the lower level. Most of the original data is stored there, and additionally we have extra capacity in a data warehouse, for the older data."

"Where is that located?"

"Isle of Man. At least for now. We're considering moving once the British leave us, so that the data stays in the family, ha ha, if you understand what I mean."

I don't understand anything, but I'm wary of asking about it. It seems Arocha has fallen silent, and I'd like to enjoy this doubtlessly fleeting moment. We get into an elevator that takes us to the lower level. From there, Arocha leads me into a data room, telling me uninteresting details about Carris all the while. This clearly isn't an office where local technicians work, but a special collocation room for the police and RR. It's outfitted with a few tables, monitors, and a huge media wall. It smells as if no one other than the cleaning drone has been here for years.

Arocha says something. The media wall lights up and shows two colorful circles crossed over each other, the Carris logo.

"What exactly would you like to see, Chief Inspector?"

"All data about a tram on line 28, trip 27182-030654, 6:04 p.m."

He calls up the requested data for me. "May I ask what it's about? What are you looking for?"

"That's classified, due to the investigation," I reply, smiling cordially. "Many thanks, Mr. Arocha, that will be all for the moment. Could you please leave me alone now?"

Arocha nods, reluctantly, since he's not only talkative but also curious. Then he leaves the room. I look at the trip data. Carris's system allows me to view the death tram's journey on a 2D map and simultaneously see the sensor data, updated every hundredth of a second, about the outside temperature, number of passengers, speed, and rolling friction as either raw numbers or in the form of charts. I scroll through the data, over and over, but can't find anything worth noting. Eventually I stand up from the amazingly uncomfortable desk chair and stretch. I walk back and forth for a few minutes until the muscles in my lower back have relaxed enough that I can stand up straight again. I activate my specs and call Ava. She answers almost instantaneously.

"Hey, Aart. So, do you have something?"

"Still nothing yet. If I send you the raw data, can you find out if there are discrepancies with Terry's replication?"

"Sure, send it on over."

I direct the Carris computers to send the raw data directly to Ava over a double-secured Europol connection. Then I wait. It takes about five minutes before I hear Ava's voice again.

"Something's not right here. The data Terry got from Carris and the data you sent me don't match up exactly."

"How so?"

"The movement data deviate from each other. How much exactly, I can't say yet. To know that, we'll have to build a new replication based on this data and go in."

"Did you already take another look at the other replications?"

"I'm still working with the one in Westrem. It's insanely expensive to go through so many petabytes and check them for errors. First I have to have the entire crime scene surveyed by drones and mollies again and enter all other applicable data—for example, the Autobahn sensors. Though I do already have something about our tree."

"And? Was it cut down after the accident?"

"Yes. The most interesting detail, though, is that the path of the shot is still correct."

"How can the path of the shot be correct if there's no tree it could have been fired from?"

"Don't know. But I spoke with our clinical forensics team, including with good old Pierre Mochard."

Pierre Mochard was already on the forensics team when crime scene replications were just the obsession of a few crazy criminologists. He still had to crawl through the mud to collect bone splinters and projectiles with tweezers.

"Pierre took another look at Pazzi's injuries and

determined the path of the shot the old-fashioned way, with a pen and a ruler, entirely without Terry's help. And he says the shot must have come from there, from a height of around three-and-a-half meters above the ground, over the tree stump."

"Then our murderer must have been able to fly," I say. I look at Ava. "A drone. A weaponized drone!"

She nods. "If someone used an assassin drone in that kind of bad weather, he must have stayed a certain distance away from the trees, as a buffer. On the west side of the field, the gap in the thicket was a logical shooting position, since from the treetops, the angle would have been too steep. A drone with a targeting computer would also explain the unlikely kill shot."

"And afterward," I say, "someone added the tree to the replication so we wouldn't realize a drone was at play. But why?"

"Probably because the drone took a relatively long time arriving or leaving, and the murderer believed we'd be likely to find it on some recording or other if we went looking for it."

I'll have to apply to the public prosecutor to have the case reopened. Because this proves without a doubt that it couldn't have been the hacker from Hamburg. The entire indictment, after all, was based on Winterfuhr being at the location at the time of the murder. Theoretically, it'd be possible for this to be true, that he piloted the drone on that morning. But why would he leave his cozy ruin in the Hafencity for that? He could have steered it remotely from there just as well. I'd bet my last licorice stick we'll find more manipulations if we take another look at Winterfuhr's digital corona.

"Ava, are there more errors in Terry's replication or the associated files?"

"I'm not totally . . . finished yet."

As she says this, she gives me another one of those we-shouldn't-talk-about-it-over-the-net looks.

I nod. "Okay, got it. I'll be back tomorrow, and on Monday we'll take a look in detail. Then we'll go to Vogel."

Once Ava hangs up, I waste another fifteen minutes trying to wring something out of the Carris data, but without any results worth the effort. When Arocha comes back to see if everything is all right, I'm happy enough to leave the data room. There's nothing else to do here.

After he's given me a wordy farewell and coaxed me into accepting a miniature model of an eléctrico, I go to my hotel. It's still too early for lunch, but I could use a second shower. Lisbon is hotter and muggier than I remember. My blood is just too thick for the south, and retrospectively it's a mystery to me how I managed in Africa for so long.

My hotel is near the Parque da Bela Vista, which sounds better than it is. The time when Union officers stayed in five-star hotels has long since passed. At this point, we're mostly housed in nameless robotels, completely automated hutches without charm or human personnel. It's another reason most of us use replications whenever possible.

I have the rental car drop me off in front of the main entrance, where I cross the deserted lobby. In my room, I take off my suit and go into the bathroom. I don't know how long I let the cold water run over my body, but probably long enough that the hotel will put a separate line item for water usage on my bill. But since I've solved so many cases in the shower, I allow myself this luxury. The only thing that occurs to me, though, is that Tallan still hasn't gotten back to me.

After I've dried off and draped myself in a robe, I lie down on the bed and watch TV. The hotel room isn't set up with media screens or a 360-console; instead, there's an old-fashioned 3D television set. At first, I keep it on a Brazilian gameshow whose participants, more or less naked, are racing across an obstacle course in colorful little wagons. I continue channel surfing and, to my delight, find *Casablanca* on another channel. Not the Korean remake, the original, even if it's been colorized. The movie's already been on for a while. But that doesn't bother me—after all, I've seen it at least twenty times.

I get myself a beer out of the fridge and sit on the edge of the bed with it. Underworld boss Ferrari is trying to shake Rick down for the transit visas, but he's not bothered by it. The best part, as always, is the end, which in my opinion can only be properly appreciated by police officers. Rick shoots the Nazi major Strasser. When the corrupt French police chief Renault arrives with his men, the jig seems to be up. But instead of ordering Rick's arrest, Renault tells his guys: "Major Strasser has been shot. Round up the usual suspects."

I have to think about whether I tried doing the same thing in the Pazzi case. Before I can ruminate on this interesting hypothesis, though, my specs report an incoming call. It's John Tallan.

"Good afternoon, Sir John. Thank you for calling me back."

"Is this about the creeper-feeds?" In the background I can hear the sounds of a city. "My IT manager is on it."

"Yes and no, thank you very much. Ms. Stähler is very helpful. This is about something else that might be related to our investigations. There was a military project implemented by Tallan Consolidated a few years ago."

"And which one would that be?"

"Tares."

A short pause follows, then Tallan says, "One moment." I hear steps and the clattering of a door.

"The Tares project, yes, I remember that, vaguely. It was a long time ago, almost ten years. It was also quite secret. How did you come across it?"

"In connection with the file of a certain parliamentarian we questioned. Unfortunately, I'm not allowed to share the name with you."

Not that I have to.

"Jana Svensson," he murmurs.

"Many of the people involved either can't or apparently don't want to remember this project. And I'd really like to know why."

"The project is under military classification, as I'm sure you already know." He laughs. "They don't want to let you look at the files, right?"

"No, not even the boring parts."

"And why should I help you, Chief Inspector?"

"Tares concerns a case that doesn't have anything to do with your problem, but unfortunately takes up a lot of time. If you help me to move forward with Tares, in return I promise you the highest discretion in the creeper-feed case. As much as possible, we'll also forego a search of your corporation's databases."

"I'd very much like to tell you a thing or two about it, believe me. But breaking the confidentiality clause is no trivial matter."

"Oh, come on, Sir John. The classification was ten years ago. No one will hold that against you now. In any case, you have the best legal minds money can buy."

"All right, then. But don't expect me to go into too much detail." He clears his throat. "Tares was a surveillance project."

"What was being surveilled?"

"Rebels in North Africa. At that time, the Union had massive problems in the solar territories."

"That was a dark time for me. I was one of the people who had to take the rap for it."

"Then you must remember that at a certain point we started to bug everything down there. Clouds of dust-sized mites were sent out over the cities. The first panopto systems were installed to keep tabs on every movement in the Sahara in real time. All communication was intercepted and stored."

"My impression was it didn't add up to much. The first thing every rebel learned was how to hide his true intentions and wipe his data trail. Terrorists aren't dumb."

"No, that they're not. But aspiring terrorists are, in a way."

"I'm not sure I follow."

"The idea behind Tares was this: with enough data about a person, it's possible to draw conclusions about their political views, sexual orientation, or other characteristics. In short, with the help of their corona, it's even possible to read their minds a little bit. And to prognosticate whether they'll become radicalized in the foreseeable future."

"Predications," I say.

"That's it. Thanks to Tares, the RR and military could identify terrorists before even they themselves knew what they'd become in a few months. Before they became cautious, before they subjected their own communication to a kind of self-censorship."

My throat feels dry. I can't get a word out.

"If you'd excuse me now, Chief Inspector? That's everything I can tell you about it. I need to get to an important replication in Rio."

Then he hangs up. I sink back against the pillow and stare up at the ceiling. It's possible Pazzi knew something about Tares he shouldn't have known. But what? I close my eyes. I can guess the answer.

In my mind's eye, I see masked men in desert camo, the bull cocarde on the arms of their jackets, busting open a door in some nameless alleyway in some nameless medina. Despite his mother's wails, they throw a young man onto the ground and tie him up, though he's barely more than a child. In computer-translated Arabic, the colossal blonde milpol officer informs the weeping family that their son has to be brought down to the station because he's under suspicion of terroristic activities, in accordance with the Union regulation on preventative aversion of danger in the case of self-defense, article 7, line 2. The men drag the crying boy outside as he yells over and over in broken French: "I'm innocent. I didn't do anything. I didn't do anything."

I open my eyes. Still in my bathrobe, I sit in front of the minibar and take out of it all the hard liquor I can find, tiny little bottles of Japanese whiskey, French cognac, and Brazilian sugarcane schnapps. First, I drink down the two whiskeys, then take a stab at closing my eyes again. The medina seems to have gone away. But instead I hear Ava quoting from the Bible: "In the time of harvest I will say to the reapers, Gather ye together first the tares, and bind them in bundles to burn them: but gather the wheat into my barn."

A computer program to identify the chaff. Milpol personnel to separate it from the wheat. Personnel like me. What can be done with a person who will, with ninety-five percent likelihood, blow a barracks or checkpoint sky-high within a year? What did they do with all the people we arrested back then?

After I've emptied all the little bottles, ten in total,

I stand up. I manage it, but it takes a big effort. Then I let myself fall backwards on the bed. My stomach, almost empty except for the schnapps, rebels for a moment against the commotion. But then I feel how it all vanishes. Tares, Pazzi, the creeper-feeds, Terry's mendacious hall of mirrors, my time in North Africa, everything dissolves into the alcohol and I sink into a dreamless sleep.

CHAPTER 18

They were somehow able to sneak into my hotel room without being noticed, which is conceivably a bad sign. Normally the robotel doesn't admit anyone who isn't a guest, and even a guest would have to pass at least a half-dozen biometric checkpoints to gain access to this room. It's difficult to deactivate those. That means the two men watching me in disgust from the foot of the bed must be from the police, from an intelligence service, or from a major syndicate.

They both look athletic, in their mid-thirties and wearing dark sport jackets under which their high-caliber pistols in shoulder holsters are visible to a practiced eye. The one on the left, a man with a mustache and a shaved head, growls, "The place smells like schnapps. This guy is wasted."

His associate, who has more hair—but, if his dull gaze is anything to go by, fewer brain cells—shrugs his shoulders and runs his hand through his buzzcut. "Then we'll freshen him up."

I try to sit myself up. It'd be easier without the schnapps potpourri in my veins, but as it is, the room is swimming before my eyes. "Now is generally the best time to shove your badges in my face," I say.

They look at each other for a moment. Baldy smiles icily, while Buzzcut thinks really hard about where he left his identification. It takes a few seconds before it clicks. Then his expression darkens.

I stare at him. "You're the quick one on the team, is that right?"

Instead of answering, he pops me one. He doesn't look very powerful, more like a stripling, the kind of guy whose entire skeleton I could break without breaking a sweat if I had less alcohol in my system. But his appearance is deceptive. He catches me straight on the chin, and when I come to again, he's already schlepping me into the bathroom. He tosses me in the tub, which also hurts. Baldy comes into the bathroom as well, reaches for the showerhead, and starts to spray me down with cold water.

"No more shenanigans. Get dressed, we're going for a little stroll."

"What do you boys want from me, anyway?"

Baldy considers me. "At the moment, just for you to shut your mouth, Westerhuizen."

I get dressed. I'm almost grateful for the ice-cold shower, since it made me halfway sober. That in turn affords me the opportunity to think about how I'm going to get out of this mess. It goes without saying that they relieved me of my specs and my larynx mike, so there's not much for me to do at the moment except follow orders from these gangsters, if it turns out that's what they are. Unfortunately, I've developed another hypothesis.

They both escort me to the ground floor. I feel very

queasy. All the doors open as though held by a ghostly hand, and the receptionist avatar looking out from a media wall wishes us a wonderful afternoon. I'd say the chances of that are extremely low. We take the elevator down to the underground garage where the men's car is parked, a souped-up Tesla Lightning, not exactly an inconspicuous vehicle.

They bundle me into the back of the sports car. I have to bend over quite a bit, since the backseat isn't much more than an upscale place to drop a handbag. Then we pull away. The bald guy drives it himself, with a steering wheel that pops out of the front console. I wonder why they haven't covered my eyes. And I'm worried it isn't a good sign.

We head east, taking the E80 out of the city. Neither of them says a word, and definitely not to me. After a good half hour, we reach a suburban estate located in a little park. The bald guy steers the Lightning through a gate, then along a narrow avenue lined with date palm trees. At the end there's a whitewashed villa, newly renovated but not particularly spectacular to look at. In a city as rich as Lisbon, there are hundreds of similar mansions.

We stop in front of a flight of steps leading to the main entrance. The house is set too far back from the street for there to be any point in calling for help. So I climb the steps like a sacrificial lamb, followed by my two guards. Buzzcut opens the house door via a fingerprint scanner and pushes me through. The villa is decorated in a country casual style, everything inside looking as if it corresponds directly with the virtual catalogue of an interior designer. It doesn't look as if real people actually live here. The visible portions of the house are likely a façade for something else that takes place in secret.

"Downstairs," growls one of the men.

They bring me to a windowless room about forty meters square. It's tiled. A plush wingback chair stands in one corner, looking out of place. When I see the man sitting in it, I know it's going to be a very bad afternoon for me. It's Ververke. He doesn't look happy.

Piet Ververke, Lieutenant Colonel of the Récupération de Renseignements, is forty-five, the same age as me. Since he's significantly wealthier, though, he looks at least ten years younger, thanks to various rejuvenation therapies. He wears an expensive slate-gray double-breasted suit with a blue cravat, no specs, no accessories. His sky-blue eyes look at me sadly. He indicates I should take a seat on the only other available place, a stark aluminum chair.

"What do you all want from me, Piet?" I ask.

"For you to finally keep your nose out of things that don't concern you."

"Özal and Vogel have told me something similar already. Is this about Tallan?"

He smiles mildly. "Hmm, for someone sitting with the shadow police in an interrogation chamber you ask an astonishing number of questions, Arthur."

Ververke makes a careless hand gesture, at which one of the two men, whom I can no longer see, comes at me from behind. The force of the impact throws me forward, sending me toppling off the chair and falling hard against the tile floor. Before I can stand by myself, the two men yank me up by the arms and dump me on the chair again.

In the meantime, Ververke has stood up and lit himself a cigarette.

"Listen to me very carefully now. You will not move around in the mirror space again. You will not carry out any more research about Tares. And you will not speak with anyone about it either. Did you get all that?"

I hurry to nod. All the same, a fist comes from somewhere outside my line of sight, coming into contact with my right cheek. Everything spins around. Someone yanks my upper body upright so I don't tip off the chair.

"Understood?"

"Yes, got it," I gasp.

Ververke, still smoking, looks me over from a few meters' distance. "Hmm, I hope so. But I'm still not sure, Arthur. You're as stubborn as a goddamned mule, always have been. But I want to help you, for old times' sake."

I glance up and look him in the eyes. "I'm on pins and needles, Piet."

"I'll make it easy for you. Your Internal Affairs will issue a motion to suspend you tomorrow. Because of the shooting in the Zoniënwoud, hmm? On suspicion of excessive use of force, not to mention your refusal to cooperate with the review."

"What? That's all bullshit."

"Of course it is. It's all made up, we falsified some evidence here and there. But as a result of my pulling you out of action for a few weeks, it'll be easier for you to keep your mouth shut. You'll have a chance to avoid piling up any more shit that might cost you your head."

"You wanted to get me out of the way before, in the Zoniënwoud. What's changed?"

Ververke shakes his head. He looks offended. "Slipshod work, that wasn't us. If it'd been us, you'd be dead now."

"Who was it then?"

"Probably the Britskis, since you're after them because of these creeper-feeds. How should I know?"

He throws his cigarette on the ground and uses the tip of his foot to nudge it in the direction of the drain in the middle of the room. "I have to go now. Think about what I told you. It's your last chance."

"Can I leave now? Your boys have already made your message loud and clear."

"Hmm, not yet."

He saw right through me, but it was at least worth a try. Just like me, Ververke was in Milpol down south for years. After bullet wounds and landmines, one of the biggest hazards of the job is the likelihood of being kidnapped and tortured by guerillas. Every officer goes through a sophisticated course in pain before he's sent to the desert. As a result of this conditioning, I can hold out against any number of things. The kicks and punches dished out by the two RR guys were barely more than pinpricks to me. If things are going to get really uncomfortable, they'll have to take it to the next level. Above all, though, they'll have to take their time.

Ververke knows this. As the door latches behind him, the bald guy is already tying me to the aluminum chair with plastic zip ties. In the meantime, Buzzcut retrieves a folding table and a case full of instruments from a corner of the room.

These two don't want to kill me. But in the coming hours, I wish over and over that they would. I think I even go so far as to beg for it.

CHAPTER 19

When I come to again, I'm not sure where I am at first. I'm lying in a room, on a mattress, my torturers seem to have dumped my lifeless body here before they made themselves scarce. Everything hurts, and I seem to have a slight fever.

Then I realize I'm still in my hotel room. I look at the clock. It's 8:11 p.m.

I lift myself up on my forearms and look at my bare chest. Someone's attached an escape patch over my heart. The little green LED on the outside indicates it's already been activated. Clearly the patch only just released the monoaminoxidase cocktail to neutralize the hypno in my brain and bring me back out of the mirror space.

I sit up completely and take the replication headset off my head. Slowly, I stand up and stagger to the mirror. I look over my unscathed naked body in disbelief. I see no brand marks, no cuts, no welts. Even the area between my legs is unharmed, although they, although they . . .

I run into the bathroom and vomit over and over. Once my stomach and my head have calmed down somewhat, I get dressed and pack my bag. I really wanted to fly home tomorrow afternoon. I wanted to take a look at the Port and Douro Wine Institute and take a stroll through the Bairro Alto. But now nothing strikes me as more urgent than catching the late flight to Brussels.

I ignore the robotel receptionist and her question about whether I've had a pleasant stay, making a beeline for the parking garage. If Ververke wasn't making empty threats—which, after four hours in a torture chamber, I can safely rule out—I'll have to give up my badge first thing tomorrow. For now, though, I'm still a Europol investigator, and so I tell the car to drive to the airport as fast as possible.

At the airport, I zip through the Express Check-In reserved for travelers with Union passports. The sooner I get to the gate, the more time I'll have to get drunk all over again at the bar in the waiting area. A voice in my head whispers this isn't a good idea, that alcohol has already gotten me into trouble once today. But who listens to voices anyway.

At the gate, there's a branch of Copacabana Cocktails. Better than nothing. I sit down on one of the stools and the bartender sizes me up. "You need something strong, right?"

I nod wearily.

"Whiskey? Vodka?"

"Do you have genever?"

"We have Bols."

"Give me a double."

He brings me a chilled glass filled with a colorless liquid. I resist the impulse to toss back the schnapps in one go, and instead sip it carefully. When I put the glass back down, I see a drop running slowly from the surface down to the bottom, leaving a viscous trail in its wake.

When they let us on board the aircraft an hour later, the captain shares with us that we'll be staying on the tarmac for at least another half hour due to "mechanical difficulties." With the help of my specs, I piggyback on a police feed from Lisbon. The difficulty seems to be that a group by the name of "Liberators of the Sahara" carried out a bloodbath at a shopping center in Porto a few hours ago. In light of this, the Portuguese air traffic security are checking everything two and three times over before they allow flights to take off.

It's almost ten o'clock before we finally move in the direction of the runway. Shortly after we've taken off, Ava calls me.

"Hello, Aart. Should I pick you up from the airport?"

"Not necessary, my Mercedes will get me. What's new?"

"Quite a bit."

She has that look again, the one that says, "Not on the phone."

"Do you want to come back over to my place now?"

"Can it wait until tomorrow, Ava? I had a really bad day."

But then I remember that by tomorrow I might be a Chief Inspector emeritus, and Ava won't be allowed to tell me anything about the investigation. "Forget what I just said, Ava. I'll come to your place straight from the airport."

"You got it."

I hang up, lean back, and close my eyes. I drift off immediately. Fortunately, I don't dream about the guys from the RR, but about a city in the desert that looks familiar to me, although it seems strangely old-fashioned. I sit in a nightclub drinking an Americano with lots of ice. The other patrons look as if they come from the previous century. The men wear wide ties instead of cravats, the women lacy blouses. Clouds of blue smoke billow through the establishment. In one corner sits a group of loud Union soldiers wearing their dark blue dress uniforms, apparently celebrating something. One of them sits down at the piano and the men begin to belt out "Joy Thou Glorious Spark of Heaven." The rest of the patrons look at them with hostility. It looks as though a fight will break out at any minute. Then the Embraer 797 touches down at the Brussels airport with a jolt, the squealing of the tires tearing me from my dreams.

My Mercedes is waiting at the exit. I order it to extend the steering wheel, since the episode in Westrem has made me wary. For the first time in years, I drive the car myself on the Autobahn, taking the exit for Ava's neighborhood. I park in front of the house and run up to the door in the drizzling rain.

Ava opens the door. She looks at me with tired eyes, dark circles visible below them. In her right hand she holds her analyst's glasses, indicating that she was still working, though it's almost midnight.

"It's good you came by, Aart. Even if you look like you've been through a meat grinder."

I can feel the sweat building on the nape of my

neck in light of this observation, but I don't say anything in reply. Instead I follow Ava into the living room, where an oriental mezze has been laid out on the dining room table. It covers almost the entire table, with tiny candles and a carafe of red wine standing in between.

"Are we expecting more people, Ava?"

"No, just you and me. But I thought maybe you'd be hungry. And anyway, chopping vegetables calms me down, so I always make way too much."

"And what has you so stressed out?" I ask. "Our two cases?"

She nods. We sit down and eat in silence. Although we don't say so aloud, it's clear we won't talk about the case in Ava's unsecured living room. Someone could be listening in. It's possible some RR agent is in the mirror space at this very moment, standing near our table and eavesdropping. Maybe he even sat down on one of the empty chairs and is trying Ava's tabbouleh.

I decide not to let this mental image spoil my appetite. After I've polished off a large portion of mezze, I say, "Where?"

"Come with me. Sergio, the Brazilian guy who owns the house, had a panic room put in. We won't be disturbed there."

She stands up and goes into the hallway. I follow her. We head to the basement via a flight of creaking wooden stairs. Ava stops in front of a thick steel door and begins to type on a keypad on the wall.

"Why would someone in the most secure city in

the Union build a panic room? Is this guy paranoid?"

"Sergio is from São Paulo. All affluent people have them there, because of the gangs. He didn't want to go without one here, force of habit."

"Apparently money was no object."

She shakes her head. "Not really. His father is a big shot at Solobras Shell."

The bunker opens with a hiss. An airlock stands behind it. We walk inside and Ava bolts the door after us. Vents hidden in the floor and ceiling come to life, and a current of warm air sets my pants and cravat flapping. After about a minute there's another hissing sound, and the inner door of the airlock opens. Behind it is a small room, not even fifteen square meters, with whitewashed walls and a lighted ceiling made out of media screens. It doesn't look like any of the shelters we had in the military; it looks much cozier. There's a three-piece furniture suite made of leather, two armchairs, a small workspace with a media table and chair, additional shelves with actual books, and a big refrigerator. There's even an espresso machine on hand.

Ava indicates I should sit. I take a seat on the sofa and watch as she prepares two espressos in her own graceful way. After she's set the cups in front of me, she opens a browser on one of the walls and makes some kind of adjustments on a menu.

"This room is physically difficult to access and is equipped with a separate HVAC system and filters against biological weapons," she clarifies. "And it has other advantages, too."

"For example?"

"The airlock will have sucked away ninety-five percent of all mites that might have been swarming around us. In addition to that, the room is covered in a non-ferromagnetic metal."

"A Faraday cage?"

"Exactly. It shields us from electromagnetic fields. There are also thousands of tiny senders in the paneling that continually produce white noise, a sort of disruptive radio broadcast. It's like we're whispering when a heavy metal band is giving a live concert right next door."

"That means no one can keep us under surveillance? What if someone bugged the room right from its initial installation?"

"You weren't this paranoid before, Aart."

"There were also no unexplainable apparitions in my replications before, and I could trust our police computer."

Ava closes the browser on the wall and sits beside me on the couch. "I'm afraid that's the crux of the matter."

"What did you find out?"

She sips her espresso. "Something isn't right with Terry, with his replications. To start with, the case in Lisbon."

"Milar's accident."

"If it actually was one. I took another look at the crime scene replication from back then and compared it with the original data from Carris."

"And?"

"Do you remember the sick pigeon? It was the reason Milar didn't make it over the tracks in time and got hit by the tram. I'm quite certain someone added it in after the fact."

"How did you find that out?"

"You know how a few days ago we just so happened to learn that the panopto-surveillance system in Brussels is continuously active now?"

"Yes, because of the elevated threat level in advance of the constitution vote."

"It was an obvious next step to assume these measures don't affect just Brussels, but other large cities as well. I checked into it. Lisbon, Paris, Berlin, Warsaw: high-definition pictures have been shot in real time in all of them for about three months now."

"What exactly is being recorded here?"

"It's always the entire region around the city, as a video, from a height of about seventy-five-hundred meters. The resolution is so good it shows pieces of gum on the pavement and people, cars, or animals in the same detail. Besides the topography, all movements inside the city were also collected. The complete history was stored and can be analyzed when needed. It doesn't happen automatically, though, since the amount of data is so absurdly huge even Terry wouldn't be able to handle it."

She leans back and exhales audibly. "It wasn't difficult to call up the clip from the Praça Camões and take a look at the seconds in question individually, frame-by-frame. The tram is there, Milar too, just like all the other objects we saw in the crime scene replication. Only the pigeon was missing. I found something else in its place."

"And that was?"

"The thing that killed Milar. Here, take a look for yourself."

Ava takes a papyrus tablet out of the inside pocket of her track jacket and rolls it open. Then she plays a video. It's an aerial view of the west side of the Praça Camões apparently taken directly from the panopto system. From this bird's eye view, I can see Milar, a tiny dot with swinging arms. He crosses the street while the tram draws closer from above. It looks as though he's correctly assessed the speed of the tram and will cross the tracks in plenty of time. But then the tram speeds up suddenly. It leaps forward and runs over Milar.

"I analyzed it," Ava says. "The tram normally travels at twenty-five to thirty kilometers per hour. And then it suddenly accelerated to sixty."

"Was that the driver's doing?"

"I'd be more willing to bet someone hacked the tram's software. The eléctricos are normally capped at fifty kilometers an hour, you see? Even if the driver wanted to, he wouldn't have been able to accelerate that much. That would only work via direct access to the tram's computer. Later, someone put the brakes back on in the replication and inserted the pigeon."

"What was the driver's testimony?" I ask.

"Nothing."

"What do you mean, nothing?"

"He suffered a severe shock and wasn't coherent

for days afterward. And then," I can hear Ava sighing, "he committed suicide."

"Of course."

So that means we have two dead MEPs. And I'd bet my service weapon that this Swiss guy's golfing accident would also turn out to be a hushed-up murder if we looked over the raw data, not to mention the tram driver. If Ava has even more bad news coming, I might have to start looking at my forthcoming suspension as a positive development.

"What about Pazzi?" I ask.

"Hard to say, since there's no panopto data in Westrem and also no drones that happened to be present and might have been able to record something. We only have what Terry was able to collect. I just have a feeling."

While we've been watching the video on the papyrus tablet, Ava's moved closer to me. She's sitting cross-legged beside me and her knee keeps touching my thigh.

"What kind of feeling, Ava?"

"That something else was added in, not just the tree."

"The assassin drone?"

"Yes, but not only that. After all, we still don't know what Pazzi was actually doing there. The most likely explanation would be that he was meeting someone."

"And you think he or she was later airbrushed out?"

"Yes, although that's just a feeling. I still haven't

found anything in the data. It's difficult, I've . . . I've been having problems with Terry."

"Lovers' quarrel?"

"You really can be dumb sometimes, Aart."

"Sorry. What kind of problems?"

"Ever since this new version has been in operation, Terry functions differently."

"You mean his character is different?"

"No, his software architecture. Before, it was easier for analysts to access his raw data. That was necessary, too, since at the end of the day he's an idiot, though admittedly an idiot with lots of computing power. But since the new version of Terry is supposed to be more autonomous and self-sufficient, it's also not as easy to control. It directs itself."

She looks unhappy.

I smile at her. "Sometimes I don't understand exactly what you mean."

"It's like with cars, Aart. With the old vehicles, you could still adjust everything yourself. I used to have this ancient Golf, a 2019 model. You could plug in your tablet and modify the vent controls or adjust the individual tire pressures. It was even possible to open the hood. But in today's models, not only is the hood closed tight, but all the interfaces, too. No one knows what goes on inside. It's the same thing with the new Terry. It's no longer possible to reconstruct how he came to a conclusion."

"Very handy for someone who wants to falsify or erase evidence. Any other kind of irregularities? Or progress toward solving . . . anything?"

"The creeper-feeds. We still keep finding them."

"More and more video clips."

"Yes. Terry's search routines are still combing through the net and have found five thousand data files by this point."

"That many?"

"That number is from this morning, so there may be even more by now. I'd bet he'll end up finding even more. They seem to be scattered across the entire net."

Özal will be thrilled. All of the affected people will eventually have to be informed about the damage to their data integrity. Given that there are tens of thousands of cases, this matter won't stay under the radar for long. The media will rip Tallan to shreds.

"Did you already tell Tallan's people about this?"

"No, I wanted to talk with you first, Aart."

"Tallan was very cooperative. I'll send him a message as soon as we're out of this cage. But I have to tell you a few other things first."

I look at Ava. I'd prefer to keep everything far away from her, but that won't work. And then I tell her about my impending suspension. I tell her about Tares, about software utilized in the protectorates to separate the wheat from the chaff. She listens without asking questions, her dark-brown eyes looking at me with concern. I tell her only the most important details of my encounter with Ververke, sparing her everything I can. And then I tell Ava now might be a good time to take that trip to Sardinia she's been talking about for months.

She wrinkles her brow. "You want to give up now?"

"I don't want anything to happen to you."

She takes my hand. "I can take care of myself. Or you could come to Sardinia with me, it's part of Southern Italy, so it's outside Union territory. We'd be able to go underground there for a while. I know a godforsaken beach close to Zinnibiri with only four bungalows."

"That won't work, Ava. I'd be putting you in danger. There's something big going on here, and I know the RR. They'll stop at nothing. It'd be better if you stayed out of this. Away from me."

"That," she answers quietly, "is what you're always telling me."

Instead of answering her, I take her in my arms. We sit for a while in a close embrace. I feel Ava starting to caress my neck. My hand runs through her thick hair as our lips move toward each other. And then we're kissing. I'd almost forgotten how that feels. I can hardly believe it's been eight years since the last time—it always felt like cheating to me, kissing a woman other than Janet. But as Ava's mouth opens and first our lips touch, then our tongues, it doesn't feel like cheating at all.

I can feel Ava's hardened nipples pressing against my chest through my shirt. A voice in my head says it'd be better to shift to a lower gear after such a long, self-imposed celibacy and such a horrifying day. But it's already too late for that, we've waited for each other too long, and time is running away from us besides. This might be the only night we have left, and we're alone, more alone than we're ever likely to be again. And so we tear each other's clothes from our bodies and make love, on the sofa, on the floor, in a cage made out of aluminum and ceramic, far from the all-too-inquisitive world outside.

CHAPTER 20

I leave Ava's house the next morning. I'm guessing Internal Affairs is already waiting for me and might even show up as soon as I arrive at my apartment. Even though it's Sunday, I can't imagine Crolo would let a chance to personally take my service weapon away from me slip through his fingers.

I'd really like to speak with Vogel one more time before I'm finally withdrawn from circulation, and I ask Terry to locate the Commissioner.

"Commissioner Vogel is in his office at this time, Chief Inspector."

"On a Sunday morning?" I ask in disbelief.

"Could you rephrase the question, Chief Inspector?"

I ignore Terry. Rumor has it Vogel only needs a total of four hours of sleep per night, besides which he has neither family nor hobbies. In light of that, maybe it's not so implausible he'd go into the office on Sundays, and definitely not considering the heap of trouble brewing at the moment.

I go to the Palais, making my way to the upper floor of the building completely without incident, a sure sign my suspension hasn't gone through yet. Upstairs, I march past the Union landmarks, the Temple, the Eiffel Tower, and Buckingham Palace, which will have to be switched out for another tourist attraction in not quite four weeks. I think a burning solar tower or a killer drone would be fitting.

At the end of the hallway, the doors glide open, providing a view into the office. As always, Vogel is sitting in his servo chair; he has his specs on and is gesturing in the air. He's stuffing himself full of information, his everyday morning ritual. A dozen windows are open on the wall, playing news videos, feeds from Europol and Interpol, and clips from the panopto surveillance. I see a live feed of a police raid in Budapest, in another video I can make out a burning building, probably in Madrid, possibly in the government district.

Vogel doesn't seem particularly pleased that I'm interrupting him. On the other hand, he never looks particularly pleased about anything.

"Good morning, Commissioner."

"Morning, Westerhuizen." He points to a chair for visitors. "On a Sunday? Something urgent, I take it."

"Several urgent somethings."

He folds his hairy paws in front of his belly and releases a heavy, audible sound, but doesn't say anything. Then he states, loudly and distinctly, "Whisper mode. All systems on. Now we can talk without being disturbed."

I look at him. "Do you know about my impending suspension?"

"What?"

"Apparently Internal Affairs is going to order my

suspension later today. Because of excessive use of violence."

"Those bastards! Where'd you get this information from?"

I smile grimly. "From a friendly agency."

"Those sons of bitches!" Vogel is invariably foul-tempered, but he almost never swears. The fact that he's doing it now, especially in connection with the RR, is a clear indication he's on the cusp of an explosion. He stares at me for a few seconds, while his hands creep along the desk like tarantulas, on the hunt for something they can grab. The first victim is a pen, which refuses to yield at first but then cracks and bursts apart.

"Is this because of Count Krolock's crap? Do the guys at the RR have something to do with this suspension business?"

"Probably the latter. But I'm afraid no one will be able to prove it."

Vogel throws the pen carelessly away and starts to strangle a notebook instead. "I'll see what I can do for you. I'm about to get on a call with Müller, she should call her people off. Why are they after you anyway?"

"The RR recommended I not say anything about it. They were very . . . emphatic."

He stands up, a sign of highest agitation. Vogel's face is scarlet red, his teeth bared. "It's because of this Tares story. It can't be anything else. I should've known! You poked a hornets' nest."

"Explain it to me."

Vogel waddles around his desk and stands near

my chair. He fills almost my entire field of vision, a hundred and forty kilos of furious blubber. The Commissioner folds his hands behind his back and looks at the ceiling.

"Many people are of the opinion the shadow police have become too powerful in the past few years. The Solar Wars made these guys into major players, and now they're everywhere. And since the invention of the mirror space, they can look over any of our shoulders, twenty-four hours a day. But that'll change soon."

"Because of the new constitution?"

"That's right. Everyone's been fighting for months over how much power the Commission should keep, if the national states will be rendered completely powerless, how the voting rules in the government should be reformed, over the institutional balance. But the small changes in the appendix are even more interesting, hundreds of pages of legal jargon almost no one has read through. According to the final draft, the RR will be put in front of a parliamentary supervisory committee. Not a toothless kangaroo court like before, but a board of hand-selected MEPs. The inspectors are supposed to get access to GORGON, and in the process all RR files, all their operations. And then we'll clip their wings."

"That means the RR is against the new constitution. But what does that have to do with Tares?"

"The RR headquarters in Bonn is afraid a few of their less-honorable activities will come to light right at the moment when Parliament is discussing whether or not the intelligence service should be massively shrunk and taken in hand. And Tares is one of the darkest chapters in the RR's history."

I already know what's coming next. I've known it ever since my discussion with Tallan. If I'm being honest with myself, I've known it for years, since my time in North Africa.

"If I know you, I'm guessing you've already found out about it, in spite of all the red tape and dead ends?"

I nod. "Partly. The RR carried out complete surveillance in the occupied territories. Then a computer identified possible troublemakers with the help of predictive algorithms. And then they were taken into custody."

"Correct. But that's the unremarkable part. When the boys in Milpol—I guess that means you, too—got the signal from the military courts to arrest someone with an unfortunate predictive criminal record, that's when the problems actually started."

"The moral problem that these people really hadn't done anything in the first place?"

Vogel laughs humorlessly. "You're forgetting that we lost over five thousand soldiers in the associated territories the year Tares was first put in place. And you're forgetting the RR carried out these operations. They sidestepped the moral question of what percentage of the detainees were innocent and would continue to be so in the future."

"How many innocent people do you think there were?"

He looks at me piercingly. "Legally speaking, they were all innocent, at least at the time of their arrest. If we leave that out of the conversation, I'd bet the predictions were correct in eighty-five to ninety percent of the cases."

"Still too many innocents."

Vogel shakes his head. "You're right, but that's not what I'm getting at. What I'm getting at is the incredibly large number of suspects. You see, for example, if Scotland Yard wanted to, they could routinely identify all citizens whose predictive criminal records contained a murder. Could be thousands every year. They'd then have to be locked away preventatively. Morally and legally questionable, but logistically possible."

Vogel leans toward me and looks me in the eyes. "Apart from a few Scottish separatists, Great Britain is a prosperous, peaceful country. But how many murderers does a predictive computer cough up for a region where war has been the order of the day for years?"

"Tens of thousands," I say.

"Possibly. No one knows how many it was anymore. And no one knows where these people went, the ones who were never brought in front of a court, not even a second-tier military court. According to the rumors, there were special prisons on the Arabian peninsula."

"But everything there is still contaminated by radiation," I reply.

"I know. None of it can be proven, but it could

finally come to light now. If it did, the RR would be finished. And that's why the gloves are coming off."

"Is it possible the RR also has Pazzi on its conscience?"

He looks bewildered. "Explain it to me."

I tell him what Ava found out: that Pazzi's, as well as Milar's and possibly Füßli's, crime scene replications were tampered with.

"And, in your opinion, what's the RR's motive, Westerhuizen?"

"All three were involved in the same scandal, the Golden Trail corruption affair. That's also a largely unprovable rumor. But if the story's true, then about ten years ago, the three dead MEPs helped John Tallan's company get an enormously important Union weapons contract: the Tares project. At first, I'd have guessed Tallan was getting rid of co-conspirators involved in the affair. But why now, after so many years? Especially because he made sure at the time that no journalist would ever conduct research into the case again. The German news magazine that published the Golden Trail story went under because of it. Not to mention Tallan had enough time to wipe away all data traces. But maybe Pazzi, Füßli, and Milar weren't dangerous co-conspirators in Tallan's eyes, but in the eyes of the RR. Maybe they knew secret details about Tares. Maybe they stayed silent for years out of fear that their involvement in a corruption scandal would still become public. But now, since Parliament is trying to put the intelligence service on a tight leash, knowledge of a long-forgotten military project is suddenly a weapon that could be used against Yvonne Müller. And the representatives are suddenly an incalculable risk for the RR."

Vogel walks a few paces, looking out the window in the direction of the Commission Palais. "Your theory is plausible, unfortunately. It's just as plausible that the RR manipulated the replications. The intelligence service is one of a very small number of agencies that have an analytical computer on par with Terry: they'd be in a place to do so from a technical standpoint."

He turns himself to face me. "We're not going to contest your suspension."

"But—"

"Listen up, Westerhuizen. This is a political game now, not an investigation. Let the RR think they've won. Clean out your desk and look sad while you do it. I'm about to speak with the Commission president. And afterward, I want to see your analyst, what's her name again—"

"Ava Bittman."

"—I want Bittman to come and see me, around one o'clock. You should come too, if you haven't already been withdrawn from circulation by then. The chief prosecutor will also be there."

"What are you planning, Commissioner?"

"I theoretically trust the anti-eavesdropping features in my office, but I'd prefer not to say everything, only this much: I'm going to set off a bomb, possibly two. And the RR should consider themselves lucky if they're still around afterward."

He comes over to me and claps me encouragingly on the shoulder. He's never done that before. "Don't worry too much about it. In two weeks at most, you'll be back in your office. And now leave me alone. I have a war to unleash."

CHAPTER 21

After my conversation with Vogel, I tell Ava the Commissioner would like to see her. Then I take a seat in my office. I don't have to wait long. At 10:17 a.m., Count Krolock appears, flanked by two colleagues in their traditional garb. Without knocking, he waltzes in and recites his sentence: "Chief Inspector Arthur van der Westerhuizen, in the name of the Internal Affairs of the European State Police, I hereby relieve you of your duty until further notice, according to Paragraph 37b of the Police Code of Conduct. The decision takes effect today at 11:00 a.m. Central European Time."

The two uniformed colleagues watch me warily, as if they're waiting for me to pull out my H&K and shoot Crolo down. I'd prefer not to know what he told them about me. Instead, I stand up, walk around my desk, and sit on the edge.

"Why?" I ask.

Crolo murmurs something. The written statement provided by the public prosecutor appears on my specs, documenting the reasons for my suspension. It states that one of the amateur killers in the Zoniënwoud indicated he wanted to speak with me before I shot him down. Furthermore, there are "numerous existing indications" that I didn't have to shoot all five of them. Should I only have taken one of them out? And then just calmly looked around to see how the others were taking the demise of their colleague? I swipe the document away and try to remain calm, even forcing a small smile to my lips.

"And where do we go from here, Crolo?"

I can see on his face that he'd hoped for more surprise and consternation on my part.

He needs a few seconds to collect himself before he answers, "I'll take your service weapon now."

I give it to him.

"My specs?"

"You're permitted to continue using them for a maximum of twenty-four hours, without the Europol features, of course. Then they'll deactivate automatically. Your access to Terry and your vehicle has already been revoked, your entry clearance for the Palais lapses at 10:45 a.m. on the dot. In the next few days, possibly as soon as tomorrow, you'll receive a new appointment for the outstanding crime scene inspection, and a hearing through the Committee for Internal Investigation. If you ignore the summons," he pauses for effect and looks sinister, "I'll have you dragged back here in handcuffs."

I stand up and get my coat. "That won't be necessary, I'll cooperate. Anything else, Crolo?"

"You may take any essential personal effects with you now."

I stick my bag of licorice under my arm and look at the two cops expectantly. "Shall we, gentlemen?"

Crolo is just about to lose his cool. "Don't you have anything to say, Westerhuizen?"

"To you? Not really, no."

I walk past him and allow myself to be led out by the two officers. I stay standing on the stairs out front for a moment, then walk through the driving rain across the Jacobsplein in the direction of Regentschapsstraat. The place under my left shoulder where I'd normally keep my service weapon feels strangely empty.

Once I've arrived at the Poelaertplein, I look back at the Palais de Justice, whose enormous gilded cupola stretches out into the Brussels sky and almost seems to scrape the heavy-hanging clouds. The washed-out façade, unrenovated for decades, is the color of bleached bone.

According to my specs, it's 10:58 a.m. I take my white-and-blue ID badge from the inner pocket of my jacket and look at it until I hear the ringing of the bells at Nôtre Dame de Sablon nearby. The media screen on my badge begins to change colors, the hologram of my head and the background both taking on a dark red tint. In the middle, the word "SUSPENDED" appears in bright yellow letters. I put the badge away again and trudge on in the direction of my favorite haunt.

Since nothing better occurs to me, I hole up at a corner table in the Café Amsterdam, drinking black tea and reading the paper on one of the large-format media screens I picked up at the entrance. They're made out of coarse, crumpled material. This retro texture is supposed to be reminiscent of the cheap paper the news used to be printed on. I read *Le Monde du Figaro*, *Delors*, and also a British daily paper before I turn to the table and ask it to show me a selection of new episodes of the Johnny Random show.

A notice pops up on the screen stating that this program is unfortunately not available in my country.

"News about Johnny Random," I say.

The table shows me a list of articles. It looks as though Vogel and Özal really meant business. One *VNN* report states that Random was accused of illegal hacking activities and the European Information Agency revoked his journalism license and blocked his feeds across the entire Union. Several citizens' rights groups and a few leftist parliamentarians are already protesting these "censorship measures." Allegedly, some activists are even trying to circumvent the ban through guerrilla actions, though they aren't described in any detail.

It's not surprising that they'd only touch on the subject via the official channels. I tell the table to show me what the droggers have to say about this topic and prepare myself for the flood that's about to wash over me.

"Four screens, refresh every fifteen seconds, Union-wide results, with source labels."

Four video feeds appear on the table; they're from Madrid, Gdansk, Cologne, and Toulouse. In the Castilian capital, a few hundred people in the Plaza Mayor are demonstrating against the broadcasting ban, the same in Gdansk. A drone video from Cologne shows a black woman in a track suit kneeling beside a case of spray paint. She's surrounded by passersby who are more than willing to take the cans off her hands.

The media table keeps showing more and more new videos. The majority include no commentary and haven't been edited. They're raw, unfiltered photos, so it takes me awhile before I understand what's happening out there right now. These white, unlabeled cans of spray paint are visible everywhere, the same kind the woman in Cologne was handing out. Young people are standing in front of walls and spraying them with paint, though not with classical graffiti. Nobody's writing "Free Johnny Random" or anything like that. Instead they're painting the walls with a symbol I'm already familiar with: white rectangles in all conceivable sizes.

I stop the videos and mark the rectangles on them with my pointer finger.

"Show me more feeds with these in them. With location and date. Refresh every ten seconds."

The table does as I tell it. I watch the rapidly changing videos in fascination for a few minutes. They're coming from all corners of the Union, and they confirm what I already suspected: these rectangles didn't just show up suddenly in the past two days. The whole thing started almost exactly two weeks ago, without anyone thinking anything of it. In the meantime, they've shown up all over the place. White squares in the Marais district in Paris, in the historic district in Milan, on a park bench in Düsseldorf.

"Table, are there official posts about this graffiti story?"

A video from "Drogging Brussels" comes up on the table. It shows the spray painters, as I've already seen multiple times, in this case at the Brussels fish market and at a train station, maybe the Noordstation. Two moderators discuss the images.

"And what exactly is happening here, Paul?"

"That isn't any normal graffiti, Veronique. These cans contain a sprayable polymer. As soon as they're dry, after about ten seconds, you're left with a media screen, receivers and all."

"Super wicked! Not exactly cheap, but this media spray can theoretically be bought anywhere, right?"

"True, though the stuff being used here must be a custom-build. According to our research, this special spray formula contains a receiver integrated and preset to a specific, secure net protocol."

"And what does it receive?"

"Right now, nothing. The whole world is waiting for these rectangles to be activated and show images. Maybe it has something to do with the forbidden Johnny Random show."

"But I thought the cops had completely blocked *Random Discoveries* on the Union net?"

"That they did. You can no longer receive it via specs, 360-TVs, or other devices, since Random's feeds are caught and wiped clean at all net nodes. But all of the spray screens are unlicensed, making tens of thousands of tiny pirate broadcasters. The data stream to this media graffiti would be difficult to block, since it would be the equivalent of the cops turning off the entire civilian net, Union-wide."

"But how can one man make something like this happen?"

"No idea, Veronique. It's just a rumor, after all. The latest episode of the Johnny Random show is supposed to air this evening at 7:00 p.m. We'll know more then. If the graffiti lights up with Johnny's face, then our suspicions were correct. It's just as likely, though, that the whole thing is only guerrilla marketing for some shitty Korean energy bar."

"That would not be wicked, Paul! But if it is actually Random's doing, won't the cops try to stop it? It's still an illegal broadcast."

"And how would they do that, Veronique? They'd have to remove thousands of pieces of graffiti."

"Or keep the audience away from them."

"Since when is it illegal to stare at a white wall? In any case, we've ordered a few extra drones to keep watch on these pirate screens all across the city and stream the events—live, only here on 'Drogging Brussels!' And now on to another story: hermaphrodite surgeries are becoming ever more affordable in the Union. Will the big sex trend make its way from Brazil over to us next? Veronique, what's your take? Would you like to have something else to go with your hoo-ha? Maybe a thick, fat—"

I turn off the feed and debate whether I should call Ava. But she's probably already been told about my suspension and our communication is likely being closely monitored. I don't want to cause her any problems. And I'm worried RR agents are still hanging around me via the mirror space. One of them is probably sitting on the other side of the café and watching me without even having to hide himself behind a newspaper like they used to do in my favorite old films.

Besides, if I know Ava, her stable of retrieval programs has reported the newest developments to her already, and she's having Terry keep an eye on all of it. If I end up getting my job back, I'll be able to watch the replications of it.

I turn the table off and stay seated for a while, staring out at the rain and trying not to brood about the abrupt end of my career. To take my mind off it, I think about Ava's curves.

CHAPTER 22

Since they took away my Mercedes, I use the metro to get to Beursplein in the early evening and walk in the direction of the Dansaert district, at the end of Kartuizerstraat. There, the alleyway opens up to a beautiful plaza, where the absolutely heinous prewar buildings were torn down a few years ago and replaced by new buildings in the New Nouveau style. The main attractions, though, are the numerous bars and restaurants. Asian and South American tourists who want to eat mussels and frites seldom come here, sticking instead to the joints around the Grote Markt. That's good. I don't like mussels and definitely not tourists.

On my left, there's a brasserie named Jansen & Janssen. I sit down at one of the covered outdoor tables and read the daily specials, more from habit than anything else, since I don't really have much of an appetite. I order a beer from the waitress. I take a gulp and watch the goings-on in the plaza. It's a beautiful summer evening, 25.3 degrees Celsius, hardly any wind, only light spitting rain falling almost like an aerosol spray. The Bloemnhofplein is bustling—I can see a group gathering on the other side. There are about twenty people standing in front of a collapsed fin-de-siècle house whose lower floors are covered by a green construction fence. At first, I think a tour group lost its way and came into the Dansaert after all, but these people look less like tourists and more like locals. The crowd is getting bigger by the minute, and I ask myself what these people are doing.

There's really only one explanation: they're waiting. They're waiting for something that's supposed to take place promptly at 7:00 p.m. It suddenly occurs to me that a large part of the fence is covered with snow-white rectangles seeming to glow from the inside out.

The waitress brings me a little plate with chips and pretzel sticks. She looks somewhat bewildered when I stand up.

"I'll be right back," I assure her. I take another gulp of my beer, then leave the bar. I cross the plaza quickly, walking in the direction of the crowd. It's grown to at least forty people. Many of them have set their rain jackets down on the damp cobblestones and sat down. Most of them are young, almost none of them looking to be older than fifty. All of them are staring, transfixed, at the white spray screens, where small green numbers have appeared: 03:43, 03:42, 03:41.

I position myself amongst the onlookers and activate the recording feature on my specs. Then I wait along with the others for the show to begin. Two drones have gotten into position above the crowd—not one of ours, something from the media or droggers.

The countdown ends and the numbers disappear.

All of the screens flare harsh white for a minute, followed by a multicolor explosion, a psychedelic attack of color lasting for about thirty seconds. After all that, there's a matte white screen, where the logo of the Johnny Random show appears and, shortly after, Johnny himself. He walks into the image from a distance, at first barely distinguishable in a white suit on a white background. But after just a few seconds, his face fills the entire image. "His face" is not an entirely accurate description. Who even knows what Johnny Random really looks like? The countenance on the construction fence doesn't at all resemble the man I spoke with in the replication in the Zoniënwoud. The Johnny du jour has a long horsey face with thin cheeks worked through with furrows. They look as if they were carved with a knife. There's also a shock of brown hair, though it's hardly worth mentioning; his eyes are hidden behind a pair of silver-blue mirrored Lennon glasses. I tell my specs to access the info from the screens, probably emitted via ultra-short-wave audio, and translate it into Dutch.

The roughly fifteen Johnnys of various sizes bare their horse teeth. "Welcome to a new episode of *Random Discoveries*! If you've just wandered in, ladies and gentlemen, you'll gape at corrupt ministers, criminal billionaires, and other sensations! As you've probably heard, the government's lapdog—apologies, of course I meant the Union's broadcasting control center—has cut me off. And so some of my fans have installed a few new screens and I'm broadcasting direct from Manila!"

The crowd of people has gotten even larger. Around sixty or seventy people are listening to Random's tirade. I ask myself how long it could be before the metro police show up. Technically, no one here is doing anything illegal. As the droggers put it, it's not forbidden to stand in front of a white wall, after all. But spraying a media screen coupled with a Filipino pirate channel is guaranteed to break a half-dozen laws. There may be enough of these white rectangles, though, that we don't have enough drones to stop all these improvised public viewing events.

"This week, I have an especially juicy tidbit for you. There's been a rumor circulating for a long time that high-ranking political and economic leaders throughout the Union have been maintaining close contact with certain Russian-British crime syndicates commonly referred to as the Britskis—"

"Hey! Down here!"

I turn around, looking for the man that just spoke to me. Then I realize the voice came from my headset.

"To your left, Westerhuizen. It's me, the little Johnny on the streetlamp."

A small square, hardly larger than a pack of cigarettes, has been painted on a lamppost two meters to my left. Johnny Random is visible on it. Although all of his larger counterparts on the fence gesticulate and speak simultaneously, the remote Johnny has his arms crossed and stands completely still. I have the feeling he's staring at me. Then he raises his left pointer finger to his lips and indicates with his right that I should come closer.

I force my way through the crowd until I stand directly in front of the lamp. The small Johnny considers me. He looks sad, even disappointed.

"Didn't I say you should proceed discreetly, as discreetly as possible?"

"I don't trust you, Random."

"Instead, you're trusting the wrong people. But no hard feelings, you've already paid for that bitterly."

"What are you really doing here, Random? All these illegal screens—are you trying to instigate a popular uprising?"

The small head moves back and forth. "No. And if it happens—it's completely unimportant. What's important is that you disappear, and quickly."

"What do you mean by that, get away from here?"

"From the face of the earth. You're the subject of a 36A sent out a few seconds ago." Random holds something up. It's a Europol alert poster with my photo on it. Underneath, in large red letters it reads: "Armed and dangerous."

"Get out of here, Westerhuizen. When you've found a hiding place, call this number: 1-777-EIDO-LON."

"What's Eidolon?"

His forehead forms into angry wrinkles. "Run, you idiot!"

I pull my sou'wester closer over my face and push my way through the crowd. Once I've put it behind me, I quicken my steps and walk along Fabriekstraat in the direction of the Charlesroi canal. I don't know if this is another red herring on Random's part. If I stopped moving at the next intersection and waited a few minutes, I'd get the answer all on my own. Instead I take my privatizer out of my jacket pocket. The battery's almost dead. Without stopping, I activate the device, set it to maximum strength, and hold it clutched in my right hand.

Thirty-six is the police code meaning a manhunt for a suspect. Level A is the highest-possible level of urgency. The entire arsenal of digital search methods is brought into play for an A-level case, a Taurus unit standing at the ready for an arrest. Level A normally means the target has committed a felony, in most cases a recent homicide. Despite my best efforts, I can't remember having killed someone in the past few hours. Maybe Ververke decided I'm still too big of a risk even without my dog tags and wants to wash his hands of me.

As I cross over the canal via Vlaamespoort, a taxi shoots past me. For a moment I debate calling a car but dismiss the thought right away. Taxis, busses, and subways are moving jails, as every minor criminal on the lam knows. Sensors routinely collect Pay-Passes from all riders as they board. Terry compares the names with a criminal database in a fraction of a second. If he finds a match, he takes control of the onboard software and locks all doors. Anyone who wants to get away from the entire police apparatus would be best advised to do so on foot.

By now, I'm finding myself in one of the more dilapidated neighborhoods near the West Station, if the concentration of sex shops is anything to go by.

As I walk past one of the bigger ones, the Ministry of Love, my gaze lands on one of the media screens near the entrance: "Viewing booths—100% discreet—privatizing fields." I enter the shop and walk past the shelves full of dildos and latex suits to the booths. Gaining entry requires inserting a five-hundred euro coin into a slot. I dig one out of my pants pocket and toss it in. Past the turnstile, I enter a dimly lit common area with multiple hallways leading to around thirty booths. There are men, women, and other people of indistinct gender standing in front of a few, smiling at me invitingly. I ignore them and search for an empty booth.

The windowless, soundproofed boxes are barely bigger than two by two meters. As I lock the door, a lascivious-sounding computerized voice informs me that every half hour costs an additional thousand euros, and that the booth is protected against electronic scanners. I shove a bill in the slot.

"I hope you have a satisfying time," the computerized voice breathes.

I sit down on one of the plastic benches affixed to the walls. To start with, I take off my neutered service glasses. It's hardly worth it to deactivate them, since they're the property of Europol and Terry could turn them on and locate them at any time. So I need to remove the battery, which means I have to break off the left side of the frame. Then I toss the specs in an overflowing garbage can full of tissues and condoms.

That was the pleasant part.

I roll up my left pant leg past my knee. Then I take

off my right shoe and sock and place them on the floor. I take a small jackknife with a ceramic blade out of the inner pocket of my trench coat.

There are essentially three possible ways to catch a criminal in flight. The first is his specs signature. Based on net usage, every wearer's location can be pinpointed to within a few centimeters. Once Terry's placed him, surveillance cameras, drones, or panoptos take care of the rest. In case the man on the run doesn't wear glasses, the second-best data trail is his face. Since Terry can analyze feeds from any camera recordings, he can find the wanted person within minutes as a rule, no matter where they are in the entire Union. The only way to avoid it is to wear a mask or hole up somewhere.

Many people believe they can't be caught if they keep both of these things in mind, while also making sure they don't use their PayPass to order kimchi-pizza delivered via courier drone to their hiding place. But it's not enough to give up specs and wear face masks, since Terry naturally has other tricks up his sleeve. His best one is motor analysis. Retinas and fingerprints aren't the only things unique to every person. Our gaits, the way we carry ourselves, how we move a fork to our mouths can all be matched up if there's sufficient observable material on hand in the form of video recordings.

Terry must have stored tens of thousands of hours where I'm concerned. Even if I moved through the capital completely mummified, he'd find me. He'd just have to search through the feeds for my movement patterns. That doesn't work quite as fast as the other methods—I'd bet Terry would need at least fifteen minutes before he found me.

And so I have to use an old trick I learned from the guerrillas in North Africa: I'll change my movement patterns.

I swing my bare foot back as a wind up and then kick it against the wall. Shooting pain rushes up my instep in the direction of my shin; I have to brace myself so I don't lose my balance. I set my right foot down cautiously and put weight on it. As anticipated, it hurts like hell. Still sitting on the bench, I take a look at my toes and try to move them. None of them appears to be broken, but there's discoloration already setting in on the middle digit, indicating a capsular tear.

Then I pick up the little knife and use it to slash the skin underneath my left knee. The pain isn't too bad, and the wound won't have any long-term implications for my ability to move. But from now on, every stride, just like every step on my right foot, will produce shooting pain strong enough to change my motion pattern so Terry won't be able to find me, or at least not as quickly.

I've done enough now to go back out on the streets. Only my ID still needs to be jettisoned. A few years ago, when I gave up my Dutch citizenship in favor of Union citizenship, I had myself chipped, since it makes life easier in many regards: hardly any customs screenings at the airport, simplified payment methods, almost no more biometric scans. But now it has to come out. I take a few deep breaths in and out, then roll up my left sleeve slightly. The ID chip is a thin plastic rod located about three finger-widths above my wrist. It's so small I have to poke around my forearm for almost two minutes until I find it. I make a cut. Blood wells out and I dab it away with a tissue. I pinch the rod, milk-white and slippery, between my fingers and clean it off. Then I wait until the cuts on my arm and leg stop bleeding. In the meantime, I loosen my cravat, roll it up, and smooth out the crumpled silk as best I can. Once I'm done, I tie the scarf in front of my face. With my wide-brimmed sou'wester pulled down over my forehead and the bandana pulled up over my nose, I look like someone who wanted to dress up as a cowboy but didn't have money for a costume. Passersby will do a double-take when they see me. It doesn't matter—the only important thing is that Terry doesn't recognize my face.

After I've left the booth, I spend a bit of time wandering around the main room of the sex shop looking at the displays. I pick up a transparent polyethylene package containing a shrink-wrapped item made of glittery green rubber. It looks like a radioactive pickle, but in any case I'm only interested in the "Sale!" sticker on the front of the blister pack. I peel it off carefully. Then I stick my ID chip on the adhesive backing and affix the sticker to my privatizer. The display indicates that, at full signal strength, there are twenty-nine minutes left until the battery dies.

I leave the shop and walk along the street heading west. More precisely, I hobble, since the swelling in my toes is proving more uncomfortable than expected. When I come to the next big intersection, my entire right foot is throbbing. I'm standing along a major thoroughfare, trucks thundering past. Once the light turns red, I make my way through the stopped traffic, on the hunt for an ideal vehicle where I can deposit the privatizer. I'd hoped for a truck with a full load of freight or an empty cargo bed, but there aren't any. Shortly before the light turns green, I see a fire-red electric scooter with a basket attached to the back. In passing, I throw the privatizer inside and murmur a quiet apology. In about twenty minutes, when the device's battery is drained and my ID chip logs on to the net again, it'll transform into a magnet, attracting things like half a dozen drones from Europol, innumerable policemen, and even a skyship full of Taurus apes. The driver, a man in a yellow helmet, will get the shock of his life, but also a story he'll be able to use to entertain his buddies down at the pub for the next two weeks.

I hurry up to reach the other side of the street. With gritted teeth, I hobble further west, in the direction of Little Tehran. The neighborhood is among the worst-surveilled in all of Brussels, since its unruly inhabitants shoot down any police drones they catch sight of. A charming locale, to be sure, full of street robbers and gangs. It's never struck me as more enticing. It's a long walk to get there on foot, about five kilometers. I could theoretically travel as a hitchhiker, but I don't think anyone would stop.

Who would pick up a man almost two meters tall, broad-shouldered, trying to cover his face with an improvised cowboy headset mask? So I walk along the Avenue Van Damme, ignoring the pain in my foot and my leg, until I can make out the Aurore high-rise apartment complex, better known as the Rose of Tehran.

My destination is a dive bar, Che Khabar, close to the Place de la Cohésion. I was there once during a raid years ago, and I'm fairly certain it has neither surveillance cameras nor undercover officers. Maybe I'll be able to find someone at the bar who'll drive me out of the city, no questions asked, or anonymously rent me an apartment where I can stay until I know exactly what the game is here.

Che Khabar is located on the ground floor of one of the Aurore buildings. Subsidized apartments are piled up for twenty floors above the bar, and trash is piled up on the surrounding streets. I'm probably the only one in this bar not armed to the teeth. As the door closes behind me, I loosen my scarf slightly. No one here would call the police, even if he'd seen my wanted poster on a screen somewhere. I go to the bar and order a double genever. I hole up in a dark corner with it and open a window on one of the tables. I find what I'm looking for in the local news.

"—a Union-wide manhunt was issued today for forty-seven-year-old Europol inspector Arthur van der Westerhuizen. According to police reports, he stands under strong suspicion of having murdered his colleague, thirty-three-year-old data forensics expert Ava Bittman. The woman was his lover, according to a statement from the public prosecutor, and all traces of her have disappeared. According to his digital corona, Westerhuizen was in her apartment shortly before Bittman's disappearance, leaving early this morning. At the scene, recovered traces of blood and semen indicate a violent crime.

"Westerhuizen made headlines recently when only a few days ago he shot and killed five suspects in a police operation. Raoul Farani, on behalf of the Initiative for Citizens Against Police Violence, clarified that it wasn't the first time a Europol officer has come unhinged. 'Many Jacobins are veterans of the Solar Wars. These guys are ticking time bombs.'"

To my regret, Ava's face isn't shown in the report. And yet I still see her clearly in front of me: sitting on her ergonomic chair, her head gently nodding backwards, the area around her eyes hidden behind her analyst's glasses; sitting next to me on the poplar and looking out over the abandoned field, or lying in the sun beside me on a reclining chair; smiling at me as she shovels far too much hummus on my plate; digging her hands into the sofa, gasping, her bare bottom stretching upward. My hands ball into fists and I can feel the wound on my wrist splitting open again. The bar blurs in front of me and tears stream down my cheeks.

They didn't say anything about a body, which might indicate Ava is still alive. It could also mean, though, that the RR kept themselves occupied with her for a few hours before they made her disappear forever. What did you find, Ava? What's so important it means two cops have to be taken out? I'd feel better if I at least knew what this was all happening for. Why did the intelligence service let me go if they were planning to pin a murder on me shortly after? Nothing about it makes any kind of sense.

I'm pulled out of my thoughts by the sound of screams coming from outside. The door to the bar is flung open, banging against the wall with such force that plaster trickles to the floor. The man in the doorframe is in his early twenties, Persian, wearing the yellow-green colors of the Lion Ancients, a local street gang. The kid looks worked up and starts talking right away, unfortunately in Farsi. Without my specs I don't understand anything except the word "Polise." He gesticulates and keeps on talking. I'm relatively sure he wants to let the small-time criminals here know that the cops are on their way.

I'm not the only one who scatters on hearing his observation. At the mention of the word "Polise," half of those present leapt up and hustled to the back exit. I follow them. The back exit turns out to be a rolling door, leading via a loading dock to an inner courtyard. These men apparently know where they want to go. They quickly clamber down the ramp and head for a trapdoor on the other side of the courtyard. One of them yells something to me in Farsi. When I don't react, he says in French, "You not through here."

"But the cops are after me, too," I answer, which makes him shake his head energetically and move his right hand behind his back.

"I can pay." Carefully, so he can see, I rummage in my pant pocket and pull out the last of my cash, five blue bills featuring the image of Robert Schumann, ten thousand euros in all. I hold it out to him. He nods shortly and points to the hatch. From the far side of the building, light is coming through into the courtyard, probably from floodlight drones. Besides that, I can hear the characteristic hissing of Taurus skyships from a distance. I climb through the opening, a staircase leading down into a dark tunnel. I can hardly see my hand in front of my face. All the others are probably wearing specs and can turn on residual light amplifiers, infrared, and mapping functions. I, on the other hand, have to slowly feel my way forward.

My helper pushes me from behind. "Go faster!"

"I don't have any specs," I pant.

He curses in Farsi and reaches for my arm. Then he pulls me through the darkness behind him. I'd estimate we go along for about five hundred meters, although it's hard to say, since the underground passageway seems to be made solely out of curves and turns. After a few seconds I no longer know in which direction on God's green earth we're moving. After some time, we reach another ladder with an opening above it. Pallid light shines down. I wait until the other men have climbed up, then follow them.

We've come to the surface in a small storage room; cardboard boxes with Korean lettering are stocked around us. A few of the men give me evil looks. They speak with each other for a moment and my helper evidently clarifies that I've paid. It seems a few of them take issue with my now knowing their secret. Their discussion goes on for a while, apparently debating whether it wouldn't be better to put a bullet in my brain and pack me away in a box. Eventually the conversation comes to a standstill without anything happening. A man with a mottled gray beard and a dark linen jacket goes to the only visible door, opens it cautiously, and walks through. The others pull out cigarettes and wait silently with arms crossed.

"Can't we go through?" I ask no one in particular.

"Wait," my helper says. "One goes every three minutes."

I nod. It makes a lot of sense that we shouldn't all walk into the store or bar on the other side of the door at the same time. If the police are looking for a group of people on the run, the panoptos will report all assemblies in Little Tehran to Terry. So it's better to leave the building one at a time. Another man goes to the door.

I lean against one of the stacks of boxes and close my eyes. There's a probability of about zero that the sudden appearance of the police was a coincidence, a routine raid. Taurus bulls don't hunt down pickpockets. They came because of me. But how did they find me?

When I open my eyes again, I'm alone in the storeroom. I walk to the door and pull it open a crack. A shop awaits me on the other side, the kind usually referred to as an import-export. The shelves hold an eclectic assortment of rice cookers, ugly 3D paintings of Isfahan, not to mention yapping children's toys, containers of rose water, housewares made from brightly colored plastic, and all kinds of other kitsch. Traditional Persian music jangles from a speaker in the ceiling. I'm the only customer.

I walk along the overstuffed shelves to the exit, an old-fashioned scanner checkout next to it. Behind it sits a wrinkled old man with snow-white hair, wearing a thick wool cardigan despite the summer weather. He looks through me, clearly hoping I'll leave his store without bothering him.

"Good evening," I say.

He doesn't react.

"I'd like to buy something. Do you carry disposable specs?"

His head performs a barely perceptible nodding motion. His left hand disappears under the counter. When it comes back into view, it's clutching a small cellophane package. Inside are the ugliest specs I've ever seen. They're neon green, their frames adorned with lopsided trails of wine-red flowers. They're the cheapest things money can buy, and it's questionable if they'll even hold up for the twenty-four hours promised on the label. But they're not coupled with a net signature. If the wearer is careful what kind of data to ask for, it's possible to stay anonymous.

"How much?"

The shop owner murmurs something in Farsi. I shake my head. He takes a pad of paper and writes, "10,000." Too much for this crap. But at the end of the day, the price is irrelevant. I gave almost all the cash I still had to the guy in the bar, so there are only a few coins left. I still have my PayPass, but if I were to use that, I might as well go to the nearest police station and turn myself in. I take my wallet out of my pocket and look inside. Not only was my police badge rendered useless, but they've also blacked out the passport coupled to my ID chip, so I can't flee the country. My PayPass, on the other hand, still looks intact. Not a surprise, since the investigators are clearly hoping I'll use it at some point out of sheer desperation. I lay it on the counter in front of the man. As he picks it up and starts to run it through the slot in his register, I say, "Wait. I'll take the glasses, you keep the PayPass."

He shakes his head.

"You keep the PayPass. And I'll give you the PIN that goes with it. But don't run the card through the scanner. Got it?"

He doesn't react for a moment. He's probably debating how much money he can get from his dealer for an active credit card with access codes. Then he nods and slips the PayPass away. It doesn't seem to sit well with him, which I can understand. It's not the crime making the old guy restless. It's the fact that, on the black market, the card is worth at least a hundred times as much as these shitty North Korean specs. The enormous inequality of our little bargain strikes a nerve with his sense of honor among thieves. Instead of saying anything, I wait and look at him.

Without another word he gets two more pairs

of specs from under the register. One is pink, the other eggplant-colored. He packs them in a plastic bag printed with "Super Pars" in large letters, along with two cartons of Mogul cigarettes and a bottle of rose water. I take it. Then I turn around and leave the shop, first pulling my cravat up over my nose.

As I can see now, the store is located on the Boulevard Hallstein, also called Boulevard de Bazaar by the locals, since the street is almost entirely made up of small shops offering all the necessities of everyday life. There's everything a suburbanite might need: vegetables, meat, liquor, illegal cigarettes, pirated copies of 360-videos, handheld weapons. It suddenly hits me that I'm unbelievably hungry. The last time I ate something was this morning, well before my involuntary march out of the city center. I'm somewhat dizzy, and although I'm reluctant to remain on the street too long or go into a shop probably under surveillance, I have to eat something. Otherwise this will be a very short getaway.

I walk along the Boulevard Hallstein in the direction of the Graanmarkt. When we still conducted patrols here, there was a shish-kebab stand that took cash. I hope the few coins jangling around in my jacket pocket will be enough for a bite. After I've gone a few hundred meters, I can already see the street cart. As I walk, I reach into my jacket pocket and pull out the coins. I look at my opened hand. In it are several euro coins as well as an I Ching coin. Pazzi's I Ching coin. Unlike the silver currency, its metal shimmers gold.

The enigma of my profession, or maybe my ex-profession, is its irrationality. There's a popular belief that police work is a thing of pure reason, a sort of mental exercise like it is for Sherlock Holmes or Amadeus Cho. Puzzle pieces are pushed back and forth, connections are made, alibis are verified. In this way, the bigger picture—and also, somewhat incidentally, the murderer—is gradually revealed.

It's all nonsense. Thinking, and above all brooding or rumination, is overrated in my line of work. One of our professors at the police academy in Leuven always said that difficult cases are never solved through continuous deduction, but through epiphanies. It's a Greek word, and I've forgotten the exact translation. But in essence, it means something is revealed, is shown, to the investigator, suddenly and without warning. Usually there's a trigger for these epiphanies, although that doesn't mean they can be made to happen consciously. Put another way: it's pointless to chase after a discovery. You have to wait for it to come to you.

And now one is coming to me, suddenly and unsolicited, in the form of this small coin I've already held in my hand many times. Pazzi used it to ask the Chinese oracle what he should do. Heuberger told me his lover wasn't formerly so superstitious. Pazzi only began to show an interest in tarot and I Ching a few months ago. Why would a grown man, firmly of the here-and-now, suddenly be interested in clairvoyance? Why would he trust important decisions to dice, cards, or coins? Why would he give himself over to chance?

The question has been cropping up since the beginning of my investigation, even if I never deliberately posed it. And now, suddenly, the answer to the riddle is showing itself. I don't like it one bit.

I tear open the plastic casing on the specs and activate them. After I've put them on, I duck onto a stoop and watch the shish-kebab stand from there. White smoke drifts around the metal cart as the owner turns the skewers. I zoom in. The man grabs one kebab after another with a pair of tongs, turning them 180 degrees before putting them back on the grill. More than once, the barbecue slides away from him in the process. His movements aren't fluid enough for someone who's spent years of twelve-hour days turning lamb meat on skewers. His apron is covered in grease stains, but the rest of his clothing looks conspicuously clean in contrast.

I turn on the residual light amplifier and look at the surroundings. After being in this line of work as long as I have, certain clues become noticeable that normal citizens completely overlook: an unshaven guy with greasy hair and a tattered surplus jacket, a genever bottle in one hand and the most cutting-edge model of specs on his nose. A black Maybach Bolivar taking its third turn around the plaza.

In total, the Graanmarket is being surveilled by at least six plainclothes detectives. They're waiting. They're waiting for a suspended inspector under suspicion of murder, who, according to the movement, camera, and PayPass data stored in Terry's archive, bought a shish-kebab here a total of seventeen times six years ago during his tenure in the Brussels vice squad. And since people are creatures of habit and unknowingly fall back into old patterns, above all in times of stress, it's likely he'll show up here. If I were the mission leader and had an indication my target was somewhere in Little Tehran, I'd ask Terry to compile a list for me. A list of the five or ten places in this area the target would probably seek out, since he knew them and felt safe there, whether he knew it or not. That's classic predictive forensics, a textbook example.

I should have realized much sooner that my colleagues would take this approach in the absence of a spec signature or other data trail. Now that I know it, though, I ask myself if the knowledge is any good to me. I can try not to head to any places where I have a past connection, but that's easier said than done. As every predictions expert knows, free will is a fiction. People do over ninety-five percent of all things unconsciously, mostly running on autopilot. That's why it's hardly possible to outfox Terry for a long period of time. He knows what we're thinking of doing more precisely than we do ourselves. Terry is a master of getting to know our patterns of action and, with their help, prognosticating our next steps.

And sooner or later, we always fall back into our old patterns.

I turn the I Ching coin back and forth between my fingers. Pazzi must have had the same train of thought. Maybe he saw clearly that, once someone had his complete data history, he was as transparent and predictable as a lab rat in a maze. He must have realized there's only one possible way to break out of predictive patterns, and that's chance. Pazzi wasn't superstitious. He somehow found out someone was looking through his files and observing him and predicting his every move. And so he made his decisions by chance to try to outwit his opponent. I can see him in front of me, sprawled on the field, faceless. It could be said his coin trick didn't work too well.

I'd already pictured the lamb skewer in my hands, could almost taste it—it's a shame. I turn around and walk along the Boulevard in the opposite direction. I have to speak with Random, but I need a quiet corner to do so. I can tell I'm barely feeling the wound on my knee and my damaged toes, the pain having ebbed away. That means I'll gradually fall back into my old patterns of motion. Patterns are fatal. I have to get off the streets as soon as possible.

In my head, I take a survey of several restaurants, boardinghouses, and shops I can remember. They're all part of my mental map, another pattern to be avoided. I ask the specs for a list of all video shops in the area. It shows a total of fourteen.

"Random generator," I say. "A number between one and fourteen."

A large "6" appears in the air before me, at which I steer toward the sixth shop on the list. It's located on a side street I normally wouldn't enter without a weapon even in broad daylight, not to mention in the dark of night. This is gang territory, Lion Ancients or the Zoroastrians, I'm not sure which. Pairs of eyes watch me from unlit entrances, scanning me to decide if I'm worth jumping. I'm lucky no one wants to fight with a masked giant in a scruffy trench coat. I only have to maneuver around a gutted motorcycle and an unconscious junkie to reach the video shop.

I hurry to find myself a booth. There won't be any camera surveillance here, or at least I hope not. There's a very practical reason for not having them: a video shop owner who filmed his customers going at their favorite activity—that is, masturbation—would quickly go broke. As I close the door to the little booth, the media wall in front of me flares up and asks me for my PayPass.

"I'd like to place a collect call," I say.

"What is the number of the participant?"

"1-777-EIDOLON."

A few seconds go by. Then the computer voice tells me the other participant has accepted the charges. The screen changes color. Johnny Random appears across from me. Behind him stretches an old library with immensely tall shelves and real books made out of paper. Random has his version of a Peter Lorre face on again, the one he was wearing for our meeting before last. He's taken off his bright white suit, though. Instead he wears a slate-colored corduroy jacket, a button-down shirt, and a sweater implausibly knitted in a zigzag pattern. If it weren't for his eyes, with a certain mischievousness shining out like always, he could be mistaken for a librarian. Maybe this is Random's idea of an undercover assignment.

He looks at me with a satisfied expression. "You look like shit, but you're still alive. I'd hoped you'd shake them, Westerhuizen. You know all the tricks. Only a Jacobin can outwit a Jacobin."

"About time you tell me what's going on here, Random."

He lifts his hands in a placating gesture. "Of course. But everything in its time, and above all in a discreet location. If what I see is correct, you have nothing left—no money, no ID, not even a face you can show."

"Bingo."

"That's bad. After all, you're supposed to solve a case for me. First, we have to make sure you're back in action again, Aart. I can call you that, right? I think our relationship will deepen in intimacy considerably over the next few hours."

I suppress the desire to pound away at the face on the wall with my fists. Instead I say, "Call me whatever you want. But how will you swing it so I can go out on the street again? Half of Europol seems to be after me, and the RR to boot."

"It's simple. From now on, you'll only investigate in the mirror space."

"They'll find me even faster there than they would out on the street. Probably at the exact moment I went in."

Random shakes his rounded face. "You're not going into the Union's mirror space. That would, in fact, be unwise."

"Is there another one of some kind?"

"I'll explain it to you as soon as you're there. First

you have to get off the street."

"But I don't have any money."

"That's an easy problem to solve. I didn't know exactly where you'd show up again. So I prepared a courier drone to bring you a few things that might prove useful."

"And where would that be?"

"Do you know the street heading toward Ghent? Not the main road, the bypass that goes around Zottegem and Oudenaarde?"

"Yes, of course."

"It'll land there, on an adjacent field. It's outside of the Brussels panopto surveillance. You'll have to walk a decent way from where you're currently stopped, but it's not too far."

"And what I am supposed to do way out in a village?"

"You'll go to a little country inn called the Groene Hunter, which is in the parish of Appelterre. I've reserved bungalow 8 for you and paid a week in advance. The keycode is 8419. The Hunter is a proper, old-fashioned establishment. Hardly any cameras: they still understand what it means to be discreet. If you stay in your room, no one will bother you."

"Okay, Random. But how do I know you're not leading me into a trap?"

"You don't know. But if I wanted to set a trap for you, God knows I've had plenty of opportunities for that. Besides, as I see it, you don't have another choice."

"I could turn myself in. I didn't kill my analyst.

The whole thing will sort itself out."

"I fear your former colleagues are interested in another form of resolution."

Random plays a clip. It shows the Brussels city center, a street near the Halleepoort. Traffic is jammed in all directions. It's due to a terrible accident. In the middle of the intersection, something is burning; above the clouds of smoke, there are the dancing sparks characteristic of a burning lithium-ion battery. Scorched pieces of metal are strewn across the intersection. It takes a moment before I recognize the destroyed vehicle as a motorized scooter. It's fire-red. Somewhat off to the side, a yellow, blood-smeared helmet lies on the street. I feel my mouth going dry.

"Come on, Aart. Go to the rendezvous point now. It's your only chance."

"My chance for what?" I ask flatly.

"For the truth. And maybe even for a little bit of justice."

Then he nods encouragingly to me one more time and hangs up the connection. I stay seated for a moment. On my specs, I call up the exact location of the transfer point. It feels like it takes an eternity, since the burner specs are as slow as they are ugly. I can see on the map that I have another march of about three kilometers ahead of me. A borrowed bike wouldn't hurt, but I'd need a PayPass for that. It's not a good idea to steal one either. Most bikes are chipped and set off alarms as soon as they're taken more than five hundred meters away from their rightful owners.

Slowly, I stand up from the hard plastic chair, pull

my scarf around my face, and leave the booth. Once I'm outside again, I head westward and walk as far as the Ghent bypass, keeping away from the main roads. The city here is already unraveling into a loose collection of subsidized apartments, industrial zones, and fallow land, but it finally stops entirely. The main street runs to the northwest, lit by a group of green algae lamps stretching to the horizon through the Flemish marsh. I walk along them, a number in the upper right corner of my visual field showing the remaining distance. After a solid twenty minutes I leave the road and tramp the most direct route across a field that hasn't been mowed in some time. When I reach the position given to me by Random, I crouch down. I'd really like to lie down in the grass and close my eyes for a few minutes, but the ground is soft from the eternal rain. How long has it been since I've lain down in a dry summer meadow?

A hissing sound announces the arrival of the courier drone. It doesn't belong to any of the big logistics services; its sides are unmarked. According to my specs, it's an Embraer Swiftjet, licensed by a Brussels firm I'm not familiar with. Terry would be able to tell me who's behind it right away. But I can't even pose such a complex research question to the pea brain inside my shitty North Korean glasses.

The Embraer is about the size of a refrigerator, though shaped much more aerodynamically. It moves in a circle over me, then sets out to make a landing. Small steering jets on the side start to hiss, then the drone's feet spring out and it lands in front of me. I wait for it to say something, but it remains silent. Instead a little rolling window opens and reveals the storage area, where a backpack is waiting. I take it out and verify that the cargo area is completely empty. Then I tell the drone it can head out from the field.

Once it's disappeared, I open the backpack. It contains clothing, as well as an envelope presumably containing a roll of money, if its bulge is anything to go by. I decide to go through the contents at the hotel. As I close the backpack and lift it up, I notice something made of hard metal in the front pocket. I pull open the zipper and see the plastic grip of a gun. If the weapon is meant as an indication of the severity of my situation, then I really need to start worrying. It's a Česká Skorpion II with an under-barrel grenade launcher, outfitted with tiny seeker missiles that follow their targets around corners and through buildings. A very illegal weapon only the military has access to. I shoulder the backpack and tuck the Česká under my coat. I call up the coordinates of the hotel on my specs.

I arrive at the Groene Hunter a short while later. It's almost three in the morning and no one is around. The inn looks like an old Flemish estate, though the bungalows behind it are, in contrast, horrifically modern things made of ceramic and glass. But I'm at the point where I'd spend the night in a ditch on the side of the road. I trudge across the puddle-covered courtyard to bungalow number 8 and enter the keycode. With a click, the door opens.

My new domicile is practically furnished—lots of plastic, not much wood, with a kitchen and a holo-fireplace in the living room. I tell the bungalow to roll down all window shades and make the space impermeable to light. I barricade the door manually from the inside and double check there's no back exit. Then I take off my jacket and sit in a chair across from the fake fire cheerfully flickering in the fireplace. I spread out the contents of the backpack on the floor in front of me. Johnny Random may be a lunatic, but he's no idiot. The gear leaves nothing to be desired. Aside from fresh clothes, toiletries, energy bars, and plenty of bullet clips, I find a first-aid kit and a bottle of strong pain medication. Additionally, there's a pair of prepaid specs, not a crappy pair, but a comparatively efficient model made by Earl. As anticipated, I find money in the envelope, a million euros in all, in used bills and single-use debit cards, and also small amounts of the major foreign currencies: won, real, Australian dollars. There's a small case at the bottom of the backpack. When I open it, I unexpectedly have to laugh. It contains a selection of fake beards, colored contact lenses, wigs, and containers of makeup.

Since my gut tells me this isn't everything, I check over the pockets and compartments of the backpack again. In one of the lower pockets, probably meant for rain gear, I do find something else. It's a small black nylon pouch. When I open it, replication gear tumbles out: a headset, several escape patches, and, instead of the usual inhaler, an injection device and accompanying liquid hypnoremerol in ampoules. There's at least four hundred milliliters, enough to beam a sperm whale into the mirror space. The pouch also contains a note. It reads: "Sleep a few hours. Come when you're ready. Activation word: 'Eidolon.' R."

As if I'm being controlled from afar, I stand up and go to the big double bed, an energy bar in one hand and the Skorpion in the other. I sink down onto the wool bedspread. I chew lying down and stare up at the ceiling. I don't even make it through eating the entire bar before I pass out from exhaustion.

When I wake up again, it's 8:30. I'm longing for breakfast, a proper Dutch breakfast with eggs, aged Gouda, gingerbread, and a pot of steaming coffee. Instead I eat another energy bar and drink tasteless black tea out of the bungalow kitchen to go along with it. After I've showered, I sit on the bed again and look over the replication gear. I pull on the headset slowly and peel back the film on an escape patch. I set its timer to sixty minutes. Then I let myself fall back, hold the injection pistol to my arm, and press it. The hypnoremerol shoots through my veins. But nothing happens, probably because the headset is still inactive and hasn't been powered on.

Then I remember the note with the activation password. "Eidolon," I whisper. And the world disappears.

CHAPTER 23

I find myself once again in my usual haunt near the Palais de Justice. This fact gives me a real scare, since there are few places in the Union watched over as thoroughly as Galgenberg. After a few seconds it becomes clear to me that I'm not really here.

I'm sitting at my corner table with a big Dutch breakfast in front of me, including eggs and gingerbread. I reach for a cup of steaming coffee and take a drink. According to the clock on the wall it's just past nine in the morning, and the usual suspects are sitting at the bar. It's raining outside, and through the downpour I can see the front of the Palais de Justice. Demonstrators are already assembling in front of it. Everything seems to be going through its routine, everything like normal.

Almost everything. Something is strange, although it's difficult for me to say what that could be. The simulation Random has replicated me into is top-notch. All the details are consistent. I pull the bread basket toward me, pick up a piece of gingerbread, sniff it, and take a bite. Very realistic olfactory and tactile experiences, making the hairs on the back of my neck stand up. It's not nausea plaguing me—it's something else. But what? Maybe it's my new constant companion: the fear of being discovered.

Before I can think about the subject further, the front door opens and a man walks through. It's Johnny Random, this time appearing again in his usual white suit, but with a new face, a Southern European one with coal-black eyes, dark hair falling to his shoulders, and a considerable nose. The most noticeable thing, though, is his skin tone. Random looks pale as a corpse. When I look at him more closely, I see there's no hint of color apparent anywhere on the man. Johnny Random is in black and white. He looks as if someone copied and pasted him into a color film from one of my old 2D flicks.

He nods amiably and sits down on the chair across from me.

"Good morning, Aart. Welcome to Eidolon."

"Morning, Random. I take it that's the name of this replication."

"Yes, Greek for a ghostly manifestation. Only moderately original, I know. But the name does the job."

"Who's running this replication? The Brazilians? A syndicate?"

Random shakes his head. Without my noticing, breakfast utensils have materialized on his side of the table. Random takes a croissant for himself and dunks it in his milky coffee. After he's taken a bite with a chomping sound, he answers, "Neither of them. Let me tell you a story, a story that goes back in time to when there was still no such thing as a replication true to reality."

"I'd prefer a couple of quick answers," I say.

"The less you interrupt me, the faster you'll get them."

He looks at me defiantly, but I don't reply.

"Good. A good decade ago, when the Tares program was already being carried out in Union-occupied territories, it became clear to a few programmers that a copy of the world, a virtual world, could be built with the abundance of live data our sensors were already using to absorb the nooks and crannies of reality and record them on hard drives. These programmers, above all a brilliant chap named Peter McDoyle, worked for Tallan Consolidated. They built the first prototypes. When they showed these to the EU army command and the RR, they were beside themselves. The ability to send invisible spies to practically any place in the world would mean unbelievable power. The military wanted these ghosts, the sooner the better. An enormous budget was allotted, and McDoyle's people got to work. After two years they'd come far enough that the ghosts began to float through the mirror space. As I can tell by your impatient expression," a derisive smile plays on Random's lips, "this part of the history is familiar to you."

"More or less."

"As the other major industrialized countries caught wind of the situation, they naturally introduced themselves to TalCon. The Koreans, Brazilians, Japanese—everyone wanted their own mirror space. But Tallan wasn't allowed to sell anything to them. The Union had classified the technology in question as a sensitive military matter, and the Earl had to decline contracts worth billions of euros."

As he speaks with a calm voice, Random crumbles up the bitten croissant. Butter-yellow flecks trickle down on the table, on his pants, on the floor.

"I believe that, around this time, John Tallan made a decision with many consequences. It was of course clear to him what kind of power access to the mirror space could bestow. If he wasn't permitted to sell this unbelievably valuable technology on the open market, he'd at least use it for himself. And so he tasked McDoyle with a secret project, codename Eidolon."

"He had a mirror space built for himself?" I ask skeptically.

"That's right. Eidolon is a simulation completely independent from the Union mirror space. Of course, Tallan had to make sure no one got wind of his private replication. Neither the RR nor the military would have found it especially funny that someone was developing an alternative option, even if that someone was a business partner loyal to the Union. So Tallan's head programmer McDoyle couldn't simply build a copy of the EU mirror space. After all, Eidolon couldn't tap into any official government data sources. That would have attracted attention sooner or later. So Tallan needed another data source. I don't want to keep you in suspense, Aart. Eidolon's data came and continue to come mostly from—"

"—from specs."

"That's right. All specs manufactured by Tallan Consolidated secretly record images, sounds, and position data."

"All of them? But that must be in the millions."

"Billions is more like it. In the Union alone, five hundred million people wear specs by TalCon. Five hundred million pairs of eyes, five hundred million involuntary spies watching everything all the time. And Tallan is also the market leader in many other countries. With the help of this gigantic amount of data, Eidolon's simulation computers generate a very accurate live replication. Furthermore, they tap all sources with open access—for example, drogger videos. When you and your colleague began to investigate these creeper-feeds and hypothesized that someone had hacked Tallan specs, the Earl understandably went into a panic. He was afraid that everything would be laid bare."

"Did he sic the killers on me?"

"Those Russians? Those were Orelovs, elite contract killers from the Britskis. Yes, I'd bet my virtual suit Tallan sent them. He has good contacts in the Britskis."

"So how did all these creeper-feed videos end up on the net, then, Random? We found vast quantities of them."

He sighs. "I mentioned that Eidolon is built differently from the Union space. It's much more decentralized, the computers aren't in TalCon headquarters, but are strewn and hidden throughout the net. The data inventory is so gigantic that a few terabytes seeped into the normal net."

"It's just that simple? But Terry's mirror space databases never run over."

"That's because the Union space is much less extensive than Eidolon. You see, Aart, Terry's replications function, in principle, just like a map. From a distance, everything appears grainy. The image only becomes richer in detail upon zooming in. Or, to put it another way: tiny drones are only dispatched to the areas where an observer is located, and a high-definition virtual reality is only created there. Terry doesn't construct a simulation anywhere someone isn't looking."

"And it's different here?"

"Yes. This is McDoyle's masterpiece, a comprehensive replication, and a continuous one. Eidolon is four-dimensional, it has the three dimensions of space and one in time. Pay close attention for a moment."

Random stands up and goes to the bar. He appears to murmur something. I think I can detect a very gentle vibration, then everything is as it was before. The clock shows ten minutes past nine. I sweep my gaze from table to table. The usual suspects are still hunkered over the counter reading the news. A pretty young woman has taken a seat at a table in the corner. She makes a face as if she's already had to turn down a dozen invitations for coffee. I'd guess it was three at the most.

A man comes inside, a big guy with an angular chin, a receding hairline, and a crumpled trench coat. He greets the woman and gets something to drink at the counter. She watches him expectantly, arms crossed in front of her chest. After he's hung up his dripping coat and sat down across from her, he says, "I'm sorry."

"Good. You owed me an apology. And if you follow it up right now with an explanation for why you behaved so strangely, we might be able to be friends again."

"An informant made themselves known to me."

"When?"

It's difficult to endure any more. "Cut it out."

Random nods, snaps his fingers, and goes back to his place. He's standing so I can no longer see Ava and the other Aart. Another light shiver goes through the room, as if the subway is going by us far below. Random sits down. Ava and Aart have disappeared.

"That was last Tuesday," I say.

Random nods. "The replication goes back for many years. We have more data in total than Terry, even if it's not as high definition. Did anything about Eidolon stand out to you?"

"Something is different than normal, but I couldn't say what."

"Take a look under the sink behind the bar."

"What's that?"

"Do it. After all, no one will see you."

I stand up and walk past the bartender behind the counter; if I did that in real life, I'd pay for it with a round of drinks for everyone on me. I kneel down in front of the sink and open the cabinet. Inside, as expected, there are cleaning products and rags, and also the plumbing. In contrast to the public space, however, everything seems strangely imprecise. It looks as if it were painted by a late Impressionist. The scene comes across like a still life, Scrubbing Powder with Sponge in oil, by Vincent van Gogh. I close the cabinet and go back to our table.

"Your simulation has too little data in certain places."

"That's right," Random says. "Although there are plenty of people going back and forth out front here, most of whom wear specs from Tallan, only the cook and the bartender look in the cabinet under the sink." He swipes his right pointer finger over the table and looks at his now-darkened fingertip with a furrowed brow. "And that's only when they absolutely have to. Anyway, both of them wear specs from Arirang. Your police computer would send out its mites in such a case. Eidolon, however, can't do that. In cases where there's too little live data, our computer inserts its best estimates and makes these visually apparent to the user. When only a few data points are missing, the result is a blurring effect, with everything swimming just slightly, like the Mona Lisa. This Impressionistic distortion, on the other hand, indicates that the computer has had to, well, guess."

It takes a moment for me to understand what Random is telling me. "But if you're storing and archiving the information from all these specs . . . the amount of data must be astronomical."

"It is, and that's a problem. Eidolon is threatening to burst. And so old raw data is always slipping into the open net—the raw data you found. In the beginning, McDoyle only had the data from the greater

416

Brussels metropolitan region replicated, but Tallan wanted a bigger replication, more countries, more power. The point of the entire initiative, after all, was to spy on competitors as well as movers and shakers in politics and justice. If you've looked at TalCon's history, it will have been apparent to you that the corporation is always one step ahead of its rivals and opponents. That's because of Eidolon. And once someone goes down that path, they'll always want more information. Tallan didn't just want to know what the members of the Commission or the government thought; he wanted to be present at confidential conversations in Warsaw or Vienna, as a ghost. And so Eidolon got bigger and bigger."

"Then why doesn't he dial the project back to a manageable size?"

"He can't do it anymore."

"Why not?"

"The only person who had even half a handle on the situation was McDoyle. But he died in an accident three years ago."

"Tallan had him eliminated."

"An obvious suspicion, but in fact I don't know. I know for sure that Eidolon has gobbled up a lot of money since then, since the amount of data grows bigger with every passing year. The inventory increases, petabyte by petabyte. And more and more people are wearing TalCon specs, making the mountain of data increase even faster. In a way, Tallan is a victim of his own success. In order to shoulder the enormous expenditure, the Earl had to find a partner, one outside the Union. But the aforementioned nations were, of course, out of the question. The Britskis were the only ones left."

"The biggest crime syndicate in the world has its own mirror space?"

"Yes. If you walk around out there a bit more after this, watch for people who look like me, monochromatic people. That is to say, the black-and-white people you come across in Eidolon aren't simulations, but ghosts. They're lying on a couch somewhere, their synapses full of hypnoremerol, and are going about their business here."

"How many are there?"

"No one knows exactly. But it must be thousands. The Britskis have since sold access to all possible interested parties. And the demand is enormous. Moving around in Eidolon is, after all, one of the few possibilities to avoid the total surveillance inside the Union."

Random leans back. "Now you know what that means for your creeper-feeds. The fact that there were so many violent videos probably means Terry didn't find the original data leak. He found the creeper-feed collection of a dealer who's known for years that, in certain dark corners of the global net, videos of unknown origin are constantly showing up. You also know now how you can move freely again. Now, if you'd help me in return—"

"Not so fast, Random. I have a few other questions first."

"Of course. Should we take a stroll while you ask

them? I have to confess your local haunt isn't exactly to my taste."

We leave the Café Amsterdam and walk along the Regentschapsstraat in the direction of the Commission Palais.

"First, I have to know what happened to Ava."

Random's expression gets serious. "As long as she wore her service specs, I had an eye on your analyst. But about an hour after you left her house on Sunday morning, the feed cut out. It looked to me like she turned off her glasses herself. She was still working with Terry beforehand."

"What exactly was she researching?"

"I'm not too familiar with your police computer. But what I did get indicates she found something unusual."

"What?"

"That I can't tell you, I don't know. But she cursed, many times, in English and Hebrew. My guess is Ms. Bittman found something iniquitous enough that someone pulled the plug shortly after."

"Someone liquidated her."

"Someone decided to get rid of her immediately and put the blame on your shoulders. But your analyst strikes me as too clever for that—and too paranoid. Maybe it became clear to her in time that her life was in danger, and she fled."

"But how? And where to?"

"That's the hundred-thousand-won question. And, by the way, it leads us back to my request."

"And that would be?"

We reach the Koningsplein, the Commission Palais towering to our right. Random steers us toward the Park van Brussel behind it, where a neatly mown green covered in pigeons shines in the morning sun.

"The dead MEPs, Aart."

"Pazzi, Füßli, and Milar?"

Random stands still and makes a hand gesture. A list appears before us in the air. It's long. On it are the names of the three representatives, as well as the names of other people, twenty or thirty total.

"Are those all dead MEPs?"

"Yes, those who have died since the beginning of the last legislative session forty-seven months ago— accidents, fatal illnesses, natural causes. But according to my research, they were all murdered. The crime scene replications and associated forensic data were manipulated, just as with Pazzi, Füßli, and Milar."

"Do you have a theory of who could've done it, Random?"

He sighs. "I had one. When I only knew about the three cases, just like you I assumed it had something to do with Golden Trail. All three men were involved in it. But when I discovered the other strange deaths a few days ago, it became clear to me this old corruption scandal couldn't be the common thread. Some of these MEPs are too young for that, others never came into contact with the Union's military-industrial complex. It has to be something else, but I can't figure out what." Random smiles worriedly. "I'm not as original a thinker as you are, Aart. And so I'm hoping for your help."

"It would make sense to have the data coronas of all the deceased run through an analytical computer that can identify statistical similarities."

"Already done, although there were no results."

"But that might be because you asked the wrong questions, Random. Get me access to a high-performance computer that can carry out congruence analyses. Then I'll try it myself."

Random has started walking again, and I follow him. By now we're in the middle of the park, which is empty except for a few joggers and dogwalkers.

"Okay. I use a very satisfactory analytical computer for my journalistic research, and you're welcome to use it. I'll share the access codes with you. Does this mean you already have a working theory?"

"Yes. But I'll keep it to myself for now."

"That's not very cooperative. Not to mention useless. I'll know everything you do in Eidolon."

I take a look at him. Normally I'm very good at reading people's faces and gleaning the things they'd rather not expose. But it's different with Random. It must be due to the masking software he's using. The man is capable of making his face appear as emotionless as a strip of wallpaper. It's the best poker face I've ever seen. Same with his eyes. I've seen glass eyes reflect more about the souls of their owners.

"Before I agree to work on this case, you owe me another answer, Random."

"What's your question?"

"Who the hell are you?"

We're coming to the large pool surrounded by statues of the twelve Roman emperors. Random stops and looks up to the sky.

"Do you remember the journalist who exposed the Golden Trail scandal once upon a time?"

"Arne Jürgensen? You're Jürgensen?"

"Tallan destroyed everything I'd built for myself. He wanted to make an example and so he made use of the truly new, rigid Union media laws to extort a gigantic amount in punitive damages. Our magazine went under, all the writers were let go, myself of course above all."

"And since then you've been researching into your nemesis's past?"

"Since then, I've worked for him."

"What? You work for Tallan?"

"A few months after I was let go, he invited me to London. You can imagine I was very wary. Tallan made me an offer. The kind of offer that couldn't be refused. He offered me the chance to become his head researcher. There was a new technology that made possible the kind of research I could only dream of before as an investigative journalist. My budget and salary were supposed to be similarly dizzying."

"But why did you let yourself get mixed up in it?"

"Because I could keep working at my job, a job I love. No media organization in the Union would have given me another chance. Tallan, on the other hand, promised me I would be allowed to research and publish anything I wanted, as long as it didn't have a bearing on his business interests."

"And so you became Johnny Random."

"And so I became Johnny. And you know everything he's uncovered. The most powerful people in the world tremble in fear of me."

I throw a doubtful glance at him. "Unless they're under Tallan's protection. Or unless they belong to the Britskis. And how many of his enemies did Tallan set you on?"

He makes a dismissive gesture. "Yes, I know, you're right. I always convinced myself that the end justifies the means. With Eidolon I was able to eavesdrop on secret conversations, I had unlimited access to the halls of power. Nothing remained hidden from me. I still believe, now as always, that I did plenty of good, uncovered plenty of scandals. But after McDoyle's death—I always considered him a friend—and after Tallan opened Eidolon to the Britskis at the latest, it became clear to me that this guy is much worse than anyone I unmasked in *Random Discoveries* over the past few years."

"Couldn't you already have realized that based on the Tares project? Tallan's technology led to countless people being thrown in jail."

"Yes, Tares was a staggering transgression. I lied to myself for too long." He looks me in the eyes. "Just like you, Union Lieutenant, retired, sir."

"Touché, Random. But what are you doing now? Giving your notice?"

"You know as well as I do that that would be the end of me. As soon as Tallan noticed I was becoming too independent or even rebellious, he'd shut me down, or rather his Orelovs would. And so I need your help. I'm under intense surveillance, my hands are tied. I can help you in your work, as I've been trying to do since you were tasked with the Pazzi case. But you're the only one who can find out if Tallan murdered these MEPs and, if so, why. Only then will I be able to bring him to his knees."

"All right then, Random. I'm about to disappear into thin air, I set the escape patch to an hour. But then I'll hook myself up again right away and be back on the case. I think Pazzi is the key. In the cases of all the other victims, the murderer clearly had time to conceal his crime. With Pazzi, though, it had to be done quickly. That indicates he'd found out something compromising."

I tell Random about the I Ching coin and about my hypothesis that Pazzi was being surveilled with the help of predictive software.

"Sounds plausible. And it speaks in favor of your theory that Pazzi wanted to meet with me. He contacted me and set up an appointment, although that never came to pass."

"At the Lotte. He wanted to meet you at the Lotte."

"Correct. He shared the meeting place with me shortly before his death."

"With you and Heuberger."

"Heuberger had nothing to do with it. I falsified the message Pazzi sent me after the fact and changed the recipient to Heuberger. It was believable and inconspicuous for Pazzi to send his lover an invitation to dinner. That way I was out of the line of fire."

"Destruction of evidence. Punishable offense. And

it makes you suspicious to boot."

He shakes his head reproachfully. "Your mistrust has pathological overtones. Look at the crime scene one more time, then you'll see I wasn't the only one who erased my tracks."

"Who else did?"

"Just look at it again. Unfortunately, I have to go. My lord and master, the Earl of Mertonshire, demands my service. In the past few days I've rattled my chains too much already, and I don't want him to become suspicious."

Random gives me a friendly nod and begins to walk along the sandy path in front of us with brisk steps. I don't follow him, instead standing still and watching him. He walks down the alley in the direction of the Delorsplein. Then he disappears behind a Roman emperor. By rights, he should reappear on the other side a second or two later. But he stays gone.

CHAPTER 24

Since I don't know how to activate the escape patch from here, I have to wait until the hour is over. I sit down on a park bench between Augustus and Justinian and watch the gardening drones as they trim the lawn border and the conifer bushes.

A beeping sound informs me a priority message is coming through. I call it up in front of me. It's the access data for the analysis computer Random promised me. I set up a link and wait.

While Terry takes pains to remain discreetly in the background, this analysis device has an avatar. He looks like a British butler and resembles the servant who recently opened the door for me at the Club Dupont. He comes along the gravel walkway and stops in front of the park bench.

"Good morning, Mr. Westerhuizen, sir. Jonathan, at your service."

"Hello. I have a few requests. First, I'd like to know if my escape patch can be triggered on command."

"That is possible, sir. Provided you haven't set a timer."

"I did."

"Then I'm afraid you can only go back into Tellurium after its appointed time has run out, sir."

"Into what?"

"Tellurium, sir. Derived from *tellus*, Latin for Earth. This is the term Eidolon's programmers chose for the real world."

"How prosaic. Anyway, when I come back, I'd like to appear somewhere else."

"As you wish. Simply tell me the time and place, sir."

I consider a moment. "July 4th, five o'clock a.m., on the field near Westrem off the Autobahn E40, kilometer 537.4."

"Very good, sir."

"How much time do I have until it pulls me out?"

In all seriousness, the butler raises his left hand, pulls back the double cuff on his shirt with his gloved right hand, and looks at his wristwatch with a frown.

"According to my watch, you have twelve minutes and nine seconds remaining, sir."

"Why this song-and-dance?"

"Sir?"

"You're a manifestation of an optic computer with how many petaflops?"

"I'm a pythia-subroutine with 123.4 petaflops at present, sir."

"What I mean is, you don't need to look at a watch. Or is there really any doubt that the cesium watch keeping time for your servers is running slow?"

"You are completely correct, sir, and I must sincerely apologize for it. The original programmer of Eidolon, Mr. McDoyle, placed great value on all interactions between human and machine seeming as natural as possible."

I'm not exactly sure how I should respond to that. Nothing about this joker seems natural to me.

"Let's forget about it. I have a few questions about all of these dead MEPs."

"Of course, sir. What may I analyze for you?"

"Are there notable connections of a geographic, religious, sexual, or economic nature between any of the victims?"

"I'm afraid not, sir. This is a very heterogeneous group."

"Basic statistics, please."

The butler pulls a notebook from his vest pocket. Then he pulls off his right kid glove, licks his pointer finger, and begins to leaf through.

"Of the thirty-one people in question, seven are from Germany, one from Northern Italy, five from Switzerland, three from Portugal, eight from France, two from Israel, four from Poland, two from Sweden. Three of them sat on the Defense Committee. Two more of them were on the Cultural Committee. Three—"

"That'll do." Too many details, mountains of meaningless one-variable statistics. What I need are connections.

"What about their political orientation?"

"Nine belonged to the Conservatives," the butler answers. "Three to the Liberals—"

"To put it another way," I interrupt him, "did they all belong to the progressive wing of their party? Or to the conservative one?"

"It's mixed, sir."

I bombard the butler with question after question, but it's pointless. It almost seems as if someone picked these thirty-one MEPs so there were as few similarities between them as possible. I don't have even the faintest glimmer of an idea why someone killed these parliamentarians, of all people.

I only have thirty seconds left. Time for one final question.

"Can you use the recordings and actions stored in Eidolon for these MEPs to calculate which of them were for the new Union constitution and which were against it?"

The butler flips intently through his notebook. "I regret to say it, sir, but there is too little data available for me to predict within an appropriate confidence interval how the thirty-one deceased would have voted."

He looks up from his book. "Good-bye, sir."

I regain consciousness on the bed in the bungalow, though more slowly than usual. I have the feeling I'm trapped in a nightmare. I frantically try to reach the surface and leave behind my sleeping state. I'm successful, finally, but it's more arduous than it should be. At first, I think it must have something to do with some kind of special technological feature of Eidolon. But then my gaze falls on the injector on the nightstand. There are two fingers' worth of green liquid missing from the syringe.

It's more likely I've overdosed myself with hypnoremerol.

It's a strange substance. Thanks to it, consciousness can go into the virtual realm, with the body sinking into a kind of coma. Even pain or other sensory experiences aren't enough to bring a person out of it. Only the counteragent can do that, concentrated monoaminoxidase-C17. Abbreviated MAO, it's also naturally occurring in the human body, a sort of flushing mechanism for the brain. The synthetic version found in escape patches neutralizes the hypno within fractions of a second—assuming the doses of the two chemicals are optimally balanced.

Failing that, it's a difficult trip back, like in my case. Someone who overdosed on hypno could only be brought back with a lot of effort. Neuroscientists would have to put them on an MAO drip for a long time, since it can't be pumped directly into the human brain in the preferred doses without frying the synapses.

I lift myself up. It's cold—the HVAC control system clearly decided to cool my bedroom down to a subpolar temperature. I tell it to make it warmer. Then I stand up and waddle into the kitchen. I turn on the tap and fill a glass with water. I drink it down in one gulp, then a second and a third glass. The difficult return trip has given me something to think about. Who knows how long I'll stay in Eidolon on my next trip? If a patch fails, there's only self-produced MAO to rely on to work off the drug.

That can take days. Dehydration would be the biggest problem in that case, so I drink water until I have to go to the bathroom. In an office, a ghost could be hooked up to an IV drip and muscle stimulators for multiday missions. There are supposedly guys, especially in the RR, who are able to spend weeks or months in the mirror space that way, without their bodies withering.

Since I have neither a catheter nor adult diapers, I make sure to go to the bathroom one more time before I take an escape patch out of the black pouch. There's a tiny media screen attached on the front side where the setting can be adjusted so the chemicals aren't released by a timer, but by a radio signal. I pray it works. Then I stick the patch on my chest and lie on the bed again. Since I'm still freezing, I crawl under the down blanket and wait until I'm warmed up. I say, "Eidolon." The ampoule on the injector is still half full. I hold it to my upper arm and pull the trigger.

CHAPTER 25

From the shoulder of the Autobahn, I walk along the muddy gravel path to the place where Pazzi lies. Even in Eidolon he's still by far the best-dressed corpse I've ever come across: welted calfskin shoes; a bespoke Milanese suit worth more than what I take home in a month; and a Steinkirk tied with deliberate disregard—including a matching pocket square.

I kneel down next to him and look at the sandy ground splattered with blood and brain matter. The rain's already washed away some of the mess. The blend of blood, brain matter, and bits of flesh creates a pinkish halo around Pazzi's shoulders.

"Display time," I murmur.

It's 5:01 a.m. The time point is identical to when I showed up at the crime scene for the first time. I stand up and walk around the corpse somewhat indecisively. I wish I had an unbiased computer to compare the Eidolon replication and Terry's reconstruction with each other. Since that's not available at the moment, though, I have to rely on what I remember and what I see. I walk across the field to the thicket from which Pazzi was shot. In Eidolon, there's no poplar like the one Ava and I climbed in Terry's crime scene replication, just like there isn't one in the real world, in Tellurium, as the butler would call it.

I ask myself where he's gone off to.

At the west end of the field, there are a total of seven trees. The available data doesn't seem to be particularly good, since the poplars aren't rendered in detail. They look as if Monet painted them. The same is true for a large part of the field. I remember Ava telling me almost no survey drones ever look in here, much less people. No people means no specs. And in Eidolon, no specs means no data. And so I'm standing in this strange Impressionistic landscape.

Wait a moment.

With a hurried step, I stomp back to the corpse. When I reach Pazzi's body, I can tell that he and the surrounding area are being displayed in high-definition—no Impressionism, no sfumato, but razor-sharp, true-to-life images.

"Jonathan?"

"Yes, sir?" The butler approaches solicitously from behind.

"How is this replication so clear in this area?"

"Because current spec data is available, sir."

"From what sources?"

"Two glasses filmed the area in the past few hours, sir."

"When you say the past few hours, do you mean in real time or replication time?"

"The information was based on the point in time in which we find ourselves now, last Monday at 5:06 a.m., sir."

"Can you send me a bit further back in time? Without making me feel sick, if possible."

"With the greatest pleasure, sir. Don't be concerned, most people do better with temporal changes inside Eidolon than with so-called superhero effects like levitation or teleportation."

"Fantastic. Same day, 2:10 a.m."

There's another one of those small shudders, this one seeming to go through the whole field. Pazzi's body has disappeared. The field lies there, quiet and dark, gusts of wind whipping at our faces. One minute passes, then another.

"How long is it until something happens?" I ask.

The butler looks at his wristwatch. "Two minutes and eight seconds, sir. Should I fast forward?"

"Absolutely not."

We wait. Then the light of a car headlamp flits across the field. A dark Bentley stops at the far end of the gravel path. A man steps out of it. He's of compact stature and wears a gray plastic jacket over his suit. As he comes closer, I can see he must be around fifty years old, and the hair peeking out from under his sou'wester is fire-red. He gives the impression of being anxious but not fearful. His hands are buried in his jacket pockets, and I think I can make out the bulge of a weapon under his left shoulder.

"This is the man who called Pazzi here," I whisper.

"What makes you say so, if I may ask the question, sir?"

"His shoes. Pazzi wore welted Budapests, which indicates he didn't think he'd end up having to trudge through mud. This guy is wearing waterproof duck-boots. Because he knew what the conditions at the rendezvous point would look like."

"Understood, sir."

"Identification and précis," I say.

"Alan Thompson, fifty-two, born in London. Two years as an MEP from the electoral district of Croydon. Member of the Conservatives, sits on the Foreign Commerce Committee. Married to Emily Thompson-Parker, two children—"

"He was a good friend of Pazzi's. I remember Terry saying so."

"That aligns with my information, sir."

"What did he do before he became an MEP?"

"He was an Air Commodore in the Royal Air Force during the first Solar War. Later, he worked in the foreign service of the United Kingdom, for over ten years. Stationed in Delhi, Cairo, and Buenos Aires."

"As what?"

"Cultural attaché, sir. In Buenos Aires he was also a deputy ambassador."

"So, intelligence service, probably MI6."

"Sir?"

I ignore Jonathan. A British flying ace who, just before the British exit, changes over to Union service after a decade in the diplomatic service? What kind of person would do something like that? Only a fool. Thompson, though, doesn't look like one. I'd bet MI6 sent him, and probably not just him, to Brussels for the final legislative period. The British likely want to weigh in on a few more things before their little island kingdom untethers from the mainland and drifts off into the Atlantic. If Thompson was able to hide his status as an agent from the RR for two years, he must be good.

Thompson remains standing in the middle of the field and looks toward the street. He doesn't have to wait long. After another two minutes, a dark limousine stops at the edge of the street. Its side door swings open and Pazzi gets out. With a furrowed forehead, he stomps along the path, while the limousine disappears into the darkness. When he reaches the field, he lifts up his legs like a stork so his shoes get as little as possible on them.

Thompson nods at him encouragingly. "Good evening, Vito. Or, better put, good morning."

"Hello, Al. Why did you pick this godforsaken place?"

"Because according to our calculations, it has the lowest amount of surveillance in a hundred-kilometer radius."

"We could have gone into a privacy box in the city."

"No. That would have been noticed by certain people."

Pazzi looks like a drenched poodle, and not just because of the water running down his dark curls and into his collar.

"You all have to help me, Al. I think I've found out why the others had to die. And I'm sure I'm supposed to be one of the next to go. They're watching our every move, our immunity isn't worth anything anymore. They want to push through the new constitution at any price."

"I know. But my government won't be able to stop it. Nor will any other."

"Maybe not. But in spite of that, I've decided to go public with the whole thing. And afterward I'll have to disappear."

"That's not so simple."

"I realize that. But if Great Britain offered me asylum, or at least hid me from the RR for a little while, you'd get everything I have, and it's a considerable amount: military info, details about our security apparatus, political dossiers."

I look at the digital clock in the upper-right corner of my visual field. Only fifty-eight seconds left. "Get on it with, already," I growl.

Thompson furrows his brow at that. "I'd really like to help you, Vito. But I have to speak with London first. When are you going to make the story public?"

"As soon as possible. I'm meeting Johnny Random tonight, at the Schönbrunn. I'd hoped you'd come too."

Thompson doesn't look enthusiastic. "A dangerous game, Vito."

"I know. But do you have a better idea?"

The Brit apparently can't think of a good answer to that one. Then he says, "Have you found out who created this congruence profile yet?"

Pazzi nods and stares at the ground.

"Spit it out!" I yell. "Say the damn name!"

He opens his mouth. I look at the display. Only four seconds left.

"At first I thought John Tallan was involved. But it's—"

Pazzi's face explodes. Thompson throws himself down into the muck. In the space between the poplars, I can see an EADS assassin drone, a terrifying monster made of matte black ceramic. It's round, with four rotors at the top and eight circular muzzles on the underside. The drone has enough firepower to turn the entire field into a blazing inferno. But it doesn't do that. It's already climbing and moving away toward the west. A few seconds later, it's disappeared into the night sky. Thompson, in the meantime, has clambered to his feet and subvocalized something into his larynx mike. He doesn't waste any time checking on Pazzi. Instead, he runs in the direction of the street, where his Bentley picks him up a few seconds later.

I look yet again at Pazzi lying on the ground. "You could have helped me. But you talked too much and said too little."

I turn to Jonathan. "I could use a drink right about now."

"Perhaps a genever, sir?"

"That would be wonderful."

The butler reaches with his right hand into the inside pocket of his striped vest and brings a bottle into the light of day that, realistically, would not have been able to fit inside. It's covered by a thin coating of ice. Jonathan twists off the top, pours two fingers in a similarly iced glass that he's gotten from God knows where, and offers it to me.

"To your good health, sir."

I sip. The sensors are quite true to life. Then I tip the rest back in one go.

"Is it possible to get drunk in a replication?" I ask.

"Not to my knowledge, sir."

"Shame. Then we're done here."

"Very good, sir. Where would you like to go next?"

"Where can I go?"

"Well, wherever you'd like, sir."

"To any place in the Union?"

"To any place on the planet, sir."

I lower my head and close my eyes for a moment. I feel how the rain runs down my neck and think about Ava's words: "I know a godforsaken beach near Zinnibiri."

I don't have much hope. But I have to at least try.

"Take me to Zinnibiri."

"On Sardinia, sir?"

"Yes. There's a beach in a bay close to Zinnibiri with only four bungalows. I don't know the name."

"That doesn't matter, sir. In the vicinity of Zinnibiri there are many hotel facilities, but only one bay that matches your description. How would you like to travel there? Teleportation? Autopiloted airplane?"

"By boat, Jonathan. By boat."

CHAPTER 26

The motorboat approaches the coast from the east. It's early afternoon, the sun at my back casting a golden and ochre light over the hills and hinterlands of the Costa Smeralda. There must have been a wide sand beach here before, a draw for plenty of sunbathers. But the sea consumed most of it and only a narrow, rocky strip is left. Based on the nearby driftwood, I can tell the water sometimes comes up to the base of the embankment.

About twenty meters above the floodline, four boxy bungalows cling to the slope. I have no idea which one she could be keeping herself in. From down here, it's not clear if all the houses are occupied. As soon as we've landed, I'll ask the analysis program about it. The boat is now at most fifty meters away from the shore, the electric motor whining indignantly at the crest of every new wave. From the bench at the rear, I watch how the butler steers the boat onto the beach. With a crunch, it comes to a stop.

I stand up and walk along the gunwale to the front of the ship. Jonathan is already waiting for me in the shallow water and offers me his hand. I ignore it, jump onto the dry sand in one movement, and keep walking. The butler hurries to follow after me. I point

445

in the direction of the bungalows.

"Do we know which of them are occupied?"

"In the bungalow all the way to our left, there's a man with Tallan specs, James Whitney, Irish, forty-three years old, single. I'm not receiving any signals from the second bungalow, nor from the third. A woman is living in the fourth. She's using prepaid specs from Felton, no ID signature."

I can feel my heart beating nervously. "Show me a video."

A creeper video appears in front of us. It shows Ava standing in front of a bathroom mirror putting her hair up. She looks tired and worn out, as if she hadn't slept for days.

As fast as possible, I climb up the narrow path to the bungalow on the far right. The summer rains have dug deep ridges in the sand and washed out the path in many places. After ten minutes, I make it to Ava's little house. It's an ugly modular building, which the azure-blue coat of paint and begonia-filled flowerboxes under the huge Plexiglas windows can do little to change. There's no perimeter wall and no fence. I walk up to the front door. It doesn't have a keypad, but a mechanical lock and a door handle made of worn brass. I push it down.

Inside, it looks like a predictable Sardinian vacation bungalow: knotted rugs, media frames with seascapes that change by the minute, earthenware vases. From somewhere I can hear quiet music—it sounds like a classical concert. Not one of my strong suits, so I call it up: "Mahler, Symphony I, 'Titan,'

First Movement: Slowly, dragging. Like the sounds of nature."

Cautiously, I step further into the apartment. The hallway leads past a bedroom with an open door, one half of the bed rumpled and the other half untouched. Past that, the hallway opens into a large living room with windows reaching to the floor, looking out over the sea. Ava is sitting motionless on the sofa. I go to her and look over her face. She doesn't seem to be looking at the sea, she's not looking at anything in particular with her thousand-yard stare. I can see she's been crying. I kneel down in front of the sofa and stroke her right cheek. My fingers glide right through.

"Oh, Ava. If only I could talk to you."

I hear someone clearing his throat behind me. It's the butler.

"It pains me to disrupt you in this situation, sir. But theoretically, communication should be possible."

"How?"

"The control system of the bungalow is comparatively, ah, primitive, if you'll permit me the liberty of saying so, sir. I should be able to bring one of the media screens under my control. I could display you there. As soon as Ms. Bittman is aware of our presence, a high-quality interaction should be possible. If Ms. Bittman assigns us the use of a particular signature, I can project you via a preferred device."

"Can she come to us, to Eidolon?"

"Unfortunately not, sir. I beg your greatest pardon,

but that's only possible with the help of a special data headset. We would have to send one to Ms. Bittman by courier drone, although that could attract unwanted attention."

He's right. True, we're not in Union territory, but this area is likely still surveilled, possibly twice over: by the RR and by the gendarmes of the Vatican, who, although they don't have any official jurisdiction here, still control wide swathes of Southern Italy de facto.

"Okay. Hack your way in."

"With the greatest pleasure, sir." A few seconds pass, then he says, "If you'd please make your way to the kitchen, sir."

I do as he says. I've hardly stepped foot inside when I hear an irritating cheeping sound. It's the timer on the oven. After about ten seconds, Ava appears in the kitchen to see where the noise is coming from. She tells the stove to turn the timer off. But the cheeping continues undeterred. She looks at the little touchpad near the back burners and starts to type on it. Suddenly the media screen hanging on a panel over the oven starts to shine brightly. Normally it'd probably be used to display recipes or cooking videos. Now it shows my face, which surprises me as much as it does Ava.

"Aart?"

"I'm so happy to see you, Ava. I thought they got you."

"And I thought I'd never see you again, Aart. Where the hell are you?"

"That's a long story. Listen, we might be able to speak to each other directly. My butler says he can set up a projection if you clear a signature for us."

"Your butler?"

"The avatar of an analysis program."

She nods. "I have a small holoprojector in the living room."

"Okay, go into the living room. I'll—I'll be right there."

As a ghost, I follow Ava into the living room. She takes a small drone folded into an icosahedron out of the desk drawer and gets it ready to go. Then she activates the little flying device. It rises off her palm and positions itself half a meter below the ceiling. Ava says, loudly and clearly, "1719.2729.9272.9273."

"I'm almost ready, sir," the butler says, indicating I should stand under the holoprojector.

"Why do I have to go over there?"

"I could generate a copy of your Eidolon avatar that would be projected into Tellurium under Ms. Bittman's projector. But then you would appear twice, at least from your own perspective. And that would be a somewhat confusing situation, wouldn't it, sir?"

I nod. Better not to think about my divided self anymore, since that can only lead to a headache. I go ahead and position myself directly under the holoprojector. Right away, Ava comes walking over to me.

"Oh, Aart!"

She wants to hug me, but stops halfway through the motion. Instead she runs her hand over my right forearm, her hand gliding through my jacket. She starts to laugh.

"What is it?" I ask.

"We're at the beach again. And you're wearing a fucking suit again."

"I could ask the computer to generate shorts and a Hawaiian shirt for me," I reply.

The smile disappears from Ava's face. "That means this projection is coming from a replication? You're in the mirror space? But how—"

"I'm not in the Union space. I'm in Eidolon."

"What's that supposed to mean?"

I indicate Ava should sit on the sofa, then I take a seat next to her. And then I tell her everything. My escape from Brussels to Eidolon, my renewed acquaintance with Johnny Random and everything the crazy journalist told me about Tallan and the creeper-feeds. I also report to her about my latest visit to Westrem.

"Pazzi wore specs by Earl, a TalCon make," I say. "The way I see it, whoever falsified Terry's crime scene replication didn't know about Tallan's creeper-feeds and Eidolon. He or she believed they could manipulate our police computer and camouflage certain details, like the arrival of an assassin drone, and cast the blame on separatists or a syndicate. But the murderer couldn't have known that, thanks to Tallan's illegal spec surveillance, we have a data source independent from Terry. And in addition to showing the assassin drone shooting Pazzi at the crime scene, it also shows another man: Alan Thompson."

"Pazzi's friend?"

"Exactly. Although I'm not sure if it was a true friendship. Thompson most likely worked for MI6 and it's possible he was assigned to Pazzi. He was a deputy party leader, after all, and an important economic politician. Pazzi, by the way, said that in his view, Tallan had nothing to do with the murders. The way I see it, it means the compromising data still exists in Eidolon. If Tallan were Pazzi's murderer, he could have gotten rid of the evidence for sure—at the end of the day, he has full control over the replication."

"Do you know where Alan Thompson is now, Aart? He'd be an interesting guy to talk to."

"No idea. But definitely not in Brussels anymore."

She nods grimly. "The drone."

"Yes. Thompson must have seen the assassin drone in Westrem, and vice versa. So Pazzi's murderer knows there's a flesh-and-blood witness. And he's probably found out in the meantime that Thompson works for British intelligence. I noticed Thompson spoke with someone as soon as possible after the assassination. Maybe a cleanup crew from MI6 got there only a few minutes after he disappeared, wiped away as many traces as possible, and then got him out of the country. He's sitting in an embassy somewhere far away from the Union. Europol still has executive powers in British territory through the 30th of August and could arrest Thompson, at least theoretically. Which means our murderer's hands are probably tied. If he went after Thompson, Thompson would spill the beans on all kinds of compromising material everywhere he could."

I look at Ava. She still looks tired and worn out, but at least she doesn't seem as desperate as before. Ava pulls a window up on the coffee table and starts to murmur to herself.

"What are you up to?"

"I'm setting up a search routine for Thompson," she answers. "Without access to Terry's database it's tricky, though, especially since he has immunity as an MEP. But if we scour all public outings, sightings through droggers, and other openly accessible data sources, we might get an idea of where he could be. Or if he's already dead."

"It'd be good if we could speak with him—a chat between fugitives from the republic. How did you make it out of Brussels, anyway?"

"In the end, it was sheer luck. After you went away, I took a few pieces of data out of Terry's inventory again, stuff I was already working on before your visit. By that point I was sure someone had manipulated a large amount of digital evidence and forensic replications. This someone must have extremely good knowledge of the system architecture. Only one of Europol's top programmers came to mind."

"Why only one?"

"Because the falsifications are almost too perfect. If you didn't know they were there and had no clues about what could have been changed, it'd be practically impossible to find them. All the logfiles where changes are usually recorded were changed after the fact in the same way, a masterpiece of digital counterfeiting."

"So that rules out a whole group of suspects."

"That's how I see it, too. In my view, apart from the Europol programmers, the only other option is the RR. They have an almost identical analysis computer. No one else could do it. That means it must have been the RR."

"Why are you ruling out our people?"

"Because of a lack of certain indications. That's classic logic, the principle of Occam's razor. It says that, in the case of multiple possible explanations for the same set of facts, the simplest theory is preferable to all the others. In our case, it's that the RR has been throwing stumbling blocks in your path from the start, probably because of this camp in the desert. The RR has been in the game the whole time and had a motive because of Tares. The intelligence department at Europol, in contrast, was never opposed to our investigations, not even in a rudimentary way, not with Pazzi or with the creeper-feeds. Therefore, the simplest explanation is that it was the RR."

"You forgot Tallan."

"I didn't forget him. Tallan appears to be a bastard of the first order, but he and his people couldn't have carried out a manipulation of Terry's database, it's not even a possibility. It follows that he isn't Pazzi's murderer. And that's who we're really still looking for, right? The thing with the creeper-feeds has been cleared up, even if it was admittedly in an unusual way. But there's something else."

"Which is?"

"I had an idea on Sunday morning. What if Pazzi,

Füßli, and Milar had all been fervent proponents of the new Union constitution, possibly in secret? Could that have been a motivation for the RR? Wouldn't they have wanted to lower the number of yes votes?"

"To do that, they would've needed to kill a lot more than thirty-one MEPs," I argue.

"That's true. All the same, I did a little more research into the question. I didn't know anything about Random's other dead guys then. But I could use everything on the three murdered MEPs I already knew about to my heart's content, since their data coronas were completely unsealed."

"And?"

"I had Terry draw up comprehensive political congruence profiles for the three of them. Now I know what the representatives thought about asylum politics, budget consolidation, or transgendering. Not what they gave as their official statements, but their actual opinions. But Terry couldn't tell me how they'd vote on August 30th."

"Jonathan, the Eidolon analysis program, said the same thing, that he couldn't calculate how any of the thirty-one deceased would have voted."

"That's the way it should be, Aart. Predications don't always work. The chances were fifty-fifty for Pazzi, sixty-forty for Füßli, same for Milar. Keeping in mind the statistical margin of error, the only conclusion is that Terry just doesn't know."

"But why not?"

"The experts have been fighting amongst themselves about this for years, Aart. A small number of human behaviors seems to be very difficult to determine with predictive algorithms. The phenomenon is called the Markov anomaly, and no one knows when exactly it'll turn up. There are usually a few people in any given group that you just can't get a read on."

"What percentage in this cross section?"

"Unknown. That's the bizarre thing about Markov anomalies—it's never once been predicted what percentage of a group is affected. It could be five percent, or it could be twenty percent. Since I didn't get anywhere with Pazzi and Co., I tried something else."

"I'm on the edge of my seat."

"All members of the Union Parliament have immunity from criminal prosecution. And their data is retroactively sealed, different from a normal deceased person. That's a protective measure. No one should know what individual representatives think. Otherwise, voting by secret ballot would be pointless."

"So far, so good," I say. "We're only able to get their data if they agree to the unsealing, if Parliament rescinds their immunity, or if they die an unnatural death."

"I posed a hypothetical question to Terry. I asked him if he could calculate a better prognosis about the voting behavior on the Union constitution for Pazzi and Co. if I could get him the unsealed data for all remaining MEPs."

"And what was his answer?"

"He said no."

I stare at her uncomprehendingly. "Yeah, so?"

"Terry said no, although he should have been required to say yes. More data is always better for an analysis computer. He needs control groups, he needs all possible points of comparison, you see? If Terry were allowed to vet the data coronas of all MEPs, he'd know even more about Pazzi's political preferences. Terry should have had to answer my question with a yes. But he said no."

"You mean he lied to you?"

"Aart, he's a computer. The golem can't lie. Terry always tells the truth and he always means what he says. You of all people know the problems he has with sarcasm."

"Sure, but—"

"I asked him if the entry of these data points would improve his results. He answered truthfully that they wouldn't. Why? There's only one logical answer: because Terry had already analyzed the data of all MEPs. Although it was sealed."

She falls silent for a moment, giving me time to digest this information.

"That was on Sunday morning. When Terry said no, I knew it wouldn't be long before someone found out he'd opened his big mouth, if it can be put that way. I didn't even pack a bag, just went straight to Zaventem and took the next flight to Palermo, most importantly out of the Union. Then I came here. I threw away my service specs in Brussels, and since then they've blacked out my Union passport."

It all fits together. I see Alan Thompson in front

of me, how he stands across from Pazzi and asks, "Have you found out who created the congruence profiles yet?"

I tell Ava about it.

"It was Terry. He looked through the data of all Union parliamentarians and created congruence profiles from it," I say. "So he knew who would vote yes. Pazzi seems to have caught wind of it and was liquidated because of it. Thompson clearly also knew the story. But why did Terry do it?"

"You're making the mistake of treating this golem like a person again, Aart. He definitely didn't come up with the idea by himself. Someone used him to screen the MEPs."

"It must have something to do with the yes votes. It's the only logical explanation, Ava."

"Occam's razor? Maybe. But what I don't understand is that none of the three men whose deaths we examined seems to have been a reliable proponent of the new constitution. But then why did the RR have it in for them?"

"That is strange. Where do we go from here?"

"The question is whether we can do anything else at all, Aart. I'm stranded here, maybe I can get away to Brazil, but even that might be difficult without a passport. And you can only get around in Eidolon, your body is stuck too. Where is it, anyway?"

"Somewhere outside of Brussels," I answer. "Listen, I have an idea. Do you trust me?"

Instead of answering, she lays her forehead on my cheek. More accurately, in my cheek.

"I'm going back to Eidolon now. You wait here."

"What are you planning to do?"

"Talk with a couple people. It's better I don't tell you the specifics. As soon as I get it settled, I'll come back for you."

She smiles worriedly. "As a ghost?"

"If everything goes according to plan, hopefully in the flesh."

CHAPTER 27

There's an audible click as the bungalow door falls into the lock behind me. I head out across the parking lot. There are hardly any cars in front of the Groene Hunter. It's not raining anymore. Large patches of the ground are actually dry, so the sun must have been shining for hours. It might have been the longest rain-free period of this entire sopping summer. And I missed it.

But there are a few other things the blue sky is good for. The first advantage of this weather is that I'll be able to see them a few seconds sooner. I stay standing in the parking lot for a while, searching for cameras. There are only two, looking somewhat weather-beaten but still capable of functioning. I walk a few steps. The cameras follow me. I look in one of the lenses and smile. Then I turn around and cross the main street of Appelterre, patched over many times and barely wider than a bike lane in Amsterdam. On the other side there's a row of old farmhouses, the village already starting to taper off behind them. Then there are fields all the way to the horizon. The field stretching out in front of me is not unlike the one near Westrem. I walk onto it and go as far as its middle. This all began on a nameless field.

It seems fitting to me that it's also ending on one.

I stay standing and wait, head down, hands in my coat pockets. My temples are pounding. Small wonder, I've never been able to stomach the stuff. The headaches brewing behind my forehead will soon grow into a first-class migraine.

Even more suspenseful than the question of how fast they'll get here is who will show up when they do. I'm betting the first guys from the RR are already here. Two minutes and twenty-one seconds have gone by since the parking lot cameras first caught sight of me, more than enough time to set off an alarm and teleport an agent already in a replication here from another corner of the mirror space. Maybe the guy is already standing beside me and speaking excitedly with his superior. Yes, Lieutenant, it is Westerhuizen, no doubt about it. We need a team for physical extraction right away, before the assholes at Europol get here and fuck everything up.

In the real world, as expected, a jet drone gets the ball rolling. Right after I've first spotted it as a far point on the horizon, it's already thundering over me. The drone turns a tight circle and gets into position over the farmhouses. It immediately begins to fill the field with sound: "Attention, attention! This is the police! Aart van der Westerhuizen, you are under arrest! In the name of the European Office of Public Prosecution, you are hereby ordered to give yourself up! Resistance is futile! Your face has been logged."

I comply with the police drone's orders, remaining motionless on the field and doing nothing that could make the thing hovering over me pepper me with bullets. The drone came from the direction of Brussels. More black dots are drawing closer from the same direction, though not quite as fast. After a few minutes, I can make out the outlines of two skyships. I turn back to the jet drone. If I want to say anything else, I have to do it now, before the field transforms into pandemonium.

"Message for the mission leader: tell your boys they should keep a calm trigger finger. I made sure to have some life insurance."

Then I watch as the two skyships brake over the field, hissing angrily. One starts to land, and a whole train of commandos repel to the level of the village out of the other. Twenty-five masked guys in black suits run in all directions, weapons at the ready. They secure streets and buildings as if Appelterre were a Moroccan hideout for terrorists. Then they start kicking in the farmhouse doors. Suddenly, humming-drones are everywhere, along with other small scout drones. The stabbing pains behind my temples get sharper. I feel bile rising in my throat.

While the first team terrorizes the locals, the second occupies itself exclusively with me. In perfect wedge formation, the men run toward me, weapons similarly drawn. As they come closer, they section off and surround me.

"Hands where I can see them!" yells the platoon leader.

I raise my hands, though otherwise I'm not paying him any attention.

I have eyes only for the person waiting on the edge of the field. I can make him out clearly, but I can't—I don't want to—believe it. So much for Occam's fucking razor, so much for all of our useless theories, so much for my original plan. I'm going to have to improvise. I hate improvising. Especially when my head is right on the brink of exploding.

My former colleagues dispense with forcing me to the ground and putting me in cuffs. They just take my specs off and search me for weapons. Clearly, they've been given explicit instructions. On the platoon leader's signal, the man walks toward us from the edge of the field.

"You took long enough," I say as a greeting.

Police Commissioner Jerôme Vogel grumbles something unintelligible. "This is no time for jokes, Westerhuizen. I'm arresting you for the murder of Ava Bittman, numerous counts of manipulating evidence, and conspiracy with a foreign intelligence service."

"That last charge is new to me. Which one?"

"The British one. Terry has incontrovertible evidence for it."

"Of course. Terry proves everything you want him to, right?"

Vogel contorts his hippo face. "Say your piece so we can be done here."

"How's that?"

"You intentionally stuck your face in one of Terry's cameras and waited for us here. You mentioned life insurance. Clearly, you think you have some kind of opportunity for negotiation or leverage. I think it's another case of self-delusion. That's your biggest weakness, Westerhuizen. But anyway, I'm prepared to listen to you for two minutes before—"

"Before what?"

"Before I take you away and hand you over to the RR."

"Didn't you tell me the head of the RR was against the new constitution and therefore your arch enemy?"

"It was true, then. Those nosy sons of bitches caused us a lot of frustration and almost ruined everything. But, luckily, we were able to come to an agreement at the last minute, a kind of cease-fire. The RR is holding back. In return, we'll make sure the planned monitoring of the intelligence service turns out more lax than planned. The new Union will be big enough for all of us."

"How magnanimous of you, Vogel. But now, about my life insurance: I know your game. You had first access to the new version, to Terry IV. You ordered him to go through all of the parliamentarians and find out who would vote for and against the new constitution. And you liquidated Pazzi when he got wind of the plot. I don't know exactly what the Commission president promised you in return for doing the grunt work. But I assume it was worth it. After Pazzi's death, you falsified the evidence so it seemed as if the usual suspects were responsible for the murder. To be exact, you made the new Terry do it. At first, I thought you had an accomplice in the

Europol IT department or at the RR. But you really didn't need those. Since Terry IV is so smart, he can self-program, so he was able to do all of it himself, any layman could have given him those instructions. At the same time, he's dumb enough not to second-guess anything underhanded, since he doesn't have a moral compass. You didn't need any awareness of programming to commit all these crimes, as I'd wrongly assumed, just the authorization to give orders. Terry carried out all of your instructions to the letter. They were definitely unlawful, but from his perspective they came from the highest-possible authority—the police commissioner. That alone was enough for him. At your command, Terry covered up the murders of at least thirty-one MEPs by falsifying the digital evidence. You got me access to the mirror space—not to help me, but to keep me in your sights more easily. Once we found out that Füßli and Milar's supposed accidents smelled fishy and furthermore could have something to do with the Pazzi case, things got dicey for you very quickly. So you went and did the same thing as Louis Renault."

"Who's that?"

"Renault is the corrupt head of police in *Casablanca*. He uses the 'usual suspects' to deflect attention from the real trail. Just like you, Vogel. You needed a guilty party, and fast, so the Pazzi case would be closed. Terry dug up the separatist Thomas Winterfuhr, who had recently finished up a bizarre, inflammatory anti-Union video. You quickly presented that to us as a claim of responsibility and set up a data trail leading to Hamburg. And, so Winterfuhr wouldn't be able to talk his way out of it, you had him killed via manipulated drone."

"An unprovable theory."

"There's an abundance of evidence."

"Which wouldn't attract the attention of any prosecutor in the world. Is that all you've got, Westerhuizen?"

"I—I passed along that data to Johnny Random," I say, my voice hoarse. "If anything happens to me, then . . . "

"That's a given. And then this madman will air a story about a malicious police computer and its murderous bosses on his pirate show? Don't make me laugh. Even if that led to a media frenzy or a formal inquiry—by the time they find out anything, the vote will be long over. Most of our representatives and their planned yes votes are completely secure."

Sweat runs down my forehead. "I thought it would be political dynamite—"

"You don't know the first thing about politics, Westerhuizen. And there's not much damage a journalistic bombshell can do when it's based on a fairy tale."

Vogel makes a hand gesture. Two of the men come toward me. They grab my hands and put me in handcuffs.

As the handcuffs click, I say, "I'd like to ask one final question, out of professional curiosity."

"And what might that be?"

"Why did all of these representatives have to die?

According to the congruence profiles, none of them were definitely against the new constitution. They just seemed to belong to the undecided group. Like Pazzi. Shortly after his death you told me the likelihood of his voting yes was only fifty-seven percent."

"That's right."

"But then why did they have to be eliminated?"

Vogel waddles toward me. His face is at most a handbreadth away from mine. And yet he doesn't look directly at me as he begins to speak quietly.

"It was Jana Svensson's idea to modify an old military project for our purposes. With the help of Terry and the political algorithm from Tares, we could predict who would vote for and against the new constitution. As an ex-soldier, you understand that the enemies you know are only half as dangerous as the ones you don't. We could try to convert known no votes with threats or promises. You have no idea how much money Özal and her supporters invested in this project. But, as always with predictive software, there were a few people who couldn't be pinned down, blank spots on our political map. There are always a few people who are impenetrable, unpredictable, erratic, part of human nature."

"The Markov anomaly," I throw out.

"Yes. And as calculated in this case, the anomaly was unexplainably large. Over forty representatives whose voting behavior Terry couldn't calculate—too many for such a close vote. That was a magnitude of uncertainty we couldn't tolerate. These people were unknown variables, they were a risk. And so we had to clear them out of the equation."

My head feels as if it's going to shatter. Everything starts to spin. "You had all these people murdered," I wheeze, "because you didn't have a mathematical consensus?"

Vogel shrugs his meaty shoulders. "Anyone who isn't with us is against us."

He turns and heads in the direction of the skyship. One of the Taurus guys grabs my cuffed hands and drags me after him.

"Eidolon!" I yell.

Vogel turns around. "What did he say?"

"I didn't quite understand it, Commissioner, sir," answers one of the platoon leaders. "It sounded like a foreign language, maybe Greek."

The pain has become unbearable. I notice how my knees are giving out. It's all taking too long; after I said the activation password, I was supposed to enter instantaneously. But second upon second is going by, and I'm still here. My visual field is narrowing.

I'm starting to black out. For a moment I think I've crossed over, but then I come back to myself. I'm lying on the field, I'm still in this fucking Flemish backwater. It's not a pretty place to die, not even a peaceful one. The skyships and the drones make a terrible racket, and the police are yelling at each other. Above me, I can make out the silhouettes of multiple people as if through a fish-eye lens. One of them is bigger than the others. It belongs to Vogel.

"What's that there under his sou'wester?" I hear him ask.

"I don't know, Commissioner, sir."

"Then take a look, damn it!"

I feel someone tearing the rainhat off my head. A new wave of pounding pain shoots through my temple.

"Looks like a replication headset, Commissioner."

"Why is he wearing one of those out here? And why is he smiling?"

I didn't know I was doing it, but I seem to have largely lost control over my body. My arms and legs are little more than a vague memory, there's just my head, pulsing with pain. Am I still here? Maybe . . .

"I think he's crashing, Commissioner. He's sweating profusely. No pupil reaction."

Someone pulls my eyelid up and shines a small lamp inside.

"We need an emergency doctor—this is odd."

"What do you mean?" Vogel asks.

"The man is wearing strange contact lenses."

"What kind of contact lenses?"

"Specs," I hear myself gasp out, "a gift from the Earl of Mertonshire."

And then, as if someone threw a switch, the pain has suddenly disappeared, and with it the cops, the skyships, Vogel, and the damp ground beneath me.

CHAPTER 28

"How long am I going to be stuck here?" I ask.

Johnny Random looks me over. In addition to his white jacket, he wears a black bowtie, his hair slicked back with gel. The getup makes him look a little bit like Rick in *Casablanca*. Though he's wearing a run-of-the-mill face to go with it, not Bogey's, which I'm thankful for. We're strolling along a narrow beach as the sun is just about to disappear into the Impressionistically blurred Tyrrhenian Sea, a light breeze blowing over the water.

"Without a counteragent, Aart? Considering the extremely high dose you injected yourself with, probably two, three weeks. But you're being put on an MAO drip over on the other side in the Saint Pierre Hospital as we speak. Even with that, though, it'll take a few days before you're back in Tellurium. Why exactly did you do it, anyway? You could've killed yourself with that dose. It's a miracle it didn't give you an aneurysm."

"I didn't have any other choice. I knew my Tallan contact lenses would record Vogel's involuntary confession. But of course that wouldn't be enough. How could I be certain the video-feeds would get in the right hands afterward?"

"You could have relied on the fact that I'd receive them."

I bend down, pick up a stone, and toss it into the water. "But I couldn't be sure you'd actually release the material."

Random squints. If I'm reading his expression correctly, he looks bewildered. "But why wouldn't I have used the video, Aart? That was our arrangement in the first place."

"No. You wanted Tallan to get it, and I was supposed to send it to you, that was our arrangement. You didn't have any interest in Vogel. I knew if these video-feeds were made public, the existence of Eidolon would also come to light. And, to be honest, I wasn't sure if you were ready for that, Random. You also could've just let my recordings disappear. So I had to go back into Eidolon to send copies to Ava and Alan Thompson. I knew British intelligence would do everything they could to make sure the matter went public, and Ava as well. Hence the trick with the replication headset under my sou'wester. I also had to take enough hypnoremerol to stay in Eidolon as long as possible. Not just because of the video-feeds. I wanted to give the torturers at the RR the slip for as long as I could. I'd also hoped to find a way out from here, even if my comatose body on the other side is lying in an interrogation chamber somewhere."

"I understand. I'm still shocked you don't trust me, Aart."

I don't answer. Instead I think about a certain

document Ava showed me two days ago in the panic room under her house. One of her search routines had coincidentally dug it up earlier, a stroke of luck. The document was the only tangible thing we ever really found about the ousted editor-in-chief Arne Jürgensen, alias Johnny Random. It was two or three years old, a scan of an archaic-looking paper form, with a real stamp and the signature of a medical examiner. It certified the death of an undocumented man without a country named Arni Jurgensen. Place of death: George Town, Socialist Republic of Tanzania. Cause of death: suicide by hanging. The attached picture bore hardly any resemblance to earlier records; in the end, life apparently hadn't been good to Jürgensen. But Ava's facial recognition software established a match at 95.78 percent. It couldn't tell if the scan's underlying paper document was authentic or if we were dealing with a fake.

We walk along a little farther. I'm not sure if this beach is true to the original, or if Random has made some modifications. At the end of the bay, he leads me along a narrow path winding up the hills to a little restaurant. Once we're there, we sit at a wooden table that was once painted yellow, where a tub filled with beer bottles on ice waits for us. No drops of condensation are running down the emerald-green glass, so someone must have placed the cooler here only a few seconds ago.

Random offers me a bottle. "Let's have a toast."

"To what?"

"To your solving the case, of course."

Our Heineken bottles clack as they touch. After I've had a drink, I say, "What'll happen to Vogel?"

"He's in custody awaiting trial. Thanks to your videos, he can't worm his way out of this one. Svensson is on the run, though I can't imagine where she's planning on going."

"And the Commission president? In the end, it was all her plan."

"Vogel confessed, he's trying to drag Özal into it. Doesn't want to go down alone. My feeling, though, is that she won't be implicated." His eyes flash. "Something more will be needed for that. I'm working on it."

"And Tallan?"

"Tallan is burning in hell."

"Do you mean that metaphorically? The public prosecutor—"

"Forget justice with this one. Tallan has disappeared. The RR came for him. As I've already mentioned once before, they see his private mirror space as high treason, as a threat to their power. Personally, I doubt he'll ever be seen again."

"And his company? I heard stock prices dropped sharply after the creeper-feed affair was made known to the general public."

"Yes, and it looks like new investors will take over the business. A mostly unknown hedge fund bought up a large stock portfolio shortly after the drop in price."

"I have a feeling I know who's behind the purchase, Random."

He laughs. "Despite the current problems, I see great potential for TalCon. Of course, it remains to be seen what kind of complaints will be lodged because of the specs. And if sales will take a hit. But I don't think so. Human rage evaporates quickly."

"And Eidolon?"

"Since its existence has become widely known, the number of ghosts has increased exponentially."

"How?"

"I allowed a large number of access codes to be distributed. Eidolon can no longer be kept secret. But many people were just waiting for the opportunity to outwit the total surveillance inside the Union and elsewhere. So they're offering us their feeds and their servers. Now that there's no more reason for a secret market, we can open up Eidolon. More and more data sources will be available to us. Even if specs suddenly stopped providing data, this replication can still continue to exist. It'll be even better than ever before."

Random gets ready to stand up. "If you'll excuse me now, Aart. I have a lot to do. The Norwegian and Mexican governments have just gotten in touch. They want to make their public data-feeds available to Eidolon in exchange for access. I thank you for your help. Have a wonderful time as long as you're here. Don't think about tomorrow. It's a blessing not to know exactly what will happen next. I envy you that."

"Just a moment. What exactly did you really need me for?"

"I don't understand your question."

"Oh yes, you do. You knew almost everything before I did, Random. You have eyes everywhere. I couldn't get you any information you didn't already have. So, then, what did you need me for?"

"I had all the data, that's true. But I didn't have a solution. Information isn't the same thing as ideas. As I said to you during our last conversation, I'm not as original a thinker as you are."

"That's hard to believe when it comes to someone who marches to the beat of his own drummer like you do."

He shrugs his shoulders. "But that's how it is. The rest is just appearances."

"Golems don't have original ideas."

"You heard that from your analyst, I mean from your girlfriend. A very two-dimensional view on the matter."

Johnny Random is now standing up and smiling down at me from above. The sun shines on his reflective suit; he seems to glow very brightly. "A golem is just clay. The rabbi breathes the *ruah* into it. That's Hebrew and means 'breath of the bones' or 'animal spirit.' Ruah is the energy flowing through all living things, nothing less, nothing more. A golem can move like a person. But there's nothing spiritual about it. And why not?"

"Listen, I—"

"—because a golem doesn't have a human soul. That's why it doesn't even have a name." He looks me in the eyes. "But I have a name. My name is Johnny Random." Then he turns around and walks down the hillside. A few seconds later, he's disappeared.

I stay seated on the woven chair, motionless, as the beer in my right hand gradually gets warm. My gaze wanders over the empty terrace. I notice a woman in a straw hat sitting at the other end. She must have just arrived. The woman wears a floral-patterned sundress which, like everything about her, is in black and white. I jump up and run over to her.

"Ava!"

When she hears my voice, she stands up. I try to take her in my arms. My fingers touch her warm back without sliding through. We hold each other for a long, long moment.

"He said I should wait for you here," she whispers. "I wonder who he is."

"What he is would be the better question. But where exactly are we, anyway? Is it far to your bungalow?"

"Not far. It's in the next bay, maybe a kilometer from here."

She takes my hand. "Come on, let's get going."

I just nod, since we have no time to lose. We might have only a few days left. I hope to see Ava again on the other side, but that's by no means guaranteed. And so we walk, hand in hand, along the narrow path that leads over the crest of the hill to the next bay. At the top, we linger for a moment, looking out at the mirror-smooth sea until the sun sinks into it.

ABOUT THE AUTHOR

Tom Hillenbrand was born in Hamburg, Germany. He has an MA in European Politics. After working as a reporter and section editor for the online edition of DER SPIEGEL and others, he became a full-time author. His thrillers and science fiction novels have won him various prizes and are bestsellers in Germany. He currently lives in Munich without any cats.
http://www.tomhillenbrand.de

ABOUT THE TRANSLATOR

Laura Caton was born in California and spent her childhood living across the United States and near Stuttgart, Germany. After graduating from the University of Pittsburgh in 2013 with an MA in German Language and Literature, she moved to New York, where she worked for several years in international and nonprofit theater. In 2016, she was awarded the Gutekunst Prize for Emerging Translators. She currently lives in Pittsburgh.